THE ANARCHIST

A Novel

JOHN SMOLENS

Three Rivers Press
New York

Copyright © 2009 by John Smolens

This is a work of fiction. Names, characters, places, and incidents
either are the product of the author's imagination or are used
fictitiously. Any resemblance to actual persons, living or dead, events,
or locales is entirely coincidental.

Published in the United States by Three Rivers Press,
an imprint of the Crown Publishing Group, a division of
Random House, Inc., New York.
www.crownpublishing.com

Three Rivers Press and the Tugboat design are registered
trademarks of Random House, Inc.

Cataloging-in-Publication data is on file with the Library of Congress.

ISBN 978-0-307-35189-0

Printed in the United States of America

Design by Elizabeth Rendfleisch

1 3 5 7 9 10 8 6 4 2

First Edition

In memory of my mother, Mary B. Smolens

Generally, men judge by the eye rather than the hand, for all men can see a thing, but few come close enough to touch it. All men will see what you seem to be; only a few will know what you are.

—Niccolò Machiavelli, *The Prince*

BOOK I

THE TEMPLE OF MUSIC

You will never stamp out anarchy any more
than you can keep down the waves of the sea
with a broom. You may kill an anarchist but
you will never kill an idea.

Emma Goldman
Chicago Tribune
September 11, 1901

I

AT FIRST LIGHT a carriage stopped on the towpath above the Erie Canal. Four men climbed out and walked single file across a footbridge, Captain Lloyd Savin leading two uniformed police officers and Pinkerton detective Jake Norris, who followed a ways behind, his head lowered as he gazed down at the water. He had recently arrived from Washington, D.C., and this was the first time he'd seen the canal. He expected it to be wider. Though it was August, a raw wind blew in from Lake Erie, a reminder that in Buffalo winter was never far off, and an occasional drop of rain tapped on the hard dome of his bowler. He took great pride in his hat, which had white satin lining and cost him five dollars.

On the far side of the canal a barge, the *Glockenspiel*, was tied to a pier in front of a brick warehouse; it was a shallow-draft, broad-beamed vessel, a good seventy feet in length, designed to negotiate the low bridges that spanned the canal. The four men descended on a narrow plank to the deck and went astern, where two other uniformed policemen stood over the body, which was covered by a frayed blanket.

Savin didn't appear interested in the body; instead, he approached the man who was standing in the open pilothouse door. "This your boat?"

"It is."

"Your name?"

"Bruener. Klaus Bruener." He had a heavy German accent and was easily over six feet tall. His nose was large and crooked, no doubt broken several times, and his hands were enormous.

Savin took a pack of Turkish Delights from the pocket of his raincoat and lit a cigarette. He had a perpetual grimace as though he were enduring constant pain. "Where'd you find her?" He flicked the matchstick into the canal.

Bruener nodded toward the footbridge. "Floating under there. We are just coming in from Rochester when my son spots something from the bow. So he climbs down and pulls her out." He smiled, revealing brown teeth. "Don't think the boy ever touched a naked woman before. Kind of upsets him—more 'n that she be dead. If you take my meaning."

Norris cleared his throat to get Savin's attention, and then he asked Bruener, "Where is your son now?"

Bruener tugged on his wool cap a moment. He looked like he wasn't going to bother to answer, but then something seemed to make him reconsider. "Below in the cabin."

Savin went to the blanket now and lifted one corner. Norris was trying to determine whether his hesitance was because he didn't want to see what was underneath or he wanted to hold the moment of anticipation a moment longer. When Savin tossed the blanket aside, he glanced down at the woman's body, and then looked away as he drew on his cigarette.

"It was dark," Bruener said. "He might not a seen her if it wasn't for the hat."

She was only wearing a yellow felt hat, pulled down snug on her scalp. Her flesh was pale blue and bruises stood out on her arms, neck, and face, which was badly swollen.

"Look at them nipples," one of the policemen whispered. "Big as fried eggs."

"She called herself Clementine," Bruener said.

"You knew her?" Norris asked.

Bruener nearly smiled. "Worked in the house run by Big Maud."

"She come down here a lot to work the barges?" Norris said.

"You might say that," Bruener said. "She knowed a lot of canawlers."

Norris gazed up at the small group of men who had collected in front of the warehouse. They stood watching, hands shoved in the pockets of their jackets and bib overalls. The country was full of such men, day laborers who laid railroad track, constructed buildings, loaded goods on and off boats and wagons. Just by looking at them Norris could tell which ones had only recently arrived in the United States. Some Washington politicians believed that it would take a good war to prune the immigrants.

Savin took off his felt hat and shaped the indented crown with his forefinger; it was a surprisingly intimate, sensual gesture, and when he saw Norris watching his hand he winced. His black hair was heavily oiled and so smooth against his scalp that it might have been painted on. Like Norris, he understood the advantage of dressing well—tailored suits, a topcoat, and leather shoes that take a regular polish. It was the first thing Norris had noticed about him, along with the fact that the man smoked cigarettes almost constantly. He was several years younger than Norris, who was thirty-eight. Looking around at the other policemen, Savin said, "Anybody here buy sheet time at Big Maud's lately?" The men stared off as though they hoped not to be noticed.

Savin put his hat back on and grimaced around his cigarette. "Now I want all of you to start knocking on doors—every house, every business from here down to Black Rock Harbor. Find somebody who saw or heard something."

The policemen appeared relieved to get away from Savin as they rushed off the barge. He turned to Norris and said playfully, "Want to go, too, Detective? Try your hand at some mundane police work?"

"I'd rather talk to Bruener's son."

Savin looked as though he'd been insulted, but then he said to Bruener, "Get your boy up here."

Norris went over to the body and leaned down for a closer look. In some places the skin was raw and bloody, but there were no cuts or gashes. The bruises were purple and black, and her left eye seemed to have collapsed in the socket. "Whoever did this used something that wouldn't break the skin."

"Like a fist?" Savin said.

Norris bent down closer until he was within inches of her face. "Look, in her hair."

Reluctantly, Savin leaned over her as well. "I don't know what that is—the doctor will tell when he shows up. It's not hair, but something else." He straightened up, took Norris by the arm, and walked him to the stern of the barge. Quietly, he said, "This is one?"

"Yes."

"She get anything for you?"

Norris shook his head. "She only just started working for me."

"When's the last time you saw her?"

"Two days ago, in a café, the Three Brothers."

Savin flicked his cigarette butt into the water. "So she was working for you down here—or was she just providing her usual services?"

"Both, probably. I asked her where she could find anarchists in Buffalo and she said anywhere—the saloons, the whorehouses, the churches, the slaughterhouses, the factories. But she said to try the canal first. It's how people come and go from Buffalo."

Savin nodded as he glanced at the body for a moment. Turning to Norris again, he asked, "Ever fuck her?" Norris stared back at him, and when he realized he wasn't going to get an answer, Savin took out his pack of cigarettes. "Right," he said. "You're a real professional."

"What I am is back where I started when I first got here from Washington," Norris said. "I'll need somebody else. Soon."

"Another whore? Well, we've got plenty of those in Buffalo."

"No. Not this time. I want a man—one that works down here on the boats, a canawler, as they call themselves. I need a canawler."

Savin dragged deeply on his cigarette; he held the smoke down for a moment and then released it, saying in a tight voice, "I don't know if informers and spies are ever going to help you catch anarchists."

"They have in Washington."

"This isn't Washington, Norris."

"On that we agree."

Bruener and his son climbed up a ladder from below and stepped out through the open pilothouse door. "This is Josef, my son."

Savin walked over to the boy, who was very lean, with a long, sullen face. He might have been eighteen. Warily his eyes drifted toward the naked body, then back to Savin.

"You pulled her out of the canal?" Savin asked.

The boy nodded.

"And you first saw her where?"

Josef raised a long arm and pointed toward the footbridge.

Savin stepped closer to the boy. "You're the loquacious one, aren't you?"

"He don't speak," Bruener said. "Been mute since birth, and he don't hear too good."

"Isn't *that* grand," Savin said. "Can you tell me what *time* you saw her?"

The boy held up four fingers.

"Four this morning," Savin said. "About two hours ago."

The boy nodded.

Norris leaned against the stern rail of the barge. His hand touched something coarse and he looked down. Beside him was a cleat, with a dock line attached. The rope had to be as thick as his wrist, and he plucked at it with his fingers, pulling away hemp fibers, stiff, like bits of straw. "Savin," he said. "I think I know what the killer used on her."

Norris got up and went to Clementine's body. Leaning down close to her face, he removed some fibers from her cold wet hair. Holding both samples out, he said, "Rope. Whoever did this beat her with a rope like that."

"Maybe, Detective." Savin appeared angry now as they watched a heavy man, carrying a black bag, walk gingerly across the footbridge. "But why don't we let Dr. Rivard gather the evidence?" Savin went to the bottom of the plank and offered the doctor a hand as though he were a woman.

Dr. Rivard wore a pince-nez and was winded from the climb down to the boat. "In the future, Captain, I would prefer it if you would arrange that the dead bodies in Buffalo turn up on dry land," he said. "I detest any vessel that floats—because I do not." He alone laughed at his joke, and then he put his bag down on the deck and began to inspect the body.

One of the policemen Savin had sent up to the houses above the canal came back to the pier. "Sir, if I could have a word with you?"

"All right, Cullen." Savin climbed the plank up to the pier and the two men talked quietly, their backs to the barge.

It began to rain lightly, each drop making a hollow sound on Norris's bowler. He looked directly at the boy and said slowly, "Josef, how was she positioned in the water?"

The boy appeared nervous as he watched Norris's mouth.

"Was she faceup?" Norris held his hand out, palm toward the sky, and then turned it over. "Or facedown?"

Josef nodded.

"And she was just like that," Norris said. "No clothes, other than the hat?"

The boy nodded vehemently, his eyes growing wide.

"I wonder when her clothes were taken off," Norris said. "Before or after she was dead." Turning to the doctor, he asked, "I don't suppose there's evidence of sexual activity?"

The doctor said pleasantly, "We can find out."

When Cullen left the pier again, Norris climbed up the plank and joined Savin. The rain was becoming steady.

"This is a lot of work over a whore," Savin said as he lit another cigarette. "Dead ones aren't much use to anyone."

"I doubt she was killed because of her abilities as a prostitute," Norris said. "Bruener has assured us she was well qualified. She must have learned something."

"About anarchists?" Savin said skeptically. "But of course she was killed before she had a chance to report to you." Norris only looked at him in the rain. "Why they sent you out from Washington, I don't know," Savin said. "Because the president is coming to Buffalo next month? What can you do here in a month? You Pinkertons aren't . . ." Savin hesitated, and then he said, "You aren't necessary."

Norris understood Savin taking offense; in his position, he too would resent an outsider. With Savin, it was important not to ask for something, and he said, "It will be necessary for me to find another one."

"Right—another spy, who can infiltrate and inform on the anarchists in Buffalo." Savin's face grew tighter, like a fist. "To ensure our president's safety while he visits Buffalo."

"Find me one."

"Sure I couldn't just get you another whore?"

"No," Norris said patiently. "I said I want a canawler, one who goes to places like Big Maud's."

"There must be a few of *those* in Buffalo," Savin said. "The anarchists, the bastards, they'll probably kill him, too."

"I need one that can stay alive long enough to be useful."

Before Savin could answer, the doctor called up from the barge. "Well, that's done."

They looked down at Rivard—to stay dry he had stepped under the pilothouse roof next to Bruener and his son. Clementine's body lay facing them in the rain, legs parted, knees at odd angles. The rain had matted the pubic hair against her skin.

"This woman has entertained recently." Rivard had to raise his voice now because the rain was beating loudly on the deck of the barge. "There's plenty of you know what, you know where."

"Some spy." Savin exhaled smoke. "Just down here on the canal, doing her job."

"If so, why kill a whore?" Norris said.

"Ethical or moral reason?" Savin said. "Or maybe she just wasn't very accommodating."

"No, she found something out."

Norris looked at the group of men who were now leaning against the brick wall of the warehouse, trying to keep from getting soaked. They gazed sullenly down at the barge, as though the police were the guilty ones, responsible for everything from the rain to the death of a prostitute. One of the men was holding a mule by the reins, and when the animal brayed, the sound echoed out over the canal, plaintive and sorrowful.

∽⊃C⌣

HYDE was early.

If you wanted something in St. John's Protectory, if you needed something, you learned to get there first. The nuns always ladled out full bowls of soup to the boys at the head of the line, but with time their arms tired and the portions grew smaller.

So he arrived early and waited a good ten minutes in the doorway of Fallon's Apothecary across from the Three Brothers Café. Though he'd never met Jake Norris—and Captain Savin had offered no description—the Pinkerton detective was easy to recognize when he walked down Market Street: a large, well-fed man in a black suit and hard collar stood out in the Polonia section of Buffalo. As Norris approached a vendor's cart that sold noisy chickens, several old women in babushkas instinctively scattered out of his way. Norris entered the café and sat at a table by the front window. Hyde wished he'd found a place that wasn't visible from the street. Norris removed his bowler, which left a neat indentation in his short blond hair. His skin was the color of a peeled potato. He opened the morning edition of the *Buffalo Courier,* and for several minutes did not look up from reading. His actions were calculated and deliberate, and suggested that he knew he was being observed—and that he welcomed the fact.

Hyde glanced at his own reflection in the window of the apothecary. His thick dark mustache concealed his mouth, and the hollowness of his cheeks suggested that he could use a good meal. Though it was August, his jacket was buttoned, with the collar turned up. When he faced the café again Norris had put down his paper and was staring out the window directly at him.

Hyde crossed the street, almost as if drawn. When he opened the door and entered the café, Norris said, "I've ordered you coffee. Come, sit."

Hyde approached the table. "Detective Norris?"

"Jake Norris, but just Norris is fine."

"People usually call me Hyde."

"No first name? Your folks gave you one, didn't they?" Norris touched his own cheekbones. "They're prominent—Eastern European, perhaps, but I can't quite place—"

"I don't know where my family's from. I'm certain I was born in the United States, here in Buffalo, or nearby." Hyde sat at the table as the waiter, an old man in a soiled apron, brought the coffee.

"Something to eat?" Norris asked.

"Maybe later," Hyde said, and the waiter retreated.

"But your mother and father . . ." Norris began.

"I never knew my mother," Hyde said, "and I suspect she never really knew my father." He waited for the detective to figure it out.

"Orphaned," Norris said.

"I'm told that when the nuns found me on the steps of St. John's Protectory it couldn't have been more than a few hours after birth. There were hundreds of boys—Italian, Polish, German, Russian, you name it—and they stuck with their own kind, a lot like the neighborhoods in this city. I don't know who my parents were, let alone where they were from."

"An outcast among outcasts," Norris said with satisfaction. "So you learned to fend for yourself. Well, the thing is you know how to survive." He nodded toward the window. "I saw something out there when you crossed the street, something invisible about you. You can disappear into a crowd, go unnoticed—that's an excellent trait. It's useful."

"You spotted me."

"It's my job." Norris took out a cigar case, a penknife, and matches, and laid them on the table. He opened the silver case, removed one cigar, and then with the penknife began cutting the tip. "I like to make a little bird's mouth, see?" he said. "Garcias. You read the newspapers?"

Hyde nodded.

"Then you know who smokes these—William McKinley. You can say what you want about the president, but the man knows cigars." Norris studied his workmanship for a moment, and then picked up the box of matches. He might have been performing a magic trick, the way he struck a matchstick and puffed slowly as he lit the cigar, sending blue smoke across the table. Suddenly, he said, "I'm sorry—would you like one?"

"No, thank you." Hyde sipped from his cup, and then sucked the beads of coffee from the bottom of his mustache.

"According to the papers, the president smokes twenty of these a day," Norris said as he studied Hyde. "You seem unimpressed. Let me guess. You're in your late twenties. But there is nothing youthful about your face—the cheeks, already sunken and deeply creased. At the rate you're going, most men wouldn't make it to thirty-five." He exhaled smoke, which hung in the air, coiling, slow and languid. "I like to think of myself reaching sixty, when I will retire to a wide front porch and smoke twenty cigars a day."

He took a cigar from his case and placed it on the table next to Hyde's coffee cup. "For later on, then. You strike me as a patient man. You can wait to eat, you can wait for a Garcia—or perhaps you don't smoke?"

"No, I like a cigar," Hyde said. "But usually at night."

"Yes, with a glass of beer. What else, Hyde? Whiskey?"

"Not to excess."

"Not usually, you mean." Norris smiled around his cigar. "Women? You like the women? Or maybe you're married? Captain Savin didn't say."

"I'm not married."

Norris moved his shoulders slightly. "You like the saloon dancers? The upstairs girls in the houses of assignation? You frequent places like Big Maud's, a real palace of carnal pleasure, I understand, except one of the girls was found in the canal a couple of days ago."

"Clementine," Hyde said. "I heard."

"Yes, it's been in all the papers. She one of your girls?"

"No."

"Never?"

"Never."

"Any idea why someone would beat her to death and throw her in the Erie Canal?"

"No idea."

Norris placed both elbows on the table. "I can tell you why. It had nothing to do with sex. She found something out about someone down there on the canal, and they killed her before she could tell me." Norris leaned even farther over the table, speaking in a whisper. "It was anarchists. That's why I'm here."

"She was working for you?"

"*Very* good, Hyde." Norris sat back now. "So Savin sends his men around to Big Maud's and other places like that, and they question men who work on the canal. I know how that goes. When a man is afraid you can tell inside two minutes if he really knows anything." Norris rolled the ash of his cigar on the edge of his saucer. "But you—Savin says you were different."

"I don't know anything about Clementine."

"Tell you the truth, I'm not interested in a dead prostitute," Norris said. "I'm interested in what she found out." He paused a moment. "Savin sent you to me—he said you knew something, and you seemed willing to help. So tell me, Hyde, why is that?"

Hyde glanced around the café, which was full, with most of the customers speaking Polish, and then he leaned forward and spoke quietly. "I was picked up when the police raided a workers' meeting at a hall here in Polonia and they questioned me for a long time. At first Savin was—he was like all the police, but then he seemed to change his mind and had a meal brought in. He even offered me a cigar afterward."

"But it wasn't a Garcia."

"He smokes a lot of cigarettes."

"You must have impressed him. You must have said something interesting."

"Savin was skeptical, like you."

Norris glanced down at the table a moment. "Your hands," he said. "They're unusually large, and calloused—powerful hands for such a lean man. You get hands like that from working on the barges. I'll tell you, with the proper diet, I'm convinced America could be a country of strong men. This could be a great nation." He regarded the smoke that hung in the air, and then asked, "You live on a barge?"

"Depends. I have a room in a boardinghouse, when I'm in Buffalo."

"Certainly. Come and go. And you've been working on the canal for years?"

"Since I was twelve."

"You ran away from this St. John's Protectory." Norris smiled. "And hid on the Erie Canal. It's not much of a life."

"Being a canawler's better than working in the slaughterhouses—I've done that, too."

"Granted."

There was a moment of silence. Norris seemed to be waiting, and Hyde finally said, "Savin said he knew someone who could help me."

"That's right. You sure you wouldn't like a cigar?"

Hyde picked the cigar up off the table. "All right."

"I find they steady the nerves." Norris slid the penknife and matches across the table. "Now let's talk about what you told Savin. If he was *too* skeptical, he wouldn't have recommended you to me."

As he lit his cigar, Hyde surveyed the café once again. "You Pinkertons—you're always looking for someone on the inside."

"Inside the workers' movement, yes. You are one of them and they trust you." Norris hesitated. "And you told Savin, who smokes a lot of cigarettes, that you met a man who talks about assassinating the president."

"I did."

Norris waited, and finally said, "He has a name."

Hyde looked out the window a moment, and then back at Norris. "Leon Czolgosz. Very quiet usually, but then sometimes he starts to boast about changing history. He talks about how it should be our duty to kill the president. That's his word, duty."

"And you believe him."

"I rarely believe what people say, but I believe their eyes. And he has these pale blue eyes. They are—they tell you he's very quiet, but inside there's a great deal, you know, going on in his head." Hyde leaned over the table slightly and whispered, "Savin said I should tell you this because you're here to help protect the president."

"That's why I was sent out from Washington. McKinley will visit Buffalo next month."

"What will you do?"

"It depends," Norris said, "on whether I believe you."

Hyde leaned back, insulted.

Norris took his cigar from his mouth and smiled. "At heart, you're honest, and you're a realist, Hyde. I don't think you'd make this up. The number of death threats against the president has increased considerably since he began his second term last March. Anarchists are trying to kill leaders here and in Europe. Last year they shot the Italian king, and that has only made them more determined."

"So if Czolgosz is a threat, you can arrest him?"

"You're talking about a potential threat. If that's the case we should arrest half of Buffalo—and Cleveland, and Paterson, and entire neighborhoods in Chicago, too. But where do we start? With the Italians, the Russians, the Hungarians, the Jews? No, we should watch this Leon Czolgosz—see what he does, who he associates with. If he is a threat, he can't be doing this alone. That will be your job." Norris worked on his cigar for a moment. "The fact is, Hyde, I don't want you to do anything different from what you're doing now. Keep your ears open down on the canal and at Big Maud's. Continue to go to workers' meetings. Read *Free Society,* and listen to impassioned speeches about the virtues of socialism and communism. Keep close to these people. And if you can get Emma Goldman in the sack, which I understand isn't too difficult, give her a good poke for me."

Hyde removed the cigar from his mouth. "You want to know what they talk about? But you already know this. They talk about improved working conditions, better wages—they talk about freedom."

"Fine, let them talk all they want—it's a free country and people can be as stupidly idealistic as they want," Norris said. "But people like Czolgosz talk about presidents and kings. The reason you're here is because you have come to the realization that you're not dealing with idealists. What would you call them, these people who plot to kill their leaders?"

Hyde considered the tip of his cigar. "Wrong. They are wrong."

"Absolutely. And your worker is going to remain cold, hungry, and sick, no matter how many speeches Red Emma gives. These people, they don't want to *earn* anything, they just want it *handed* to them. We're really talking about taking responsibility for one's own life, Hyde. *Then* freedom will follow. I believe that, and I think you do, too—that's what you did when you ran away from that orphanage. Otherwise, we wouldn't be here now." Norris cleared his throat. "I can give you five dollars a week to start." He leaned back as though he himself were stunned by such a figure.

"That's not enough," Hyde said.

For the briefest moment, Norris's eyes turned hard, and then he smiled. "What can you make working on the canal—four, five dollars a week? Listen, show me what you can do, and then we'll see what you're really worth."

Hyde turned his head and stared out the window. The vendor who had been selling chickens was pushing his cart down Market Street, the wooden wheels leaving deep furrows in the mud.

"You know the Pinkerton motto?" Norris asked.

"'The Eye Never Sleeps,'" Hyde said, still gazing out the window.

"Good. You can become a part of that, if you handle this for me."

"The eye that never sleeps grows weary, tired."

"Not if there's enough of us looking—then we grow vigilant and strong."

"We become a great nation." Hyde finally turned to Norris.

"Very good," Norris said. "You are a patient man, Hyde, and patience is a useful quality in this line of work. It keeps the mind clear, the eyes sharp."

Hyde crushed his cigar out in his saucer. "So does hunger."

THE air in the crowded hall was stifling hot, smelling of sweat and damp wool clothing, yet windows were kept closed for fear of alerting the police. The speaker, Johann Stefaniak, was a glassworker from Milwaukee whose forelock danced on his damp brow as he thumped the podium with his fist. People forgot their discomfort in the heat, raising their arms, cheering, and applauding as Stefaniak raged on about wages, eight-hour workdays, and better conditions in mills and factories. He might have been a preacher at Sunday meeting, the way he led the crowd like an orchestra, building it to a fevered pitch, only to bring it back down to absolute silence, so that when he whispered the name of J. P. Morgan there was a collective horrified gasp, as though he had spoken the name of Satan himself. When he was finished, everyone was standing as they shouted with fists raised—and then it was over, and, exhausted, they began to file out of the hall.

Leon Czolgosz remained seated on a wooden bench next to a window near the back of the hall. He liked to let the others leave first; something about the emptiness of the room appealed to him. Same thing on a train—he was often the last to leave.

He turned to Hyde and said, "Been listening to speeches like that since I was a boy."

"This was a good one," Hyde said. He sat with his arms folded as he stared toward the now empty stage.

"There used to be gatherings in the room above my family's grocery store in Cleveland," Czolgosz said. "The entire neighborhood would come to hear some socialist or communist. It wasn't like the Catholic masses we attended—this was the true passion play."

"At least the police didn't break things up tonight."

"If any blood would be drunk, it would be our own."

They were alone now except for a few old women who swept the floor and collected discarded handbills. "Well, it makes me thirsty," Hyde said as he got to his feet. "A speech like that makes you want a cigar, a beer, and whiskey—the good whiskey."

"Right, top-shelf," Czolgosz said. "Who has time for that five-cent stuff?"

"Ta hell with the temperance people."

Czolgosz continued to stare at the podium. "He was good tonight, but he's no Emma Goldman."

"So we'll drink to her."

Czolgosz turned toward the window next to him, and he could see himself dimly reflected in the glass. There was an unusual grace to the angle of his jaw. His hair, parted on the right in the reflection, was blond, and most disconcerting was how his lips appeared full and even curvaceously feminine. But it was the eyes, his pale blue eyes, that often seemed to transform people, as though he possessed some unique, perhaps even magical power over them. Standing up, he said, "Yes, a dram for Emma Goldman."

The cool night air was a relief as they walked through Polonia. Mud caked their boots and there was the smell of horse manure, chimney smoke, stale beer, and cooked sausage, onions, cabbage. Voices burst from open saloon doors—places with names such as Mick Pickle's Palace and the Erie Strutters' Dance Hall, where English was seldom heard. The alleys were littered with pickpockets and prostitutes, lingering in the shadows.

"You know I heard Goldman speak in Cleveland last May," Czolgosz said. "I'm telling you, she can set an audience on fire. She often causes riots and the police have to break them up."

"She could make a man commit murder," Hyde said. "She convinced Alexander Berkman to try to kill Carnegie's manager, Henry Clay Frick."

"What a botched job. Berkman gets into Frick's office in Pittsburgh with a gun—but he can't even shoot straight! Then he pulls a knife and stabs the man, but still he lives. When workers struck at the Homestead mill, Frick sent in the scabs and hundreds of Pinkertons to protect them. And because he survived the assassination attempt, Frick became a hero. So how do you get close to them? Men like Frick are surrounded by guards all the time now."

"With your light hair, you could almost pass for a Pinkerton."

"Men like me, or you—we are not going to be mistaken for those bastards."

"You really think so? Then how do you get close enough? You must have help."

"Not necessarily. You blend in—you become Mr. Nobody," Czolgosz said. "Nobody but Poles can pronounce my name, so I tell people my name is Fred C. Nieman. Then they don't even see me. This is a war of ideas. Invisibility can be a weapon."

"True," Hyde said. "But be careful, Fred Nieman, or Emma Goldman will make a good weapon out of you."

"I would like that," Czolgosz said.

"Really?"

"Really."

"You've mentioned this before, that it's your duty," Hyde said, "and sometimes I think you're—"

"It is my duty," Czolgosz said. "We defeated Spain in Cuba and the Philippines, and now America's preparing to conquer the world. But look around us! To walk through these neighborhoods it appears that the world has sent its defeated to Buffalo. And it's the same in Cleveland, Detroit, and Chicago—they're importing a whole new slave class. Industry thrives on our cheap labor."

"This is true, and this is why the socialist and—"

"A few more pennies per hour is not the solution. Socialism, communism—they don't . . ." Czolgosz stopped walking. "Do you know what historians will make of 1901? They'll say Americans were a hardworking, industrious people. They'll remember men in boiled white shirts and stiff collars, and women in satin gowns with their hair tied up under a big hat with a plume. They'll remember Anna Held and Gibson girls. They'll hardly mention the conditions in the factories, children working all day instead of going to school. The socialists and communists, they're just talk, they're just speeches and handbills. The anarchists— they're something else, and they're not talking about a few more pennies."

"I work for pennies," Hyde said. "And right now I just want to think about a strawberry blonde—not so much on the plump side. But still, you know, with nice high ones, and hips like this—" He carved the figure of a woman with both hands. "Sometimes you should concentrate on something else, Leon—a glass of whiskey or maybe a girl's hips."

"Perhaps."

"It's not exactly free love."

"No—more women should practice free love." Czolgosz seemed baffled, embarrassed, but then he blurted, "There is no such thing as 'free love.' You're talking about a decent woman, you're talking about marriage. That's neither free nor love. It's just procreation, making a bunch of babies who will grow up and go to work for you—listen, I come from a family of eight, and there would have been more except that my mother died at forty when she was giving birth to my sister Victoria. The family as a capitalist unit—create your own workforce. That's the only way to survive."

"Then maybe it's better to simply pay for it." Hyde seemed to be smiling, though it was difficult to tell with his full mustache. "What do you say?"

"Do you—pay for it?"

"Sometimes," Hyde said, and he nodded toward the clapboard house at the end of the block. "It's run by Big Maud, and it's certainly not free. But it's honest—at least until all women are like Emma."

∿〇∾

BIG Maud's house had a bowl of fruit—peaches, grapes, oranges, and an enormous banana—crudely painted on the clapboards above the front door. As they stood on the front stoop, Hyde could sense Czolgosz's reluctance. But then the door was opened by Mr. Varney, the bouncer, and Big Maud welcomed them in the vestibule; she wore a bustle and seemed to drift across the floor without actually taking steps. In the parlor "Hello, Central, Give Me Heaven" was being hammered out on the player piano, which was in need of tuning. The room was smoky, and the heavy, tasseled drapes suggested a hint of pageantry. Hyde and Czolgosz ordered whiskey at the bar and within minutes the available girls hovered around. They concentrated on Czolgosz, knowing that Hyde was interested only in the strawberry blonde named Motka Ascher. By the time Hyde finished his whiskey, Czolgosz had been maneuvered to a stuffed chair next to a large potted fern. A stout redhead with a creased neck sat on the armrest talking in his ear, but he didn't seem to be listening; instead, he stared at the carpet and held his glass as though he could crush it in his fist.

Motka came down the stairs, carrying the bottom of her long green dress in one hand, and entered the parlor. She had enormous blue eyes, wasn't too plump, and had what was called good carriage. Without saying anything, she took Hyde's hand and led him up the stairs. They climbed all the way to the third floor, passing closed doors. There were the sounds of bedsprings, of coughing, of giggles and laughter, of a headboard knocking on the wall. The top floor was quieter, though the music from the parlor echoed up the stairwell. They entered her room, which was small, with a sloped ceiling. She lit candles, and then sat on the chair next to the bureau. She undid his trousers and, using a fresh cloth and warm water, washed him gently. When she was done, they undressed and got into bed. Overhead rain began to fall on the roof, and it was soon pouring—drumming on the shingles so hard that the protests from Motka's bedsprings were nearly drowned out.

When they were finished, she said, "I have cigarette, mind? Big Maud does not let us smoke in the parlor. Only the men."

"You go ahead."

She got up, opened the bureau drawer, and came back with a pack of cigarettes, matches, and a flask. "Your friend, he does not come here before," she said, climbing back under the sheets. "What's his name?"

"Fred Nieman."

"He is a nice-looking boy, but I bet you a dollar—he does not leave the parlor the whole time." Motka liked to make little bets and she usually won. She opened the flask and took a sip, and then handed it to him. Compared to her warm skin, the silver flask seemed absurdly smooth and hard.

"You really think so?"

She lit her cigarette and exhaled slowly. "He will be right there sitting by that plant—ignoring every girl that talk to him. Big Maud even sit with him a spell, try to make him relax." Shaking her head, she said, "He just look holes into the carpet."

"You could see that?"

"Moment I saw him."

"But not me?"

"You?" She laughed as she placed a hand over him. "You could knock on front door with this stick of wood."

"Why do you suppose Fred is that way?"

"You the kind that think a lot. He the kind that think too much. Or maybe he has too much Catholic."

"Not anymore," Hyde said. He drank some more whiskey before giving her the flask. She took it with the hand that held the cigarette, while her other hand continued to fondle him. Motka was a three-dollar girl, the most expensive in the house, other than Bella Donna, who had been there the longest. Ordinarily you were given a half hour for three dollars; and if you could go more than once in that time, it was an extra dollar for Motka. "How long you been in America?" he asked.

"Four years. I come over at sixteen."

"From where?"

"Smolensk. Russians throw Jews out. That or they kill you."

"Pogroms?"

"Yes. Both my parents dead. My brother and sister leave with me, but she die on the ship. First I go to Pittsburgh, then come to Buffalo because my brother, Anton, is here. He has wife and child and does not like much my life here." She took a drink from the flask. "I cannot blame him. Maybe someday I will not have to live this life. There is either something better, or you are dead. No in-between. Like Clementine."

"I heard they found her in the canal."

"She was sweet girl," Motka said. "Here one day, dead tomorrow. Girls come and go from house like this. And nobody care. The madam tells us never to speak about her." She tapped her forehead with a finger. "But I remember."

They didn't talk for a moment but only passed the whiskey back and forth, while Motka smoked. There was something very deliberate about the way she held her cigarette, how she examined the ash before taking another drag. Her other hand continued to caress and stroke him, and he couldn't help but watch her small, delicate fingers, which seemed to possess full knowledge of him.

"Why do you think Fred won't come upstairs?" he asked.

"Who knows? He is afraid?"

"Everyone is afraid."

"What does he like?"

"I don't know," Hyde said. "Whiskey. He likes good whiskey, but not too much. And cigars—he likes a stogie. And he once mentioned trains."

"Trains?" She crushed her cigarette out in the ashtray she kept on the nightstand. "Maybe he find women ugly? Or maybe he think he is too good for us. Maybe that is his problem."

"You're very smart, Motka. Too smart to stay in this place forever."

"We cannot all be ignorant immigrants." She threw back the covers and got on her hands and knees, facing toward the foot of the bed. Looking around at him, she said, "Now, for another dollar, I am engine and you be caboose. Like choo-choo train."

~つ⌒~

THIS time Norris was early. He liked the fact that Hyde had arrived at their first meeting before him; it suggested that he had good instincts. This is how it goes, little distinctions, small observations. Don't miss anything. Everything is important. And this time Norris sat in a booth in the back of the Three Brothers Café. When Hyde finally arrived, he was reluctant to sit down. He stared at the folded newspaper on the table.

"You look like you need a good night's sleep," Norris said. "Sit, will you?"

Hyde slid into the booth. "You promised more. Five dollars is not enough."

"You'll like what's in this edition, Hyde. Don't sound so desperate." He took out his silver cigar case, knife, and box of matches and laid them on the table. "I was wondering, you being an orphan and all, where do boys like you get your name?"

Hyde prepared a cigar, and Norris struck a match. "The nuns just give you a name," Hyde said once his cigar was lit. "I was left on the steps in an apple crate. The name of the farm was printed on it: Hyde."

"And the first name?"

"The nuns often gave the boys the names of saints. If you were taken in at the protectory on Saint Bartholomew's Day, chances were that would be the name they'd put down in their records.

But I was a bit of an exception." Hyde appeared reluctant as his fingers stroked his mustache. "It had to do with the weather. They tell me it was pouring and I was sopping wet. They thought it was a miracle I didn't drown, so they wrote down Moses." He took his hand away from his mouth. "But I don't use it much."

"Moses Hyde," Norris said. For a moment, the two men sat in silence, enshrouded in blue smoke. "Tell me about Czolgosz."

"I lose him," Hyde said. "He comes and goes. The man does not stay in one place. Sometimes he says he'll be at a meeting, but he doesn't show. I ask where he's been and he laughs and says Chicago or Akron or Columbus. I think he makes a lot of it up. With him there is no difference between the truth and a lie. That is the danger, you see."

"But—"

"There's something about him. Or maybe he's just a lonely man who can't find decent work. The city's full of them."

"Do you think he suspects you?" Norris asked.

"No. He told me that sometimes he goes by the name of Fred C. Nieman. He's unpredictable. Very quiet, shy. But then after a meeting he'll talk forever. He can find strange things to laugh about."

"He drink?"

"Of course. And good stuff, but he's no drunk."

"Women?"

Hyde almost smiled. "He sees a decent woman on the street and he crosses to the other side to avoid her. That's the truth. I took him to Big Maud's but he's afraid to go upstairs. Sits down in the parlor and listens to the player piano."

"How do you know? You sit down there with him?"

"No. I lost a dollar bet on it."

"Maybe his problem is virginity?" Norris asked. "Can't Big Maud cure that? Something with big pink nipples? Your first time you want to have pink."

"You're right," Hyde said. "I should take him to Big Maud's again."

"Listen, I was sent out here from Washington to do a job, to protect the president. I talk to people like you every day, and every one of them has some conspiracy to sell me. You come to me with one man, Leon Czolgosz, and I'm starting to wonder if this is about nothing more than the act of fornication."

Hyde was considering the ash on his cigar. Norris sensed he was grappling with something. Hyde would be a good spy if he could only get rid of his conscience—but then without one he wouldn't be able to get close to people like Czolgosz. The problem was, Hyde still half believed all that socialist crap.

"What is it?" Norris said. "Tell me."

"He told me he has met Emma Goldman and Abraham Isaak—all the people in Chicago connected to *Free Society*."

Norris put both elbows on the table and leaned forward. "Yes, your workers' bible," he said. "Emma Goldman often stays at Isaak's house when she's in Chicago. We don't think he's screwing her. Isaak has a wife and family, but with Emma you never know. How a woman who looks like that can get so many men in the sack, I don't know. She must talk them into bed."

"Czolgosz says he saw her speak in Cleveland last spring."

"That would be the first week of May." Hyde looked surprised. "We keep tabs."

"Czolgosz talks about her often."

"How?"

"It's like he's made up his mind about something."

"And you think Goldman has something to do with this?"

"I don't know," Hyde said. "It seems no one gives a speech like her."

"Red Emma is an ugly little Jew from Lithuania. Maybe she gets up on the stage and raises her skirts? Bends over for the crowd and spreads her fat legs?"

"She believes marriage is a form of enslavement."

"Maybe she's not so crazy after all." Norris smiled, but Hyde didn't. "What happened between Czolgosz and her?"

"He said in Chicago they rode the train together. In Cleveland she gave him some reading material on the Haymarket martyrs."

"Martyrs," Norris said. "You hang people for inciting violence that kills officers of the law and it makes them martyrs. That was Jesus's role. The rest of them ought to be a message, an example of what you get when you break the law." Norris finished his coffee and tucked his cigar case inside his coat. In his experience it was usually more effective to keep these meetings brief. "I can't use this, Hyde. Two people discuss reading material? It's not against the law. This is a free country, so they can complain about our government all they want." He started to get out of the booth but then paused. "Jesus, I'm irritable today myself. Maybe I should pay a visit to one of Big Maud's girls."

"Czolgosz wants to meet Goldman again."

"He told you that?" Norris stabbed his cigar out in the ashtray.

Hyde nodded. "You and Czolgosz, you have something in common, you know?"

"Really? What's that?"

"You are both obsessed with Emma Goldman."

"You got that right, comrade. I'd like to fuck her good." Norris slid out of the booth and picked up his newspaper, letting the envelope drop out from its folded pages onto the table. "There's something extra in there, like I promised. But you listen to me: don't you lose Leon Czolgosz. Or Fred Nieman. Or whatever he goes by. Keep close to this one. And meet me here tomorrow morning." Norris turned and walked toward the door.

⌒つC⌒

THE next time they went to Big Maud's, Czolgosz decided against the whiskey.

"I get it," Hyde said.

"Do you?"

"Some don't want to get liquored up," Hyde said. "They can't . . . you know."

Czolgosz stared at him, helpless.

Hyde seemed to understand. "You want to have all your powers of concentration."

He went across the parlor to the Russian girl, Motka, and spoke to her a moment before bringing her to the bar. She was so petite compared to the other girls, with their heavy thighs and ample arms. There was a look of expectation on her face that frightened Czolgosz.

"I thought you always went upstairs with her," Czolgosz said to Hyde.

"It's all right," Hyde said. "Tonight you take her upstairs."

Motka put her hand on Czolgosz's forearm, startling him. "I'll make to you a little bet, darling." She spoke English slowly, with care, trying to compensate for the angularity of her Russian accent. He liked her voice, which was soft and had the slightest quaver, as though she were chilled. It made him want to offer her his coat. "My room is very quiet," she said. "We can just talk a little—would not you like that?"

Czolgosz looked at Hyde. "A bet?"

"A small wager," Hyde said. "Just go upstairs. You'll see."

"Sometimes I wonder if you are a true comrade," Czolgosz said.

Hyde shrugged, as though he did not wish to take credit for a small accomplishment.

Motka led Czolgosz out of the parlor and up the staircase, her skirts rustling about her hips as they climbed to the third floor. There, in her room, she had him sit in a straight-back chair and watch as she went around the room lighting candles. She made small talk, about where he was from, how long he'd been in Buffalo, speaking now in a combination of Russian and Polish—and when she hit upon an English phrase it was as though it were a great discovery.

"You are studying English?" he asked when she had all the candles lit.

"I buy an English newspaper every day. I have much used with the dictionary."

"That's good," he said.

"But I do not always *buy* what I read." She smiled at her joke, but then with great concern asked, "Is this the correct English word—'buy'?"

"Yes, very good."

"Perhaps I should find more lovers who speak English?"

"We can speak only English, if you like."

She sighed dramatically. "With you, it will be good. So much times I think that a man's vocabulary to be most limited." She came over and sat on the bed. Her knees were almost touching his left thigh and he moved his leg away from her. Yet her hair was beautiful in the candlelight and he fought the urge to reach out and touch it. "You like a whiskey?" she asked.

"No." He coughed into a handkerchief, and then blew his nose.

When she reached out toward his face, he began to withdraw, but then allowed her to lay her hand on his forehead. "You are ill? You seem most warm."

He started to get up from the chair, but she caught his arm and guided him to sit next to her on the bed. "Is there something I do wrong?"

"No, of course not. It's just this catarrh." He leaned back into the pillows, exhausted. "I can't breathe, and my sinuses hurt. I get headaches so bad they make me dizzy."

"Is there a favor you want?" she asked. "Just tell me what it is, please. What do you like to do?"

"Do? Well, I like to ride trains." She stared at his mouth, trying to comprehend what he was saying. "It's something about the speed, the noise, watching the countryside pass by."

"Trains," she said vaguely.

He turned his head away. "What was this bet you made with Hyde?"

"It is of no importance now. I have already won." He looked at her and she giggled. "It was only for me to get you up to this room."

"For how much?"

"A dollar. You are disappointed it is not more?"

"No."

After a moment, she said, "Then let me ask you to do this favor for me?"

"What?"

"Read," she said. "Read with me. Help me. My pronunciation is—it's not good, I have been told many times."

"I can understand you."

"No. I must make better."

"What do you want to read?"

"I have newspaper, but it is a week old. You are not interested in old newspapers? What would you have me read, Fred?"

He wiped his nose again with his handkerchief. "My name isn't Fred. It's not Fred Nieman. It's Leon Czolgosz."

She smiled then. "I make false names, too. But this is America and now I know it is no matter. My real name is Motka—Motka Ascher is who I was and who I will be." She leaned toward him. "You have the interesting blue eyes, Leon Czolgosz. They are most beautiful. Like two dreams. You almost seem in a trance, and when you stare at me I feel—powerless? What makes your eyes to be like that?"

For the first time he smiled. "Because I read a lot. I've always liked to read."

"Will my eyes be like that if I learn to read good English?"

"Maybe."

"What will you have me to read?"

"There's a book I've read over and over for . . . eight years or so—a novel called *Looking Backward*. Have you heard of it?"

"We have not time for books here."

"It's very popular."

"One book for eight years? What is it about?"

"A man named Julian West. He lives in Boston, he's well-to-do. It's 1877 and there are strikes and workers' protests everywhere," he said. "Then he falls asleep—and he wakes up in the year 2000."

"Two thousand!" She laughed. "That is ninety-nine years from here."

"*Now*. From now," Czolgosz said. "He finds that Americans have reached a solution to all their differences, all their problems, and they've done it without some bloody revolution. He discovers a workers' utopia." He could tell she didn't know the meaning of the word. "There is no competition between factories. No difference in salaries. Everyone has enough to eat, a decent place to live."

Her eyes drifted up to the sloped ceiling above their heads. "Women do not work in houses like this?"

"No," he said. "Everything is perfect. The strange thing, though, is that Julian West discovers that he has somehow lost his own identity, but he realizes that this is a necessary step, and like everyone else he is happy."

"Do you think we are headed to this . . . *you-top-e-a*?"

"Utopia," he said. "Yes, maybe it's a step."

He reached into his pocket and took out the article he'd been carrying for the last year. Motka watched him unfold it carefully—it was about to fall apart along the creases. Slowly, she read the headline, "Bresci Assassinates King of Italy," and then leaned away from him. "You knew him?"

"No."

"You read this over and over, too?"

"I admire this man. Gaetano Bresci believed in utopia." She looked confused as she reached out for the article, but Czolgosz folded it and put it back in his pocket as he got up from the bed. "I must go now."

"But why?"

"I don't know—I need to go. It's not you," he said. "I must leave Buffalo."

"Now?"

"Yes." He looked around the small room, its slanted ceiling. "You say you hope you don't have to live this life anymore someday. I hope so, too. You believe in the future. I believe in the future, but the difference between us is that I don't have one."

"Please," she said, looking confused. "Where do you go?"

"I don't know," he said. "It's more like I am taken."

"Will you come to see me again—and bring this book to help me with the reading?"

"I can do that."

She put her hand on his arm and said regretfully, "Of course, to give me the reading lesson you still must to pay three dollars to Big Maud."

HYDE spent half an hour upstairs, talking with Bella Donna. Because he only sought the favors of Motka, he was treated differently by the other girls; some showed jealousy or contempt, while others, like Bella Donna, who was Motka's best friend, treated Hyde as she would her brother. She was responsible for the well-being of all the girls who worked at Big Maud's, which meant that she ran the kitchen, the laundry, and the maintenance of the house, and provided what passed for medical services— handling everything from hangovers to overdoses to abortions. Her room on the second floor had flocked red wallpaper, a green velvet fainting couch, and a Victrola on which she played scratchy Italian opera recordings. She hummed along with the aria by Giuseppe Verdi that always made her eyes well up. Her wavy black hair hung to her waist and she liked to have Hyde brush it while she sat on the edge of her bed and looked at herself in the dressing-table mirror.

When the record was finished, he went down to the parlor and found Motka sitting on a sofa, avoiding the stares from the men at the bar.

"Where's Nieman?"

"He's gone." There was a hesitance in her voice.

"He didn't say where?"

She shook her head, distracted. "Did you know he likes to read? He is the real dreamer. He talks about . . . *utopia*? He would not hurt the fly." Raising her eyes to him, she added, "You owe me one dollar."

Hyde found a dollar in his pocket and gave it to her, and then he sat down heavily on the sofa. "I should stop making bets with you."

"He is not like most men."

"No, I believe you're right."

"He keeps his pants on, and his mind, it work like the fever. He says he has the catarrh and he takes medicines for it all the time. Maybe that is why he has beautiful dreams in his eyes. You know that he carries a—how do you say?—article from the newspaper in his pocket?"

"An article—about what?"

"Gaetano Bresci. The man that kills the king of Italy because he believes in this utopia, too."

Hyde sat forward, his hands on his knees. "He didn't say where he was going?"

"No."

"I must go."

"You must to find him?"

"Yes."

"I don't think that will be easy."

"You are a good judge of men, Motka."

"If they do not make talk. He said he is leaving Buffalo."

"Not again. He say where?"

"No, but you are right. He likes trains." Hyde started to get up off the sofa, when she said, "He did promise to come back and give to me a reading lesson."

"But he didn't say when?"

"He said he believes in the future, but he does not have one. Do I say that correct?"

"Yes, it's perfect."

They stood up and Motka took his arm and walked him out of the parlor to the front door. She went as far as the front stoop with him, her arm still curled around his elbow. "Big Maud tell us that if we step into the street with a customer at night, we lose a dollar."

"But you earned a dollar from our bet."

"I would only then to break even."

"That's true," he said. "I missed going upstairs with you."

"You went with Bella Donna, no? She is like the mother to all women. Is she not good to you?"

"Of course, but it's not the same. I brushed her hair while she cried to her opera."

"I think you be just a little jealous?"

Hyde was embarrassed and he looked away, but then he said, "Yes, a little."

Light from the transom window above the door slanted down on Motka's hair. Her eyes were large and sad. He had a sudden urge to kiss her, even though the one thing she would not allow was to be kissed on the mouth—like stepping out into the street and smoking in the parlor, it was against the house rules. But now he suspected that she might not resist, and would even welcome his kiss. As he leaned down to her, she lifted her face toward him, but then he heard a sound behind him, quick footsteps, and he was struck on the back of the head. A second blow caused him to see shooting white streaks. He fell off the stoop, landing on his side in the street, where he was kicked in the ribs. He managed to get to his feet and confront his attacker, a stocky man with curly hair who reeked of whiskey. He swung at Hyde but was so drunk that he missed and staggered against the stoop railing. Hyde hit him in the stomach, doubling him over, and when he straightened up, Hyde punched him in the face, once in the nose, followed by a roundhouse to the chin. The man fell to his knees, blood gushing from his nose and mouth. Hyde moved toward him, but Motka came between them, her hands on his chest, saying, "*Please, stop!* Anton, he is my *brother!*"

Hyde stepped back from her. Someone opened the front door, and the three of them were suddenly cast in the gaslight from the vestibule. Big Maud, Mr. Varney, and Bella Donna peered out, and Motka said, "It is over, it is a mistake! This is my brother and . . ." She began to cry as she held Anton, keeping him from falling.

"Well, get him in off the street," Big Maud said, but then she laughed. "We don't want to give the impression that I run a house where brawling is encouraged." She led Mr. Varney back to the parlor, her bustle floating behind her.

Bella Donna came out on the stoop and helped get Anton upstairs to her room. They laid him on the fainting couch and sat Hyde at the small table by the front window. Both women tended to the men's wounds, washing cuts and cleaning bruises. Though Hyde had a lump on the back of his head and his ribs ached, Anton was in worse condition. Motka wrung out the washcloth in the basin and tried to clean the blood from his face. "Anton, be *still*. You are stupid with this fighting. Always you lose." She turned and explained to Hyde, "He has been this way since we are children."

Her brother said, "I am defeating my sister's honor."

"Defending," Hyde said. "You were defending your sister's honor."

"Yes, that is correct," Anton said.

"Honor," Bella Donna said. She had Hyde's shirt off and she was wrapping a bandage around his ribs. "There's another capitalist lie. It's an excuse for losing."

Anton tried to raise himself up on the fainting couch, and

said to his sister, "You must leave this house. Or you end up like that girl in the canal."

Motka pushed him back down and continued to daub at the encrusted blood around his nose and mouth. "And you are not to come here every time you get drunk and—"

"This has happened before?" Hyde asked.

Motka only sighed.

Bella Donna said, laughing, "Usually he comes into the parlor, drunk, and shouts at everyone. In this moment it is like the opera, *è vero?*"

"Big Maud will throw me out," Motka said.

"Good," Anton said.

"Then what?" Motka dropped the cloth in the pan of pink water. "I live in the street? The girls work there do not live very long."

"You stay with me and my wife and son," he said. "I say this before."

She began to dry his face with a towel. "You cannot feed three mouths now, and I know how Katrina thinks for me."

Hyde buttoned up his shirt and got to his feet slowly.

Anton watched him and said, "You pay to be on my sister?"

"You might say that."

Anton made a little pushing gesture with his fist. "How do you like it for me to be on your sister?"

"I don't have a sister, Anton."

"You do not get my point."

"Neither do you."

Anton looked away, insulted.

Hyde went to the fainting couch and Anton stood up quickly. "Listen," Hyde said, "I'm sorry. I wish it were not this way."

He held out his hand, and after a moment Anton looked squarely at him. He was sober now and his nose was probably broken. He shook hands firmly, and then let go, nodding once. "You are the good fighter," he said. "Who teaches you to box?"

"A nun," Hyde said, and then he smiled. "A Sister of Charity."

"This is why I never understand Catholics, maybe?" Anton said, smiling, too, though it was clearly painful. "Rabbis do not teach children how to box."

"Sister Anne Joseph got tired of seeing me get beat up by other boys," Hyde said. "So she taught me what she called 'the art of self-defense.' " He went to the door and opened it, but then hesitated and looked back at Motka, her blue, woeful eyes. "You're lucky to have such a brother."

∽⌒∽

CZOLGOSZ did love trains. He rode them often, but rarely with a clear destination in mind. Within hours he'd be in Chicago— or Detroit or Akron or Cincinnati. No one in his family would know where he was for weeks at a time. He liked the power of a locomotive engine, the immediacy of travel, and he was content to sit in a Pullman car forever, staring out at farmland where neat rows of corn flickered by with such uniformity and speed that it created the optical illusion that the earth was spinning while the train wasn't moving at all.

Though he was born in Detroit, Czolgosz was conceived in Europe. He imagined that it happened the night before his father left for America. Nearly eight months later, his wife and three children followed him across the Atlantic. A month after they arrived in Detroit, Leon was born. The year was 1873, though no one in the family could remember the exact date of birth. His family moved about Michigan frequently, but his father only managed to find laborer's work up north: Rogers City, Alpena, and Posen, isolated lumber towns that attracted many Poles. Month to month it was a struggle to pay the rent and keep the family fed.

When Leon was ten his mother died while giving birth to her eighth child, Victoria. His mother was forty years old. Less than two years later, his father married Katren Metzfaltr. She was hard on all the children and cruel to Leon. He was quiet and withdrawn, and she distrusted how he would be idle for long periods of time. She accused him of stealing food from his brothers' and sisters' plates. He attended school less than six years, but had learned to speak and read English so well—better than any of his siblings—that it intimidated her.

His father couldn't keep in steady work in northern Michigan, so when Leon was in his teens the family lived for a couple of years in Pennsylvania, and then finally settled in Cleveland, where they ran a grocery. When all the children were old enough to work, their father collected money from each of them to buy a fifty-five-acre farm in Warrensville. They kept the house and store in Cleveland, but the farm was their father's dream: to own land in America.

When he was twenty-five, Czolgosz suddenly quit his job at a wire plant in Cleveland. He was skilled at repairing machines, as well as operating them, but he didn't look for another job. For the next three years he spent most of his time at the farm, tending to the animals, hunting, and fishing. At dinner he usually piled his plate with food—he was a voracious eater—and ate alone in his room. He could spend an entire day in bed, sleeping and reading; he read newspapers constantly, in English and Polish. Often he demanded money from his family and there were frequent arguments. They didn't know what was wrong with him, and mostly left him alone.

After leaving Big Maud's, Czolgosz boarded the Lakeshore Line express for Chicago, with the hope of seeing Emma Goldman. He knew she also traveled by train a great deal, giving speeches around the country and selling stationery products to stores, but she had spent the past few months at the home of Abraham Isaak, the editor of *Free Society*. Czolgosz couldn't stop thinking about her. He didn't feel well—he seldom did. His catarrh caused severe sinus pain and shortness of breath; he constantly took elixirs and lozenges, but eventually they made him lethargic, dazed, and nauseous. As the train traveled west across northern Ohio, he was lulled into a stupor, his head lolling against the window glass. He saw Goldman's round face, her intelligent eyes behind her rimless glasses. He had spent a great deal of the summer of 1901 in Buffalo because he believed she wanted him to go to the Pan-American Exposition. That year thousands of people were traveling to and from Buffalo, the city of electric light, the city with the bright future. Even President McKinley had been expected to visit the exposition when it first opened in the spring, but his wife had taken ill and their trip was canceled.

Czolgosz didn't know exactly when he decided to shoot the president, but the idea had first gripped him the night before he left his family's farm earlier in the summer. He was in the barn, cleaning rabbits. His sister Victoria came across the yard from the house, followed by his older brother Waldeck. Czolgosz could tell by his sister's long stride that she was angry, and though Waldeck was taller he was having difficulty keeping up with her. She worked as a maid for a wealthy family in Cleveland and she was still wearing her black uniform with the white lace collar. Her face was so pretty, her waist so small, her breasts full and round.

"Waldeck says you're going away again," she said. "Why, Leon?"

"Maybe I like trains?"

No one spoke as he peeled the skin down the rabbit's back. His brother and sister, repulsed by the smell, kept their distance from the workbench.

Then, wearily, Victoria raised her arms to her head, removed the pins, and let her long hair down. *"Leon, gdzie idziesz tym razem?"*

"This time? Where am I going *this* time? Chicago?" he said. "Or maybe Buffalo?"

"*Again?*" Waldeck said. "How many times you been to Buffalo this summer? You spend weeks there. You ignore the company of decent women, but I think you go to whorehouses."

He looked up at Waldeck. "Tell me you never have."

Embarrassed, his brother lowered his head and rubbed the back of his neck.

"You just ain't been to one in Chicago or Buffalo." He laughed, but it made him cough again, and he had to inhale slowly until his breathing calmed.

"What you *should* do is go to a good doctor," Victoria said. "That catarrh is getting worse. Your lungs sound like they're drowning in fluid. All the medicine you take doesn't do a thing. Except make you sleep a lot. You haven't really worked for, what, three years? You lay about reading all hours of the day."

"Maybe I like to sleep? Maybe I like to read?" he said. "And besides, I shot my dinner. I provide for myself. We should all quit our jobs and hunt for our food." The first rabbit was done and he held it out to them, soft and pink in his greasy hands. "Smooth as a girl's thigh." He put the rabbit aside on the bench and took the second one out of his pouch.

"Well I just think you're crazy," Victoria said.

"That's because you work for those rich people. You put on that uniform and tuck your hair up under your little cap, and you wait on them, clean their house, polish their silver."

"At least I have a *job*."

"And the sad thing, Victoria, is you believe in it," he said. "You believe it's right, it's good that there are some people who can live like that. But it demeans you, that uniform." With one swift motion, he cut open the second rabbit. "At least Waldeck understands what I'm talking about. He knows what's happening to the working people in this country. We've only sought the truth. Remember when we sent away for that Bible in Polish? We read the whole thing. Everything the priests had told us as boys was a lie—they said expect nothing but pain and sorrow in this life and you shall be rewarded in the next. Catholicism, like capitalism, is just another means of oppressing working people."

"Attending socialist meetings isn't the answer to anything." Victoria sat on a barrel as though she no longer had the strength to stand.

"I agree," Czolgosz said. "I go to the meetings, but socialism isn't the solution. It's another system, a yoke designed to harness working men and women." He began removing the organs. "Anarchists believe in a beautiful absolute: all political systems, all religions, all leaders, all laws enslave people. We need to live free, without restraint. Anarchists ask the hard question: When will we be capable of lifting ourselves up to the point where laws and rules and leaders are no longer necessary?"

"Leon, they *kill* people," Victoria said.

"The right people," he said. "Like the president of the United States."

"They shoot them, stab them, blow them up," she said.

"Not you, not me," he said. "Only the kind of people you work for."

"It's still murder," Waldeck said. "They're criminals, they're murderers."

"No," he said. "They're doing their duty. It's all any of us can do."

Disgusted, Victoria got up off the barrel and left the barn.

"Waldeck, I need money."

"You always need money, Leon. You take it from me, from Victoria, and then you go away, and when you come back you need more." When Waldeck struck out like that, it was a sign that he was weakening, and after a moment's hesitation he reached into the pocket of his trousers and put some folded bills down next to the first rabbit. "What *are* you going to do?" he asked.

"Maybe I'll shoot the president."

Waldeck stared at him, incredulous. "You're always making these . . . these claims."

"You don't believe me?"

"They're outrageous."

"It'd be easy—easy as shooting a rabbit. It would make history. That's what I should do: make history." He picked up the bills—eight dollars—and then continued to clean the second rabbit. "And this money will smell of rabbit in Buffalo."

"And then you'll be back for more. The way you borrow money and never return it, maybe you should become a capitalist."

He watched Waldeck leave the barn, and in the distance there was sound of cow piss driving into the mud.

Cows rarely looked up from their grazing to watch the train pass by, and Czolgosz often envied their sense of purpose. They were only concerned with eating; locomotives meant nothing to them.

Turning from the window he saw the conductor working his way down the aisle of the Pullman car, punching tickets as he went, speaking briefly to each passenger. His box cap had a blunt shiny bill, and his dark blue uniform gave him an air of authority. Czolgosz had seen him on the train before, but he knew the conductor would never remember him, which he found comforting. As the conductor approached the two elderly women sitting several rows in front of Czolgosz, something changed in their posture; they squared their shoulders and sat up straight, as though presenting themselves for inspection. The conductor punched their tickets with his silver clipper, and as he returned the slips he said something in an Irish brogue that made both women nod their heads. When he moved down the aisle, their shoulders sagged with relief.

Though he was a stout man in his fifties, the conductor swayed easily with the train's sideways movement, and his feet shifted in graceful little dance steps as he maintained his balance.

"Ticket," he said.

Czolgosz stared down at his hands, resting in his lap. He just wanted to close his eyes and go back to sleep.

"*Ticket,*" the conductor said impatiently.

Slowly, he reached into the pocket of his jacket and took out the ticket, which the conductor snatched from his hand.

"Chicago?" It sounded like an accusation. "Can't talk, boyo?"

He glanced up at the man, who had muttonchops and a mustache, black with gray, waxed at the corners. Czolgosz had worn a mustache until recently, and regretted shaving it off. Now he looked younger than twenty-eight, but what he missed was the sense of concealment those whiskers provided. Without the protection of a mustache, his mouth, his face, even his thoughts seemed more exposed.

The conductor held the ticket as though it were a ransom. "Can't talk English?"

Czolgosz looked the conductor in the eyes, and the man's thick eyebrows tilted inward as the hardness of his expression dissolved into fear, or perhaps awe. Since he was a boy, Czolgosz had known that his light blue eyes could have this power over people. As the train started around a curve, there came a screeching of metal from below the car. The conductor rocked back on his heels, though this time he lost his balance momentarily and his other hand reached out instinctively for the back of the empty bench in front of Czolgosz—and in doing so he dropped his ticket punch into Czolgosz's lap.

Czolgosz picked up the nickel-plated tool, studied it a moment, and then extended his arm toward the conductor; he might have been holding a gun the way the conductor leaned away.

"I speak English," Czolgosz said. "Better than you."

The conductor pulled himself upright as the train came out of the bend. He took the clipper, and as he punched the ticket there was a precise metallic click. He returned the ticket and moved down the aisle to the next passenger.

Czolgosz laid his forehead against the cool window glass and closed his eyes, and at that moment he realized what his duty was: he was supposed to shoot the president. He had thought about this before, many times, but now there was an absolute certainty to it—as though Emma Goldman had whispered in his ear.

~つC~

AS Norris walked down Market Street, he saw Hyde standing at the head of the alley next to the Three Brothers Café, looking impatient and worried. Norris decided against going inside the café, and they walked toward the back of the clapboard building. He listened to Hyde and finally stopped him when they reached a cabbage patch. Throughout Buffalo there were such fields between buildings, where people grew vegetables.

"What did I tell you?" Norris said.

"I know."

"But you went and lost him." Norris stared across the cabbage field; on the horizon he could see a series of tall stacks rising above Lake Erie, thick smoke angling into the blue sky. He was so disgusted he didn't want to look at Hyde. "And where does he get the money for all this traveling?"

"I don't know."

"Is he working?" Norris waited. "You don't know that, either."

"No."

"Did he *say* he was working?"

"No." Quietly, like a child.

"Then maybe someone's giving him the money? John D. Rockefeller says he received his money from God. Who's giving it to Leon Czolgosz?" He took out his cigar case, removed a cigar, and put the case away. He didn't light it but just held it between his fingers, where Hyde could see it. "And according to this Russian whore, he's an admirer of Gaetano Bresci?"

"Yes."

"You said Czolgosz wouldn't even go upstairs with a girl."

"He did last night."

"So he likes women."

"I said he's often shy around them."

"He fuck her?"

"I'm not sure what they did up there in her room."

"So what does that tell you, Hyde? Maybe they're plotting something together."

"No."

"With Russians, you never know."

"I don't know exactly what they did up there, but she's no anarchist."

"Why *don't* you know, exactly? You find *out*, that's what you *do*. It's hard work, this is, but sometimes it has its little rewards. You get her in the sack and you get her to do to you what she did with him. See? You become him. You got to *become* Leon Czolgosz, also known as Fred C. Nieman, which is goddamned German for 'nobody.' "

Hyde stood perfectly still. Norris realized this was a man who was accustomed to being chastised; he suspected it had to do with the orphanage. There was a time and place to just take it, to bend but not break. Hyde was smart enough to hold his temper.

Norris removed his bowler hat, inspected the white satin lining, and then seated it on his head, tapping it down until it was snug. "I was starting to think he was an onanist." He glanced at Hyde, who was clearly baffled by the word, and he made a back and-forth gesture with his fingers around the cigar. "And then I was half expecting you to report that he, you know—" Norris sucked on the end of the cigar before biting off the tip, which he spit on the ground. "So now it appears our friend enjoys sexual intercourse like any normal man." He struck a match with his fingernail and took his time lighting the cigar. "You're both just a couple of normal, God-fearing American men, that it?"

"He's left Buffalo," Hyde said. "I'm sure of it."

Norris exhaled cigar smoke and asked, "You know the story of Daniel, the prophet?" He was looking down at the packed dirt and he watched Hyde's shadow shake its head. "Well, I'll tell you, Daniel was at a feast in Belshazzar's court when some writing mysteriously appeared on the walls. No one could read this writing except Daniel, who said it predicted Belshazzar's death, followed by the division of his kingdom. That's why we still say 'read the writing on the wall.'" Norris took his billfold from his coat, counted out five one-dollar bills. "You should study your Bible." He handed the money to Hyde and said, "You find him. Or you don't get another penny from me."

~~OC~~

IN Chicago, Czolgosz spent an entire afternoon pacing the sidewalk in front of Abraham Isaak's house on Carroll Street. Isaak's wife, Mary, a heavyset woman who wore a cardigan despite the heat, frequently peeked out from behind the curtains. Finally, Abraham Isaak came outside in his shirtsleeves.

"I know who you are," he said. There was a bit of scrambled egg in his full beard.

"I wish to see Emma Goldman."

"She's not here."

"When will she be back?"

"That's none of your business," Isaak said, looking up and down the street.

"I only want to talk to her."

"Who are you working for?"

"No one."

"She's not here. She's not in Chicago."

"Where is she?" Czolgosz pleaded. "You remember me, don't you? I came here in July. She was preparing to go to the train station with your daughter. I helped you with the luggage. They were going to Rochester, to visit Emma's family, and then they were going to visit the Pan-American Exposition in Buffalo. She hasn't returned?"

"I know what you're up to," Isaak said. "They send men to watch us all the time, but they don't have the *nerve* to stand right here in front of our house!"

"I only wish to speak to her—"

Isaak started up the stairs to his front door, saying over his shoulder, "You keep away from her. You keep away from *us*!"

Czolgosz returned to his boardinghouse and spent much of the next few days in bed because his catarrh was particularly bad. He had clogged sinuses, a sore throat, sneezing fits, a hacking cough, headaches, and dizziness. Though he tried various remedies, nothing worked. He was convinced he would die young, which caused him to worry about his place in history.

At night, when a cool breeze came in off Lake Michigan, he felt a little better and he walked the city streets. He brought English and Polish newspapers back to his room and read everything in them. There was little truth or comfort in the opinions expressed in their pages, though he was particularly drawn to advertisements for elixirs, nostrums, and other health aids: Lydia Pinkham's Vegetable Compound; Syrup of Figs Laxative; Dr. McLaughlin's Electric Belt, which "stops the drain upon a young man's vitality." But it was next to a Sozodent Tooth Powder advertisement ("Good for Bad Teeth. Not Bad for Good Teeth.") that he read that the president's visit to the Pan-American Exposition had been rescheduled for the first week of September. The original plan had been that McKinley would pay a visit to Buffalo on his return from his tour of the western states in the spring, but Mrs. McKinley had taken ill. In El Paso the president's physician,

Dr. Presley Rixey, lanced a bone felon on her finger, but when the entourage reached California the first lady collapsed. The president's train sped north to San Francisco, where the first lady could rest. Her condition grew worse and the press reported that arrangements had been made for a funeral train. The president's entire schedule had been canceled. But the first lady, as she had done before, rallied, and her health stabilized. They returned to their home in Canton, Ohio, where they spent the summer while she recuperated. Czolgosz wasn't sure what a bone felon was, but he realized that the first lady's illness had given him an opportunity.

On the last night of August he returned to Buffalo. Previously he had boarded at the Kasmareks' house out in West Seneca, but now he wanted to stay in the city, near the exposition. He entered Nowak's Hotel on Broadway and asked for lodging. He was wearing the gray flannel suit he had bought in Chicago, and a black shoestring tie. He carried his valise and brown fedora with a yellow band. John Nowak studied his face, and for a moment it seemed he was going to refuse to rent him a room.

But then Nowak said, "Weekly rate is two dollars, in advance."

"Sounds fair," Czolgosz said.

Opening the register book, Nowak asked, "Name?"

"John Doe."

Nowak raised his head but he couldn't meet Czolgosz's stare, and his eyes drifted toward his assistant. "Frank, you see any women with this fellow?" He smiled, to cover his unease. "I suppose if there was a little woman in that valise, you'd tell me your name was Smith." He laughed.

Czolgosz was tempted to tell him he had a single-shot pistol in his valise. Instead, he put two dollars on the counter. "I promise you, no woman in here."

Nowak picked up the bills. "You can pay, you can stay. You make trouble, you go. No refund."

Frank led Czolgosz up the stairs, and when they reached the second-floor hall, he said over his shoulder, "John Doe?"

"Well, I'm a Polish Jew and if I told him that do you think he'd let me stay?"

"Doubt it." Frank unlocked the door to room number eight. "Besides, I don't believe you're Jewish. What's your real name?"

Czolgosz entered the room, which had a single bed, a straight-back chair, and a bureau with a water pitcher and a basin. The furniture was old but the bedspread looked clean. "Nieman," he said. "Fred C. Nieman."

Frank had a hollow right cheek and it appeared that he was missing some teeth back on that side. He placed the room key on the bureau and turned to leave.

"You want to know the real reason I gave a false name?" Czolgosz asked. "My mother's maiden name was Nowak. If I got into my family tree with your boss, I'd never get up here, and I really just want to rest. This heat, you know."

Frank appeared skeptical, rubbing his jaw with his hand, but then he seemed to come to a decision. "Well, there must be a lot of them's come over, 'cause you see the name Nowak a lot."

"Swear it's the truth," Czolgosz said. "If there's one thing a man can't lie about, it's his mother's name."

The next day, the first of September, he read the announcement in the new issue of *Free Society*.

Attention!

The attention of the comrades is called to another spy. He is well dressed, of medium height, rather narrow shouldered, blond, and about 25 years of age. Up to the present he has made his appearance in Chicago and Cleveland. In the former place he remained but a short time, while in Cleveland

he disappeared when the comrades had confirmed them-
selves of his identity and were on the point of exposing him.
His demeanor is of the usual sort, pretending to be greatly
interested in the cause, asking for names, or soliciting aid
for acts of contemplated violence. If this individual makes
his appearance elsewhere, the comrades are warned in
advance and can act accordingly.

He wasn't surprised. This was Abraham Isaak's doing. It was just like what happened to Gaetano Bresci—none of his comrades in Paterson believed he was capable of killing the king of Italy until he had accomplished the deed.

Czolgosz could do nothing but go about his business. He arose early and was downstairs by seven. He never took meals at the hotel—the portions were small, the meat greasy. He would buy cigars from Nowak before setting out for the day. When he returned in the evening, with a bundle of newspapers tucked beneath his arm, he usually went straight up to his room. Occasionally he paused briefly in the saloon for a whiskey, always top-shelf. Several times he visited the Pan-American Exposition grounds. The streetcar was a dime; admission fifty cents.

In his valise he carried a single-shot pistol, which he knew would not be sufficient. One morning he went into the Walbridge Company Hardware Store on Main Street and bought a small, nickel-plated .32-caliber Iver Johnson five-shot revolver for four dollars and fifty cents. Manufactured in Fitchburg, Massachusetts, it was identical to the pistol Gaetano Bresci had used to kill the king of Italy.

September 3, the night before the president was to arrive in Buffalo, Czolgosz went by himself to Big Maud's.

When he told the madam that he wanted Motka for the entire night, she said, "Splendid choice, darling, but it will require twenty-five dollars."

To her surprise, he produced a roll of bills and peeled off three tens.

"You can have drinks on the house at the bar," the madam said. "Motka should be able to receive you soon."

"Who is she with now? Hyde?"

"You understand that we respect a gentleman's privacy in this house," she said.

"Of course."

He spent about half an hour at the bar. During that time several men came downstairs, but none of them was Hyde.

When he went up to Motka's room, she was wearing a black silk bathrobe with red flowers. She was lighting her candles, a ritual she must perform for each man who came up to the third floor. "I am most pleased to see you again," she said.

"One day you won't have to use candles," he said. "Everywhere you will turn a switch and the room will be lit."

"Electric lights will never come to houses like this." She waved out the matchstick. "Maybe in—what was it?—the year 2000?" He tugged the book from the pocket of his suit coat and gave it to her. "You brought it!" she said. She took his hand and they sat on the bed. She studied the cover and read slowly, "*Looking Backward.*"

"I brought it so you could practice."

She raised her head, her blue eyes concerned, even fearful. "This is really about life in the year 2000?"

"Yes."

Motka got up off the bed, went to the bureau, and opened the top drawer. She turned around, a silver flask in her hand, and then came back to the bed and stood in front of him. "Let's drink to the year 2000."

He was about to begin reading, but she took the book and put it on the nightstand. She stood close to him as she untied her robe and let it slide down her arms. The material dropped to her hips, where it bunched momentarily before falling to the floor. She was wearing a silk slip with a tiny flattened pink ribbon stitched to the border between her breasts. Her nipples, pushing against the sheer fabric, were enormous. She knelt on the bed, straddling his thighs, and whispered in English, "This cannot be the same with electric lights."

She took a sip from the flask, and then held it to his lips. The whiskey sent him into a coughing fit. She helped him lie down on the bed, and after a few minutes he could breathe normally, but he was coated with sweat.

"You need to get out of these," she said, as she began to unbutton his shirt.

It was unusual—he did not feel the shyness that ordinarily plagued him around women. The room was very hot. After she removed his clothes, Motka set a pan of water by the bed and washed him with a cool, damp cloth—all of him, starting by dousing his scalp.

"It is not just your eyes," she said. "You are a lovely man. Not fat, like so many, and you don't smell. You are like the virgin."

"A virgin," he said, correcting her.

"Tonight you seem different. Maybe there will be the reading lesson later?"

"All right."

But when she lay down next to him, he tried to sit up. His breathing suddenly became shallow, which usually preceded another bout of coughing. She placed her hand on his chest and he lay back on the bed. "Slowly," she whispered. "Slowly."

He breathed through his mouth, and after a few minutes the congestion in his lungs and the tightness in his throat began to disappear.

"We have all night," she said. "As long as you don't decide to leave."

"I'm not leaving Buffalo again. Ever."

"Ever?" she asked. "What does that mean?"

"It means 'ever.' "

She moved so that she brought her breasts to his mouth. He sucked on one, and then the other, and then he took them in his hands. Periodically she reached down to the pan, squeezed water from the cloth, and rinsed both of them. Water ran down his face; it pooled in the little depressions behind her collarbone.

~ つC~

BECAUSE of the heat, Hyde was sitting out on the front stoop of his boardinghouse when Lottie Bender came down the street. She was wearing a blue dress and a bright red hat, and walked as though invisible hands were pushing her hips this way and that—and everyone sitting out on the stoops turned to watch. She might not have been sixteen.

"Big Maud sent me to fetch you," she said. "It's about some man."

"Nieman's returned?"

Looking away, bored, making eyes at the men on the next stoop, Lottie said, "She knows you'll be good for the two dollars you promised." She held out her hand. "Ordinarily I don't do house calls, not in this heat."

Hyde got up off the steps and handed her a dollar. "That's for you. I will pay Big Maud when we get to the house."

He began walking down the sidewalk, but paused when Lottie couldn't keep up because of her high heels. "What's your rush?" she said. "Your friend has bought Motka for the whole night. He peels ten-dollar bills off like they was a soiled shirt." Taking his arm, she said, "Listen, for another dollar you and me could take our time—it's so much cooler out here."

Hyde looked back down his block, where half the neighborhood was watching, fascinated. "You sure he's there all night?"

"And it's still young. Now let me take you down this alley here and"—she ran her tongue around her puckered her lips—"I'll do you *sooo* right, love."

He pulled her along the sidewalk, going at a pace that made her half trot.

Mr. Varney opened the door and Big Maud was waiting in the vestibule. Hyde let go of Lottie's arm—she was breathless by the time they reached the house—and he gave two dollars to the madam. "Thank you for sending for me," he said. "Is he up there now?"

Big Maud tucked the folded bills in the little purse that dangled from her wrist. "He is," she said, smiling warmly, "but, as you know, the policy in this house is to honor a gentleman's privacy." He took another dollar bill from his pocket, but she held up her hand. "Please, I have the reputation of this house to consider," she said. "If my people thought that I'd let anyone else interrupt their assignations, I'd lose the faith of my most cherished customers."

Reluctantly, Hyde took out another dollar bill.

Big Maud accepted the money with her usual grace, and said, "You are, of course, welcome to wait here in the parlor. Or perhaps enjoy the company of one of my other girls?" She drifted away, glancing once over her shoulder, her bustle bobbing gently behind her.

Hyde went into the parlor, where "Camptown Races" was playing on the piano. He stood at the bar and kept his back to the girls who were seeking his attention. The room was stifling and he ordered a whiskey with a chaser of beer. He drank the first and then the second glass of whiskey fast, before returning to the vestibule. Big Maud was fanning herself, as she sat on a dainty chair next to a small table with a vase of flowers.

"This heat," she said. With her fan she indicated the chair on the other side of the table, and Hyde sat down. "I understand," she said. "It's really this girl, Motka, that brings you back again and again. You must not lose sight of the true nature of such relationships."

"I don't like the idea that she's upstairs with a man all night."

"But he's your friend. You brought him here."

"I know." He leaned forward, placing his elbows on his knees. "Any man."

"Oh, my. Has it gone *this* far? Really, one mustn't drink so fast in this heat."

He turned to her. The powder was caked around her eyes. "You sell your women."

She laid her fan on the table. "You are interested in a . . . business transaction?"

"No. I wish to have a family."

"I see. A family." She exhaled slowly, in anger. "Mr. Hyde, this is an illusion and, well, some illusions are dangerous."

"How much would you sell Motka for?"

"She's one of my most popular girls—*why* would I want to do such a thing?" She paused a moment, listening to laughter coming from the parlor. "And, I assure you, girls who are stolen from me, who are coerced by a man to believe in certain dangerous illusions—they come to no good end." She glanced toward the front door, where her bouncer sat on a stool, his thick arms folded. "Mr. Varney takes particular pleasure in returning lost or stolen goods to me. It's a source of pride, like a good hunting dog."

"I understand."

"What's mine is mine."

"But—"

"I have no intention of selling, and even if I did you wouldn't have the resources."

She picked up her fan and began waving it in front of her face. Hyde got to his feet and went back into the parlor, where he ordered another whiskey and beer.

~ᑐᑕ~

THERE was a knock on the door. Czolgosz awoke and Motka stirred beside him. After the knock came the second time, she got out of bed and pulled on her bathrobe. When she opened the door, Hyde came into the room. Only one candle remained burning, so everything seemed unreal, dreamlike to Czolgosz.

"Big Maud does not tell you I am busy tonight?" Motka whispered angrily as she closed the door behind Hyde.

Hyde's movements were unpredictable and exaggerated because of drink. He seemed both determined and exhausted as he sat in the chair that was piled with Czolgosz's clothes. "I have been looking for you, Leon."

"And why is that?" Czolgosz asked.

"I read something in *Free Society* the other day—a warning about a spy, and the description made me think of you."

Czolgosz started to laugh, but it quickly broke into a cough. When it subsided, he said, "Funny, I saw that, too, but it occurred to me that the description might fit you as well. Except you have dark hair. This spy is reported to be blond. Perhaps I have been too trusting? I should have watched you more closely? Should I report you?"

As Hyde leaned back in the chair, Czolgosz's jacket slid off the armrest and fell to the floor, making a heavy knock on the wood. He looked down at the coat, and then reached into the side pocket and took out the Iver Johnson revolver. "What have we *here*?" he asked. "This seems new, brand-new." He looked up at Motka, who had stepped back into the corner, frightened. "Maybe he is a spy. Don't spies carry these?"

"Put it back." Czolgosz wanted to get out of bed, but he was naked and couldn't bring himself to throw off the sheets with another man in the room.

Hyde studied the gun closely. "And it appears to be loaded. Of course, what's the point of carrying a gun, if it's not?"

"What do you want?" Czolgosz asked.

"*Want?*" Hyde said. "Tell me what you plan to do, *comrade.*"

"Why?"

"Maybe I can help."

"No one can help me," Czolgosz said. "Not now."

Hyde stood up suddenly, holding the pistol at his side. He was very drunk. "You have a plan, I know you do. There's something about you—it's frightening, but I must admit it's also admirable. There's a . . . a purity to the way you operate." He laughed. "You have purpose." Leaning forward, he said, "You move about so. Where are you going next?" When Czolgosz only stared back at him, Hyde grew angry and pointed the gun at him. "I think I know."

Czolgosz said nothing. He seemed unable to get enough air into his lungs. He often had trouble breathing but now he was only aware of a painful tightening in his lungs. He kept watching Hyde, the gun in his hand—though he noticed that Motka, who was standing in the corner behind Hyde, had picked up something.

"The president arrives in Buffalo tomorrow," Hyde said.

"Perhaps you do know," Czolgosz said. He inhaled slowly, filling his lungs, and as he exhaled he gasped, "But do you understand?"

"Understand? Understand *what*?"

"Necessity." Czolgosz inhaled again, deeper this time. "Necessity and history."

"Then I'm right?" Hyde straightened up, his face became more alert, as he aimed the pistol at Czolgosz's chest. "Anarchists, they always talk about eliminating all leaders. You don't really want to help the worker, do you? You only want chaos."

"I have my duty," Czolgosz said.

Hyde seemed to lose his resolve for a moment, and the gun

appeared to weigh down his arm. Then he took careful aim again. "So have I—"

Motka stepped toward Hyde and swung with both arms, and when the porcelain chamber pot struck the back of his head it rang with the tone of a bell. Hyde fell forward onto the bed, his arms lying across Czolgosz's legs. He was out cold and blood matted his hair.

Czolgosz removed the revolver from his hand.

II

EXPRESS ORDERS HAD been given regarding noise. When the three-car Presidential Special pulled into Buffalo the afternoon of Wednesday, September 4, it was expected that there would be tens of thousands of people gathered to welcome William McKinley. There would be marching bands; there would be a military gun salute. McKinley had just been sworn in for his second term of office in March, and he was clearly the most revered president since Abraham Lincoln. However, McKinley's personal secretary, George Cortelyou, was concerned about two things: the fact that since the second election there had been, despite the president's popularity, a marked increase in the number of death threats directed toward him; and the health of the first lady, Ida B. Saxon McKinley. Cortelyou consulted regularly with Dr. Presley M. Rixey, the president's personal physician, who accompanied the McKinleys everywhere. Rixey insisted, as he had in the past, that care had to be taken concerning noise when the train arrived in Buffalo. Thus Cortelyou had forwarded specific instructions that the welcoming ceremony—and in particular the twenty-one-gun salute—had to be conducted at a safe distance from the train. The president's health was consistently robust and satisfactory, though Rixey would have liked to see him lose weight. The doctor's attention was largely taken up with Mrs. McKinley's condition, which was frail at best. She could not, Rixey insisted, be subjected to loud, unexpected noise.

Rixey was standing by her chair in the president's coach as the train crept into the city. The plan was to stop briefly at Terrace Station on the outskirts of Buffalo and allow members of the Pan-American Exposition committee to board the train, and then continue on to Amherst Station, which was at the north end of the exposition grounds. It was a warm afternoon and some windows were partially opened. Even as they pulled into Terrace Station a throng was being held back by a security line consisting of police, soldiers, and Pinkerton men. It never ceased to amaze Rixey, the planning and coordination and, increasingly, the security measures that were necessary for any public appearance by the president. He sympathized with Mrs. McKinley, who had said more than once that she would prefer that they all remain in the tranquillity of Canton until it was absolutely necessary to return to the Executive Mansion in Washington. The whole idea of passing the summer in Ohio was in response to her near fatal collapse during the trip they had taken to the West Coast in the spring. McKinley had canceled many events and appointments as a result, and this two-day visit to Buffalo had been rescheduled, primarily to give the president an appropriately large audience to deliver what he considered a major speech, one that would establish the goals for his second term of office. It was an opportunity that could not be missed; seldom was there an event outside of Washington where so many Americans would gather to see and hear their president. Newspapers speculated that when McKinley addressed the audience at the exposition on September 5, he would appear before the largest crowd to ever hear an American president speak.

As the train drew to a halt, the crowd cheered and applauded while arms and flags waved in the brilliant September sunlight. A marching band was vigorously playing the last bars of a John Philip Sousa tune that Rixey had been hearing all his life but still did not know by name. He looked down at Ida McKinley, dressed in black despite the warmth of the day, and watched her raise her handkerchief to her forehead.

"Can I get you anything, Mrs. McKinley? A glass of water before we alight?"

"No, Presley, thank you." She offered him the faintest smile. "I'll be fine."

"We have arranged for a wheelchair to be at the platform."

"You are always most considerate."

The band concluded its number, and just as the crowd broke into applause there was a loud, percussive explosion. Dr. Rixey instinctively crouched down and turned his back toward the impact, which seemed to come from the depot platform. There followed another explosion, and then another. There was screaming inside the coach. Security men were moving, shouting; Mrs. McKinley's niece Mary appeared to have fainted on a sofa—or perhaps she had been wounded. The explosions continued, developing a precise rhythm, causing Rixey to realize that it was only the military salute. The soldiers were too close to the train and their rifle fire was deafening.

But the salute continued, and just as Rixey looked down at the first lady the windows on the platform side of the train blew in, raining glass on everyone, amid more shouts and screams.

And then it was over. Outside, the cheering swelled to a nearly ecstatic pitch, the crowd not realizing what had happened on the train. Passengers got to their feet, glass crackling beneath their shoes. Rixey leaned down to Mrs. McKinley, who was deathly pale.

"I'm all right, Presley."

"Are you sure?"

But then she raised her head and looked past him, and a brightness, even a faint joy, entered her weary eyes. Rixey knew who it was, stood up, and turned around. William McKinley's broad, soft face was absolutely serene as he gazed at his wife. His

blue-gray eyes, as Rixey had noted many times, maintained startling clarity and focus.

Standing a little behind and to the right of the president
was Mrs. McKinley's youngest nurse, and a look of panic had
taken over her face as she stared at the first lady. Rixey turned
quickly and saw that Mrs. McKinley was showing the first signs
that she was about to have one of her seizures. Her left eyelid
had begun to droop and there was a rapid twitching in that
cheek. A series of deep furrows had developed in her forehead,
and her mouth trembled as spittle foamed from the corners.
Her pulse was visible in the side of her gaunt neck. Aghast at
such a sudden transformation, everyone around her seemed to
have frozen—this too Rixey had seen on numerous occasions.
No one seemed able to do anything to help her. Even Rixey still
felt somewhat helpless.

The president stepped toward his wife's chair. Calmly, yet
deliberately, he removed his handkerchief from inside his frock
coat and unfurled it with the slightest snap of the wrist, as though
he were an amateur magician who had developed such little dra-
matic flourishes to conceal his lack of technical skill. Leaning
down, he carefully draped the handkerchief over Mrs. McKinley's contorted face, and then he said quietly, "It will be over in a
moment now, dear."

Rixey looked about at the others—staff members, Cortelyou,
several security officers. They returned his gaze expectantly, hoping he could make this silent, awkward moment pass. But Rixey
did nothing. Though he was the doctor, he'd learned to simply do
nothing during these quietly tense moments, for this was, perhaps
as it should be, a uniquely intimate occasion between husband and
wife. Long ago Rixey had learned that it was best not to interfere.

The handkerchief seemed to have a life of its own, quivering
as it rested over Mrs. McKinley's face. Her husband remained
close to her, supporting himself with both hands on the armrests
of her chair.

A good minute passed and no one moved. Though there was still the noise of the crowd outside, it was as though an eternal silence and stillness had descended upon the coach. Only the handkerchief trembled, as if by some spiritual force.

Finally, the handkerchief became still, and McKinley gently removed it by the upper corners, uncovering his wife's face: her eyes were closed, her mouth slack but calm, set in its usual frown. She might have been asleep.

But slowly she opened her eyes—the left lid still slightly recalcitrant—and gazed up at her husband inquiringly.

"Better now, dear?" he asked.

"Yes, Major," she whispered.

He straightened up and smiled.

Suddenly, Rixey moved toward the sofa, where Mrs. McKinley's niece was beginning to stir. The doctor took her hand, which was warm, and gently placed his fingertips over her wrist to feel her pulse. The girl's eyes were not dilated; her cheeks were pleasantly flushed.

"I'll bet you could use a glass of water," Rixey said.

The girl nodded slowly, awed, it seemed, by such remarkable perception. Rixey himself was surprised at how calm he sounded. But it wasn't so—the explosions seemed to have ignited his nerves.

There was a beverage tray on the table next to the sofa; Rixey poured water into a glass and gave it to the girl. He noticed, as he put the pitcher back on the tray, that his hand was not shaking. She took a sip of water, and then smiled at him.

"You see?" The president's baronial public voice addressed everyone in the saloon. "Does anyone question why we always keep the good doctor near at hand?"

There was polite laughter, which more than anything seemed to express a collective sense of relief.

George Cortelyou approached McKinley, his face slick with perspiration. "Mr. President, we might attempt a different mode of transportation into the city, and I could begin to make arrangements."

McKinley looked at his wife, and then turned to Cortelyou. "Everything is fine now, George. Why don't we proceed as planned? I gather there will be an even larger crowd waiting for us at the exposition. If we keep them waiting too long, they might all turn into Democrats."

~ఎC~

CZOLGOSZ was in the crowd when the president's train arrived at Amherst Station in Buffalo. He had never been in such a noisy, suffocating crush of people. He was pushed and jostled as everyone pressed toward the tracks, where a line of security men and uniformed police blocked the crowd from surging across the platform. He held his right arm tight to his side, to protect the revolver in his coat pocket.

Slowly he found openings in the crowd and inched toward the front. He was not a tall man, only five foot eight. Parasols held high made it difficult to see the train, which was at least fifty yards away. It was impossible to tell which coach McKinley was in, and there was nothing to indicate where or when he might descend from the train. A line of carriages stood waiting, to be led through the exposition grounds by guardsmen on horseback wearing plumed hats. Finally, Czolgosz reached the front of the crowd and came face-to-face with a burly policeman.

Somewhere to the left there was a scream. Turning, Czolgosz saw a tall man take a swing at one of the policemen, his fist glancing weakly off the round helmet—the only result was that the brim was knocked down over the officer's eyes, causing people nearby to laugh. But the policeman in front of Czolgosz shouted "Here now!"—and shifted to his right, reached through the crowd, and took hold of the pugilist's upper arm. The pushing and shoving increased to the point where Czolgosz was unable to keep his balance, and he fell forward past the guard, his hands scraping the brick platform.

He was hit several times on the back of the head and shoulders, and then he was lifted up by both arms by two policemen. They hustled him along the front of the crowd and then heaved him off the platform, as one of them shouted, "Here you go now!"

Czolgosz landed on his hands and knees in gravel. He felt his coat pocket—the pistol was still tucked away. Getting to his knees, he turned and saw the two policemen working their way along the platform, continually shoving back at the crowd. He stood up and staggered away from the noise and confusion.

~ɔC~

THE McKinley administration's best-kept secret was the first lady. Soon after Presley Rixey became the president's physician, he learned that one's political importance could really be determined by the extent of one's knowledge of Ida McKinley's condition. The public had no idea, of course, because the press corps assigned to cover the Executive Mansion had little understanding of the first lady's history of ailments. When the McKinleys had married, William was a young Ohio lawyer and a retired Civil War major who had served under Rutherford B. Hayes, and his bride was the independent, spirited daughter of one of Canton's wealthiest bankers. They had two children, one who died within days of birth and another while still a baby. After the loss of the second child, Ida McKinley became extremely withdrawn, and over the years suffered bouts of depression, which were complicated by various illnesses, including epileptic seizures. She was obsessively dependent upon her husband, who always came faithfully to her aid.

During McKinley's first term as president, his staff realized that perhaps their greatest obligation was seeing to the first lady's constant needs. Though remarkably frail, she insisted upon being included in the endless ceremonies and duties that were incumbent upon the president. At the frequent large dinners held at the Executive Mansion, the president broke with protocol and sat next to his wife. At receptions she would be placed on display in a chair, holding a single flower in her lap as an indication that guests should not attempt to shake her hand. Through it all, the president was ever the doting husband, but such constant solicitude was clearly a burden.

As the president's physician, Rixey had as his primary responsibility the first lady's comfort and health. Her seizures were frequent and could last a few seconds or several minutes; when they occurred in private, either the president or Dr. Rixey would stand behind her chair and gently massage her temples. When the seizure ended, she was usually confused and often didn't know what had just happened. It could quite naturally sour her disposition and make her demanding and even obstinate. Rixey knew he was retained as the McKinleys' physician for his patience and discretion as much as for his medical expertise.

Thursday, September 5, had been declared President's Day in Buffalo, and well over one hundred thousand people were expected to pass through the gates of the Pan-American Exposition. The president's schedule was, as always, coordinated by his personal secretary, George Cortelyou. It was commonly perceived within the administration that McKinley was able to function so well as president because of Cortelyou's meticulous care and attention to detail. During their visit to Buffalo, the McKinleys and their staff were staying in the home of John G. Milburn, president of the Pan-American Exposition. That Thursday morning after breakfast Rixey took Cortelyou aside in the front hall. "George, you must cancel the entire program."

"Everything?" Cortelyou asked. "Including his speech?"

Rixey, who was well over six feet tall, leaned toward Cortelyou. Years earlier as a naval officer, he had come to realize that his height gave him a unique vantage point. And often people tended to be drawn to his height as though seeking protection. But not Cortelyou. He was a man of about forty, at least a dozen years younger than Rixey, and had sleek dark hair and a full mustache. Though Cortelyou was always poised and impeccably mannered, beneath his officious veneer lay steely nerves.

Rixey glanced toward the open front door, where McKinley and several other men were enjoying their first cigars of the day on the front lawn while they waited for the carriages to arrive. "We should cancel these public appearances and get the president to Washington."

"But, Doctor, we're anticipating that tens of thousands will attend his speech. When has a president had an opportunity to address so many at once?"

Rixey's fingers stroked his full mustache, shaping it over his upper lip. "George, that's what worries me."

"You know that the president has said that this may be the most important speech of his career—it's intended to set the agenda for his second term." Cortelyou scanned the guards who patrolled the sidewalk in front of the house. "Look at the security we have—they've cordoned off the entire block. We have Buffalo police, military personnel, and of course the beloved Pinkertons."

The attempt at humor didn't take, however; if anything, it made Rixey more agitated. "You take all these precautions, and yet—do you know what the president did again this morning?"

Cortelyou knew, but he shook his head.

"He came downstairs and before breakfast was served, he went outside, and took a *constitutional* around the neighborhood—ordering the guards that he was *not* to be followed. The president, wandering alone around the streets of Buffalo, without any protection at all!"

"As his physician, you might recommend that he take more constitutionals. Nothing would be better for his waistline."

"I'm not talking about the fit of his vest," Rixey said. "He defies my every precaution. At the Executive Mansion once he was sitting by an open window—at *night* when he was in *full* view from the street. When I mentioned this to him, what did he do? He got up, pulled down the *shade,* and took his seat again. When

I suggested that he move away from the window, he was aston-
ished, and asked, 'Who would wish to harm me?'"

"He is beloved," Cortelyou said. "You saw his reception yesterday. He enjoys being among the people, meeting them. He
detests the isolation of the office, which I find an admirable, even
healthy, response."

Rixey folded his arms as though to restrain himself. "You
know what he once said to me? He said, 'If it weren't for Ida, I'd
prefer to go the way of Lincoln.'"

Out in the street they could hear the sound of carriage wheels
and horse hooves approaching the house. Behind them there was
the rustle of skirts from the far end of the hall. Rixey turned and
watched Mrs. McKinley walk from the dining room, followed by
her maid, Clara Tharin. Both he and Cortelyou stepped aside,
bowing slightly. She didn't really look at either of them, but stared
straight ahead. She passed through the front door, and the president smiled as he took her arm.

"You watch," Rixey said. "As the day progresses at some point
the first lady will . . ."

Tactfully, he let it stop there. It wasn't necessary to go further;
they both knew what would happen, for Mrs. McKinley could be
quite exasperating and predictable. To be sure, at some point during the day's events she would grow tired, and suddenly special
arrangements would have to be made to accommodate her.

"Presley," Cortelyou said, placing a hand on the doctor's forearm. "We're all fortunate you're here."

Then they both followed the others down to the waiting
carriages.

∽⊃C∼

CZOLGOSZ had never seen such a crowd, thousands gathered
in the Triumphal Causeway before a stage built especially for the

president's speech. He was so far back from the platform he could barely hear the president. He worked his way forward slowly, gazing across the sea of hats and parasols. It was so rare to actually *see* the president that people didn't seem bothered by the fact that they couldn't hear every word he said.

Czolgosz kept his right hand in his coat pocket, holding his revolver tightly, but as he neared the stage he realized it would be impossible to get close enough. There were soldiers in full-dress uniform lined up in front of the platform. He got to within twenty yards of them, but he stood shoulder to shoulder with two men, and it would be impossible to take aim and fire accurately before one of them made a grab for the pistol. It was very hot and he was sweating heavily. All around him people wiped their faces with handkerchiefs—he'd left both his handkerchief and his fedora in his room at Nowak's.

McKinley did not seem affected by the heat. He held a sheaf of papers before him as he spoke, while his other hand was casually tucked in the front pocket of his striped trousers. He was fatter than Czolgosz had expected, but somehow that didn't make the man an easier target. Nor did he seem particularly threatening. Even from this distance, his face was wide and fleshy, but his voice was deep, clear, and remarkably precise as it drifted out over the hushed crowd. He was simply a man who ate well and dressed formally— when he first stepped up onto the stage he had been wearing a silk top hat, which he removed before delivering his speech. He was talking about things that meant nothing to Czolgosz. He used the word "reciprocity" numerous times, and it seemed to have something to do with America's trade relations with other nations. Behind him on the stage sat dozens of foreign dignitaries; some wore their native clothing, shiny pastel silks from the Orient, and one man wore a red fez. Compared to these other government representatives, the president was as bland as he was fat.

This huge crowd, all these ornate buildings in the exposition—it seemed so distant from the dim, noisy, foul-smelling factories where Czolgosz had worked in Cleveland. He tried to imagine what Emma Goldman would say if she were up on that platform. She would talk about the children whose youth was being destroyed by endless days on the factory floor. She would talk about the city streets where tenement buildings did not have electric lights, where the squalor, filth, and lack of sanitation led to disease and death. She would talk about women bearing children until it finally killed them. Gesturing with her arms, her glasses glinting in the sun, Emma Goldman would shout down this fat man. She would insist that instead the president look closely at the daily lives of American citizens.

∽つC∽

AT Norris's insistence, two Pinkertons accompanied Hyde to the exposition for the president's speech. They bought three pairs of binoculars from vendors just inside the gate, and then they agreed to split up, seeking high vantage points from which to view the wide esplanade known as the Triumphal Causeway. Hyde managed to find a place on the steps to the French exhibit building, where he had a good view of the stage. The two Pinkertons— Rawley, leaning on a windowsill in the Brazil exhibit, and Miles, standing next to a palm tree rising from the flat roof above the Streets of Cairo—scanned the crowd methodically, but they frequently trained their binoculars on Hyde, as he was the only one who knew what Czolgosz looked like. The newspapers predicted that anywhere from fifty to one hundred thousand people would come to hear the president. The crowd was enormous; Hyde had never seen anything like it.

He used the binoculars, though it seemed quite pointless. The back of his head still ached, and the lump left by Motka's chamber pot was tender—it was very close to where her brother, Anton, had hit him. When he had awakened he was lying in her bed, and she leaned over him, rinsing the cut on his scalp.

"Where's Czolgosz?" Hyde had asked.

"Gone." Her eyes were filled with tears. He'd never seen her cry before. "I do not understand this. He wants to shoot the president?"

"The gun—he took it?"

"Yes." She wrung out the cloth over the pan of pink water.

He touched the back of his head and winced at the pain. "Did he give you any idea where he was going?"

"I did not understand what was happening. I thought you were going to shoot him."

"I should have."

She placed the cool, wet cloth on the back of his head again. "You must to stop him."

But it seemed impossible amid this enormous crowd. Everyone gazed toward the stage, and from this angle it was difficult to see faces. Still, Hyde believed he could spot Czolgosz's head, if not from the back, certainly in profile. There was a delicacy to his features, a dreamy expression that was unmistakable. With subtle adjustments of the binoculars, it was as though Hyde could leap across the audience and peer right at someone's face. He examined scars, pockmarks, shaving nicks at close range. Men with facial hair he passed over quickly. But it occurred to him that Czolgosz might attempt some form of disguise. There wasn't enough time, and there were simply too many men, too many faces raised, almost as if in prayer, toward the stage.

After he had left Big Maud's, he went to tell Norris. He had never been to the Pinkerton office before, but he knew it was above a men's haberdashery. When he entered the long room, detectives sat at desks smoking, talking, and like Norris they all possessed a well-fed brutality. They watched Hyde as though he were a suspect, but then a door opened at the back of the room and Norris waved Hyde into an office that was separated from the rest of the room by frosted glass.

The police captain Lloyd Savin was there, too, sitting in the corner. Norris leaned on a mahogany desk. They both listened to Hyde describe the previous night at Big Maud's, though he didn't mention Motka. When he was finished, Norris said, "So you've lost him. Again."

"After he brains you," Savin added. "That's using your head." Both he and Norris laughed, but then they stopped as if on cue.

"I don't suppose you have a picture of him?" Norris asked.

Hyde shook his head.

"A blond man, slight build, not too tall, in his mid-twenties," Norris said. "There shouldn't be too many of those in Buffalo, I imagine."

"And you're sure he has a gun," Savin said. "You saw it."

"A revolver, yes," Hyde said.

Norris got to his feet, opened the office door, and said, "Wait outside."

Hyde went out and the door was closed behind him. The detectives in the larger office all stopped talking at once; they turned and stared at him. He went over to a window that looked down into the street. They could all hear Savin's voice coming from Norris's office—something about the way he spoke more distinctly indicated that he was talking on the telephone. He was arranging some meeting for later in the afternoon. When he mentioned the Milburn house, one of the detectives said quietly, "That's where the president's staying."

After Savin hung up, minutes passed, causing the detectives to get restless, until finally the door opened; Norris came out, with Savin behind him, bringing absolute silence to the detectives in the room.

Norris said, "All of you are to go to the exposition this afternoon for the president's speech. You're to keep an eye out for a young man with blond hair, not too tall, slight build, and he's carrying a revolver."

Norris looked at him and said, "And you, Rawley—you and Miles take Hyde with you." He paused a moment, and then glanced at Hyde. "And when the speech is over—assuming the president doesn't get shot—you are then to bring him back here."

One of the other detectives snorted. "What if he does get shot?"

Norris stared long and hard at the man, who finally removed the toothpick from his mouth and looked away.

Norris and Savin went back into the office and closed the door, making the frosted-glass wall shake. The detectives didn't move at first; then slowly, one by one, they got up from their desks and began to leave, each one as he put on his coat or hat giving Hyde a hard look on the way out.

Now the president finished his speech and the crowd burst into cheers. McKinley seemed genuinely surprised by the response. He bowed repeatedly, a gesture that was formal, yet humble and appreciative. He raised his arm and waved back at the crowd, and it was this simple gesture that seemed to elevate the noise until it swelled through the Triumphal Causeway in waves, Americans cheering their president, who waved back as though he were greeting old friends. A woman standing in front of Hyde wept with joy.

Hyde lowered his binoculars and watched the president leave the stage with his entourage. The crowd shifted and re-formed itself, and quickly an avenue was created, allowing the president's carriage to move slowly down the causeway. Hyde looked through the binoculars again, and suddenly he saw Czolgosz, standing not five yards from the carriage. His head seemed to float on a sea of humanity—but while there were expressions of adoration around him, his face remained stony and unmoved.

As McKinley's carriage continued on through the parting crowd, Czolgosz was pushed farther behind, and finally he began to make his way in the other direction, toward the Lincoln Avenue gate.

Hyde ran down the steps and pushed through the crowd. He could no longer see Czolgosz, but he kept moving toward

Lincoln Avenue. Finally, he reached the gate, and through the wrought-iron bars saw Czolgosz walking down the wide boulevard. Hyde followed, weaving around groups of strollers and vendors' carts, and just avoiding being run down by bicyclists.

Then Czolgosz, not twenty yards ahead, looked over his shoulder and saw Hyde. He turned and began to run. Hyde skirted a large group of children, who were singing "God Bless America," and then he broke into a run. Czolgosz wasn't that fast; his shoulders heaved, and Hyde realized that it was his breathing—his catarrh caused him to slow and gasp for breath. Hyde was gaining, and when he was within a few feet, Czolgosz turned and looked back—his blond hair was matted against his forehead, and he appeared out of breath. He jammed his right hand into his coat pocket, and raised his arm. Hyde could see the end of the gun barrel pressing against the corduroy fabric of Czolgosz's coat, and he stopped. People brushed by them, laughing and talking loudly.

Hyde moved forward, raising his arms in front of himself involuntarily. Czolgosz extended his arm, but he was gasping for breath and seemed to have difficulty taking aim.

There was a sound to Hyde's left and he turned his head to see a boy on a bicycle coming straight toward him. The boy was looking at Czolgosz and must have noticed the gun because he yelled just as his bicycle slammed into Hyde. They both fell to the pavement with the bicycle, and all around them there were exclamations from men and women. When he rolled onto his side, Hyde saw the boy, lying on the ground beneath the enormous front wheel of his bicycle, crying in pain.

A small crowd gathered around, tending to the boy, who began to scream when he realized that the rim was warped, the spokes bent, the tire deflated.

Someone helped Hyde to his feet—it was Miles. The other Pinkerton, Rawley, arrived, out of breath from forcing his way through the crowd. "You saw him," he gasped. "You saw Czolgosz?"

Hyde touched the side of his head and blood came off on his

fingers. The Pinkertons were speaking to him but their voices seemed distant. White streaks shot across his vision. He gazed down Lincoln Avenue; it was full of people, most walking away from the exposition, some waiting for the trolley. There was no sign of Czolgosz.

~⁀つC⁀~

IT was late afternoon when the president's entourage finally returned to the Milburn house. Everyone was quite done in from the sun and heat, but there was also a muted sense of jubilation: the president's speech had been a spectacular success.

Only George Cortelyou seemed unaffected by the mood of the house, and when he found Rixey in the dining room, where a substantial buffet had been laid out, he whispered, "I wonder if you might accompany me to my next meeting. It concerns the president's security." Before Rixey could answer, Cortelyou tucked his leather-bound folder—which was seldom out of reach—under his arm and started briskly down the hallway toward the back of the house. "No, it's not the Secret Service," Cortelyou said over his shoulder. "Their job is to escort the president, and indeed they did a splendid job this afternoon."

"Then who are they?" Though Rixey was considerably taller, he had to make an effort to keep pace with Cortelyou.

"A captain from the Buffalo police, a Pinkerton detective I know from their Washington office, and one of his informers."

Cortelyou opened a door and entered a sunroom on the south side of the house. There were large potted plants and wicker furniture covered with cushions decorated with a bright floral pattern. The ceramic tile floor made every sound echo, especially the crackling wicker as three men stood to greet Cortelyou and Rixey.

"Gentlemen," Cortelyou said, shaking hands. "This is the

president's physician, Dr. Rixey. And this is Captain Savin and Detective Norris. And?" He looked at the third man, the youngest of them.

"This is Hyde, Moses Hyde," Detective Norris said. "I thought it would be wise for you to hear what he has to say."

"Indeed," Cortelyou said.

Hyde was quietly nervous, clearly unaccustomed to such company. His clothes were worn and ill fitting, and Rixey noticed what appeared to be a sizable lump on the side of his head.

They all sat in their chairs, and once settled everyone seemed afraid to move for fear of making the wicker creak.

Savin lit a cigarette and dropped the match into the ashtray on the table next to his chair. "The speech went well," he said, almost as a formality. His suit was tailored, his oiled hair tight to his skull.

"The president attracted a remarkable crowd," Cortelyou said. "It was estimated at more than fifty thousand. Dr. Rixey here has been urging us to cancel all of the president's public appearances. He believes these crowds are too large."

"The size of the crowd has nothing to do with the size of the threat." The Pinkerton detective, Norris, leaned forward, his chair groaning, and spoke to Rixey. "You might be wise to do just that, Doctor." Creases from his hat appeared to have been permanently impressed into the side of his head. He lacked Savin's polish, and there was something unsettling about his bulging eyes; they possessed a hint of humor, as though the detective thought it absurd that five men, responsible in various ways for the safety of the president of the United States, should be lounging in the warmth and comfort of this sun-drenched room.

"The president has a full schedule, tonight and tomorrow, before he leaves for Washington," Cortelyou said. "I don't think we've *ever* had more security people surrounding him. We even brought you out here, Mr. Norris."

"I hope it's enough," Norris said.

"What are you suggesting, Mr. Norris?" Cortelyou asked.

"I'm suggesting that you pack McKinley on the Presidential Special and get him back to Washington in the dark of night. Lock him up in the Executive Mansion and give him very limited access to newspaper reporters. In fact, you might line his office with lead, too."

"Bulletproof?" Cortelyou asked.

"I was thinking more along the line of bombs," Norris said.

Cortelyou shifted so that his chair creaked in disapproval. "During the last election the president conducted much of his campaign from the front porch of his house in Canton. *Anyone—not* just reporters—was welcome to gather on his front lawn and ask him about his policies regarding Cuba, the Philippines, the gold standard. He is determined to continue that method on through his second term of office. Nobody's going to 'pack' the president anywhere."

Norris sat back in his chair; he had had his say.

"That's why you're here," Cortelyou said. "We require the best security."

"Thank you," Norris said.

Cortelyou leaned toward Rixey and said, "A year ago I received a letter from a man claiming that he was part of an anarchist group that was planning to assassinate the president. He listed five names, all of them Italian. The Secret Service wasn't getting anywhere with it, so I contacted the Pinkertons and Norris was instrumental in finding one of the men who was already in Washington."

"How?" Rixey asked.

"I run spies, Doctor," Norris said. "Informants, like Hyde here." He gestured toward Hyde, as though he were evidence of a rare, seldom-captured species. "They can be our best defense against something like these anarchists."

"This is why I requested that Norris come to Buffalo weeks ago," Cortelyou said, "to work with Captain Savin so that we might learn of any plots before the president arrived."

Savin exhaled blue smoke upward into a shaft of sunlight. "We have an enormous population of Italians, Poles, Hungarians, Russians—they're pouring into the city. They have no money, most speak little or no English, and they're all looking for work. They're ill fed, poorly clothed, in the winter they're cold, they're sickly throughout the year. The women who can't find work in factories walk the streets, and the men—they spend what they have on the women and in saloons. Would some of them like to kill the president? Absolutely. There are groups all over the city—socialist, communist, anarchist, whatever. We hear of plots all the time, but it's like trying to hold water in your palm."

Hyde seemed distracted; he was gazing down at the floor tiles, as though trying to figure something out.

"Detective Norris," Rixey said, "you have not just one spy, but a network here in Buffalo?"

"I do." He leaned forward in his chair again. "Captain Savin has helped me set it up, and I think we've identified some potentially dangerous individuals."

"What do you do with these individuals?" Rixey asked.

For a moment, the doctor thought that Norris was going to laugh, but he then settled a cold stare on the space between them. "What I'd *like* to do is kill them. And the rest of the lot I'd load into ships and send back to where they came from—but that, of course, is a policy decision I cannot make." Cortelyou was about to speak, but Norris continued, his voice measured and forceful. "I'll give you one example. Hyde has identified a man who came here from Cleveland. He's a Pole and has been in contact with the likes of Emma Goldman. His behavior, according to Hyde, suggests that he's quite capable of attempting to kill the president. But he has done no wrong, broken no law. And even though Captain Savin has sent word of him out to the police throughout Buffalo, the fact is nobody knows what this man looks like, other than the most general description."

"Interestingly," Savin added, "there was an announcement in the recent issue of *Free Society* that describes a man who might be spying on the anarchists. Some of the description matches what little we do know about this Czolgosz."

"What I suspect it means," Norris said, "is that now that they've sent their man on his mission they want to sever all ties with him."

"And nobody really knows what he looks like," Cortelyou said.

Rixey turned to Hyde. "Except for you."

The young man appeared surprised to have been addressed directly. He was gathering the nerve to speak, when Norris said, "That's correct, Doctor: except for my informant."

Rixey nodded, and looked at Hyde again. "Where is this man?"

Norris sat back, glaring at Rixey; the doctor ignored him.

"I'm not sure where he is right now, Doctor," Hyde said. "But he was at the exposition during the president's speech today."

"You saw him?" Rixey asked.

"From a distance—through a pair of binoculars," Hyde said. "He got fairly close to the president's carriage, but the crowd was too . . . I followed him, but I couldn't reach him. He was armed."

"Armed?" Cortelyou said.

"Yes, sir," Hyde said. "He had a pistol."

"You saw it?" Cortelyou asked.

"He aimed it at me," Hyde said. "I followed him through the crowd." The young man lowered his eyes, and it seemed he was unable to continue.

"Well?" Cortelyou said.

Norris cleared his throat. "Hyde says he was hit by a boy on a bicycle, and when he looked up the man was gone."

Cortelyou studied Hyde for a moment. "A bicycle?"

"The gun," Rixey said. "Did he take aim at the president?"

Hyde glanced at Norris, as though seeking permission to

speak, and then he said, "I didn't see that, sir. He was in the crowd and I couldn't tell."

For a moment, Cortelyou scribbled rapidly on the notepad in his leather-bound folder, and when he closed the folder on his knee everyone understood what it meant. "Thank you, gentlemen," he said as he replaced the cap on his fountain pen and tucked it inside his suit coat. "Please keep us notified of any further developments."

They all stood up and moved toward the door, passing in and out of wide bars of sunlight angling down from the tall windows. Cortelyou walked ahead with Savin and Norris, and Rixey fell in next to Hyde. From the side, the doctor could see the considerable lump above and behind the young man's right ear, which was encrusted with black dried blood. "That looks nasty," he said. "It really should be cleaned properly."

"I'm all right, sir."

Rixey hesitated at the door, causing Hyde to stop and look at him uncertainly. "No, it might get infected and that could lead to all sorts of problems. Let me take a minute to clean it." When they were all out in the hallway, Rixey said, "You gentlemen go on. I'm going to take a minute with Hyde here."

Cortelyou nodded agreement, Savin seemed uninterested, and Norris looked perturbed. Clearly, there was something coarse, shrewd, and even brutal about the man. "Well, we can't wait," Norris said. "Other appointments, you know. You meet me, Hyde, tomorrow morning at the usual place." He didn't wait for a reply but followed the others down the hallway to the front vestibule.

Rixey led Hyde up the back stairs to the bedroom he'd been using since the president's entourage had arrived at the Milburn residence. "Here, please have a seat," he said, pulling the desk chair closer to the window.

Reluctantly, Hyde sat down and watched as Rixey made preparations at the desk: pouring water from a pitcher into a porcelain pan and opening his medical kit, a leather bag with a frayed handle. "I've been telling myself I should get a new bag for years, Moses, but somehow I just never get around to it."

Hyde turned his head and stared out the window toward the carriage house; small talk didn't seem to put him at ease. "People just call me Hyde."

"Your parents must be very religious to name you—"

"It was the nuns," he said quickly. "The nuns in the orphanage gave me my name."

"I see." Rixey soaked a cloth in the water, and then began to gently daub at the encrusted wound. "It looks like some hair has already been cut away," he said.

"Yes, sir."

"Who did that?"

"A woman I know."

"Did she put anything on it? Iodine, disinfectant?"

"She didn't have any."

"I see. Well, I do."

Slowly the water broke down the encrusted blood, revealing a deep, crescent-shaped gouge in his skin. Most patients would have pulled away or at least winced, but Hyde only continued to stare out the window. "This is quite nasty," Rixey said.

"It was a misunderstanding."

"With the woman?"

"It was just a misunderstanding."

"I see—"

"No, I don't think you do, sir."

After a moment's hesitation Rixey took a jar of ointment from his bag and began to spread it over the wound. "I'm sorry," he said. "I don't mean to pry."

There was a nervous tension in the young man's face, and he seemed both undecided and angry. "The woman, she cleaned it as best she could, but she had no medicine."

"Your girl, perhaps?"

"Not exactly. She's a prostitute, and the misunderstanding—

if you want to call it that—was with this man that wants to kill the president."

"He got away because of some bicycle mishap?"

"That's right."

"That's how you got this cut?"

"No. Not exactly. It was earlier—it's not important, not now."

"Tell me something." Rixey waited until Hyde looked up at him. "Norris says you're an informant. Obviously, it's dangerous. Why? Why do you do it?"

"I get paid," Hyde said. "I get paid, and Norris said I might get to join the Pinkertons." He began to turn his head away, but he looked back up at Rixey. His eyes were different now, not angry but vulnerable and sincere, like a child's. "But I don't trust Norris, not one bit. Or Savin either. You can't trust any of them." He seemed at a loss for words suddenly and looked as though he regretted having spoken at all. But then he went on, speaking with vehemence now. "But, you see, *somebody's* got to stop Czolgosz. He wants to shoot the president—I *know* it. He's an anarchist and he feels it's his duty." Hyde looked down, appearing weary and exhausted.

"So you've made it your duty, too," Rixey said.

"I suppose I have," he said regretfully. "Besides, I know what he looks like."

As Rixey put the lid on the jar of ointment, he said, "To do this sort of thing, it takes fortitude, a rare kind of fortitude." There was a notepad next to the telephone on the desk; he picked up a pencil and scribbled the phone number on it. He tore the page off and handed it and the jar of ointment to Hyde. "If I can help you—perhaps look at this wound again—you can always call me here at the Milburn house."

Hyde stared at the jar and slip of paper a moment, and then he took the jar and stuffed it in his coat pocket. "Thank you, but I will not use this." As he placed the slip of paper on the desk, he smiled, revealing some embarrassment. "The truth is, sir, I have never used a telephone."

∽ↄC∼

NORRIS knew that Savin naturally resented the fact that he, Norris, had been brought in from Washington—perfectly understandable. But Savin was smart and circumspect. Rather than try to make Norris's job difficult, he was too helpful. He sent numerous stoolies and collars to Norris, but they were bogus. Norris met with them in bars and cafés and at newsstands, and they all tried to sell him on plots: Italians planning to blow up city hall, Poles scheming to kidnap the mayor. A man who called himself Bluenose Brudnoy swore that he'd seen Emma Goldman on more than one occasion at the Pan-American Exposition, talking to a group of Russians about shorting the electrical system and setting on fire the Edison Company's Electric Tower, which loomed above the grounds.

Hyde was different. He wasn't hawking his wares. He wanted the money, yes—they all wanted the money—but Norris felt he was holding something back. Unlike the others, who would say anything for another drink, Hyde was cautious and shrewd, qualities that were necessary to survive a childhood in an orphanage. And he was obsessed with this Leon Czolgosz. It was in his eyes; the man was playing a hunch and in his mind there was no question. He had conviction.

Norris needed to get closer to Czolgosz himself. He realized that Hyde and Czolgosz had one thing in common, so he went looking for the Russian prostitute. Buffalo was full of declared brothels and he had been to several of them. He would never have gone to Big Maud's on his own. It wasn't a bad place as such houses go—it was relatively clean and in the parlor the madam put on some air of Victorian gentility, which was ironic since most of the girls and their customers were Slavs or Italians. But that was the kind of thing that attracted a certain client, the potted ferns, the player piano, a rug on the floor. The girls dressed up while they were downstairs, unlike in some houses where they just sat around in their bathrobes between sessions.

The girl's name was Motka Ascher and she wasn't exactly his style. He liked them bigger, more robust, probably because they reminded him of girls he knew when he was a teenager back in Iowa. But Norris spent the afternoon up in her hot room. Periodically, they would pause and she would have him sit on the straight-back chair in the middle of the room while she slowly sponged him down with cool water from the basin. The window was open and he could look out across the rooftops. On the sill was a paperback copy of *Looking Backward*.

"You read English?"

"I try," she said. "I learn."

She ran the sponge across his shoulders and up his neck to his scalp. "How many languages you speak?"

The girl shrugged. She seemed to enjoy bathing him. Her eyes were clear because she wasn't using anything. Drugged girls had little enthusiasm for their work.

"Let me guess," he said. "Your customers here are Russian, Polish, German, Croat, Italian, so you speak a little of each."

"*Si, signore, parlo italiano un po',*" she said. "And English."

"You believe that crap?" he said, nodding toward the book.

Her hand paused and she smiled. A girl's smile, still. Full lips and a mouth with all its teeth. "Utopia," she said as she dunked the sponge in the basin. "The year 2000 is a long time away, so must we get it now in little pieces."

"Well put." He laughed. "You believe in utopia, you must be a socialist."

"No."

"No? Maybe an anarchist."

"No," she said. "No political."

"You're all anarchists, don't kid me. You'd shoot Andrew

Carnegie right now if he walked in the door. I probably would, too. Those bastards own everything."

"Maybe *you* are the anarchist," she said.

"No. Worse."

Her hand paused as she worked down his chest with the sponge. "How?"

"I'm going to show you in a minute, I'm going to give you another little piece of utopia."

She smiled uncertainly.

"Let me see that," he said, nodding toward the book.

She put the sponge in the basin on the bureau and went to the window. The faintest ridge rolled beneath the skin on her calf.

"It is difficult," she said, handing him the book. "Not like reading a newspaper. I take a page or two at a time and do not understand all the words."

"But you figure them out, don't you. You're smart and you can figure out what the words mean. It's called context."

"Context?"

"The words you understand around the words you don't."

She nodded and picked up the sponge again.

"I'm cool enough for now," he said. "How about a drink?"

She opened the top bureau drawer, took out a silver flask, and handed it to him. He unscrewed the cap and took a swallow of warm whiskey.

"Nice," he said, looking at the flask. "Somebody give this to you?"

"Left it." He handed the flask to her.

"Couldn't pay."

"It was a gift." She took a pull and swallowed without wincing.

"You like gifts?"

She nodded.

He held up the book. "This a gift, too?"

He watched the caution flood her eyes.

"Don't calculate," he said gently. "Just tell me who gave you the book."

"What is 'calculate'?" Norris waited. "Is it important?"

"It might be. Was it Leon Czolgosz? Or Fred Nieman?"

Leaning a hip against the bureau, she said, "Leon."

"Which is his real name. He must be fond of you. When'd you see him last?"

She shrugged.

"It was last night, right?"

"Yes, and Czolgosz cracked Hyde's skull." She looked nervous now. "You know all about this," he said. "You knew about Czolgosz and his gun, and the lump on Hyde's head."

The girl stared back at him.

"Here, it happened here, didn't it?"

She didn't say anything.

"All right. Good. This is very good," Norris said. "Czolgosz goes around giving books like this to little Russian sluts like you, talking about utopia and workers' paradise and, my favorite, free love." As he raised his voice he could see that she was becoming more frightened. "You believe in *free love*?" he nearly shouted. "You ever give a man a piece of utopia for *nothing*?" He got up off the chair and moved toward her.

"You do not have to pay," she said, frightened. "We can have this free love now."

"No, I have money," he said. "I don't mind paying. I'm an *American*. I be*lieve* in capitalism, *see*?" He hit her on the top of the head with the book, and then tossed it on the bed. He was impressed that she didn't start to cry. "Where is Leon Czolgosz now?" he said, then louder: "You know—don't you?" She shook her head. "You *know* what he's going to *do*?"

"I *don't* know where he is, please. He was gentle. Like a boy."

"And he brought you that damn book about utopia."

"To teach me to read."

"I'll teach you." Grabbing her by the upper arm, he pulled her over to the open window. "Now put your hands on the sill."

She resisted but he got her bent over so she had to put her hands on the sill or fall out the window. He entered her from behind and took hold of her hips, and each time he shoved she gasped as her head and shoulders went a little farther out the window. Looking down into the fenced yards behind the houses, he saw two boys staring up at the window with their mouths open. With each shove, she cried out in pain. Toward the end he tried to knock her right out into midair, but her arms were strong, braced against the sill.

It was early evening when he went downstairs, where Big Maud greeted him in the vestibule. "Everything was satisfactory, I trust, Mr. Norris?"

"There some place we can talk?"

She raised a hand and touched her hair. "Of course. Is there a problem?" When he didn't answer, she led him down the hall to an office that was appointed with book-lined walls, a mahogany desk, leather chairs. "Sir, I gather that you're not with the police, because we are on good terms with—"

"No, the Pinkertons."

"I see."

"This isn't some shakedown for money," he said. "It's your girl, Motka."

Big Maud gestured toward one of the leather chairs. "Please, sit down, sir."

He sat down and waited until she was seated behind the desk. "I understand that Motka has entertained two men recently—"

"I'm sure you appreciate, Mr. Norris, that we respect the privacy of our clients—"

"I do, but in this case you're going to make an exception. Because it involves security issues of the highest order."

"Security?"

"National security," Norris said.

"I see. Who are these two men?"

"One's named Hyde—one of your regulars." She nodded. "And Leon Czolgosz."

"I don't know this—"

"He also goes by Fred Nieman."

Big Maud placed her elbows on the desk and pressed her palms together as though in prayer. "Nieman. Yes, he has been here." She stared back at Norris with the cold eye of a seasoned cardplayer.

"He and Hyde, together?"

"Yes."

"Recently?"

She wetted her lips. "Well—"

"Motka says last night."

"Did she?" Big Maud sat back, looking slightly offended.

"Was she lying?"

Big Maud took a deep breath for effect. "The fact is, sir, something rather strange occurred during the night. And I will tell you in the strictest confidence."

"Of course."

"This man, Fred Nieman or Leon Czolgosz, at first he came here with Hyde—but last night he was by himself and he arranged to spend the entire night with Motka. She is one of my most popular girls, and the cost of such services is—well, he produced a fat roll of money. But that is not what's peculiar about all of this. Early this morning I came out of my suite—here, next to the office—and who do I see coming down the stairs from Motka's room on the third floor? Hyde."

Norris got up and went to the window, which looked out on the backyard, where several of Big Maud's girls were hanging bed linen on clotheslines. "I thought you said Nieman came alone."

"He did. But Hyde had been looking for him—in fact, he had made arrangements with me to let him know if Nieman came here. So I sent one of my girls to get Hyde. He waited down here, but sometime later when I was busy he must have snuck upstairs to her room—it is difficult to keep track late at night. If you would like, I will have Motka come down here and explain this."

"No, that won't be necessary."

"Well, I have to say this is most irregular. You understand that I can't have my girls involved in things that threaten national security."

"I understand."

"I have a good mind to bring her down here and tell her to clear out of my house—"

Norris turned to Big Maud, who was trying to strike a balance between indignation and complicity. "I'd appreciate it if you wouldn't do that. In fact, it would be best if no one knew of this conversation."

"But of course." She watched as he took his wallet from his suit coat. "And please, Mr. Norris, do not feel obliged to offer compensation. This is, after all, a question of national security, is it not?"

"Indeed, madam, indeed. Yours is an act of true patriotism." He put a twenty on the desk. "And such vigilance will not go unrewarded."

~⌒⌒~

THAT evening the president's entourage returned to the exposition to view a fireworks display created by Henry Pain, the acknowledged master of the ancient Chinese art. An enormous crowd again awaited the president. As in the afternoon, the crush of citizens greeted McKinley with screams and shouts and applause; flags waved and arms were raised as though people were hailing a beloved god. McKinley clearly enjoyed every moment, but the doctor was deeply concerned. Despite the fact that lines of police and military personnel constantly surrounded the president's open carriage during the ride through the exposition grounds, there were several incidents where someone in the crowd managed to approach the president unimpeded. Women swooned; men did silly things to get McKinley's attention—one man walked on his hands alongside the carriage until two security men grabbed him by his airborne legs and dragged him away. On another occasion an elderly man stepped forward and the president stood to shake his hand and greeted him by name; they had served together in the Civil War.

Even Cortelyou, usually unflappable, was disconcerted by such outlandish public displays. Rixey could see it in his face as he hovered near the president, his dark eyes constantly scanning the horde around them. Other members of the president's staff appeared genuinely frightened. No president had ever been exposed to such a large crowd of people. There simply were not enough guards to adequately protect him, and by the end of the evening everyone returned to the Milburn house, weary and exhausted.

The McKinleys occupied adjoining rooms on the second floor, and in the morning Rixey was summoned upstairs by the first lady's maid, Clara Tharin.

"Is there a problem?" he whispered as they reached the first landing.

"Not that I knows of," Clara said. She and her husband, Charles, who both resided at the Executive Mansion, were devoted to the McKinleys. "She slept good, far as I can tell. No calls in the middle of the night. It's the president wants to see you."

They went down the second-floor hall, boards creaking beneath thick carpeting; Clara knocked on a door and said, "I've got Dr. Rixey, sir."

"Yes, come ahead."

She turned the knob and held the door open for Dr. Rixey and closed it behind him. The sitting room overlooked the backyard and the windows were rimmed by ivy, giving a green tint to the early-morning sunlight that filled the room. The president was staring curiously at some objects on top of the bureau. He was dressed as he was most every day—boiled white shirt, starched collar and cuffs, black satin cravat, white piqué vest, and pin-striped trousers. His frock coat was draped across the back of a chair. "God has granted us a splendid morning, Presley."

"Indeed, sir. Did you sleep well?"

Without looking away from the bureau, McKinley smiled. "You mean did Mrs. McKinley?" He glanced toward the closed door that led to their bedroom. "She did, and in a few minutes it's going to be Clara's enviable task to arouse our fair maiden." The president smiled at his little joke. It had often occurred to Rixey that most of the people who came into contact with William McKinley had no idea who he was—his stern, bland expression was designed to conceal the man within. Rixey always felt a deep sense of privilege when the president shared a few minutes alone with him—something he did often, largely because their joint task was to see to the well-being of the first lady. McKinley picked up a fine silver chain, to which his eyeglasses were attached, and hung it around his thick neck. Somehow Rixey had the feeling that he was witnessing a sacred ritual, as though the president were a priest or minister donning the vestments for a religious ceremony. "Look," McKinley said, holding out several coins in the palm of his hand. "Our president is going forth on this fine day with a dollar twenty in his pocket." He tucked the change away in his trousers. "Do you suppose our vice president would be caught dead with a dollar twenty on him?"

"No, sir."

"Indeed! It might tarnish his office, not to mention his family's good name. No wonder he thinks of me as having the spine of"—McKinley turned his head toward the window a moment—"what was it? 'The spine of an éclair'? Only the strong shall inherit their family's wealth, Doctor." Looking down at the bureau again, he collected keys clustered on a small heart-shaped ring, and then two that were separate, which he put in his other pocket. "I carry these around and I don't remember what half of them are for."

"People usually open doors for the president," Rixey said.

"Only if they're Republicans." McKinley then picked up three small folding pocket knives and distributed them—one to each front trouser pocket, and the smallest tucked into the pocket of his vest. "National defense," he murmured. "We're on a budget, you know."

"You have a more relaxed schedule today, sir. No speeches to a throng. And according to the morning editions, your speech yesterday was a great success."

The president was a genuinely modest man and it was not the first time Rixey had seen him respond in silence to a compliment. As McKinley pulled on his frock coat his shirt crackled pleasantly. Returning to the bureau he took two neatly folded handkerchiefs from a stack of linen and then, after a moment's thought, he gathered up a third. "It will be hot today. And I imagine we'll do some walking out at Niagara Falls. We mustn't let anyone see the president perspire." He stuffed all three handkerchiefs inside his coat, which had satin lapels. "I really think that for a hike to see one of our most splendid natural wonders I might be able to dress . . ." McKinley hesitated.

"Less formally?"

"Yes."

"Like the vice president when he's off camping and hunting."

"Precisely, Presley. You know, jodhpurs and one of those hats, with the brim turned up on one side. How do you suppose I would look in such a getup?"

"Sporting, sir," Rixey said. "Why don't you wear something lighter?"

"Because if I have occasion to do as Mr. Roosevelt did and pounce on a mountain lion—or was it a bobcat?—I want the beast to know that he's dealing with the president of the United States."

"Certainly," Rixey said.

"Presley, would you know a mountain lion from a bobcat?"

"I doubt it, sir."

"I see. And you, a man of science." There was a gold watch on the bureau, which McKinley tucked in his vest pocket. "We do have a good schedule today, though I understand that some members of my staff would prefer it if we would all stay shuttered here in the safety of this house. But it will get warm, and I know at some point Ida will need to rest." He tilted his head as though he were listening intently. Women's voices could be heard in the adjacent bedroom.

"We have arranged for a suite for you at the International Hotel in Niagara Falls so that you might relax for a while after luncheon."

"Excellent. We must keep an eye out for the first sign that she's tiring."

"Of course, sir."

McKinley rotated slowly, aiming his girth at Rixey. There was something officious in his posture, as though only now could he formally address him. "I suppose there are days, Doctor, when you would appreciate more challenging duties."

"I don't know what you mean, sir."

McKinley smiled. "Of course you do. And one day you'll be relieved of the tedium of your current responsibilities, and you'll be able to continue your brilliant career in medicine."

"I'm honored to serve," Rixey said. "Truly."

McKinley placed a hand on Rixey's shoulder. He often touched people as he spoke to them, as though he were bestowing a gentle benediction. Rixey had experienced this before, but he still felt a rush of emotion.

"Truly, I'm appreciative, Doctor," the president said, looking up into Rixey's eyes. "Ida has never had such fine care. God bless you."

Rixey was about to speak; there was more to say, but the president's sincerity and the grip of his hand conspired against him. He was speechless—and embarrassed. He could feel his face flush.

"Now," McKinley said, delighted, "I believe that my bride awaits me."

The president turned slightly to the left, and taking his cue, Rixey went to the bedroom door and opened it for him.

Rixey closed the door behind McKinley, crossed the sitting room, and gazed out the window. As was their custom, the president and first lady would spend a few minutes alone before emerging. While he was dressing, the president had been waiting for his wife to beckon him to the next room. Rixey had witnessed this tacit form of communication before, but he had never determined exactly how the signal was conveyed. He had never seen a man so attuned to a woman's needs.

When the McKinleys had first retained Rixey's services, he assumed it would be a temporary arrangement. The president was clearly exhausted, and the first lady was experiencing frequent and severe bouts of depression. They asked Rixey to accompany them on a vacation at Hot Springs, Virginia. During those ten quiet days, Ida McKinley's health stabilized, and the president looked more rested. By the time they all returned to the Executive Mansion in Washington, it was understood that Rixey would remain in constant consultation with the McKinleys. The president's official physician, Surgeon General George Sternberg, was seldom seen at the Executive Mansion except on social occasions. Quietly yet increasingly, Rixey came to notice the subtle deference that was paid to him by the president's staff and cabinet members.

The McKinleys were an extraordinary couple in the way they exhibited their affection for each other with the utmost sincerity and, at times, even a childish abandon. William McKinley was a man torn between two duties, one to his country and the other to his wife. Rixey knew that few if any beyond the president's staff and advisers understood just how much influence the first lady had over her husband. It was clear that it had been this way since they had first married. Often while in the private quarters of the Executive Mansion, Rixey had paused to study the McKinley family photographs, and the portraits of the young Ida Saxon were simply stunning. She had bright eyes, a fine jaw, and long dark tresses. Friends in Canton still talked about how high-spirited and even rebellious she had been while growing up. Yet after the loss of their second child, she descended into a state of illness and depression that only deepened with age. Her husband became even more doting and protective, despite his ever increasing responsibilities, first as a lawyer, then as a senator, and now as president. The burden of despair was something that they both shared. Though in his public duties the president was always temperate, and in private he could be truly jovial, it was clear to Rixey that he never strayed far from his wife's dark, delicate state. There were times indeed when the president's advisers—and, in truth, Rixey as well—would have liked to see the first lady not even attempt to make public appearances, for they almost invariably turned awkward, and yet not once had the president considered not accommodating her in every way possible.

This placed a great deal of stress upon the president, which was Rixey's gravest concern. These past few years had been tumultuous. Not five years ago the country had been in deep economic depression; then a new threat emerged in 1898 as war with Spain seemed inevitable. Under McKinley, America was becoming a world power, and he proceeded with his usual caution. As a naval officer, Rixey appreciated how delicate the situation was between the United States and Spain. Cuba and the Philippines were both possessions of Spain, a poor nation desperately dependent upon its colonies. In Cuba, fighting broke out as revolutionary forces sought freedom from Spanish occupation. Americans became appalled at reports from Havana, and the Hearst and Pulitzer newspapers stoked the fires of patriotic fervor. Increasingly, Americans believed that such political and economic repression should not be allowed in their hemisphere, and war seemed inevitable. McKinley, a veteran of the Civil War, patiently tried to negotiate a peaceful settlement with the Spanish government, one that would improve the situation for Cuban nationals and protect American economic interests throughout the Caribbean.

The navy was central to all of this. The secretary of the navy, John Long, was a cordial, frail New Englander who wore spats and had suffered at least one nervous breakdown. Like McKinley, he was a proponent of restraint, whereas the assistant secretary of the navy, Theodore Roosevelt, saw the current impasse with Spain as an opportunity for the United States to finally exert itself as a significant force on the world stage. While Long was in retreat at his farm in Maine, Roosevelt took the opportunity to promote expansion and development of the navy, arguing strenuously for an increase in the number of battleships and torpedo boats being built. War, Roosevelt felt, was not only inevitable but desirable, and the result could be American fleets controlling both the Atlantic and Pacific theaters, as well as the Central American isthmus, where an all important canal would finally be built.

The night of February 15, 1898, the American battleship *Maine* exploded and sank while at anchor in Havana harbor, killing more than 250 of her crewmen. Much of the U.S. population believed that Spain was responsible, and the press urged an immediate declaration of war. Yet there was no proof that the Spanish government was responsible for the explosion. While Congress reeled out of control—many of McKinley's staunchest Republican supporters joined the ranks of the warmongers—the president displayed remarkable discipline and called for an inquiry into the *Maine* disaster. The investigation took weeks and the results were not conclusive; but it didn't matter: Americans wanted to go to war. McKinley's authority had never been so challenged, and the Republican Party was dangerously close to splitting apart. There was much negotiation, with Spanish diplomats, with other European governments, and with the Vatican, which attempted to play the role of mediator. McKinley was determined to explore every avenue in the pursuit of peace. His critics, as always, believed that he was taking his orders from Senator Mark Hanna and the power brokers on Wall Street, who were concerned only about the economic effects of war. Eventually, when McKinley did submit a declaration of war to Congress, it was specifically in response not to the *Maine* but to Spain's failure to substantially alter its treatment of Cuban nationals. This fine distinction was lost on many patriotic Americans. For the president, it was essential that the United States go to war for legitimate reasons; to do otherwise would set a poor precedent.

There was a light knock on the door to the hallway, and Rixey went to the door. George Cortelyou stood in the hall. "Is he ready, Doctor?" he asked.

Rixey nodded in the direction of the bedroom. "They'll be out presently."

Cortelyou came into the sitting room and shut the door behind him. Rixey took his arm and they went to the window. "Look down through those trees, George," he said. "What do you see?"

"Carriages. Horses. Men. Police, security, some livery."

"Indeed," Rixey said. "We are surrounded. This house is an ivy-covered fortress. But it's not enough. You heard those men we met in the sunroom."

"Norris is the best of the Pinkertons. That's why he's here."

"Fine, but you heard his informer—Hyde. There are anarchists out there, waiting for the right opportunity. And you saw what happened yesterday, George. With all the military and police swarming around, countless people were still able to simply walk right up to the president—and he smiles as he shakes their hand."

"Doctor, no one questions your loyalty to Mr. McKinley. We all know his job would be all the more difficult if he didn't have you at his side—you help relieve his constant concern over his wife's health."

"It's too dangerous," Rixey said.

"The president seldom has an opportunity to mingle with the people. He's an isolated man. You know how he hates to be alone. Do you remember the occasion when Mrs. McKinley was away for a few days, and the night the president couldn't sleep? He came down to the drawing room in his nightgown—like a child! He stretched out on the sofa and encouraged us to continue our conversation—and this allowed him to fall fast asleep."

"I'm not talking about his insomnia," Rixey said.

"You can't shut him up in a room forever. He must be seen by our citizens—and, equally important, *he* must see them. It's good for his health." Rixey began to speak, but Cortelyou raised a hand. "What does he have planned today? A visit to Niagara Falls, a luncheon, and then a brief public appearance at the exposition."

"Please don't mention the Temple of Music to me," Rixey said. "I know you canceled that part of his itinerary twice."

"That's right, I did. I thought it unnecessary. And *twice* he's put it back on the schedule."

"George, it's a ten-minute engagement. Ten minutes."

"And that was *my* point," Cortelyou said. "Why bother for ten minutes? How many people will he greet, how many hands will he shake? But the president said there'll be thousands there, and even those who don't lay eyes on him will know he at least made the effort. To him, that's the point: he is their president." Cortelyou looked defeated. "I'm as concerned for his safety as you are."

"I know, George."

There were footsteps and voices out in the hall. The day was beginning.

~つC~

CZOLGOSZ didn't sleep well the night after the president's speech. He lay in bed above Nowak's saloon, and in the distance could hear the fireworks from the exposition. Though he'd had a substantial dinner of pork chops, mashed potatoes, and peas, followed by rhubarb pie topped with whipped cream, he was hungry.

At one point he sat up and lit the gas lamp; it was two o'clock. For a year he'd kept in his pocket the newspaper article about Gaetano Bresci, who had edited an anarchist magazine in Paterson, New Jersey. When Bresci demanded the money he had invested in the magazine returned, his colleagues shunned him; but then, after he used the money to sail to Italy and shoot King Humbert, they all wrote articles and columns praising him. He had done his duty. They didn't understand. They weren't true workers. Unlike Czolgosz, they hadn't spent long days laboring in a glassworks plant as a teenager. They hadn't put in years at a wire factory. They didn't understand that there was no such thing as anarchist philosophy. All that mattered was the act. Bresci understood this. Emma Goldman understood this. Czolgosz had seen it in her eyes when they had first met in Cleveland—she understood that the true anarchist was one who acts. Without question. Without remorse. Without fear. She understood it was a matter of duty, an act of love.

The president's schedule had been reported in all the newspapers. Today, his last day in Buffalo, he would visit Niagara Falls, where he would attend a luncheon at the International Hotel. Midafternoon he would return to the exposition for a public reception at four in the Temple of Music. The reception would be brief—ten minutes—and only those who got in line early would have the opportunity to shake the president's hand.

Czolgosz slept for a few hours but, as usual, he was awake at dawn. He put on the corduroy suit he'd bought in Chicago, and today he remembered to bring his fedora and handkerchief—it promised to be another hot, sunny day. His revolver was wrapped in a shirt in the bottom of his valise; he took it out and tucked it into the right pocket of his suit coat, and went downstairs, where he bought four cigars from Nowak. He walked down Broadway, trying to decide what he wanted for breakfast. It seemed he was always hungry.

~つC~

THE truth was Hyde had been afraid of Niagara Falls since he was ten years old, when he went there with the sisters and a group of the boys from St. John's Protectory. It was an outing to celebrate the end of the school year. They had a picnic and played baseball, and then they walked across the bridge to the Canadian side, which afforded the best view of the falls. They were all lined up along a railing, watching the white water cascade into the gorge. Hyde had never seen anything so powerful. The noise was constant, and a fine mist rose up and moistened their faces in the warm June sun. Something happened to people as they looked at the falls. Some had a look of awe; young couples stood with their arms about each other. But Hyde noticed one woman standing alone farther down the railing. She was in her mid-twenties and her shiny brown hair danced in the breeze. It was her eyes that made him notice her—she wasn't really looking at the falls. Her hands gripped the railing, and she seemed to be waiting.

Hyde turned his head away for a moment, and when he looked back toward the woman she was gone. He couldn't see her anywhere, and then there were voices raised and an elderly woman who was screaming, and then others joined in as people rushed to where the young woman had been standing. They looked over the railing, some pointing down into the gorge. Hyde started to move to see better, but one of the nuns took hold of his shoulder and quickly guided him away from the railing. Something had happened—he didn't know what, but something unexpected and terrible—and with sudden urgency the sisters ushered the boys back toward the bridge that would take them across to the United States.

The following day after morning mass, Hyde went into the main office of the protectory, where Father Baker always read the newspaper until the breakfast bell was rung in the dining room. Hyde found the article about a woman who had jumped into the gorge at the falls. It said she was Alma Worrell, a seamstress from Lackawanna. The names of her surviving family were listed— her mother, father, and brother. No husband, no children, and no reason given for her suicide. Hyde sat in the main office, the smell of bacon in the air and bees droning in the flowers outside the open window. Occasionally he was still awakened by a night-mare in which a woman in a long white gown descends through the mist and disappears into the roiling waters at the bottom of the gorge.

He didn't want to follow the president to the falls but he was afraid not to, so he went by cable car and another enormous throng. He could only see McKinley from a great distance, using his binoculars. The president's carriage seemed to push slowly through the crowd. His silk top hat gleamed in the sunlight.

The newspapers had treated the president's visit as though it were a circus act. As part of his visit to Niagara Falls, the president would travel halfway across the bridge to Canada. It was consid-ered a gesture of goodwill, for the benefit of the Canadians who were expected to gather on the other side of the gorge. According to the papers, there was real concern that the president not actu-ally cross the international border because no formal invitation had been extended by the Canadian government. In fact, a line had been drawn halfway across the bridge, so the carriage driver would know where to stop and turn around. Still, there was a moment of anticipation as the crowds on both sides of the gorge watched McKinley's carriage move slowly across the bridge. Near the midpoint, the horses paused; the president stood up in the carriage and doffed his high silk hat toward the Canadians— their cheers could barely be heard above the roar of the falls. The moment seemed to linger. The horses were anxious to continue, and through the binoculars Hyde could see that the driver was having difficulty restraining them. It was a moment when a sharp-shooter with a rifle would have a good shot. The president finally sat down next to the first lady. The carriage turned around on the bridge and returned to the American side of the gorge.

∽ᴐᴄ∼

BEFORE entering the exposition grounds Czolgosz stepped into an alley that ran off Lincoln Avenue, where the shade of the build-ing provided slight relief from the sun. It was so hot that people on trolleys and in the street were constantly mopping their faces with handkerchiefs. He took the revolver from his coat pocket and, holding it in his right hand, wrapped it in his handkerchief. The odds were slim and he expected to be found out and killed before he got within sight of the president. He had a bottle of Dr. Johnson's Elixir, which he took for his catarrh, and he fin-ished off the bottle. He put his right hand in his coat pocket and moved toward the street, but then paused at the end of the alley. He thought about Hyde in Motka's room—he had hesitated, and that was what Czolgosz could not do. If he did get close enough to the president, there could be no hesitation.

He stepped out into the street and joined the crowd streaming through the exposition gate. The sun was brutal. Women spun their parasols. Outside the Temple of Music the police formed people into a receiving line. At four p.m. the double doors opened and the line began to shuffle inside. When Czolgosz entered the building, there was shade but little relief from the intense heat. He removed his right hand from his pocket and held it across his chest, as though it were bandaged and supported by a sling. There were soldiers, police, and security men along both sides of the line but none of them said anything about the fact that he wasn't wearing a sling. Many people in line were using their handkerchiefs continually.

At one end of the high, domed temple a large pipe organ was being played, and a woman in line somewhere behind Czolgosz said, "That's Bach's Sonata in F."

"Are you certain, dear?" the man with her said.

"Of course I am."

Czolgosz didn't know what a sonata was and didn't understand how someone could identify the key of a piece of music. He looked around once. The woman wore a white linen dress with a large rose perched atop her full bosom. The man with her had a gray beard and a monocle glinted from his right eye.

A Negro with a thick mustache stood directly behind Czolgosz. The man stared straight ahead, as though he were afraid of attracting attention. Czolgosz realized that the security guards were looking at this black man very carefully. Two security men approached, but then they stopped and spoke to a man two places in front of Czolgosz. He was swarthy, with oiled dark hair—an Italian, from the sound of his accent—and they removed him from the line and guided him toward a side door.

Behind Czolgosz, the man wearing the monocle said, "Which Bach?"

"Johann Sebastian," the woman said impatiently. "Really, Charles."

"You're sure?"

"Behave," she said. "You're about to meet the president of the United States."

Czolgosz expected one of the guards to stop him at any moment—one of them must be curious about the handkerchief wrapped around his hand—and yet he continued to inch forward with the line of people. It was difficult, waiting. He considered shooting this man and woman behind him instead and being done with it. But he closed his eyes and concentrated on the music. In the darkness the lilting organ notes seemed to entwine and cascade, reverberating overhead. More than anything it was this black sonata that kept him calm as he waited for the moment that would change everything.

When there were only three people ahead of him in line, he got a good look at McKinley, who stood before several large potted plants, backed by red, white, and blue bunting. He was surrounded by security men in suits. His stomach, covered by a white vest, was enormous. Each greeting was brief, a quick hand-shake and a few words. No one in the line really stopped moving; everyone just filed right by the president. When the man in front of Czolgosz stepped up to McKinley, the president said, "It's a pleasure to meet you. Thank you for coming on such a warm afternoon." The man walked off to his right and was ushered along by several men.

Czolgosz couldn't believe he'd gotten this close to the president. Oddly, it made him angry—what was wrong with all these people who were supposed to guard McKinley? But the queue continued to shuffle along the red carpet, as if only to show these men in uniform, many with rifles on their shoulders, for what idiots they were.

When it was Czolgosz's turn, the president extended his right arm and smiled, though his eyes appeared bored. Everything seemed settled. Czolgosz didn't think but simply raised the gun and pulled the trigger. McKinley rose up on his toes and then leaned forward as though to keep his balance. No one moved. All the men around the president were still. The organ sonata stopped, the last notes echoing with the sound of the shot. A small flame rose from the hole in the handkerchief and smoke drifted back into Czolgosz's face. It was not an unpleasant smell. He pulled the trigger again.

Suddenly he was grabbed from behind—it was the Negro, his

black hands clutching the front of his coat. Czolgosz tried to get another shot off, but he was knocked to the floor, with the Negro coming down on top of him. Then several soldiers stood over them, and though Czolgosz was being hit with fists and rifle butts, he could see a man help the president to a chair. There were shouts and screams throughout the Temple of Music. Czolgosz tasted blood in his mouth. Someone yanked the gun out of his hand and he expected to be killed immediately. He shouted, *"I done my duty!"*

Someone punched him hard in the nose. He was stunned, and perhaps he had passed out for a moment because he suddenly realized that his arms had been bound behind his back.

But he could still look up at the president, whose white vest was now covered with blood. His hands fumbled with the buttons. One of the men leaned over him. "Be careful about my wife—don't tell her," the president said. He stared down at Czolgosz, curious. He seemed relieved, even satisfied, as though some long-held concern had finally been resolved. His eyes became fond, and there was a moment when Czolgosz felt very close to him.

The president said, "Go easy on him, boys."

~つC~

HYDE was standing next to one of the mirror pools outside the Temple of Music when the two shots were fired. The huge crowd in the esplanade suddenly became quiet, alert—it reminded Hyde of cows in a field when an unexpected sound causes them to look up from grazing.

A young man pushed his way out the temple doors. "He's been shot!" he said. "The president's been *shot!*"

There were screams and shouts. A woman near Hyde fainted into the arms of two men. The crowd surged toward the Temple of Music, but a group of marines, carrying rifles with fixed bayonets, came outside and formed a barrier in front of the doors. Amid the jostling, people cried in each other's arms.

Hyde sat on the low retaining wall that surrounded the mirror pool. A newspaper boy stood nearby, a large burlap sack, heavy with the afternoon edition of the *Courier,* hanging from one shoulder.

"Someone really shoot the president?" the boy asked.

"Yes."

"Who would do that?"

A faint mist came from the fountain in the center of the pool. Hyde's hair became cool and damp. "I should have come straight here," he said. "Going to Niagara Falls was a mistake."

"What?" the boy asked.

"It makes sense that Czolgosz would do it here."

"Show-gosh?"

"By tomorrow everyone will be able to pronounce his name. You'll see it in the next edition of your paper." Hyde nodded toward the bag of newspapers, but the boy backed away as though he just realized that this man was dangerous. "I should have come early enough to get in line," Hyde said.

The boy moved off, looking over his shoulder once before he disappeared into the crowd. Hyde scooped water from the pool and splashed it on his face. He kept his head in his hands for several minutes, waiting for the nausea to pass. The sounds of anguish around him swelled frantically—within minutes people who had been enjoying a warm summer afternoon at the exposition had been transformed into an angry mob.

Attention was suddenly directed toward the Temple of Music. Hyde stood on top of the mirror-pool wall so he could see down the esplanade: a police wagon was moving slowly through the parting sea of people. Hyde got off the wall and pushed his way into the crowd. Men had their fists in the air, and there were shouts: "*Kill the assassin!*" and "*Lynch him!*" Hyde worked his way around to the other side of the building, where the police wagon stood before an entrance. A line of policemen had difficulty keeping the crowd back.

Two men came out of the entrance, holding Czolgosz by the arms between them. His face was smeared with blood and he looked dazed, almost sleepy. One eye was nearly closed. They shoved him into the back of the wagon and slammed the doors shut. As the horses began to move forward, fighting broke out between the crowd and police. Men lay on the ground, injured and bleeding. The wagon was surrounded but it finally managed to get through the gate to Lincoln Avenue. The police closed the gate, locking most of the crowd inside the exposition.

When he reached the gate, Hyde put his hands on the wrought-iron bars, warmed by the sun, and watched as the wagon raced down the avenue, pursued by young men riding bicycles.

III

AFTER THE RETURN TRIP from Niagara Falls, Dr. Rixey had escorted Mrs. McKinley back to the Milburn house, where she could rest. Then, believing his duties were concluded for the time being, he took a tour of the exposition. There were the usual carnival oddities, such as the four-legged chicken and the Famous Diving Elks, but he was particularly impressed with the Caverns of Hell and the Trip to the Moon, which featured an airship named *Luna* and a dance by the Maids of the Moon. Two security men found him wandering the Streets of Cairo and told him that the president had been shot.

He was taken to the exposition hospital, where Cortelyou met him at the door. "We've managed to gather a team of doctors, and they've already begun to operate. A Dr. Matthew Mann was very insistent. He says he's world renowned in the field of gynecology."

"A gynecologist? What's the extent of the president's wounds?"

"Two bullets." Cortelyou tapped the center of his chest. "One seems to have struck his sternum and only grazed the flesh. They found it in his clothing. But the other penetrated his abdomen. So they decided to operate here rather than risk moving him."

"Here?" Rixey looked around the lobby. "This is little more

than a first aid station, designed to care for people with cuts and bruises—perhaps a case of heat prostration."

Cortelyou nodded. "They debated whether to move the president to Buffalo General Hospital, where they've recently built a new surgical amphitheater, or to operate here immediately. There's been much disagreement," Cortelyou said as he led Rixey toward the room where the operation was taking place. "Mann believes we shouldn't wait. He's handling the surgery. We've also located a surgeon named Park, who's performing an operation in Niagara Falls."

"Roswell Park? I know him. He's very good."

"We've arranged for him to be brought here on a special train, but it may be some time before he arrives."

"I see, George." Since learning about the president, Rixey had been sweating profusely. He considered himself a calm, deliberate man, but now he felt tense and disoriented. "I'm afraid I'm . . . It's incredible. We have talked and considered this possibility almost daily, but now—"

"I know, Doctor. I just can't believe it, either," Cortelyou said. His voice was shaking. "That reception line was surrounded by security men. Ordinarily we have someone stand just in front of the president—and his role is to observe each person's right hand before it is extended toward the president. But today we allowed Mr. Milburn to take that position, so he could introduce certain people to the president. *Still,* the number of police and military and Pinkertons—how could we *all* have missed this man with the gun wrapped in a handkerchief?"

Rixey put his hand on Cortelyou's sleeve. "I've got to go in."

Cortelyou sucked a corner of his mustache into his mouth. "Of course."

Rixey entered the room. The president lay under a white sheet on a long table and was surrounded by a group of men, who were assisted by an inordinate number of nurses. There were too many people in the room. Rixey knew none of them, but it was clear that Dr. Mann was in charge. He straightened up and glared at Rixey.

"I'm Presley Rixey, the president's physician."

"He's too fat," Mann said. "Your president is too *fat*. I have been able close the wound in the stomach, but I cannot locate the bullet. It must be in the lumbar muscles." He had a full beard, but there was something odd about his hair. Mann seemed to read his thoughts. "I was in the middle of getting a haircut when I was summoned, so I'm not even working with my own instruments. These things belong to Dr. Mynter here." Dr. Mynter, who was assisting Mann, said nothing and looked like a child who was enduring a scolding. "Plus," Dr. Mann said, tapping Mynter's fingers with a pair of forceps, "he keeps getting his hands in my way. And this *light—*"

One of the other men said, "Someone is having a power cable brought in so that soon we will have electric lighting."

Rixey went to the table against the wall, where the surgical instruments were laid out. He picked up a metal tray and returned to the operating table. He held the tray so that it reflected sunlight from the window on the long incision in the president's abdomen. "Please, Dr. Mann, continue."

Dr. Mann looked insulted that he would have to work under such circumstances, but he leaned over the president once again.

~つC~

CZOLGOSZ was first taken to an office on the second floor of the Buffalo police headquarters, guarded by two detectives in street clothes. His face was bloody, his mouth swollen, and he could barely see out of his right eye. For minutes he would pass out in his chair.

"You think he's going to die on us, Solomon?" he heard one of the men say.

"I'm no doctor."

"Wouldn't look good with him sittin' here with just the two of us."

"Suppose not, Geary."

"My God, the president." Geary's voice trembled. "He fell into my arms and I eased him into the chair. I don't believe it."

"I don't believe he got through that line, past all that security, with a gun wrapped like that."

Czolgosz opened his good eye and looked at his guards. They both wore suits and had slicked-back hair. One had a full mustache. They stared back at him and neither seemed to know what to say or do. They seemed more confused than angry. "What's that noise out in the street?" he asked, and they both seemed surprised that he could even speak.

"That's the mob come to lynch you," Geary said. There was a pitcher of water on the desk. He poured a glass and gave it to Czolgosz.

It was painful to swallow but he drained the glass. "Why are we here?"

The other, Solomon, stroked his mustache for a moment. "Waiting for Superintendent Chief Bull, who's coming with someone from the district attorney's office."

Geary took the empty glass. "He looks a bit better now."

Czolgosz turned toward the window.

"Go ahead," Solomon said.

Czolgosz had difficulty getting out of the chair. He went to the window and leaned his forearms on the sill. The street was crammed with hundreds of men. Dozens of policemen, armed with rifles, stood on the front steps beneath the window, keeping the mob from entering the station. There was a great deal of pushing and shoving. Fists were raised, and there was chanting: *Czol-gosz, Czol-gosz, Czol-gosz!* His face hurt, his lips felt as though they might burst, his ribs ached, and every breath caused searing pain in his sides. But somehow it pleased him to look down upon this mob. He had done this—he had caused them to come together. Hatred and anger were necessary to change.

He stepped back from the window and asked, "Is the president dead?"

Solomon and Geary said nothing.

Then he understood that it didn't matter.

What mattered was he had made the attempt.

~)C~

A few minutes before seven, Rixey took a carriage from the exposition hospital. He was accompanied by Richard Buchanan, the former U.S. ambassador to Argentina, who was the director of the Pan-American Exposition. Buchanan had already begun to make arrangements at the Milburn house, where the president would be taken later that evening. Power cables were being run into the house so that electric fans could be used to cool every room. He had gathered the house staff together, informed them of the situation, and told them that Mrs. McKinley should not be disturbed from her afternoon nap. Outside the house, a somber crowd had gathered on Delaware Avenue, so the police had cordoned off the entire block.

Clara Tharin, Mrs. McKinley's maid, met the two men at the front door.

"She doesn't know yet?" Rixey asked.

"She slept until six thirty," Clara said. "Her nieces have been with her since then."

Rixey climbed the stairs to the second floor and Buchanan followed. "This could kill her," Buchanan whispered.

"It's possible," Rixey said. "I want to speak to her alone."

"Of course."

Rixey knocked on the first lady's bedroom door. One of the nieces let him in and he entered the room, avoiding her stare.

Mrs. McKinley sat, as she often did, in a rocking chair, knitting. Since her husband had become president she had made more than five thousand pairs of slippers, most of which were given away to charities.

"Where is the Major?" she asked. "Why doesn't he come?"

"I have bad news for you, Mrs. McKinley."

As she struggled to her feet she dropped her knitting on the floor. "What is it?" For all her frailty, she could be very demanding; it might be the thing that kept her alive. "Has he been hurt?"

"Yes, he's been hurt." Rixey took a step closer. "He's been shot."

She took in a long breath, held it, and then exhaled. "I must go to him."

"No, please," Rixey said, taking her arm and helping her back into her chair. "We're bringing him here. Everything now depends on you—maybe his life. We look to you to help us."

∽◯∼

FRIDAY evening Vice President Theodore Roosevelt gave a speech to an outdoorsman's club on Isle La Motte in Lake Champlain. When notified of the assassination attempt, he rode a carriage some thirty miles over country roads in a hard rain to board a private train that would take him to Buffalo. By Saturday afternoon most members of McKinley's cabinet had gathered in Buffalo. A telegraph office had been set up in the Milburns' stable, extra phone lines were run into the house, and a group of stenographers were boarded next door. At one thirty word came that the vice president's train had arrived, and by midafternoon the government's highest officials waited in the Milburns' living room to receive him.

"Even in this there's a drama about the man," Cortelyou said to Rixey as they stared out the windows toward Delaware Avenue.

Despite his suit and fresh hard collar, Cortelyou looked as though he had not slept at all. "You understand what this means?" he said. "This possibility has weighed on my mind often since the last election. The president and some of his advisers—Senator Hanna, in particular—they thought it was the perfect solution to Roosevelt. Often they would talk about what to *do* with Teddy. How can we contain him? And, of course, the logical answer is to make him vice president and thereby render him useless."

"And place him within a heartbeat of the presidency."

"Exactly. When he arrives don't be surprised if he's on a white stallion, wearing the uniform he wore when he stormed San Juan Hill. Every time I see the man I think I hear bugles."

"George, the president rested comfortably through the night. Better than you did, apparently."

Cortelyou was about to respond when everyone in the room became quiet as a carriage drew up at the curb. Roosevelt climbed down immediately and walked briskly toward the house. He was wearing a silk hat and frock coat.

"Borrowed," Cortelyou said, and then he went into the hall, where one of the maids was opening the front door.

Rixey remained at the window and watched the president's staff gather around Roosevelt. Though it was a somber occasion, something about the vice president seemed to invigorate the group of men—they were animated by a strange blend of curiosity, uncertainty, and muted fear. He worked his way through the living room, shaking hands with each one of them. Behind his glinting pince-nez, his eyes were quick, and his voice, though subdued, was clipped and blunt. He seemed to speak with his teeth, biting off phrases. He was forty-two, and surrounded by men with gray whiskers.

He reached Rixey last and his handshake was surprisingly soft. "Doctor, how is the president?"

"His pulse and blood pressure are good," Rixey said. "We're reassured, though it's still too early to tell."

Roosevelt nodded. "What about Mrs. McKinley?"

The vice president spoke with such sincerity that it had the effect of disarming Rixey. He cleared his throat. "She's doing remarkably well, sir. She's bearing up."

"I know how they both rely on you, Doctor," Roosevelt said. "I should pay her a brief visit first, if you think this is a good time."

"I'm sure she would appreciate it."

Roosevelt began to turn away, but then said, "The people I saw during my train ride across New York—I've never seen such despair in the faces of Americans. Not even the wounded in Cuba. They truly love their president. This is a terrible thing."

Rixey followed Roosevelt up the stairs. People tended to underestimate the vice president. For all his energy and brashness, he had the ability to find the truth of the moment, identify its center, and articulate it cleanly, with precision. Rixey had read several of his books, and was particularly impressed by his knowledge of natural history. It was said that he read at least three books a day. Such an intellect in a man who was so physically vigorous seemed a rare thing.

One of the younger nurses stood in the hallway outside Mrs. McKinley's bedroom. The girl's face flushed when she realized that the vice president was approaching her. He stopped before her and inhaled deeply, which expanded his chest and squared his shoulders. At first she lowered her head, almost out of fear, but then, after a moment, she raised her eyes. Roosevelt stared at her, and she was somehow transformed. She herself stood up straighter.

Rixey knocked gently on the raised-panel door, and then turned the knob.

Suddenly, Roosevelt's hand caught his forearm. Unlike the handshake he had offered downstairs, his grip now was firm. "Doctor, would you object to my having a moment alone with Mrs. McKinley?"

Rixey let go of the knob, though the vice president still held his sleeve. "No, of course not, Mr. Vice President."

"Thank you." Roosevelt let go of his arm and pushed the door open.

As he stepped inside, the nurse stared back at Rixey. She seemed embarrassed by what she had just witnessed and gazed at the floor.

Rixey walked to the end of the hall and looked out the front window. The press had set up a tent in the street and dozens of reporters stood around in small groups, smoking cigars and cigarettes; the front lawn was guarded by police and military personnel with rifles.

After a few minutes Roosevelt emerged from the first lady's room. Rixey led him down to the other end of the hall to the president's bedroom. One of the male nurses was sitting with McKinley, who lay on his back, asleep. The vice president stood silently for several minutes staring at McKinley, and then he led Rixey to the far end of the room.

"Has he been awake much?" Roosevelt whispered.

"Yes," Rixey said. "And very alert, and in remarkably good spirits. Earlier today, when Dr. Mann was here—he performed the operation to close the wound—the president asked to see the newspapers. We hesitated, thinking it was too soon for him to be reading about all this. But then he made it clear that he was more interested in seeing the editorial reaction to his speech."

The vice president bared his teeth and nodded his head. He turned and stared at McKinley a moment, and then they left the room. George Cortelyou was waiting in the hall.

"Gentlemen," Roosevelt said, "is there somewhere we can talk—here, upstairs?"

"Certainly," Cortelyou said. He led them to the end of the hall and opened the door to a small office with a daybed. "I'm using this as my office, so we shouldn't be disturbed." He closed the door behind them.

For a moment, all three men stood, silent and awkward, until the vice president pulled out the desk chair and sat down. "Please, gentlemen." Rixey and Cortelyou sat on the daybed. "Let me start by telling you what I know—what I've been told or read. Then please tell me anything else I ought to know." Both men nodded. "One bullet posed no threat," he said. "The second bullet passed through his stomach and is lodged in his back muscles. The wounds to the front and back of his stomach have been closed. His current vital signs are stable, and quite good under the circumstances." Roosevelt's voice reminded Rixey of a ticker tape. His teeth chattered and the words just kept issuing forth. "There have been a great many doctors involved already—frankly, physicians can be more divisive than politicians. Remember President Garfield's assassination. Who's in charge?"

"Though I am the president's physician," Rixey said, "we have agreed that Dr. Park, who is a surgeon, should make the final assessment of any treatments. And we have agreed to only issue joint public statements through Cortelyou on a regular basis. It is essential that the public be informed accurately and honestly."

"Good," Roosevelt said. "The newspapers are already running wild in every direction." Looking at Rixey, he said, "So, is there anything else I should know?"

"This morning I noticed a very encouraging sign." Rixey hesitated.

Roosevelt's face was stone, but after a few moments his eyes turned impatient.

"Gas," Rixey said. "He's already begun to pass intestinal gas."

Roosevelt didn't appear to comprehend what the doctor had said; then he raised one hand and slapped his thigh. "The Major's farting already?"

"Often," Rixey said. "And quite audibly."

"This is the best news I've heard since I left Lake Champlain," Roosevelt said.

They all laughed, until the vice president stopped.

He leaned forward, resting his forearms on his thighs; the others did the same. "What can we expect, Doctor?"

"Our biggest fear," Rixey said, "is autointoxication. Anytime the bowels cease to function, there's the possibility that toxins will build up in the body's internal organs. So this morning we ordered a saline enema."

"George," the vice president said, "no need to put that in your public statements. And I'm impressed by how quickly you've set things up here—like a military operation. Your security throughout the neighborhood is excellent. Even the vice president had a hard time getting through to this house." Roosevelt paused, long enough that Rixey wondered if the interview was concluded. "Gentlemen," he said suddenly, "the country is in a state of panic— absolute shock. The fact is we don't know where this is headed, or whether it's over. The press has all sorts of theories about grand conspiracies, and I'm in no position at the moment to say they are wrong. Anarchism is an international movement that has been growing more powerful in recent years. It's a sign of desperation, of hopelessness unlike anything we have ever known. While coming from the train station I was told that Czar Nicholas and Kaiser Wilhelm were both sailing somewhere off the Danish coast when they learned about the president. Their yachts planned a rendezvous and they have conferred with each other about increasing security in their own countries. There's the very real possibility that this attempt on the president is part of an international plot." He looked at the floor a moment before continuing.

Rixey felt that the vice president had a number of subjects running through his mind and he was sorting and editing as he went—and that this was the way his mind worked at all times.

Looking up, Roosevelt said, "A primary concern is the financial markets. I have received word from J. P. Morgan. Ironically, perhaps, he spent last night aboard his yacht, *Corsair III,* in New York harbor, partially out of fear of an extended plot, I assume, but also as a means of avoiding the more rabid members of the press. Mr. Morgan says there is no knowing how this will influence markets. It could be devastating. We simply won't know until Monday." He sat up straight in the chair and gazed hard at them. "This is an extraordinary event: a single act that has the potential to change the world as much as when armies and navies clash."

They were all silent, until Roosevelt stood up. "Thank you, gentleman. I will be staying down the street at the Wilcox residence, so that I will be close. I'll visit the president twice a day and meet with you regularly."

Rixey opened the door and the vice president strode out into the hall. Cortelyou gathered up some papers on the desk and put them in his leather folder.

"Signatures," he said, coming to the door. "Half my time is spent seeking signatures." He tucked the folder under his arm and went out into the hall with Rixey. "Did you notice what the vice president *didn't* mention? Nothing about the security at the exposition."

"I think it's meant as a vote of confidence, George."

"I hope so," Cortelyou said. "There were so many people using handkerchiefs in the Temple of Music because of the heat." For a moment he seemed distracted and at a loss for words, but then he said, "I don't know which of us has the more difficult job— coordinating all these branches of the government that have suddenly gathered here under one roof or overseeing this medical team that has materialized out of thin air." At the top of the stairs, he paused. The murmur of voices came up from the first floor. "I never thought I'd miss that drafty wreck of an old house in Washington we call the Executive Mansion." He smiled briefly; it was the first time Rixey had seen him do so since they had come to Buffalo.

"Personally, I envy Czar Nicholas and the Kaiser," Rixey said.

"How so?"

"I'm a navy man. I'd rather be sailing a royal yacht off the coast of Denmark."

SATURDAY morning Norris went to the Buffalo police headquarters. The mob that had collected in front of the building the night before was gone, though there were still groups of people standing around in the street, simply watching the stone building. Inside, Norris found Lloyd Savin in his office.

"I haven't been out of here since early yesterday," Savin said. "Let's go for a walk."

They went out a back door and Savin led Norris down a system of alleys. Overhead laundry hanging on clotheslines fluttered in the breeze. Men and women eyed them from steps and doorways. "One of the first things these people learn when they get to America," Savin said, "is to sniff out a copper."

"It's the same all over the country. What has Czolgosz given up so far?"

"They got a signed confession out of him last night, claiming he acted alone," Savin said. "We're getting reports of conspiracies and plots all over Buffalo—all over the *country*, for that matter—and there's a nationwide search for Emma Goldman."

Several blocks from police headquarters they entered a saloon called Tiny's and stood at the bar. Though it was only ten in the morning, the place was full of men. Norris and Savin ordered beer and shots of whiskey. Savin knocked his shot back and rapped his knuckles on the bar for another.

"I haven't heard from Cortelyou yet, but I will." Savin got out a pack of cigarettes and lit one. "We need to give him something."

"Yes, something," Norris said. There was a bowl of hard-boiled eggs on the bar and he picked one up. "Hyde was right."

"About Czolgosz, yes. My men were keeping an eye out for him, as well as a number of Buffalo anarchists. But only Hyde really knew what the bastard looked like—before yesterday."

"If he had stopped Czolgosz," Norris said, "we'd be giving Hyde a medal today."

Savin watched the bartender refill their shot glasses. "So now it might be more useful if we hang him."

"Him and this Russian whore at Big Maud's—she knew both of them, Hyde and Czolgosz." Norris tapped the egg on the bar, cracking the shell.

"We've got to find Hyde."

"I know. But he'll turn up."

"You don't really think he and this whore were in on it?"

"Does it matter?"

"No, I suppose not."

Norris began to peel his egg.

~∂C~

CZOLGOSZ believed it was Sunday. Despite the fact that he had signed a written confession Friday night, the police continued to interrogate him periodically in Chief Bull's office. After each session he was returned to the basement, where he was often punched and slapped before being locked up in a dark cell. But here, in the chief's office, there were tall windows that admitted bright, painful light. He could barely keep his eyes open.

"They had to bring in the National Guard," the man named Thomas Penney said. For hours he had been sitting across the table from Czolgosz. He was a district attorney and he looked like one, wearing a gray suit and a high stiff collar. "That mob gets ahold of you, they'll hang you right away. If they don't tear you apart first. I mean it, limb by limb. They're that angry. It'd make us look pretty bad."

Czolgosz was handcuffed and he used both hands to pick up the glass of water on the table. The water soothed his dry throat but stung his bruised lips. "That collar," he said, carefully putting the glass down on the table, "it doesn't bother you?"

There was the faintest look of surprise in Penney's eyes. "No."

"Your accent—where are you from? Britain?"

"I was born in England, yes."

"I was born in America." Czolgosz smiled with difficulty. "Conceived in Europe, born in America."

Penney and the others—several uniformed policemen standing along the wall, and a court stenographer seated at the end of the table, a young man with a cowlick over his right temple—stared at Czolgosz. The policeman nearest the door leaned over and dropped a wad of tobacco juice in a spittoon. "You're some goddamned American," he said, wiping his mouth with the back of his hand.

Penney turned toward him, and then faced Czolgosz again. "You're pretty calm about all this, I'll grant you that. Since Friday you've answered all our questions. But you still won't tell us what we want to know. Who was in on it with you?"

"Nobody."

"Right. And you're Fred C. Nieman. Fred Nobody."

"I acted alone."

"Nonsense. Other people had to know about this."

Czolgosz lifted his arms off his lap, but Penney took the glass of water and slid it to his side of the table, out of reach.

"Others influenced you," he said. "With what, money?"

Czolgosz shook his head.

"When did you conceive of this plan?"

Czolgosz touched his face with his fingers. The skin was tender, and one eye was still nearly closed. There was dried blood everywhere. They had not let a doctor see him. Somehow the pain helped him remain calm, and he knew that that's what these men found most disconcerting—perhaps more than the mob down in the street, or perhaps, even, more than the act of shooting the president. He had not been charged with anything. He had not been allowed to see a lawyer. No one had said whether McKinley was dead.

"I read in a newspaper that the president planned on visiting the exposition in Buffalo," Czolgosz said. "And it was in my heart—there was no escape for me." He looked at the stenographer, to make sure that he was getting it all down. Slowly, Czolgosz said, "I could not have conquered it"—he waited as the man wrote quickly— "had my life been at stake."

When the stenographer finished writing, he looked up, and he seemed to appreciate the fact that he had been given the time to record what was said.

Czolgosz told them how he had attempted to get close to the president when he arrived at the train station, but had failed. The only other sound in the room came from the stenographer, who continued to scribble furiously on his notepad.

Penney said, "Who were your accomplices?"

"I had no confidants—no one to help me. I was alone absolutely."

"What was your motive?"

"I am an anarchist—a disciple of Emma Goldman. Her words set me on fire."

"So she was part of this plot?"

"No. Only her ideas illuminated me. I have told you I am guilty for my acts. And that they were inspired by her ideas, I will not deny." Czolgosz leaned toward the district attorney. "But, tell me, can you find someone guilty for their ideas?" He sat back in his chair. "You can't, can you? Our ideas, Mr. Penney, are stronger than your laws."

Penney ran his thumb back and forth along the edge of the table as he seemed to be trying to develop an argument, but finally, he murmured, "Yes, well. That's enough for now."

Czolgosz was taken back to his cell, though this time his handcuffs were removed and he was locked up without being touched. Lying on his cot, he could hear nothing. No voices, no screams and shouts. No mob. Outside the Buffalo police headquarters there had been fierce fighting. Occasionally, he had been allowed to watch from the window as the crowd in the street swelled toward the front of the building, where it was met by police. This had been happening for years in America, masses of people surging toward a line of uniformed men, who beat them back with clubs and rifles. People wanted jobs, they wanted food, they wanted better working conditions. Now they wanted Leon Czolgosz.

⁓◯⌒

"YOU must be exhausted, Presley," McKinley said. He was awake, lying on his back in bed, staring at the ceiling. His stomach was an enormous mound beneath the linen sheet. "You've been sitting there the whole night."

Rixey got up from the chair by the window. "I must have dozed off, Mr. President."

"Indeed." Slowly McKinley turned on his side, which in itself was a good sign. He faced the large electric fan that had been installed in the corner of the room. "The breeze is wonderful. You know how Mrs. McKinley and I detest the heat. I trust she is keeping cool as well?"

"Yes, sir. They have installed fans in most of the rooms. The first lady is resting comfortably, and she'll visit you later." Rixey took the mercury thermometer from the nightstand and shook it out. "Let's see how we're doing this morning."

"I feel very good."

"Pain?"

"No. Stiffness, yes. But not pain, really."

"You slept through the night, it seemed."

"I dreamed of food." The president tilted his head back and opened his mouth.

Rixey inserted the thermometer, making sure it was under the tongue. "I realize you're hungry, but I think we'll have to wait to give you anything. The other doctors and I have consulted on that and we think it's best to continue to give you nourishment by injection for the time being."

The president mumbled something around the glass thermometer.

"Doctors?" Rixey said. "How many? Too many, perhaps. But they all agree that you are making great progress."

McKinley nodded. His eyes looked very alert.

They waited a minute in silence, and then Rixey removed the thermometer and read it. "Only slightly above normal," he said. "Good."

"Then I might have something to eat?"

"Not yet."

"Perhaps a cigar?"

"Definitely not! Now I'll bring my colleagues in and we'll take your other vitals."

"That should sufficiently exhaust me."

"Perhaps we might give you a little broth later today."

"God bless you!"

Rixey went to the door and told the nurse waiting in the hall that the president was awake. He remained by the door, and watched as the group of doctors gathered about the bed.

Cortelyou came into the room and whispered, "He's looking like he's ready to get up and walk."

"He rested well through the night and does seem stronger," Rixey said quietly. "But I don't quite have the confidence of some of my colleagues."

"Want to hear a terrible irony?" Cortelyou asked. "Do you know what was in another room at the exposition hospital during the operation? One of these new X-ray machines. It had been brought to be displayed as part of the exposition—and nobody even *knew* it was there! That might have enabled them to locate the other bullet lodged in his back?"

"It might have," Rixey said.

"Well, it gets worse. This morning an X-ray machine was delivered here at the house—sent by Thomas Edison himself. But some of the doctors looked it over and determined that it was missing a part and wouldn't work." Cortelyou raised a hand to smooth back his shiny dark hair. "At least there's good news from New York."

"J. P. Morgan?"

"Yes. Even though the stock market doesn't open for a few

more hours, he has sent word that there are no signs that Wall Street will panic."

~⊃⊂~

FOR hours Hyde sat watching the street from the window of his room on the second floor. He knew what he should do: go down to the canal and crew on any barge bound for Albany. Run, get out of Buffalo—it had been the answer since he was twelve, when the protectory wanted to put him on an orphan train. They called it "placing out." He had read letters sent back from other boys who had been put on trains and sent west. In small-town depots the boys would be lined up on the platform and local families could pick one. It was like an auction, and in most cases the boys lived on a farm, where they were worked like animals. Several of the boys wrote that they'd tried to escape, but because the land was so flat and empty, they were easily caught and returned to their owners. They were prisoners, they were slaves, and Hyde wanted nothing to do with being placed out. Every time there was talk of an orphan train, he'd run away.

And he always ran to the Erie Canal. It went east and he felt safer on water. Marcus Trumbull said you could better see what was coming at you across water. Trumbull's barge was called the *Northern Light,* and he was himself an orphan, eventually taken in by a farming family with land on Cripple Creek, north of Otsego Lake. Hyde's first job was as a hoggee—he walked the mules along the towpath, for which he received a few pennies a day, food, and a berth on board at night. By the time he was fifteen, he'd walked to Albany and back several times.

Hyde eventually became a first-rate pilot and lived on board the *Northern Light* for several years, until Trumbull got into an arm-wrestling match in Utica. One night at Dominique Picard's whorehouse it took Trumbull more than six hours to beat Red-Eye

Sam, the strongest arm on the Erie Canal. A lot of bargemen lost money over the match, and in the early-morning hours several friends of Red-Eye who took exception to their losses came aboard the *Northern Light*. Trumbull and Hyde put up a good fight but were outnumbered. In the end the boy was held down and made to watch while Trumbull's right arm was hacked off with a meat cleaver. It took him two days to bleed to death in Picard's bed. For good measure the *Northern Light* was burned to the waterline.

Trumbull used to say that a man who had no home, no family, was free to go wherever he wanted. At night they would often attend workers' meetings held in factory towns along the canal. Speakers got the audience riled up over higher wages and better hours, and then the police would usually show up and bust heads. Trumbull liked to say he believed the socialists with one ear. You don't keep your barge moving, you end up in one of them factories, where you can't see the sun rise and set on the water. So Hyde considered the canal home, but this time he couldn't run to it so easily, not while Motka was still working in Big Maud's house. He was unaccustomed to thinking about a woman the way he thought about Motka. It made him nervous, and he tried not to think of her being a whore. He supposed it was love.

In the evening he watched as a boy came down the street and climbed the porch. He knew that the boy had been sent by Norris, who wanted a meeting at the Three Brothers Café Sunday morning. Hyde also knew he had no choice. The president of the United States had been shot and there was no running from this now.

He found Norris sitting in a back booth, eating steak and eggs. Norris hardly acknowledged him when he sat down, and worked on his plate in a serious, thorough fashion. The fried eggs—at least half a dozen of them—had been broken, their yolks smeared over the blackened top of an enormous T-bone, which was blood-raw in the middle. There was a side dish of baked beans, laced with sweet-smelling molasses.

Hyde ordered coffee.

There was a stack of newspapers next to Norris's elbow. "Nobody found Czolgosz," Norris said, tapping the papers with the point of his steak knife, leaving a red-yellow dollop to soak into the page. "Nobody found Fred Nieman. He was *your* man and you didn't find him in time. It's in all the papers, you know."

"I was there, right outside that building."

"Yes, well, apparently he was inside the Temple of Music and he managed to walk right past half the U.S. Army with a gun in his hand."

"And Pinkertons. The papers say there were plenty of them, too."

"True," Norris said. "But you were the only one who knew what he looked like."

"The crowd was huge," Hyde said. "It wasn't my fault."

Norris cut into his steak and forked a large piece into his mouth. "What wasn't your fault, Hyde?"

"The whole thing. Czolgosz acted alone. He's the most solitary man I've ever seen and he never stopped moving. No one— *no one*—was going to stop him. He is what he says he is, Fred Nobody."

"Well, he's somebody now, the papers are making sure of that," Norris said, chewing deliberately. "And *you* are nobody, mister. I'll tell you something else: I don't believe he acted alone. No. Maybe, just maybe, you're in on it, too? You and that little Russian whore?" He watched Hyde's face, and smiled. "Ah, so you're sweet on her. I can understand why." Norris looked down and cut his steak. "It all fits, Hyde. You spent a lot of time with Czolgosz. I think he convinced you to help him. He recruited you. Just like I recruited you—or thought I did. You've never been certain about all this—you lack . . . conviction. I can see it in your eyes. You believe in his 'duty'—that's what the papers are saying he calls it. Maybe he convinced you to set me up so I would *think* I had him covered. Maybe you just didn't try as hard as you could to find him."

"That's not true, none of it."

"Who knows what the truth is? Do you?"

"You believe we're all the same. Ignorant criminals."

"I think it's a crime you people were ever allowed in this country." Norris took a flask from inside his coat and topped up his coffee. He put the flask away and leaned over his plate. "Now let me eat in peace."

"You owe me money."

Norris wiped up egg yolk with a piece of bread. "You and Czolgosz and I have one thing in common: Russian cunt." He paused, and ran his tongue out to collect a bit of crust from the corner of his mouth. "I know that both you and Czolgosz were with the little bitch shortly before he shot the president."

"I went there to try and stop Leon. I told you that. Czolgosz is not afraid for his own life—that's why he was dangerous. I said that to those men in that house on Delaware Avenue."

Norris put his fork down, got his wallet out of his coat pocket, and placed a five-dollar bill next to Hyde's coffee cup. He took up the knife and resumed cutting his meat. "Pick it up and we're square."

Hyde hesitated, and then as he reached for the bill Norris swiftly drew the blade of the steak knife across his wrist. Hyde stared down at his hand as though he'd never seen one before. For a moment there was the neatest straight line in the flesh, and then blood flowed out.

"Now we're square," Norris said.

Hyde got to his feet, holding his hand against his coat, and left the restaurant.

〜〇〜

MOMENTS after Hyde left the café, Norris looked toward the counter. A young man in a gray suit named Jack Feeney got up and didn't look in Norris's direction, though he briefly touched the brim of his hat as he went to the front door. He paused a moment out on the sidewalk, and then followed Hyde down the street. Norris pushed his plate aside and took out his cigar case.

~)C~

THE regular medical bulletins issued from the front steps of the Milburn house were so reassuring that some government officials left Buffalo on Tuesday and returned to Washington. The vice president also made plans to rejoin his family in the Adirondacks.

Rixey remained in McKinley's room for hours at a time. He was exhausted, but he found his nerves were even more frayed when he wasn't near his patient. McKinley's pulse held steady, between 112 and 122, and his temperature hovered around 100 degrees. His urinary output was low, but the doctors agreed that wasn't a great cause for concern under the circumstances. He received nutritional enemas three or four times a day, and was given small sips of beef broth.

The president received guests for short durations. The doctors and nursing staff rotated into the room with military precision. Mrs. McKinley came often, but the first lady was so overwrought that she had to spend most of the time in bed in a room down the hall. McKinley's brother had come out from Ohio and was a great comfort to the first lady. The son of Abraham Lincoln, Robert, who was the president of the Pullman Company, traveled to Buffalo aboard his private railway car and paid a brief visit to the president.

Tuesday night Rixey could not sleep. It was after three a.m. and he sat in the chair by the window, gazing at the president, who lay on his back under the bedsheets. He heard the creak of floorboards out in the hall and went to the door. Opening it, he found Cortelyou in his bathrobe. Without speaking, Rixey returned to his chair by the window. Cortelyou came into the room and stood at the end of the bed; after several minutes he took the chair from the writing desk, placed it next to Rixey's, and sat down.

"The other doctors are all sleeping through the night, Presley," he said quietly. "Some are talking about leaving Buffalo."

"I keep thinking about President Garfield. When he was shot in the back at that train station in Baltimore, it took seventy-nine days for him to die. From what I understand, he suffered from an abundance of physicians, too. But they could not agree on treatment and essentially he died as a result of neglect."

"That's certainly not the case here," Cortelyou said. "This procedure this afternoon—does it have any significance?"

"I don't think so. When we removed some of the sutures around the external wound, we found that a slight infection has developed there. We will continue to wash the skin with a solution of iodine and hydrogen peroxide. If the infection worsens, we'll open the wound a little more and we may have to remove some of the skin."

"Should this be mentioned in the bulletins?"

"The consensus among the doctors is that this is a typical reaction. Overall, they believe he's headed for a full recovery."

"But what do you think?" Cortelyou asked.

Rixey stroked his mustache with his fingers. "I think we should see how he is by, say, tomorrow afternoon before we say anything about this in a bulletin. Some of the doctors are even talking about giving him solid food soon. And the president seems to be very comfortable—he's not mentioned experiencing any significant pain."

"Then you should be sleeping like a baby."

"So should you, George."

"But here we are, Doctor."

Women nurses could not be asked to perform enemas on the president, so three male nurses had been brought from the nearby marine hospital. Wednesday morning they came to Cortelyou's room while he and Rixey were preparing the next press release.

"We wish to speak to Dr. Rixey in private," Palmer Eliot said.

"Mr. Cortelyou should hear whatever you have to say," Rixey said.

"All right," Eliot said.

"Come in, please," Cortelyou said.

He sat at the desk and Rixey remained standing, while the three men sat on the daybed. Eliot was a hospital steward and had clearly been designated to speak for the other two; he sat between Vallmeyer and Hodgins, who were both privates. All three men wore white tunics and had identical close-cropped haircuts.

"Is there a change?" Rixey asked.

"The enemas, sir," Eliot said. "The president's rejecting them." He gazed at Rixey, seeming hopeful that he wouldn't have to continue. "Things were going well at first. But now . . ." He shook his head.

"Which kind?" Rixey asked. Cortelyou turned to him. "George, we've given him Epsom salts and glycerin to help clear his bowels, and that's been successful. And three or four times a day we give a nutritive enema. With a stomach wound it's the best way to provide some nourishment."

"What's it consist of?" Cortelyou asked.

"Egg, water, and a little whiskey," Rixey said.

"Interesting," Cortelyou said.

"That's the one that we just gave him, sir," Vallmeyer said. "It just won't stay in him. It's doing him no good now."

Rixey said, "All right. Try again in two hours and report to me."

They all sat still.

"Thank you, gentlemen," Cortelyou said softly.

Almost gratefully, the three men got up from the daybed and filed out of the room. Rixey looked out the window at the groups of men gathered on the sidewalk and in the street: Secret Service,

Pinkerton agents, soldiers, and the ubiquitous members of the press. They smoked, they talked, they appeared bored.

"We haven't mentioned enemas in any of the press releases," Cortelyou said. "I want to give the public sufficient information, but it seems only prudent to not mention such procedures. I'm not going to change that policy, not now." He held up the sheet of paper. "This release is already written. I think we should deliver it downstairs and wait and see what happens in the next few hours."

Rixey nodded. "I don't envy you, George, always having to gauge these things."

Cortelyou got up from his desk. "I'll be damned if I'm going to issue a public announcement about the state of the president's rectum." He went to the door and, before opening it, he said, "I could use a good stiff whiskey myself."

"No egg?"

"And no water," Cortelyou said. He smiled briefly, though it seemed to require considerable effort. "And I'd prefer to have it administered in a more traditional manner."

They went out into the hall and down the main stairs. The front door was open and through the screen door they could see that a crowd of reporters had already assembled on the lawn in anticipation of the next press release.

That night the weather changed and a high wind buffeted the Milburn house, rustling its ivy-covered brick walls. Rixey dozed on and off in the chair by the window while McKinley slept peacefully. That afternoon the surgical team had removed more infected skin from around the superficial bullet wound. It was decided that this, too, should not be mentioned in the press bulletins. Instead, Cortelyou announced that the president had been allowed to eat a small piece of toast, and he was taking larger quantities of beef broth. Many of the physicians who had been hovering about the Milburn house since last Friday had now left. They believed that the president's condition had progressed beyond the point where peritonitis might develop. As a navy surgeon, Rixey had seen his share of gunshot wounds. After the initial critical period, recovery was always slow but steady. To some degree, he was relieved to see the doctors disperse. What the president needed was solitude and rest.

~⊃C~

CZOLGOSZ was under constant surveillance by at least two guards who remained outside his cell door. It was clear that this was privileged duty, something to tell grandchildren about, and the men were changed frequently, every few hours. But when he was moved from his cell, he was usually accompanied by Geary and Solomon, and they became quite friendly.

By midweek he was allowed to read newspapers. The president was alive and recovering from his wounds. The stories about Czolgosz often included the proper pronunciation of his name: *Shol-gosh*. Some papers claimed to have discovered evidence of elaborate plots developed by the anarchist group known as Free Society. These conspiracies involved secret meetings and coded communications between anarchist leaders throughout America. Emma Goldman and Abraham Isaak, the publisher of *Free Society*, were always at the center of these groups.

The press took great interest in Nowak's Hotel, where Czolgosz had rented a room. A man named Sturtz, who lived down the hall, had been arrested. Czolgosz had met him, but it was soon determined that he had nothing to do with shooting the president. Every day the papers reported that new informants had come forward and claimed that they had seen Czolgosz with various people. In one such instance, he had been seen walking through the exposition with two other men the night before the shooting. There were front-page articles about a Buffalo elementary-school teacher, a Mrs. Helen Petrowski, who had been arrested when it was learned that she had distributed anarchist literature to her students. It was a game. The police, the district attorney, the Pinkertons, the Secret Service, the newspaper reporters: they all wanted to "unravel" the plot behind the assassination attempt.

Some articles said that the Cleveland police were trying to link members of the Czolgosz family, particularly Leon's brother Waldeck, to the shooting. Across the country anarchists were being jailed or driven out of their homes and communities. There were several attempted lynchings. An effigy of Czolgosz was paraded through the streets of downtown Chicago and burned.

Most disturbing was the way he was portrayed in the newspapers. By some accounts he was "arrogant," "defiant," "cocky," and, the worst, "dainty." According to the guards, he made outrageous demands concerning food and cigars. One headline read: CZOLGOSZ EATS MUCH AND SMOKES STOGIES. The article said that he complained that the ice cream did not come in a variety of flavors, and that he insisted on cantaloupe, which he didn't even like. But other reports described him as "cooperative," "polite," and "courteous." He was a "cleanly young man." He asked the guards about these reports, and they all said they had been ordered not to divulge any information to reporters whatsoever. They believed that the reporters just made such stories up.

The newspapers were obsessed with Emma Goldman as much as they were with the shooting of President McKinley. Apparently she had gone into hiding, and despite a nationwide search she could not be found, until Tuesday, when the Chicago police had raided an apartment, where they found a woman taking a bath. According to the papers, she wrapped herself in a kimono and at first claimed that she was a Swedish servant and spoke little English. The police believed her and even showed her a photograph of Emma Goldman. As they were about to leave, they found a pen with the name "Emma Goldman" on it, but still they failed to recognize the woman in the kimono. At that point she told them that she was in fact Emma Goldman, and had planned on giving herself up anyway because many of her friends and colleagues were already being detained for no legitimate reason.

Some newspaper artists portrayed Goldman as a whip-wielding seductress, while others gave her the horns of Satan. Much was made of the fact that she admitted to being in Buffalo in the middle of August, at the same time that Czolgosz had been there—but there was no evidence that they had met. District Attorney Penney's attempts to get her extradited to Buffalo had been inexplicably thwarted by the Chicago police. Czolgosz was most distressed by the thought of Emma Goldman alone in a Chicago prison. She was being held in an unusual cell, a large, open space, surrounded by iron bars, almost as though she were a circus animal on display. She was quoted as saying that she was an experienced nurse and would like to care for both the president and "the boy." Despite the fact that she was only a few years his senior, Czolgosz liked the fact that she thought of him as "the boy."

~ɔↄ~

HYDE went to Big Maud's in the afternoon. He'd never been there in the daytime. The house wasn't yet open for business. Motka was in the front hall, with a basket of laundry, her hair pinned up on the back of her head. She explained that many of the girls were sleeping, and Big Maud was out taking her daily ride in an open carriage. When Motka saw the bloody handkerchief wrapped about Hyde's wrist, she took him upstairs to Bella Donna's room, where a recording of Verdi's *Otello* played on the Victrola.

"*Il fazzoletto*—the handkerchief," Bella Donna said, as they inspected his wrist. "It is always the sign of danger, no? For Desdemona! For you, Hyde!"

Carefully, Motka cleaned the cut with soap and water, and then wrapped it in a fresh cloth bandage.

"Tell me," Hyde said. "Norris came here?"

Motka did not look up from her work. "He is a—what do you call it, Bella?"

"*Scocciatore,*" Bella Donna said, gesturing with her hand toward her rump.

"A pain in the ass," Motka said.

"Worse," Bella said. "*Lui è un rompipalle!*" She turned the music up even louder and came and sat with them at the small table by the window. "I must to tell you both something," she whispered. "You not need just to worry about Signor Norris. Big Maud, too."

"Why?" Hyde said. When she only shrugged, he asked, "How do you know?"

"In *questa casa* there are few secrets kept from Bella Donna." She picked up a small hand mirror and studied her eyes and mouth.

"No one can be trusted," Motka said. "All over Buffalo the police hunt down anyone in the workers' cause. They have been looking for my brother, Anton, and his wife says he has gone to hiding."

"Maybe I shouldn't come here anymore," he said. She raised her eyes to him and, to his surprise, she appeared alarmed, even hurt. "Maybe you should leave Buffalo?" he offered.

"And go to where?" she asked.

"Motka, are you afraid to leave here?"

She blushed. "I told you, my father was a doctor. I helped him with some surgeries. He taught me not to be afraid. Nothing is gained with fear."

"*Le mie ragazze,*" Bella Donna said vehemently. "My girls. Safe in *la casa.*"

"Of course." He looked out the window into the street. "See that man in the gray suit, down at the end of the block—there, in the window of the barbershop? He has been following me since this morning. I need to lose him."

"You could leave through back door," Bella said, "but Big Maud would find out from one of the girls hanging out the laundry and it would not go well for me." She smiled at Motka. "I could make a little distraction?" She placed her hands under her breasts, as though offering them.

"That would certainly be distracting," Hyde said, and both women laughed.

"All right," Motka said, looking at Hyde. "But you must help me." She took a slip of paper from the pocket of her skirt and placed it on the table. "This morning I get this, delivered from my brother's son, Pavel. Anton is in the need of money. He is afraid to go to his factory job or to his family. The police look everywhere for him." She reached into her pocket again and took out a small wad of money. "I do not know where Anton is, but I think his wife, Katrina, does. You take this to her?" She handed him three twenty-dollar bills.

"All right."

"You need go to Tasczek's Tavern—you know it?"

"Yes, in St. Stanislaus parish."

"Katrina, she work there. She is one of Tasczek's nieces. But she will not believe that I send you unless you give this to her." She removed an earring, which was a small blue stone set in gold. "It was our mother's. Anton gave Katrina the brooch like it."

Hyde tucked the money and the earring inside his coat pocket.

"*Adesso*," Bella Donna said, as she opened the door to the hall. "You must give me just a little *minuti* and in this moment you will have so much distractions you can walk away from this man in the barbershop."

She went out, pulling the door closed behind her, and her shoes were loud on the creaking stairs. They watched from the window as Bella Donna emerged from the front door of the house and walked down the street, twirling a parasol. It was as though she created a wake in water, the way people—men and women—paused to watch her pass. At the end of the block, she hesitated in front of the barbershop, glanced back toward Big Maud's house, and smiled. Then she pulled from her sleeve a handkerchief and dropped it on the ground.

Within moments several men rushed out of the barbershop and competed with one another to pick up the handkerchief. The man in the gray suit was not among them; he was still standing in the window. Bella Donna spoke with the men on the sidewalk and then led them into the barbershop. She stood inside the window, her back to the street. There was much gesturing, and after a few moments she began to unbutton the front of her dress. Other men who had gathered outside crowded in the doorway, and the man in the gray suit was pushed to the back of the barbershop, out of sight.

"You better go now," Motka said.

Hyde went to the door.

Motka came over to him and did something she'd never done before. She put her arms around his neck and kissed him on the mouth.

He held her tightly and said, "I mean it, you should leave Buffalo."

"And go to where?"

"Everyone goes west. Maybe you should go east."

She pushed him away and her eyes were filled with fear. "I would only end up in another house, maybe not too good as this."

"Not if I took you with me."

It was as though she could not bear to hear him, and looking away, she said, "You must go now. Hurry."

Hyde went downstairs and out the front door. A crowd had gathered outside the barbershop, and two policemen had arrived. From inside the shop there came the sound of men cheering and applauding. Hyde walked quickly in the other direction, and only slowed down when he turned the corner of the block.

~つC~

AT noon on Thursday the president complained of pain and fatigue, and through the afternoon his condition declined rapidly. Though Cortelyou issued a series of vague press releases, the reporters encamped in the street clearly sensed that there had been a turn for the worse. Doctors who had left the previous day returned as quickly as possible. Rixey was in constant meetings with the other physicians; they all agreed that McKinley was suffering from acute intestinal toxemia. Enemas containing calomel, a strong laxative, brought limited results. His pulse was weakening and digitalis was administered, along with regular injections of strychnine, which were intended to prevent heart failure. He was given no more food. Through the night his heart continued to weaken. Members of the cabinet were contacted, and a message was sent to the Tahawus Club in the Adirondacks, where the vice president was vacationing with his family.

~つC~

WORD of the president's failing condition swept through Buffalo Thursday evening. Norris sat at his desk in the empty Pinkerton office, reading the *Courier* and the *Evening News*. All of Buffalo's Pinkertons were out working leads concerning anarchist activity throughout the city, plus there were rumors of another mob attack at police headquarters.

Norris listened to the footsteps in the hall and knew it was Jack Feeney, who tended to drag one heel. When the door opened, Feeney came in and walked down the aisle between the desks, never once looking directly at Norris.

"You lost Hyde," Norris said.

Feeney took off his bowler. "It was this goddamn whore, I tell you." He was not yet thirty, and he had a harelip, which made his mouth slant oddly when he spoke.

"What whore? Motka? You been upstairs with that slut?"

"No, no. I wasn't poking nobody. But this big Italian one, Bella Donna she calls herself. Hyde was in Big Maud's house and I was staked out across the street in a barbershop, and this Bella Donna comes over and puts on a show." His smile revealed uneven teeth already going brown with chaw tobacco. "You should've *seen* 'em."

"Who?"

"Well, yeah, the shop filled up with so many men I couldn't get out the door, and then the police showed up and they wanted to take her away but I think there would have been a riot right there." He was still looking to work through this with humor, and he smiled again. "I'm tellin' you, Norris, you never seen nothin' like 'em."

"Who?"

"They were . . ." He held his hands out in from of him, cupping an imaginary set of enormous breasts, but then he just gave up. "Anyway, Hyde took off somewheres."

Norris leaned back and stared hard at Feeney, who lowered his head and glanced toward the windows. "What's the matter with your foot?" Norris waited, and when Feeney looked at him, he said, "The one you drag."

"A horse stepped on it when I was a kid."

"A horse stepped on it. He kick you in the lip, too?"

Feeney's face reddened.

"How the hell you got into the Pinkertons is beyond me. You'd never make it in the Washington office." Norris got up from the desk and went over to the nearest window. Groups of people stood in the street, talking and reading newspapers, and their faces, even their postures were tight, gripped with a sorrow that seemed overwhelming. The president wasn't dead yet, but the country was already beginning to mourn. Behind him, he heard Feeney turn and walk back toward the door.

TASCZEK'S Tavern was a two-story clapboard house with awnings jutting out above a pair of large front windows. Inside, dim gaslight reflected off the molded-tin ceiling, and the walls were covered with handbills in English and Polish, which advertised rooms for rent, houses for sale, workers' meetings. Signs above the bar indicated Tasczek's services as a post office, a bank, and a ticket agent for the steamship lines on Lake Erie. The shelves displayed bottles of liquor, brandied fruits, hard-boiled eggs, pickled vegetables, pig's feet, wheels of cheese, loaves of bread. Several young men and women, each wearing a white apron, worked behind the long bar. They all appeared to be related—brothers, sisters, cousins—and they waited on customers with a resignation that suggested that they would spend their lives in this establishment.

"I'm looking for Katrina," Hyde said.

They all stopped working and stared at Hyde, and then the man at the cash register turned toward the woman who had been slicing meat. She was thin, pale, and in late pregnancy. "What do you want?" she said, wiping her forehead with the back of her hand.

Hyde went down the bar and said quietly, "Motka sent me." He laid his bandaged hand on the counter, and opening it he let her see the earring pinned to the cloth. "I must speak with you."

She put down her knife, glanced at her relatives, and then led Hyde to a door at the back of the bar. They entered a storeroom with shelves stacked with boxes, jars, and cans.

Hyde closed the door behind them and took the three twenty-dollar bills from his pocket. "This is for Anton."

Katrina sat gently on a crate and rubbed her back. Her eyes were a very pale blue, and now they seemed relieved; she took the bills from him and said, "All right. I can tell you they are on a barge in the river—it's tied up at a wharf north of the coke plant. I don't know how you tell it from the others. I don't know the name. You must find it, go there tonight, and show this earring to Anton." She handed two of the bills back to him. "He says they need this."

She started to get up, but had difficulty. He took her by the arm—as thin as a child's—and helped her to her feet. "You should be home resting," he said.

He turned to open the door, but Katrina took hold of his shirt and turned him back to her—her fingers were surprisingly strong and her eyes now bright with fear. "You find Anton and you get him away from them."

"Who?"

"There is Bruener, who owns the barge, and his son Josef."

"I know Bruener."

"Anton believes in the workers' cause, but he's having doubts since this outside man came to Buffalo."

"What outside man?"

"I don't know. He is planning something—"

"What?"

"I don't know, but it's going too far. I can tell Anton is afraid— and he's afraid to leave them." Her eyes began to brim over with tears. "*Please.* I have one son, and this one on the way. Please send my husband back."

"I'll try," Hyde said. He put his hand over hers, and slowly she released his shirt.

~逆C~

NINE thirty Friday night Cortelyou's bulletin read: "The president is dying."

Rixey remained with the president while Cortelyou went downstairs to deliver the bulletin to the reporters stationed in front of the Milburn house. Outside there was a high wind, as well as frequent thunder and lightning.

For the next few hours government officials came to McKinley's bedside. Toward midnight there were visits from his brother, sisters, nephews, and nieces. The president, who went in and out of a stupor, requested to see his wife twice. During her last visit she held his hand while he sang a few lines from his favorite hymn, "Nearer, My God, to Thee." When she was led out of the room, she made no display of grief or tears.

Word arrived at the Milburn house that an enormous mob was gathering in the streets around the Buffalo police headquarters, and that Chief Bull had requested that national guardsmen and army regulars encircle the building.

At one a.m. the *Buffalo Commercial* distributed an extra edition with the headline HE IS DEAD. Although John Milburn appeared on the front steps of his house to insist to a crowd of reporters that the president was still alive, other papers hastily released editions with similar headlines. Soon after, the county coroner arrived at the house, claiming that he had come to take charge of the body. He was turned away and told that he would be notified when he was needed.

A few minutes past two o'clock, the president's breathing, which had been mechanical and audible, stopped. After a short time, he took one more deep breath, and then was still. Rixey put his stethoscope on William McKinley's chest, and said quietly, "The president is dead."

BOOK II

"NEARER, MY GOD, TO THEE"

Buffalo is a staid city but it required no acute
vision to see that more than half the crowds
would have been willing and glad to have seen
a sudden and violent death meted out to the
man who fired the shot, and many a man that
before had spurned the thought of lynching as
punishment for a crime held his hands firmly
clenched, aching to pull the rope that might
have been thrown about the prisoner's neck.

Buffalo Courier
Saturday, September 7, 1901

IV

MRS. MCKINLEY WAS loath to even consider an autopsy, but after Rixey and Cortelyou discussed the matter with her at length she accepted a compromise: the doctors could examine the heart, lungs, and intestinal organs, but she was adamant that nothing be removed from the body other than small tissue samples necessary for microscopic study. The autopsy began at noon on Saturday, conducted by the Erie County coroner, James Wilson, and Dr. Harvey Gaylord and Dr. Herman Matzinger of the New York State Pathological Laboratory. Present were Dr. Rixey and many of the other physicians who had been involved in the case. The procedure lasted four hours, and before it was concluded Theodore Roosevelt was sworn in as president of the United States in the Wilcox house, which was a short distance down Delaware Avenue.

The autopsy findings proved to be controversial: a passage in the coroner's report stated that gangrene had been found on "both walls of the stomach and pancreas following the gunshot wounds." Within hours of the autopsy hysterical newspaper articles appeared across the country, claiming that the president had died of infection, not gunshot wounds; furthermore, there was embarrassment over the argument that an insufficient portion of tissue had been removed for study. The doctors disagreed about the cause of the gangrene. Dr. Park argued that the damaged pancreas caused death, while Dr. Mann was more interested in the condition of McKinley's heart. The muscle tissue was pale and extremely fatty, the result, apparently, of the president's sedentary routine. The most controversial opinion, however, came from Dr. Wasdin, the anesthesiologist, who claimed that the patient's rapid decline could only be attributed to the fact that the assassin had used poison bullets. Though there was no substantiating evidence, newspapers reported this theory in the most sensational way.

During the week following the shooting, the press had lauded the medical staff for its valiant efforts; yet within hours of the president's death numerous articles and editorials cast suspicion on the competence of the physicians involved in the case, many of whom were now prone to acrimonious statements about one another, which were quoted in the papers.

Oddly, Dr. Rixey was somewhat removed from the controversy, despite the fact that he had been at the very center of the case. His role had not been as a specialist but as a general practitioner who had acted as the one who coordinated the other physicians' participation in McKinley's treatment. This new turn of events deepened his remorse and quite exhausted him. He felt almost fortunate that most of his time and energy was devoted to the health and well-being of the grieving first lady.

~ᴑC~

NORRIS received a telephone call from Lloyd Savin asking him to come to police headquarters. With the death of the president, an angry mob had again surrounded the building, demanding to lynch Leon Czolgosz. As Norris moved through the crowd he spotted the captain, waiting beyond the cordon of policemen that were protecting the building. Norris was admitted through the line and joined Savin at the top of the front steps. The noise from the street was deafening, forcing Savin to shout, "We've requested hundreds of national guardsmen to help out."

"It might not be enough." Norris looked back down at the crowded street. "Maybe you should just throw Czolgosz out the window to them and be done with it."

"Perhaps, but I called you because I thought you'd be interested in a certain dead prostitute." He led Norris down a narrow set of stairs to the basement. "We call these the 'dungeons.'" Savin's voice echoed off the stone walls. "Ordinarily we'd hold them over in the city jail, but it's under renovation."

"Them?"

"We've been rounding up suspected anarchists. They claim to know nothing, and most hardly speak English. The one thing they have in common is they all bleed easily."

Savin led Norris to the first door, where they could look through iron bars at perhaps twenty men crammed in a cell, some sitting on benches while others were sprawled on the floor. Most were bruised and bloodied.

"We've hauled in dozens with socialist connections, but we haven't found anyone we can tie to Czolgosz." Savin lit a cigarette and the smell of tobacco was a relief. "But . . ." He continued to the end of the hall, where a young uniformed policeman unlocked a heavy wooden door and swung it open.

Norris followed Savin inside and the door was closed behind them. The room was tiny and lit by a flickering gas lamp. A man was slumped in a chair at a wooden table. He was in his late fifties, and he wore a yellow-and-black-checkered vest and jacket, and a grimy top hat that was stove in on one side. His left ear was clotted with dried blood, and blood had run down his neck and stained his shirt collar, yet he maintained a lopsided grin and a gleam in his eye, as though he were genuinely happy to see them. In a grand gesture, he doffed his hat and bowed with exaggerated grace. "As you may observe," he said to Norris in a British accent, "their powers of persuasion are without equal."

Savin and Norris sat in the chairs across the table from him.

"Haven't I seen you somewhere before?" Norris asked the man.

"Oh, it's certainly possible," he said. "In my prime I performed *Hamlet* for Queen Victoria herself, but I have now attained a vintage that seems more appropriate to the role of Polonius, who gets run through whilst lurking behind an arras in fair Gertrude's bedchamber—or even Claudius, the king, who at least gets to dally with said Gertrude before he himself is run through." As he spoke his hands moved through the air, seeming to coax emphasis and perfect pitch from each syllable. "Suffice it to say that after this interrogation I might be prepared to play the Ghost."

"No, I think I saw you in a saloon, somewhere in Black Rock," Norris said, glancing toward Savin. "Two brothers were trying to convince me that a group of anarchists from Paterson were plotting to sink J. P. Morgan's yacht in New York harbor." He looked at the man across the table. "And you, you were up on the stage, singing, dancing, telling jokes, and giving recitations between appearances by—"

"That would be Lady Godiva, of the long, splendid tresses and the ample bosom, who, *glor*iously naked, would ride bareback across the stage upon her grand white steed." He inhaled deeply, as though savoring a fine wine. "Oh, the firmness of those pale, bouncing buttocks as they jounced ever so gently on that handsome mount's quivering haunches!" He placed his hand over his heart and bowed forward slowly. "I am but a humble thespian, sir. Augustus P. Quimby, at your service."

"No," Norris said, "it was Dr. Quimby, and you sold some elixir as well."

"Ah, yes, well, even actors have to eat," the gentleman said. "That would be Dr. Quimby's Amazing Elixir, a dash of which I could use at the moment."

"That's the one," Norris said. "I believe you did recite from *Hamlet*."

"'Marry, sir, here's my drift,'" Quimby said. "'And I believe, it is a fetch of wit.'"

"The problem is," Savin said, "he's forthcoming, but only up to a point. And then we get a shitload of Shakespeare."

Norris took his cigar case from inside his coat and laid it open on the table. Slowly he prepared the tip of a cigar with his knife, never once looking at Quimby. "So you've been persuaded to help us—in what way?"

"To proffer my assistance, of course, like the good citizen that I am!" Quimby said.

"You're a drummer, a huckster," Norris said. "Why should we believe you?"

Quimby raised his chin as though to deflect the insult. "Dear sir, I am many things to many people." Then, leaning forward, he said, "'For murder, though it have no tongue, will speak with most miraculous organ.'"

Norris said, "We need information, not an entertaining quotation."

"Information, quotation," Quimby said with delight. "That makes a fair rhyme—I must remember it. Why, sir, you're a poet and you don't even know it."

Savin reached into the outside pocket of his suit coat and produced a wad of cloth, which he laid on the table.

Norris spread it out with his fingers. "Satin, I believe. Yellow with blue flowers, a pattern that suggests a woman's dress— and these brown stains: Blood? I think so. That's interesting." He handed the cigar to Quimby.

Savin struck a match and lit the cigar. "Quimby saw fit to give us this piece of material before we went to work on his other ear."

Once the cigar was lit, Quimby relaxed in his chair, his legs crossed.

Norris concentrated on the preparation of a second cigar. "This material might have been torn from the dress of a woman," he said. "Perhaps a prostitute who went by the name of Clementine and worked at Big Maud's establishment."

"Exactly—and a great loss it was." Cigar smoke enshrouded Quimby's head.

"She was working down on the canal, when somebody beat her to death. I suppose we could check with the girls at Big Maud's to see if Clementine had a dress like this."

"I assure you, sir," Quimby said, "she came down to the canal in that dress."

Norris leaned toward Savin, who struck another match and lit the cigar. "She was found naked except for a yellow hat—not unusual, considering her profession. I think she was beaten with something like rope, the kind used on the docks and barges."

"Precisely," Quimby said. "A short length of line tied into a knot known as a monkey fist. A rather popular weapon among canawlers."

"Tell him how you know this," Savin said.

Quimby drew on his cigar, and then pondered the ash.

"I must admit," Norris said to Savin, "that I'm philosophically opposed to interrogation methods that result in bloody skulls because there are other parts of the body that are far more vulnerable, and though the results aren't as apparent to the eye, the *results*—what you learn from such encounters—are invariably not only true but useful."

"You must give me a demonstration," Savin said pleasantly.

"For instance, I'm particularly fond of the dislocated shoulder," Norris said. "It's quick and easy, and there's no chance of bloodstains on your suit. It's also easily corrected. Out, in."

He pushed back his chair, but stopped when Quimby cleared his throat, and said, "There is barge called the *Glockenspiel*."

Savin said, "Belongs to that German, yes."

"Klaus Bruener," Norris added. He opened his palm on the table, a sign of mild disappointment. "That's where Clementine was found, Quimby. We know that."

"But you didn't find her dress there," Quimby said, in mock surprise.

"My men went over every inch of that boat," Savin said.

"The Bruener boy hid it," Quimby said. "That poor, dear, mute lad."

"How'd he have her dress," Norris asked, "if he found her naked in the canal?"

Quimby's eyes grew large with wonder. "That is the very question, isn't it?"

"You saw something," Norris said.

"More like what I heard, but you know how utterances can fuel the imagination." Quimby folded his arms, his stare suddenly hard and uncompromising. "I want my release, and enough money to get out of Buffalo. Fifty dollars."

"Right," Norris said. "Your comrades down the hall aren't going to take kindly to the fact that you've been in here, chatting with the police and smoking cigars."

"Indeed, this presents me with a dilemma."

"And consider another side to your dilemma," Norris said. Quimby shifted uncomfortably in his chair. "This piece of cloth," Norris continued. "If it belonged to Clementine—and I don't doubt that it did—we have to consider how it came into your possession: rape and murder, and then you throw her in the canal, where this mute boy finds her."

"Yes, a likely scenario," Quimby said. "But why would I keep the evidence?"

"A memento?" Norris said. "A reminder of a few moments of carnal bliss?"

Quimby laughed, revealing gnarled brown molars and a chipped incisor. "Surely, that theory will hold up in court about as well as my aged member."

"Give us the rest," Savin said as he got up from his chair suddenly, "and you can walk with your fifty dollars. Think it over, Quimby. We'll be back after we have a drink. Or rather, Detective Norris will be back. You know how persuasive Pinkertons can be."

"Yes, in and out." Quimby watched Norris stand up. "You're a

Pinkerton?" For the first time there was no pretense, just awe shot through with fear.

"Jesus H., you didn't mistake me for a policeman?" Disgusted, Norris turned away as Savin opened the door. "Could use that drink first," Norris said as they left the room. "I haven't separated a shoulder since I left Washington."

When Savin closed the door, he said, "That'll give him something to think about during intermission." As they walked down the corridor, the young policeman came to attention, his back to the stone wall.

They went upstairs to Savin's office, a well-appointed room in a corner of the building, which was quite dark because there were blankets hung over the windows. "In case of rocks," Savin said. He went to his desk, where he took a bottle of whiskey and two glasses from one of the drawers. "I've hardly been out of this place for days," he said, pouring them each a dram. He placed one of the glasses on the far side of the desk, and then sat down.

"Why don't you give me ten minutes with Czolgosz?" Norris sat in the leather-padded chair that faced the desk. He took a sip of whiskey, strong, peaty stuff. "I'll deliver the name of every anarchist between here and Chicago, with Emma Goldman's name at the top of the list."

"I'm afraid it's not possible at the moment. He's not here."

"Czolgosz has been moved?" Norris glanced toward the blanketed windows. "A good idea, considering this mob."

"For the past week he's been kept downstairs." Savin got up and went to one of the windows, where he held back the corner of the blanket and looked down into the street. "This crowd ever breaks through, they won't find Leon Czolgosz, but they may find a cousin or brother." He lit a cigarette and placed it on the rim of a large chrome-and-glass ashtray that was full of butts. "When word spread that the president was failing, we decided to move Czolgosz. We've told no one other than those who were responsible for the transfer."

"Where is he?"

"The county penitentiary for women," Savin said. "It's about a mile from here."

"Are you trying to reward him?"

"Hardly. Now that the president is dead, Czolgosz will be arraigned Monday, so tomorrow we'll have to bring him back here. The president's body is going to lie in state at city hall all afternoon and we want to transfer Czolgosz then. The procession will draw thousands to pay their respects."

"And the newspaper reporters will be distracted," Norris said.

"Exactly."

"I want to be in on it."

"Thought you would," Savin said. "I'm organizing the transfer, and I want to do it so that we don't draw attention. We'll have plenty of guards at the penitentiary and here, but I want to keep the trip itself very low-key. Two carriages. No sign of uniforms." For a moment he stared pensively at the sinuous filament of smoke as it rose from his cigarette. "I'll need you and one other Pinkerton."

"Of course," Norris said. "Always when there's dirty work to be done."

∽つC∽

CZOLGOSZ was kept alone in a cell in what seemed an empty wing of a large prison. There was a small window that allowed him to watch the rain on the cobblestones, and occasionally he heard voices echoing from other cells across the courtyard. They all sounded like women: some high, sweet, even angelic; others angry and demented, keening.

And the guards sitting outside his cell barely spoke to him.

Clearly they'd been given instructions to avoid conversation with him. They whispered among themselves, and he came to realize that they didn't know he was Leon Czolgosz.

Now that the president was dead, he felt an odd sense of relief. If the president had lived, Thomas Penney had suggested that the sentence for attempted murder could be ten years. The thought of a decade in a cell frightened Czolgosz. He would have failed, and he would certainly go mad. Now they would have to execute him. His work was done. It would be over soon.

He remained at the window, listening for the women. He believed Emma Goldman's voice would rise up from them. That must be why he was here now, in a place where women were imprisoned, their voices hopeless. Emma understood such despair. She would emerge to lead them all away from here. It was only a matter of time. They were all waiting, and it was in the waiting that they found belief, they found faith. The president was dead. There were no leaders. There were only themselves, and they could not be confined any longer. Together they would find freedom. That too was in the women's voices.

One of the guards brought dinner: ham, beans, potatoes, and carrots. They had cut the meat and gave him a spoon. The guard, tall, unshaven, with a prominent Adam's apple, remained in the doorway and watched him eat.

"What'chu do they send you to the women's penitentiary?" he asked.

"That's where I am?" Czolgosz smiled. "No wonder the food's better here."

"Them women can cook." The guard folded his arms and put his shoulder against the jamb. "But why they have us hold you over here, all alone? Who are you?"

"You really don't know?"

The other guard wandered over to the door. He was stout and was still wearing his dinner napkin tucked in his collar. "They just says to keep you here and don't let no one near you. Like you was something special."

The tall one said, "You don't even look dangerous. You're kind of, you know, pretty. You ain't no nancy boy?"

Czolgosz shook his head and continued to eat.

"Well," the other one said, wiping his mouth with his napkin, "he's got some appetite. And my dinner's getting cold."

"I shot the president," Czolgosz said. "I killed William McKinley."

Both guards stared at him, until the tall one whispered, "No."

He put his spoon down on his empty plate. "That's why I'm here."

The other one stepped in closer. "You're that Leon fella?"

The tall one took his shoulder off the doorjamb. "What you go and do that for?"

"So we'd all be free," Czolgosz said as he put his plate on the corner of the cot. "As long as there are leaders, none of us will ever be free."

They stared down at him, incredulous. "Free?" the fat one said. "You ain't free."

"I'm freer than you'll ever be," Czolgosz said. "Me, and those women over there."

Neither guard spoke, until the tall one said in disgust, "Shoot."

He left the door and walked down the corridor, leaving it to the fat guard to remove the dirty plate and spoon from Czolgosz's cell.

~ɔC~

WHEN Norris and Savin were sufficiently fortified, they returned to the basement cell where Quimby was being held. "Are you left- or right-handed?" Norris asked, going around to Quimby's side of the table.

Quimby got out of his chair, knocking it over, and backed up to the wall.

"Earlier you seemed to handle your cigar quite deftly with this one." Norris grabbed the man's left arm.

Quimby began to cry. There were no theatrics about it. Loudly, he said, "This is all about some harlot? What do you care about a common prostitute?"

"We don't," Norris shouted, placing his other hand on Quimby's shoulder. "We care about her killer."

"Listen to me!" Quimby pleaded.

"*What*, Quimby? Why would you kill a prostitute?"

"I didn't!"

"But you know who did," Norris said. Quimby turned his face until his cheek pressed against the brick wall. "And you know *why* they did it." Norris was about to pull the arm and shove the shoulder, dislocating the joint.

Quimby tensed, but then said, "They were there, they were there."

" 'There' rhymes with 'where,' Quimby. Where?"

"By the *footbridge!*" Quimby cried.

Savin came closer and said calmly, "Who did it?"

Norris loosened his grip on Quimby, who slid down the wall until he was squatting, his chest heaving as he sobbed.

"I still think he's acting," Norris said. "Though I must admit he's quite convincing."

"Tell you what, Quimby," Savin said. "Why don't we drive out to the canal and have a look around. Maybe you'll remember better?"

Distraught, wiping his eyes with his sleeve, Quimby nodded. Norris took him by the arm again, at first alarming the man, but then he helped him to his feet.

"That prostitute," Quimby said, regaining his composure. "I tell you, she knew what she was about. I come and go from Buffalo, often aboard one of the barges. I've performed before audiences along the canal from here to Albany."

"You returned to Buffalo aboard the *Glockenspiel*," Norris said. "Something that Klaus Bruener failed to mention."

Quimby said, "Yes, we returned to Buffalo. When I disembarked it was evening, and being short of funds for a room in a boardinghouse I elected to seek shelter as the weather was turning inclement."

Norris looked at Savin, who said, "That was one fine performance." He seemed indecisive for a moment, but then said, "All right, I have a carriage waiting in the alley behind headquarters. We'll drive out to that footbridge, and I promise you, Quimby, if you don't give us everything we want this Pinkerton detective will demonstrate the fine art of persuasion, and then I personally will push you into the canal."

"Can you swim?" Norris asked.

"Yes," Quimby said.

Savin opened the door for them. "Just try it with a dislocated shoulder."

They did not speak once to Quimby, did not even acknowledge his presence in the carriage during the ride to the canal. Savin ordered the driver to make haste through the muddy streets of Buffalo, which were filled with crowds—some were agitated and appeared hostile, while at other corners people were gathered as though in mourning. The sky was overcast—it had been raining on and off all day—and sudden gusts buffeted the carriage, causing it to rattle and creak loudly. When they reached the section of the canal where Clementine's body had been found, the three men walked along the embankment and started across the footbridge. There was only one barge docked on the far side, and it was not the *Glockenspiel*.

Savin stopped when they reached the middle of the bridge and he pointed down at the water. "She was found there, we were told, by that piling."

Quimby held on to his top hat because of the wind that rushed down the canal, and his coat collar was turned up. "It was a damp night, much like this, but a sight warmer then. When Bruener tied his barge up there on the embankment he told me I had to get off. I protested, because of the weather, but he was unsympathetic. He is the sort that's accustomed to getting his way without any argument. He seemed anxious about something, and I got the distinct impression that he was waiting for something or someone. So I bid him and his son adieu and wandered along the embankment until I came to this footbridge. I know this part of the canal well, and as it began to rain I knew I could find shelter—down there, beneath this footbridge. See," he said, pointing, "at the base of the embankment, in that shed."

"What's in there?" Norris asked.

"That's where various bargemen keep extra gear and store some of their goods. It's locked most of the time, but there's usually a window that can be jimmied."

"You got inside," Savin said.

"I did. And found myself a right snug spot in among some canvas tarps. I have trouble sleeping, so I did partake of the elixir I proudly represent. But my slumber was broken when the door was unlocked and I heard a woman's laughter."

"Clementine," Savin said, lighting a cigarette. "Alone?"

"Hardly. I was tucked up in a berth out of sight, so I lay still, hoping to get back to sleep, but from the sound of things I knew that would be impossible."

"You couldn't see what was going on?" Norris asked.

"Not well. They had one lantern, and as I said I was quite nestled down in this pile of canvas where it was warm and dry."

"They?" Norris said.

"They produced the most ardent, primitive sounds." Quimby smiled. "This Clementine was soon out of her dress—I could see enough to appreciate her considerable endowments, and she did have, shall we say, a large appetite—"

"Who was she with?" Savin asked.

"Whom?" Quimby said delicately. "First, there were several Irish lads from another barge. And then a fellow who made these distasteful grunting sounds. And then there was a brief period where nothing happened and I thought the lady had completed her nocturnal obligations. Thankfully, I began to drift off to sleep, but then I witnessed a rather unusual encounter. First, Bruener comes in and he speaks to this Clementine, mostly in German, mind you—did you know she spoke German?"

Norris shook his head. "In Buffalo I assume English is everyone's second language."

"Well, I have spent some time on the Continent, and I could understand enough to know that he had an unusual proposition for her, one which—well, at first the lady doth protest, but then Bruener's manner became more persuasive."

"He threatened her," Norris said.

"In a manner of speaking. Darling Clementine demurred, and Bruener left, but a few minutes later his boy, Josef, enters the compartment, accompanied by another man. I could not get a good look at him because he insisted that the lantern be dimmed. I did not understand at first—because he too was speaking German, and in a dialect unfamiliar to me—but I then came to appreciate that this man possessed some deformity that he did not want the lady to gaze upon. Something about his face, I'm certain, because I saw his profile—and such scars. I truly do not have the verbal powers to describe how horrible they were."

"The boy," Norris said. "What was Josef doing in there?"

Quimby leaned against the railing of the footbridge, and it seemed as though he was reluctant to continue. "Gentlemen, we must come to an understanding."

Savin caught Norris's eye, and neither spoke.

"My associating with you has already put me in jeopardy. What I'm about to tell you—well, I really must leave Buffalo."

"You'll get your fifty dollars," Savin said. He leaned over and dropped his cigarette butt into canal. "The alternative, as we said, is that you can swim to Albany."

"Albany?" Quimby said. "You don't understand. I will need to get away from the canal altogether. Word will certainly get around that I've been talking with you. Workers, socialists—they're a suspicious lot. They will assume the worst. I was thinking someplace out west, St. Louis, or perhaps Denver."

Savin unbuttoned his overcoat and took out his wallet; he removed several bills and rolled them up in his fist. "What happened down there in that shed, Quimby? Something that led to this prostitute being killed?"

Quimby studied Savin's hand a long moment, and then sighed dramatically, as though this were all a great imposition. "You see, it was the boy's duty to perform, if you catch my drift, which I must say he did quite prodigiously, exhibiting remarkable youthful stamina."

"I seem to recall," Norris said, "that when we went down to look at her body on that barge Klaus Bruener said something to the effect that his boy had never before laid hands on a naked woman."

"Right," Savin said. "So, Quimby, this German with the scarred face—he watched?"

"Indeed, sir," Quimby said.

"Is that all he did?" Norris asked.

"Well." Quimby hesitated. "Yours is a pertinent question, one which I could not ascertain with absolute certainty because it was difficult to see. I can say that while the boy and the lady were thus engaged, as dogs might be, you understand, everyone's respiration was becoming keenly elevated. Including the German's."

"He was masturbating," Savin said.

For the first time Quimby seemed clearly at a loss for words. "I thought so, at first. I tried to get a better look without revealing my presence, but it was quite dark in there. I did manage to catch a glimpse of the German in flagrante delicto. He had his trousers down around his ankles but what I observed *down there*—well, like his face, it too was deformed." Quimby took a moment to compose himself, and then he whispered, "He was indeed engaged in the practice of self-abuse, but to no avail. He couldn't rise to the occasion."

"Your voyeuristic talents are duly noted," Savin said. "But how does all this lead to Clementine's death?"

Now Quimby flushed, and looked quite frightened. "Yes, indeed. That. Well. Well, eventually the boy completed his deed with a mighty shudder, and there was a minute where no one moved. Lots of panting, you understand. And then the man tells the boy to leave the compartment immediately. He shouts this because the boy doesn't hear very well. Once the boy leaves, Clementine makes a mistake, due, to be sure, to exhaustion and drink. She—well, you see, she laughed. She looked upon the woeful condition of his manhood and she laughed. Only briefly, but clearly it stung him. And then she did something else, which I believe was the fatal mistake. She called him by name. How she came to know it, I can't say, but he was outraged."

"What was his name?"

"Gimmel."

Savin looked at Norris, who said, "Herman Gimmel. From Chicago."

"The famous anarchist—one and the same, I believe," Quimby said proudly. "He took a length of rope from his pocket, with one end tied in a monkey fist. Using this cudgel, he proceeds to beat the woman. She cries out, pleads with him, but he continues to beat her mercilessly. This goes on for a terribly long time, it seemed."

"And of course you did nothing," Savin said.

"The man was incensed! Enraged!" Quimby pleaded. "He was possessed like I've never seen before, gentlemen. And believe me, you see some hard behavior here on the canal. Even when the other man came into the shed and tried to restrain him, it was no use."

"What other man?" Norris said.

"The Jew—that's what Bruener calls him. A fellow who works on the barge, moving cargo, that sort of thing. He must have been up here on the footbridge when he heard her screams because I heard him running along these very boards beneath our feet, but when he burst into the shed it was too late. Gimmel had beaten her to death. I mean, you could tell there was no life in that supple body. He tells this other fellow—Ascher, he calls him—to help him throw her in the canal. Ascher is reluctant, but Gimmel threatened to beat *him*. They picked her up by the arms and legs—she was stark naked, except for this yellow hat—and they took her outside. Moments later I heard the splash."

"Ascher," Norris said. "I know that name. I can't remember where—"

"And that was it?" Savin said to Quimby.

"Not exactly," Quimby said. "After a few minutes I climbed down from my berth and grabbed that piece of cloth—they had torn the dress into rags and made a hasty attempt at cleaning up the blood. Then I left the shed, thinking I would get as far away from there as I could. As I walked along the embankment I could hear an argument down below in the pilothouse of the *Glockenspiel*. It was raining quite hard at that point, and there was a dense fog. They were all very drunk by then, and Bruener insisted that Gimmel leave the barge. In fact, he made Ascher take him away—Gimmel not knowing his way about. Bruener insisted they couldn't just leave the body in the canal. It was better if they pull it out and inform the authorities."

"That's what they did," Savin said. "And we arrived at dawn."

"Where did Ascher take Gimmel?" Norris said.

"No idea," Quimby said. "You can be sure I was long gone from here by then."

There was a moment when all three men gazed down at the dirty water in the canal. And then Quimby cleared his throat. Savin handed him the rolled-up bills.

"I would appreciate a ride to the train station," Quimby said.

"You can walk," Savin said.

"But certainly, sir—"

Norris turned to Quimby. "If you don't get off this footbridge now, I promise you I *will* dislocate your shoulder and throw you in this canal."

Quimby started back along the footbridge in great haste, once glancing over his shoulder in fear.

A few raindrops tapped on the dome of Norris's bowler. "Always seems to rain when we come down here," he said.

"I've heard of Herman Gimmel," Savin said, "but don't know why he's so famous."

"He's an anarchist who has never been caught, for one thing," Norris said. "And another is the Haymarket riot back in '86."

"In Chicago, the one where all the policemen were killed?"

"I've long believed that it was Gimmel who made the bomb and threw it, not any of those fools who were hung for it. It was the beginning of a long career. Herman Gimmel has been behind many anarchist attacks."

"And he's in Buffalo, where he kills a prostitute, who is working for a Pinkerton detective recently sent out from Washington." Savin looked up at the sky. "I would like to get out of this rain."

"I would like to remember where I've heard the name Ascher," Norris said as they began walking back along the footbridge toward the carriage. "And find this barge as well."

"It could be anywhere," Savin said. "Hundreds of barges work this canal. It could be anywhere—Utica, Rome, Albany."

"If Herman Gimmel's still here in Buffalo," Norris said, "the *Glockenspiel*'s here."

At the end of the footbridge Norris paused and stared down at the canal. It was beginning to rain steadily now, the drops drumming on the hard dome of his bowler. He determined that when this was over, when he returned to Washington, he would buy a new hat and wear this one only on rainy days. There was a solution to everything, and somehow this one relieved his worry about getting this bowler wet. He continued on to the carriage, but paused outside the door. "I just remembered where I heard the name Ascher." Savin didn't seem interested; he was sitting to one side of the carriage, away from the open window that was admitting rain. Norris added, "This fellow Quimby mentioned—Ascher, who helped Gimmel throw our voluptuous corpse in the canal—his sister is that Russian whore I told you about."

"The one that knows both Czolgosz and Hyde? Maybe I should have some of my men go to Big Maud's and pick her up."

"I'd rather do it myself."

Savin didn't look altogether pleased as he brushed water from the sleeve of his overcoat. "I think we'll both go."

"Suit yourself." Norris climbed inside the carriage and sat across from Savin. "This is your town."

~⁓~

ABOUT 150 yards from the footbridge a mud flat had formed on the inside crook of a bend in the canal. Barges were often hauled up there for repairs. The muck was littered with rotted wood, nails, discarded ropes of oakum caulking. Hyde stood out of sight behind one of the hulls as Norris and Savin climbed into their carriage and left. The other man, wearing the checked jacket and top hat, was one of those actors who worked the taverns and whorehouses along the canal; they did skits, danced, sang, told jokes, cheated at cards, and sold elixirs. This one sometimes also pimped for factory girls who worked the canal for extra money. He went by various names, but was most often called Quimby.

Once the carriage was out of sight, Hyde followed Quimby. The rain was beginning to come in at a hard slant. Quimby stopped briefly in the Clinton's Ditch Saloon, and then took shelter in a livery stable across the towpath from the canal. Hyde caught up with him there and they stood in the open doorway, watching the downpour.

"If it isn't Mr. Hyde," Quimby said in his fake British accent. "Mine eyes haven't rested upon your visage since—where was it—Utica?"

"Don't remember exactly."

Quimby produced a half-smoked cigar from his breast pocket. "Got a light?"

Hyde gave him a box of matches.

Quimby lit his stogie, returned the matches, and then from inside his coat he produced—a little flourish with his hands, as though he were performing one of his card tricks—a brown bottle. "Just see if *this* sublime libation doesn't help take the chill off, *what!*"

Hyde took the bottle, removed the cork, and smelled the contents: rye. The first swallow burned terribly, causing him to cough, but the second went down easier.

Smiling, Quimby said, "Ah, you'll feel right as rain in a minute."

"I noticed you," Hyde said as he held out the bottle. "Down on the footbridge with those policemen, where Clementine was found."

"Nasty business, that." Quimby's eyes grew cautious, but then he took the bottle and tipped it up to his mouth. Gasping, his breath foul, he sighed. "And tell me, how is it you know they were of the local constabulary?"

"At St. John's Protectory you learn to spot them," Hyde said. "Though the big one in the bowler—I don't know, there was something about him."

"The man's a Pinkerton." Quimby guzzled deeply from the bottle, and looked out at the rain, which was now sweeping down the canal in sheets. "I do desire to be done with this woeful weather," he said.

"That cop, the smooth one. He paid you off."

Quimby feigned being insulted. "I beg your pardon."

"What did you sell them?"

Quimby's eyes were stone now as he gazed out at the rain.

"Come on, why else would you be out on that footbridge with them in the rain?"

Quimby shrugged. "They are making inquiries, true. That is

their job." He turned to Hyde, his eyes suddenly large with cunning. "And why would you be so interested?"

"I'm more concerned with Bruener's barge."

"The *Glockenspiel*?"

"Yes. Bruener often ties up between the footbridge and the flats."

"Perhaps he's hauling a load to Albany?" He offered the bottle but Hyde shook his head. "Listen now, you know as well as I do that with our dear president's demise Buffalo is in turmoil. Agitation abounds! They're dragging the common workingman in for questioning by the dozens—dark business. Why, *I* was incarcerated at police headquarters my*self*."

"I gather that."

"It may be that Bruener is being detained, for all I know." Quimby made a grand gesture with his arm. "My good man, there are those who proclaim that we are on the brink of social upheaval, class warfare, another civil war even! And the likes of you and I are all merely pawns. The wheels of these historic events turn like—"

"They may be bringing us in for questioning," Hyde said, "but you're the one that went to the footbridge with them, Quimby. You're the one that knows something—and talked."

Quimby uncorked the bottle again and took a good pull. "I've always thought you a perceptive lad. Brought up in that orphanage, and didn't you start out as a hoggee for Marcus Trumbull? To survive on your own, one must needs have a quick wit, a discerning eye, and a fleet foot, no? I'll be out of this blasted weather soon enough. I'm heading west, I am. Someplace sunny and dry for me."

"You gave them something for the money."

Quimby corked the bottle and tucked it away in his coat. "Not much really. What's the difference?" He shrugged. "Clementine's dead—it's a shame to lose a perfectly serviceable whore like that. Were you familiar with her wares?"

"You're avoiding my question." Hyde took hold of Quimby's lapels and pushed his back against the stable door. "The *Glockenspiel,* where is it?"

"I don't *know* where it is, my good man." Quimby held still, offering no resistance. His smile was crooked. "Other than it's out there, somewhere."

After a moment Hyde released him. He stared across the muddy towpath at the canal. The rain had let up some. "You best use that money to get out of Buffalo before those other men are released from jail. They'll be coming after you." Quimby was busy straightening his clothes, but he paused and looked at Hyde, his eyes now fearful. "Say you're going west? The cops must have paid you well."

Quimby was about to speak in protest, but Hyde left the stable and walked alongside the canal, leaning into the cold rain, while seagulls cawed and wheeled overhead, white against the lowering sky.

～つC～

IN the evening Czolgosz heard women's voices—they were closer, and seemed to be coming from outside. He got off his cot, wrapping his blanket around his shoulders, and went to the small window in his cell; there was an iron grille and, beyond that, rain-streaked glass. Down in the courtyard five women were walking in a slow circle, while a guard looked on. They wore cloaks and tattered overcoats; they kept their heads down as they took their exercise, their voices echoing off the stone walls. One of them was Emma Goldman, Czolgosz was certain of it. She was heavy and short, and there was something stiff about the way her legs moved, so that she bobbed side to side as she walked. But it was also the way the other women were gathered around her, protective yet following her lead.

Czolgosz pressed his forehead against the cold metal bars in the window. He couldn't see the entire courtyard and the women would pass out of view and then reemerge moments later. None of them looked up from the ground; they might have been in prayer. Goldman gestured with her arms, and occasionally one of the women nodded her head. When he saw her speak in Cleveland the previous spring, Goldman had moved her arms constantly, her hands seeming to punctuate her words.

After about ten minutes the guard opened the door and the women went back inside the building. Czolgosz lay down on the cot again. He knew from the newspapers that Goldman had been captured by the Chicago police, and that the Buffalo authorities had been arguing for her extradition. Now he understood why he'd been brought to a women's prison. He and Emma Goldman would be questioned together. Perhaps they would be tried together. Maybe they would be executed together.

He was just beginning to doze off when there was the sound of the key turning the lock, and he sat up as the cell door swung open. He held a hand up to shield his eyes from the light but he could see the silhouette of Emma Goldman as she stepped inside. The door groaned as it closed, shutting out the light from the corridor.

Czolgosz got to his feet, offering her the cot. He removed his blanket and placed it around her shoulders, and then he sat on the stool, facing her.

We haven't seen each other in a good while, Leon.

Not since we took the trolley together in Chicago, back in July. You were going to Rochester and a group of us accompanied you to the train station to see you off.

Yes, I took the Isaaks' daughter Mary with me. Pretty girl, and smart. In Rochester we stayed at my sister's for several weeks. And we came to Buffalo to visit the Pan-American Exposition, as well as see Niagara Falls. You couldn't have picked a better place to do your duty, Leon, somewhere where many people could witness it, could experience the elimination of an unnecessary leader.

You were at the exposition?

Yes, in mid-August, Leon. You know what they will try to prove at the trial—that you and I met there, that we looked over the different exhibitions and finally settled on the Temple of Music as being the most suitable location.

I will never admit to that, no matter what they do to me.

I know, Leon. I know. Nor I. You look thin, darling.

But I eat everything they bring me. It's this cell, sitting here day and night.

You will be free soon enough, Leon. Do not worry.

I don't worry about death. I accept it.

I could see that when we first met in Cleveland. Do you remember?

Yes. After your speech there was a short intermission before the question-and-answer session. You were at the table by the side of the stage, where pamphlets were for sale. We spoke for just a moment.

You told me how difficult your life was, the years of working in that wire plant.

Then you gave me one of the pamphlets. I offered to pay for it but you wouldn't accept my dime.

It was your eyes, Leon. I could look into them forever. You have faith. It's in your eyes. When I learned that it was you who shot the president, I was not surprised. You are brave, brave like Alexander Berkman. Like Gaetano Bresci. When the workers rise up, when they have taken it all away from J. P. Morgan and Henry Clay Frick and Teddy Roosevelt, they will remember you.

It doesn't matter.

They will remember Leon Czolgosz.

I don't care for that. Truly.

I understand. But they will.

I will be glad to be gone then. My only regret is my family, how this will—

They will be fine. Your sister will no longer have to put on a maid's uniform and work for that wealthy family in Cleveland. Leon—you shouldn't weep.

Victoria is only eighteen. You should see her, she is so beautiful. Men always stare at her. She has a beauty that frightens them into silence, but I know their thoughts. I can't stand to think of her on her knees, scrubbing someone's floor.

You have freed her, Leon. You have freed your sister, and you have freed your mother. I know about her too, how she died, how long and painful it was, but believe me, it will not be that way for women in the future. That's what we will change. That will be our lasting accomplishment.

There were footsteps out in the corridor, and the tall guard's face filled the small window in the door. "You talking to yourself, Leon? Having a nice conversation with the dark?" He smiled. "Most of them women, they go off their heads, too. I just hope they strap you in that chair before you get too far gone."

Czolgosz stood, wrapped the blanket around his shoulders, and lay on the cot again.

"You know what they did at the exposition two days after you shot the president?"

"Go away," Czolgosz said. "Leave me alone."

"They tried to kill an elephant. Drew a huge crowd. They attached all these wires to it and then turned on the electricity. My brother was there. Said you could see its legs tremble, but they couldn't kill the beast. They tried again and again, but its skin must have been too tough and it wouldn't die."

There were footsteps, and the other guard said, "I've got his dinner." There was the sound of a key scratching at the lock.

"I'm not hungry," Czolgosz said. It was chicken; he could smell it.

"You sure?" the tall one asked.

Czolgosz turned on his side. "I said I don't want any."

AFTER a good steak dinner Norris and Savin went to Big Maud's. There were no customers in the parlor and only a few girls lounged in stuffed chairs and sofas.

"Assassination isn't good for business," Big Maud said. "I must say this whole business about President McKinley has been depressing. Half of Buffalo is in mourning, while the other half seems ready to burn something to the ground." She addressed Savin. "Haven't seen you in a good while, Lloyd."

"Don't take it wrong, Maud," he said.

"Moved up in the world." She smiled as she turned to Norris. "The captain and I go back a long way—to when I was on his regular beat."

But Savin appeared in no mood to reminisce. "The Russian girl, Motka Ascher. She upstairs?"

"There a problem?" Big Maud looked put out.

"Sorry, Maud, not tonight," Savin said.

"Can't give her a few minutes?"

Savin only shook his head.

Big Maud smiled at him. "You always were the bastard, weren't you?" And then, in disgust, she said, "Third floor."

Savin moved toward the stairs.

Norris nodded apologetically to the madam and then followed Savin. When they turned the landing, he whispered playfully, "Your regular beat, huh?"

"She's put on weight—she was just Maud then."

The house was quiet, except for some recorded opera music coming from a room on the second floor. They climbed to the third floor and Savin opened the door without knocking. The room was candlelit, and there was the sudden rustling of sheets as bodies flailed about and a man stumbled out of bed. Beneath a substantial belly he was fully erect, and he was clearly less than sober.

"*What* do you think you're *doing*?" he demanded.

"Alderman O'Reilly?" Savin said with regret, and then cleared his throat. "Sorry to disturb you. But we're here on police business."

O'Reilly cupped his hands over his loins as Norris gathered his clothes from the chair by the window. In the bed, Motka pulled a sheet up to her neck.

"Now, sir, if you'll just step out here with me." Reluctantly, Savin ushered O'Reilly toward the door.

"I am the commissioner of this ward!" O'Reilly said. "This is highly inappropriate, barging in on me in—"

"Sir," Norris said, "this is a matter of national security. Believe me, we are doing you a favor." He thrust the pile of clothes into O'Reilly's arms, pushed him out into the hall. As he pulled the door closed, he said, "Wait for me downstairs, Captain."

Norris went over to the bed. Motka's eyes were startled and frightened. He took hold of the sheet and yanked it away. She didn't move, and he sat down on the bed. In the candlelight her skin was golden and she gave off the deep smell of perfume and sex.

"My God," he whispered, "you are something. What are you, nineteen, twenty?"

"Yes," she whispered as though it were an admission.

"The police captain downstairs," he said. "He wants to take you in for questioning." She tried to raise herself up on her elbows, but he shook his head. "Now listen carefully. You have two choices. We can take you to police headquarters and the captain will want to question you all night. Eventually you'll be so exhausted that you'll tell us anything we want to know. Or you can cooperate with me now, and sleep here in your own bed tonight. The result will be the same—you'll tell us what we want to know."

"What is it you want to know?"

"We know Leon Czolgosz has been here with you, and we know that Moses Hyde brought him." He watched her chest rise and fall; she was nervous, and when she exhaled there was the slightest shudder, making her breasts jounce as they settled over her rib cage. "They planned to shoot the president—here, together, in this room."

"*No.*"

"Motka, you told me before that Czolgosz was here several times. He brought that book. You said he was giving you reading lessons—do you know what that book is about?"

Helpless, she was shaking her head, her red hair fanning out on the pillow.

"Do you know what he was trying to do with you? Indoctrinate your mind." Norris watched the tears run from the corner of her eyes, and with his finger he gently wiped them a way. "You don't even know what that word means, 'indoctrinate,' do you?"

She continued to shake her head. "I cannot read that book. The words—they are too much hard for me."

"It doesn't matter." Norris nodded toward the door to the hall. "It doesn't matter to the captain waiting downstairs. The fact, the mere fact that you would have that book in your possession—a book given to you by Leon Czolgosz—it doesn't matter to him whether you understand the words. You have the *book,* you know what it *means.*"

She was crying now, her nose running. He took his hand-kerchief from his suit coat and daubed her nose and mouth. It seemed to calm her down, and she began to catch her breath.

"You can be implicated—that is a word you must understand, Motka. The president is dead. We can prove you were in on it. That book is evidence enough; believe me, in this case it's enough. The captain will make sure of that."

"I hit him," Motka said. "I hit him on the head."

"Who?"

"Hyde. The night before the president was shot. With the chamber pot. It knocks his brains out. No—you know what I mean—"

"Out cold. Why?"

"He was drunk. He finds the gun—it falls on the floor out of

Czolgosz's coat. And he—I thought he was going to shoot Leon, so I hit him with the pot."

Norris had to look away from her a moment. The wallpaper on the slanted wall above her bed was faded, yellow and brown, with friezes of women carrying urns on their heads, lyres, old ruins with free-standing columns. He remembered the gash in Hyde's head. The president's physician—Dr. Rixey, a tall man with a thick mustache, who was quiet and observant—he had noticed it too and had kept Hyde at the Milburn house for treatment. "Motka, why was Hyde going to shoot Leon?"

"I did not understand then. But he knew that Leon plans to shoot the president."

"So it was planned here."

She shook her head vehemently. "No. He wanted to stop Leon, but after I make Hyde out cold Leon left."

"All right. But, Motka, you see how this would look to the captain downstairs. He would never believe you. He would say you—the three of you—planned the whole thing, right here, in this room."

"But we didn't!"

"You would be better than Emma Goldman."

"That woman in the newspapers? They arrested her in Chicago, yes?"

"Red Emma," Norris said. "She's Russian, a Jew." He watched Motka's face, the sudden panic in her eyes. "You know what I'm saying, don't you? In America it's easy to believe that all of you Jews from Russia are anarchists. Every one of you, in on it. They want to believe that—they need to believe that. It's called a conspiracy—you know that word, do you? They need to believe that killing the president was a conspiracy. Do you understand?"

She shook her head.

But he was certain that she did. "A conspiracy is necessary, Motka. It makes it easier for everyone to understand, to accept." Her lips began to tremble. Norris leaned closer and whispered, "So you must tell me—just me, Motka—where is your brother?"

"My brother?"

"Yes, Anton."

"I don't know—"

"He is an anarchist."

"No." But her eyes were doubtful now.

"*This*, this is true, Motka. You know this is true, and it concerns you. He is in with them, a group that is working with an outside man from Chicago. Herman Gimmel. A man who has been associated with Emma Goldman. See, we know all about it. People talk. Eventually, people always tell us what we need to know. This is my point: you will, too. It's just a question of method—"

"*Please*," Motka said, taking hold of his forearm. "Anton is *not*—"

"Do you know what they did?" He looked down at his arm until she removed her hand. "Gimmel and your brother, they threw Clementine's body in the canal."

"No, this cannot be?"

"We have a witness. Someone saw them, Motka. So the only way to save yourself is to tell us where Anton is."

She lay very still, gazing up at him. He placed his fingertips on the hard bone between her breasts. Gently, he ran his hand down over her stomach, pausing at the depression around the navel, and then he let his palm rest over her hair, soft and damp.

"I cannot," she whispered.

Norris moved his hand deeper, parting her thighs.

"I do not know where Anton is. That is all I can tell the captain."

Norris took his hand away, held his fingers under his nose and inhaled slowly. "Yes, I believe that is all you would tell the captain. But as I said, the only difference between him and me is our methods."

She was trying not to be afraid now. In fact, she looked brave, and he had to admire that, and the way it made her beautiful. "All right," he said, as he got up off the bed. He drew the bedsheet

over her, and her hands clutched it beneath her chin. "All right,
I'll talk to him. Maybe we don't have to bring you to police headquarters, not at the moment." He went to the door, hesitated, and
then looked back at her. "But I can't make any promises about the
future, you understand?"

She only stared at him, her eyes glistening in the candlelight.

~~♪C~~

IT took Hyde several hours to work his way along the canal,
stopping in taverns and saloons to avoid sudden downpours.
When he reached Black Rock Harbor, a dense fog had come in
off Lake Erie, making it difficult to see across the water to Squaw
Island. Dozens of barges were tied to piers and he found the *Glockenspiel* in front of the Grand Canal Warehouse. He heard footsteps
coming toward him on the pier, and he recognized Bruener's son,
Josef, a tall, lean boy still in his teens. He was carrying a club.

"Josef, it's Moses Hyde," he said slowly. "I need to see your
father."

Josef held up his hand, indicating that Hyde was to remain
where he was, and then he went back out along the pier, and
climbed down a plank to his father's barge. When the door to the
pilothouse opened he gestured with his hands for a moment to
someone holding a lantern, and then waved toward Hyde.

Once Hyde was on board he saw that the man with the lantern
was Klaus Bruener. He had known the big German for years,
occasionally crewing on his barge, and they had often attended
socialist meetings together in towns along the Erie Canal. "Anton
Ascher is here, Klaus?"

"Why?"

"I have something for him from his sister. Money."

Bruener nodded and let Hyde into the pilothouse. "I hear

she's the prettiest cocksucker in Buffalo." He grinned, revealing crooked, blackened teeth. "Too pretty to come down here to fuck canawlers."

Hyde said nothing. Bruener liked to bait people, egg them on, and draw them into fistfights. They went down the companion-way ladder to a tight cabin, where the air was thick with cigar smoke. Two men sat in a booth, a bottle of whiskey and glasses on the table. One of them stood—Anton. Hyde held up his bandaged hand, to which he had pinned the earring.

Anton removed the pin. "So, my sister sent you?"

The other man sitting in the booth wore a tattered frock coat and his hair was long, silky, and white, hanging well down below his shoulders. The right side of his face and neck was badly scarred, and his right eye was nearly closed beneath a lid that appeared to have melted. Hyde recognized him: his name was Herman Gimmel and he had given a speech at a meeting in Buffalo last spring. He was from Chicago, and word had gone around the hall where he spoke that he was a bomb expert. It was said that he had thrown the bomb that killed eight policemen during the Haymarket riot back in '86. When he stood on the stage, his scarred face was testimony to years of devotion to the workers' cause.

Hyde took the two folded twenty-dollar bills from his coat pocket and handed them to Anton, who went back to the table and dropped the money next to the whiskey bottle. He said, "Told you I could raise some money, Gimmel."

"So you did." Gimmel's raspy voice was deep and humorless, and the words seemed to bubble up out of his throat. He got to his feet slowly and came over to Hyde. "And you know this fellow, Bruener?"

"Moses Hyde's as good a canawler as you'll find," Bruener said. "Always turns out for the meetings."

"I saw you speak here last spring," Hyde said to Gimmel.

As though he hadn't heard, Gimmel turned Bruener. "You're saying I can trust him?"

"You come here from Chicago," Bruener said. "Someone gave you a few names, men you could contact. You don't really know any of us."

"They didn't mention Moses Hyde," Gimmel said.

"When you came here you said you needed help," Bruener said. "Since McKinley was shot, the police they been rounding up a lot of boys—canawlers, men from the foundries and the slaughterhouses. They've declared war on the workingman." When Gimmel didn't say anything, Bruener added, "He's all right because Klaus Bruener says he's all right."

"Well, he delivered forty dollars," Gimmel said. "That tells me something. A lot of men would have disappeared with that much money in hand." Gimmel shrugged and returned to the table, where he picked up the bills and added them to a wad that he took from his pocket. He tucked the money in his coat, sat down in the booth again, and poured more whiskey into his glass. His distorted face was illuminated by the lamp hanging above the booth. "Take a good look, Mr. Hyde," he said. "Ten years ago I was teaching somebody how to make a bomb. I have often taught this fine art, but I've lost some of my best pupils before they could graduate." His laughter was more a gurgle that seemed to originate in his lungs. He took a drink of whiskey and placed the glass on the table. "Now they send me here to organize a disturbance during the president's visit. And to my surprise—to everyone's surprise—this Leon Czolgosz up and shoots McKinley. This man, he is a true anarchist."

Bruener said, "He deserves to be free."

"We all do." Gimmel took a piece of paper from inside his frock coat; it was a newspaper clipping, which he unfolded and spread out on the table. It was an article about the assassination attempt upon the president, with a large sketch of Czolgosz. "A few days ago, when the president seemed to be recovering, I was wondering if there was some way we could get to him and finish the job. But with the security around that house on Delaware Avenue, that's impossible. So then I considered the vice president.

He moves about, in carriages, on trains, and he has a tendency to wander off into the woods—perhaps we might get close enough to him. But, again, security makes that unlikely. So I'm about ready to go back to the committee in Chicago and tell them that I've failed my mission, a distasteful task, to be sure. One hates to disappoint the committee. Frankly, I'd rather lose my other eye in a bomb explosion. But I was sent here to do a job. I haven't exactly decided what yet, but we'll just have to wait and see."

Hyde picked up the newspaper clipping. "You should have a photograph of Czolgosz. This sketch isn't a very good likeness."

"You know that for a fact?" Gimmel asked.

"I do." Hyde put the clipping on the table.

"You *know* Leon Czolgosz?" Gimmel said.

"Yes." Hyde looked at Anton and said, "Ask his sister, Motka. Ask her who brought Czolgosz to Big Maud's not long before he shot the president."

"Big Maud's." Gimmel looked at Bruener. "That's where that whore was from, no?"

Bruener nodded.

Gimmel leaned so close to Hyde now that he could smell the whiskey on his breath. "You know what happened to that whore Clementine?"

"She went in the canal."

"You know why?"

Hyde hesitated. "I gather it wasn't because she refused a gentleman's advances."

Gimmel's laughter was a combination of a cough and a wheeze, all coated in thick phlegm. "You're right, Mr. Hyde. No, it was because she couldn't be trusted. She knew who I was and she was going to use it, sell it to some policeman." Gimmel leaned even closer to Hyde. "Know how I know? It was in her *eyes*. Something about her eyes that couldn't conceal her true intentions." Gimmel studied Hyde's face for a long moment. "Anarchism,

Moses Hyde, asks only one thing: loyalty. Loyalty—not to church or government, not to some meager form of employment, or the confines of the institution known as marriage. All those fetters must be broken if we are to be truly free. Only one thing requires our loyalty—anarchism itself. We are not socialists or communists, who merely offer an alternative form of enslavement for the workingman. Our purpose, our *only* purpose is to destroy that which imprisons us. Break those bonds and we'll find a new world. One day I will die for that purpose. We all will. Do you understand that? We will not live to see that new world, but it won't come into being without our sacrifice. Is that why you're here, Moses Hyde?"

"Yes, that is my purpose, too."

"Interesting," Gimmel said, leaning away from Hyde now, as though to get a better look at him. "Maybe it's the climate, the hard winters. I've never met so many men willing to die for the cause. You put the intellectuals in Chicago and Paterson to shame."

"I'll do whatever's necessary," Hyde said.

"Even if it kills you?"

"Something will, eventually," Hyde said.

Gimmel glanced at his bandaged wrist. "What happened?"

"It was cut during a misunderstanding."

"A lot of men say they're willing to die," Gimmel said. "Few are willing to do so limb by limb." He went to the table, poured whiskey into another glass, and held it out to Hyde. Looking down at the sketch on the table, he said, "Maybe you can be useful, Mr. Hyde. We could use someone who knows what Leon Czolgosz looks like."

~つC~

IN the middle of the night Czolgosz listened to a woman shrieking. His mother screamed like that when she was giving birth to his sister Victoria. He was ten years old and they were living in a lumber town in northern Michigan, and he knew from the sound of her voice that his mother had to be dying. They had sent him out of the house. It was snowing and he stood in the small barn. His mother's cries were agonizing, like nothing he'd ever heard before, and he prayed because that's what he'd been taught to do. He prayed for everything. For his food. For the weather. For all of his brothers and sisters. But at that moment he prayed for his mother's pain to end. He begged God to let her die. She did but not quickly. He listened to her for several hours, until it finally exhausted him, and he went up into the hayloft and fell asleep with a blanket over him. When he awoke the wind had stopped. Everything smelled of horses and manure. Weak sunlight streamed through gaps in the barn roof. Such sunlight, he believed, was the hand of God. Then he realized there was silence.

He went over to the house and found his brothers and sisters sitting around the kitchen table. The smaller ones were crying. His older brother Waldeck looked angry, and he shoved Leon's shoulder, saying, Where you been? Eventually, the children were allowed into the other room, where their parents slept. A neighbor woman named Zajac, who always attended births, sat in a chair by the window, a baby in her arms, wrapped in a blanket. Their mother lay on her back in bed. There was no color in her face. She looked content. She was not in pain.

Ona jest w niebie, Mrs. Zajac said in Polish.

Leon stared at his mother's face, her long hair, which was mostly gray. No she's not, he said, and one of his sisters drew in her breath in horror. She's not gone to heaven.

Ona jest z Bogiem, the woman said, rocking in the chair.

No, Leon said, she's not gone to God.

Leon, his father said. He stood in the corner and Leon wouldn't look at him. Somehow he knew his father was responsible for this. He had watched his mother's belly grow over the months, and it was his father's fault. His mother kept saying, How are we going to feed another one? What are we going to do with all of you?

And his father would reply, They'll work. They'll grow up

strong and work, and that's how we'll get us a piece of land to farm.

And that was why I was born, Leon told Father Dubchek one day during Sunday school. Not to worship God but to work so Father could buy land. That's the real meaning of dust to dust. You work for dirt.

Father Dubchek came to the house and spoke to his father, who said, The boy's too smart. He reads. He's not like the others. He read the entire Bible in Polish.

This greatly concerned Father Dubchek. He would keep Leon after class on Sundays and try to explain things to him. There were certain things in the Bible children should not read, he said. You might take it to be literally true. He had an enormous nose with horrible burst veins, and he leaned close and asked, You know what that means, literally true? When Leon nodded, the priest sat back in his chair, defeated.

Leon stopped going to mass. His father would beat him, and he would hide in the barn for hours, his fanny stinging and his eyes smarting with tears.

His father remarried, not two years later, and his new wife was hard on all the children, which was how his father wanted it. Leon would run away and stay in the woods for several days. He'd catch a fish, cook it on a stick over a fire. He imagined getting on a train that would take him south. Look at a map—Michigan was hard to get out of because it was surrounded by so much water. You had to go down through Indiana, get around the bottom of Lake Michigan to Chicago. When Waldeck would find him hiding in the woods—it was always Waldeck who found him—he'd return to the house and none of them would speak to him. He would take his dinner plate and go out and eat in the barn with the horses. Sitting in the barn, he'd hear again his mother's screams, but now he was convinced that she wasn't in heaven, she wasn't with God. She was dead. He decided people desperately wanted to believe in God because the thought of death was too great to bear. They were wrong. They were fools. They were weak. Once you knew that there was no God, life became more important—it was life that became sacred. He believed in death. To live life you had to believe in death.

~ↄC~

HYDE and Anton kept watch, the rain drumming on the pilot-house roof. The wind pushed the barges about; dock lines groaned, dray horses and mules kicked in their stalls. Josef had gone forward to sleep in his hammock. Bruener had taken Gimmel up to McShayne's Tavern, near the Austin Street bridge. They returned and sat in the pilothouse, passing a bottle of whiskey and finishing their cigars.

"Word is," Bruener said, "the police are rounding up men from the canal, foundries, slaughterhouses."

"We got to keep moving," Gimmel said. "People talk to the police and they'll come looking for us. At McShayne's they mentioned someone named Quimby—"

"What about him?" Hyde asked.

"Got himself hauled in by the police," Bruener said. "They was all kept in the cell there, until the police take him down to another room. And they had a fine chat. It's always the dandy like Quimby, with his fancy talk. He's disappeared—last anybody saw him he was in the train station, buying a ticket." Bruener cleared his throat and hawked a wad of spit out into the canal. "There are no fucking tickets out of Buffalo."

"They'll come looking for us," Gimmel said. "Eventually. That's why we got to move quickly—tomorrow."

Hyde and Anton stared at Gimmel as he stood up and went to the stern of the barge. He undid his trousers and pissed in the canal.

"Tomorrow?" Anton asked.

"We just learned something interesting," Bruener said. "Tomorrow afternoon they're moving Czolgosz, bringing him from the women's penitentiary to the prison across the street from city hall."

"How do you know?" Hyde asked.

Bruener said, "Met me cousin at McShayne's. He's a farrier and knows just about every teamster in Buffalo. He tells us that the police are moving Czolgosz, tomorrow, while the president's lying in state at city hall. They've arranged for two carriages."

Gimmel finished up and returned to the pilothouse, his wet hair plastered to his skull. "There will be guards at both prisons," he said. "But when they move him it will be very simple—maybe just the two carriages. Nothing to draw attention to itself."

"What exactly are we going to do?" Hyde asked.

"We're going to free Czolgosz." Gimmel stared at them. "Understand? Nothing would serve the cause better than freeing Leon Czolgosz."

"*Free* him?" Anton said.

"That's right," Gimmel said. "And if it doesn't look like we'll succeed, at least we can make a martyr out of him."

Hyde said, "I thought you wanted to blow up city hall, with the president in it."

"What's the point?" Bruener said. "He's already been killed. And think of the security there—all them police and military. After what Czolgosz done, they'll be on their toes, you can bet. No, this could be easier."

"How?" Hyde asked.

Bruener said, "They'll come down Trenton Avenue."

"You know when?" Hyde asked.

"No," Gimmel said, "and we don't know for sure what the carriages will look like, though I'm sure they won't be police wagons, just ordinary carriages. So we'll have to spread ourselves along the route, and signal ahead when we think we see them." He turned to Hyde. "You know what Czolgosz looks like, so you should be nearest the penitentiary. If you see which carriage he's in, you signal on down to"—he looked at Anton—"you, and you'll pass the signal on to Josef, Bruener, and me."

"How will we stop the carriage?" Anton asked.

Bruener said, "My cousin said that when they moved him out to the penitentiary on Friday he was taken in one carriage, accompanied by only one detective. Didn't even handcuff him— they just walked out of police headquarters and got in the carriage, and nobody takes notice."

"If we do get him," Hyde asked, "then what?"

"We take the carriage." Gimmel tossed the stub of his cigar into the canal. "Josef will drive." He waited, glaring at Hyde, and when he was met by silence, he said, "The police are worried about a mob getting Czolgosz. That's why they'll keep it simple. They're not expecting anything like us." He started down the companionway. "We must get some sleep now. Bruener, you get your boy to come up and stand watch now."

"Aye." Bruener followed Gimmel down into the cabin.

Hyde stared out into the rain for a few minutes, and then he whispered, "You should get out now, Anton, go back to your wife."

"I take care of my*self*."

"Your wife worries about you, your sister worries about you."

"Don't you mention my sister." Anton looked away, disgusted, but after a moment he turned to Hyde and said, "I thought I beat you so you wouldn't see her no more."

"You couldn't beat me enough times to keep me away."

"My sister knows many men. Why does she feel this way about you?"

"I don't know," Hyde said.

"Are you in love with her?"

"Yes." Hyde knew Anton was staring at him, but he kept looking forward. "Yes, I am, and I would like to get her out of Big Maud's. She doesn't belong there."

"For some time I think my sister is lost, dead. Like my parents and our other sister, who died on the ship. But now I do not know.

You get her free, Hyde, and my dead family will smile down on you. You understand this is what I am saying?"

"I understand, Anton. And I will try."

"Good. Since I beat you in this fight, I feel I must to protect you. Like a brother."

"You didn't beat me, Anton."

"I did."

"All right, you beat me." Hyde turned to Anton then. "But I'm telling you that you should go to your wife. Katrina told me you think this is going too far. It's not too late for you to get out of this. Tomorrow will be too late."

"Now who will be the dreamer? You heard Bruener. They grabbed Quimby because he talks to the police. Who knows what will happen with him? What do you think they do if I walk away now?" Anton glared at Hyde. "Bruener has trust for you more than me."

"It's because I go to meetings."

"*I* go to meetings!"

"And because I know Czolgosz, what he looks like."

Anton shook his head. "It is because you are not a Jew." Then he laughed. "I think Gimmel is a Jew, but Bruener has trust for him—because he is a famous bomb-throwing Jew from Chicago."

"Bruener's afraid of Gimmel. He's afraid of all men who are smarter than he is."

"Then he is afraid of everybody."

"*Listen* to me," Hyde said in a hoarse whisper. "If you die tomorrow, your wife might work in Tasczek's Tavern the rest of her life. You wife, your son, and the baby, too. Then maybe next time she'll marry a Polish boy, a Catholic like her family wants. You want to die and smile down on that?" Anton was about to speak, but Hyde said, "This is wrong, Anton, and you know it. You *know* that whatever Gimmel does will not help one worker."

"No," Anton said, "it will not."

"So go, go now. They will forget about you."

"Sure, and end up like that whore in the canal? No, I stay."
Anton leaned toward Hyde, curious. "You really think you can
get Motka out of that house?"

"I can try."

"You do that, and I will not beat you up anymore." He tapped
Hyde's chest with his fist. "Anymore. Think on that!"

"It would be like I died and went to heaven."

They looked out at the wind and rain.

V

ELABORATE ARRANGEMENTS HAD been made for the Sunday-morning procession that would take the president's body to city hall. Having spent so much time administering to the president in life, Dr. Rixey wanted little to do with these preparations. His primary concern now was Mrs. McKinley, and he kept close to her throughout the morning. As always, she exhibited stiff resolve under pressure, and she was also fanatically possessive. She was adamant that her husband's body be returned to the Milburn house from city hall no later than six Sunday evening.

Before the procession there was a religious ceremony in the Milburn living room, consisting of the reading of the fifteenth chapter of First Corinthians, plus the singing of two of McKinley's favorite hymns, "Lead, Kindly Light" and "Nearer, My God, to Thee," which, since it had been the song he sang himself within moments of his passing, had become something of an anthem for all the events surrounding the assassination. During the half-hour service the enormous mahogany coffin was open; the president's head rested upon a pillow of white tufted satin, his left hand lay across his chest, and he was dressed in a black suit, with a small Grand Army of the Republic button on the lapel. His features seemed deflated, and his expression still bore the signs of suffering—this was what affected Rixey the most, the obvious tension that had gripped the president's face as he endured acute pain in his final moments.

When the ceremony was concluded, the coffin was closed and placed in a heavily fringed hearse drawn by four black horses. There was a military contingent in the procession: national guardsmen, marines, army regulars, and sailors from the U.S. frigate *Michigan*. Rixey rode in a carriage with Cortelyou and the first lady. No one spoke and Mrs. McKinley kept her head bowed, only occasionally glancing out at the crowd that lined Delaware Avenue. Rixey couldn't help but look: people stood at least a dozen deep along the curbs; many wore buttons that bore the image of the president and read WE MOURN OUR LOSS, or WE LOVE HIM, or HE LOVES US. Much of the black bunting that had been hastily draped on buildings along the avenue had been blown down overnight; a number of trees were inadvertently swathed in black, which seemed oddly appropriate. Along the route were many army veterans in uniform, standing in the rain, some with missing limbs. The size of the crowd grew as the procession neared city hall, where a queue of thousands waited patiently to pay their respects. They wore overcoats darkened by the rain, except for a number of Indians, who came in buckskin and full headdresses.

At city hall, Rixey and Cortelyou climbed out of the carriage while the casket was taken inside, where it would lie in state throughout the afternoon. As the queue began to file up the stairs, the first lady's carriage turned around and waited for the military escort that would accompany it back to the Milburn residence. It had been decided that Cortelyou would remain at city hall, while the doctor would go with Mrs. McKinley.

Rixey stared at the crowd, the police, the somber spectacle that was taking place in the rain, and just before stepping back up into the carriage, he leaned down to Cortelyou and whispered, "You know what I *really* want, George?" Cortelyou looked at him, surprised by the force in his voice. "I want to see him."

"Him?"

"I want to see Leon Czolgosz."

At first Cortelyou seemed to not comprehend, but then he nodded and whispered, "Yes, all right. I'll arrange it."

~~OC~~

THERE were two carriages in the penitentiary courtyard, each drawn by a pair of impatient horses; they snorted and stamped their hooves, jingling their harnesses, every sound ringing off the cobblestones and bricks. Norris stood with Savin as they waited for Czolgosz to be brought out. Feeney was trying to calm the horses. There were guards at the iron gates and out in the street, and riflemen stood watch from the penitentiary roof.

"I'm putting Czolgosz in the first carriage," Savin said.

"Right," Norris said. "You'd figure he'd be in the second."

"Make the bastard lie down on the floor, out of sight."

"Put me in with him, Lloyd. I'll keep him down."

Savin was smoking a cigarette. "No. And if something happens, I want you Pinkertons coming at them with shotguns. That's why I brought you. A mob sees you with shotguns, they'll back off."

Norris was afraid of this, and he knew that Savin was right. But he wanted to be close to Czolgosz; he wanted time to look him in the eye and see what was there. He felt he had earned the right. Nobody else had even heard of Leon Czolgosz before the president was shot. Nobody else had an investment in him like Norris. "What's the matter?" he said jovially. "You can't handle a shotgun?"

"Forget it," Savin said. "You Pinkertons have the reputation for dealing with mobs. You want to be part of this, then you ride in the second carriage. I'm riding up front with him, and that's all there is to it. He's my responsibility."

"You got that?" Norris said to Feeney, who was trying to keep out of it. "The mob's our responsibility." Feeney had calmed the horse he'd been patting and his face was now so close to its nose that they were practically kissing. "So if it gets ugly, Feeney, and we end up shooting anybody, they can blame it on the Pinkertons. Because the Buffalo police don't shoot citizens." ·

Savin dropped his cigarette butt on the cobblestones and said, "You don't want to be a part of this, just say so."

Norris knew Savin didn't have any choice, that he'd been given orders to do it this way. The papers were full of complaints about Chief Bull, who had restricted access to his prisoner and· had moved him several times without informing anyone in the federal government. Tomorrow morning Czolgosz would finally be charged with a crime. After today things would be very different, very public.

"All right," Norris said quietly, "but I'll tell you one thing. If somehow a mob gets ahold of the bastard, I shoot him. You understand, Savin?"

"You wouldn't rather he be torn apart in the street?"

"Shooting him would be no act of mercy. I just want to make sure he dies."

"What you want is to be remembered for the one who did it."

"You got to admit it would be some legacy."

Savin was angry now and was about to speak, but the door at the end of the courtyard opened. The three men who stepped outside were handcuffed together. The one in the middle, Czolgosz, was considerably smaller than the two guards. His shoulders were narrow and hunched forward. His fedora was cocked on the back of his head and he stared at the cobblestones as he walked toward the carriages. He seemed to Norris so insignificant that it was an insult. He didn't look up; he showed no interest in his surroundings.

Savin raised an arm and the guards brought their prisoner to the first carriage. "You put him in here." He said to Czolgosz,

"Lie down on the floor and don't sit up until I tell you to. We're leaving the windows open so people can see me and your two guards. Understand?" He waited until Czolgosz nodded his head. "You try to get up," Savin said, "I'll put the first bullet through your kneecap."

One of the guards took a set of keys from his vest pocket and began to unlock the handcuffs. Norris stepped up so that he was standing directly in front of Czolgosz. The man continued to stare down at his feet. When one cuff was unlocked, the keys were passed to the other guard. Czolgosz seemed more than uninterested in what was happening; he appeared to not even be aware of it—he could have been standing in this courtyard alone, studying the erosion of cobblestones. Norris tried to will the man to raise his head, to lift his eyes and look back at him, but he wouldn't do it. His face was quite pretty, sensitive even. Norris stepped even closer, but still Czolgosz didn't react.

Norris worked up a large wad of spit, leaned over, and dropped it on the man's left shoe.

No one moved.

The larger of the two guards said, "That's not necessary."

"You care?" Norris said.

"You care to clean it up?" the guard said.

"*Solomon.*" The captain might have been speaking to a dog. "Just put the prisoner in the carriage, like I said."

Solomon was a big man with hard, intelligent eyes. His face was broad, his skin taut and waxy, and he had a full mustache that resembled a cowcatcher on the front of a locomotive.

"I wouldn't want to ride with that piece of shit at my feet anyway," Norris said.

He looked over and nodded at Feeney, who had stopped petting the horse. They walked to the second carriage and climbed inside. Two shotguns were lying on the floor, with a box of shells. They picked up the guns, broke them open, and loaded the double chambers.

From above, the carriage driver said, "Just be careful where you point those, boys."

Norris snapped his shotgun closed, rapped the barrel on the carriage roof, and said, "You shut up."

The driver laughed as he slapped his reins on the horses' backsides, and the carriage jerked forward.

∽ↄⲋↄ∼

GIMMEL said they were to use handkerchiefs—he liked the idea because Czolgosz had used one to conceal his revolver. Hyde was to position himself the farthest down Trenton Avenue toward the women's penitentiary. He chose a street corner in front of a bakery. At least the rain had let up.

There weren't many people in the street—it was as though Buffalo had been evacuated. Hyde kept looking to his right, in the direction of the penitentiary, which was about half a mile away. In the distance he could see a small cart working toward him slowly, pulled by a ragman with a gray beard.

When Hyde looked in the other direction, he could see Anton on the next block. The plan was that when Hyde saw which carriage Czolgosz was in he would take a handkerchief out of his coat and hold it to his face. Anton would wait until the carriage reached him and do the same thing, signaling farther on down Trenton, to where Josef, Bruener, and Gimmel were waiting.

The ragman turned off on a side street before he reached Hyde. What Gimmel had not discussed was how long they should wait—there was the possibility that the police wouldn't use Trenton Avenue. Hyde studied the houses and buildings along the avenue, the upper windows, the roofs, expecting to see some sign of security, men positioned along the prisoner's route. But there was nothing, not even open windows, which had all been closed against the rain.

Then, several blocks ahead, he saw a carriage come around the bend in the avenue, pulled by two horses. It wasn't moving fast. The carriage was so far away that the horses' hooves struck the ground a moment before the sound reached him. And then beyond it, a second carriage came into sight. They were identical— two black carriages, each drawn by a pair of bays.

Hyde looked the other way—Anton had seen the carriages, too—and then he turned toward the carriages again. They kept coming, slowly. The horses sauntered, their heads bobbing rhythmically, and the clop of their hooves reverberated down the avenue. The drivers, men in long coats and broad-brimmed hats, did not push their teams. There was such a lack of urgency that Hyde wondered if these carriages were nothing more than people out for a Sunday ride.

As the first carriage drew near, he tried not to seem interested. He dropped down on one knee and tied the lace of his right boot. When the carriage was in front of him, he stood up and looked inside—there were three men, two sitting with their backs to the horses and the other sitting to the near side, his arm out the window, holding a cigarette. It was just a moment that the carriage was directly in front of Hyde, but he was certain that none of them was Czolgosz—they all had dark hair, one had a mustache, and they were all quite large men. The one smoking the cigarette, Hyde realized, was Captain Savin.

Hyde looked down the street toward Anton, but he did nothing. After a moment, he turned and watched the second carriage approach. The driver was older than the first, his cheeks hollow, suggesting he was missing teeth. Inside this carriage there were two men; the one with his back to the horses was blond, but Hyde didn't think it was Czolgosz—and he seemed to sit too erect somehow. But the other man, sitting across from the first, was Norris. Though he looked straight ahead, there was no doubt: it was Norris. His bowler was pulled down tight on his head, and in profile there was considerable flesh beneath his jaw.

For a moment, Hyde felt confused. His first reaction was to call out to Norris, to warn him, but then he realized that the worst thing was for Norris to see him, so he quickly turned his back to the road and gazed into the bakery window. Though it was Sunday, he could see men and women inside, dressed in white uniforms and hats, working around large ovens. As the second carriage continued down the avenue, he watched its reflection in the glass. He was tempted to simply walk quickly in the other direction, to get as far away as he could, and at that moment he realized he still had a choice. After this moment, though, he understood that there would be no escape, not if he wanted to stay in Buffalo.

Down the avenue, Anton was staring at him. Hyde reached inside his coat and took out the handkerchief—as they had walked down Trenton, Gimmel distributed them, new handkerchiefs—and he raised it to his face until Anton turned toward the avenue. The first carriage reached him but he didn't do anything. When the second carriage passed, he turned his back on Hyde, and he raised a white handkerchief to his face. Anton put his handkerchief away, and then disappeared down a side street.

Gimmel had said that after the carriages passed, Hyde and Anton were both to get to the barge as quickly as possible, using streets other than Trenton Avenue. But for some reason Hyde couldn't move. Not yet.

He folded his handkerchief and put it back in his pocket, and then he looked in the bakery window once more. A heavy woman stood at a table, rolling dough. Once she raised a fleshy arm, dusty with flour, to wipe her forehead with the back of her hand. She didn't notice him watching her, and it seemed an almost indecent thing to be observing her. She was completely absorbed in her work, kneading and pounding and rolling the dough, which caused her whole body to shake. When she was finished with one loaf, she slid it over next to the others on the side of the wood table and began working on another lump of dough. The finished loaves were lined up, smooth, white, identical, like something newborn and innocent.

Hyde walked quickly up Trenton Avenue and turned down the first alley.

~JC~

NORRIS leaned out the window and looked up the avenue. He could see the first carriage turning off Trenton and passing out of sight behind the corner of a clapboard house. He assumed that they were going to approach the prison on side streets that would keep them away from the crowd in front of city hall. He didn't like the idea of traveling down narrow streets, but he didn't know Buffalo well enough to say if there was a better route. Trenton Avenue was wide, open, and quiet, as he assumed it would be on an ordinary Sunday afternoon. Feeney gazed out the other window, his shotgun across his thighs.

Raising his shotgun, Norris pounded on the carriage roof and said, "*Faster!* We need to keep up with them."

The horses continued at the same pace. Norris waited only a moment, and then pounded the roof again. Still nothing happened, and then the carriage began to slow down.

"What are you *doing*?" he shouted.

The carriage continued to slow down, and suddenly two men jumped up on the runners on each side and extended their arms through the open windows. A white-haired man with a disfigured face held his revolver within inches of Norris's forehead and said, "Put it on the floor—slowly."

The other man held the barrel of his pistol against Feeney's ear. Norris considered swinging his shotgun up quickly, knocking the gun away from Feeney's head, but the man with the scarred face said, "Don't finish that thought unless you want it to be your last."

The carriage came to a complete stop. Norris slowly lowered his shotgun to the floor. Feeney did the same. There was movement up in the front of the carriage, and then Norris caught a glimpse of the driver, walking quickly away and out of sight. Someone else had climbed up on the bench and the carriage began moving again—reins were slapped and the horses began to turn around.

The two gunmen opened the doors, climbed inside the carriage, and sat down. Norris suddenly felt uncomfortably crowded, and he moved to his left to make room. The barrel of the revolver was now pressed into his neck, just below the jaw. The carriage moved back along Trenton Avenue, the horses quickly breaking into a trot.

"You're Herman Gimmel," Norris said. "From Chicago."

"My reputation precedes me," Gimmel said, not displeased. He looked at Feeney, and then said, "This is not Czolgosz?"

Norris didn't answer. The cold steel pressed harder into his neck.

The other gunman was Klaus Bruener, who said in a heavy German accent, "With a shotgun? He's blond but, this can't be him. *Shit*—he's in the other carriage. What do we do?" Gimmel didn't say anything. "Shoot the bastards," Bruener said. "We shoot them *now* and get away from here—we have no fucking choice."

Gimmel turned his head and looked back at Norris. "What's your name?"

"Norris." He continued to stare straight ahead, looking at Feeney—who was clearly frightened. "It's all right, Jack," Norris said. "The important thing is that they have already failed."

Bruener, who was holding his gun to Feeney's temple, said, "We *must* shoot them!"

"No," Gimmel said, and then he shouted out the window, "Faster! Drive *faster*!"

~っC~

CZOLGOSZ was on his back on the floor of the carriage, staring at the ceiling, where a spider had set up its web, flecked with the remains of moths and flies. It occurred to him that there was no such thing as politics in nature; it was just survival. Solomon and Geary sat in the front of the carriage, facing Captain Savin, who smoked one cigarette after another. No one spoke. Once Czolgosz tried to prop himself up on an elbow, but Solomon shook his head.

Eventually, the carriage slowed and turned to the right and Czolgosz could tell by the echo of the horses' hooves that they were moving through a narrow street. Geary leaned toward the window and seemed to become alarmed. The others didn't notice at first, but finally he said, "It's not back there."

"What?" Savin asked.

Without speaking, all three men opened their coats and drew their guns. They gazed out the windows, inspecting the houses and buildings along the street.

"We should go faster," Solomon said.

Savin considered this a moment, but then said, "No. That may be what they want."

Solomon only shook his head as he looked out the window.

"I saw nothing," Geary said. "No mob, nothing back there—what happened?"

Savin said, "It may be ahead of us."

Solomon looked at the captain. "Change our route?"

Savin considered this and said, "All right. You get up top with the driver and direct him—both of you." He glanced down at Czolgosz. "I'll stay here with him." He flicked his cigarette out the window, and then hollered up for the driver to stop the carriage.

When the horses came to a halt, Solomon and Geary got

out and climbed onto the driver's bench. With more weight forward, Czolgosz could detect the slightest increase in angle in the carriage floor. They started moving again, a little faster than before.

"It's the mob," Czolgosz said.

"Maybe," Savin said without looking at him. "Or it could be a horse pulled up lame."

"But if it is the mob, you know what you have to do."

Savin looked down then. "It's not going to come to that."

"But if it does."

"Does that frighten you?" Savin said. "What a mob would do?"

"What does the moth feel as the spider pulls it apart?" Czolgosz said. "Think how it would look in the newspapers. You'd be better off shooting me."

"You'd like that. We shoot you and you'd be done with it." Savin turned his head toward the window again. "But I'm going to see to it that you're disappointed."

Czolgosz remained still, listening to the carriage make its way through the streets. They turned again, left. He could hear Solomon and Geary talking to the driver but couldn't make out what they were saying above the sound of the horses and carriage. They were arguing about the best route to take, and then the carriage turned again, right this time, and there was the slap of reins and the horses broke into a trot.

"Almost there," Savin said.

It seemed a strange thing to say. Czolgosz was surprised at his own calm. Perhaps it was just because he knew these men guarding him were so tense. He was aware of something—he didn't know what—something large and beyond his control, beyond anyone's control. It was evident in the way the horses trotted faster, causing the carriage to buck over the uneven road. Before shooting the president, there had been moments when he had a sudden sense of the historical weight of what he was contemplating. He knew, of course, that he would die. But he tried to see what might come of it. He tried to envision the aftermath. Perhaps this one act, assassinating William McKinley, would spark the revolt and thousands of workers would rise up. Perhaps Emma Goldman, and men and women like her, would lead that revolution. Eight years he'd been reading *Looking Backward* because it portrayed a world where the workers would not be exploited, where there would be equity and free love. To hope for that was not enough. To believe in that was not enough. To act was the only course. And now he had acted, and he was lying on the floor of this carriage, rolling through the streets of Buffalo, with his guards alert, maybe even frightened. Whatever was out there, whatever threat existed, he wanted it to come, he wanted it now. He closed his eyes for a moment, and when he opened them Savin was staring down at him, still curious.

"You don't seem too worried about any of this, Czolgosz."

"Not particularly. What's done is done. Can't do nothing about it now."

"No, I guess you can't."

～♄～

ANTON was waiting for Hyde in an alley off Trenton Avenue, and they began walking toward the canal. "Listen to me," Hyde said. "I don't know if that was Czolgosz in that carriage—I couldn't tell for certain. But I do know the other man. He's a Pinkerton, and he knows me."

"A Pinkerton?"

"Yes, and we have to be careful. Don't do anything. Just go along with Gimmel and Bruener. I first want to know who they've got."

The rain started again, dimpling the puddles in the streets. They turned up their coat collars, tucked their hands in their pockets, and set a steady pace. By the time they reached the canal, fog hovered over the water. They found the *Glockenspiel* nestled in a small canal that ran between brick warehouses. Josef was standing watch on deck. Hyde and Anton went below and found Gimmel and Bruener seated at the cabin table, sharing a bottle of whiskey—neither appeared to be celebrating.

There was no sign of their hostages.

Gimmel stared at Hyde and said, "Why'd you pick the second carriage?"

"Czolgosz wasn't in the first one. The second, it was hard to tell."

Gimmel looked away in disgust, nodding toward the door to the forward compartments. Hyde opened the door and went through the hold, past the animal stalls, until he came to another door; inside was a dim, narrow space in the bow. Two men lay in bunks, both with their hands bound and tied to the iron rings hanging from the bulkhead. Their heads were covered with gunnysacks, but he knew them: the heavier man was Norris, and the other was the man who had tailed Hyde.

Hyde closed the door and went back to the cabin. "That's not Czolgosz," he said.

"We figured *that* out," Gimmel said. He took two wallets from inside his coat and laid them on the table. "Jake Norris and Jack Feeney. Pinkertons."

"They're worthless," Bruener said. "We should have shot them right away."

"It's Hyde who's worthless," Gimmel said. "You were supposed to know what Czolgosz looked like."

"I do," Hyde said, "and I didn't see him in either carriage."

Bruener picked up his whiskey glass. "We should just dump them in the canal."

"Let them go," Hyde said. "Take them somewhere and release them. They return safely, the police might not bother looking for us. Keep them and they won't quit looking."

"Even though these two have their heads covered," Bruener said, "they know they're on water. We let them go they'll bring the whole fucking police force down to the waterfront. I'm telling you it would be much simpler to kill them. Don't even have to shoot them—just tie stones to them, take them down to the harbor, and push them overboard in deep water. No one will ever find them."

"No, these are Pinkertons, hirelings of the capitalists," Gimmel said as he ran his fingers over the scars on the side of his face; it was as though he'd just discovered them. "I'm not giving Pinkertons back so they can bust the heads of workers some other day." He put the wallets back inside his coat. "Besides, this Norris, he said something interesting to me in the carriage. He said we have already failed."

NORRIS was lying in a bunk, a coarse sack over his head and tied around his neck. His wrists were bound by rope to something above him—an iron ring—so that he could only lie awkwardly on his right side.

"You pissed your pants," he whispered into the heat of the sack.

"I couldn't help it," Feeney said. "We're on a boat. You can feel it. They keep moving. Then they tie up, and then move again. You hear the horses and mules—we must be on the canal."

"Good, Feeney. Maybe you have a brain after all."

"There are barges everywhere on the canal. We could be headed to Albany. But I don't think so."

"Why?"

"The locks. There are five locks in Lockport. We'd know if we went through them."

"So we're still in Buffalo."

"I think so," Feeney said. "But there's a lot of waterway in

Buffalo. We might never be found on a barge, particularly if it keeps moving. Have your arms fallen asleep?"

"Yes," Norris said. "Move around a bit, get the blood flowing."

"What do you think they'll do to us?"

"I don't know, except they're changing their plans somehow. They thought they were getting Czolgosz, but they ended up with us."

"If they had him, they'd probably get out of Buffalo quick."

"Maybe." Norris turned as much as he could to the left, toward the sound of Feeney's voice. "Now they've got us and for the moment they're sitting tight, trying to figure what to do. The German, Bruener, wanted to kill us right away. But Gimmel, he's thinking it over, he's looking for a way to take advantage of this."

"And there are others," Feeney said.

"Right. How many you think?"

"The one who took over driving the carriage. And I've heard other voices back there—not the German or Gimmel. Two, I think."

"So there are five of them. Very good, Feeney. But there must be more, too."

"This damn sack." Feeney moved in his bunk, the wood creaking under his weight. "It's hot, it itches, and it smells of potatoes and dirt."

Finally, the sacks were removed and Norris and Feeney were brought into a cabin where they were allowed to eat at a table. Their hands were still bound and they were given spoons to eat a stew—carrots, potatoes, onions, cabbage, some fatty pieces of mutton—from an iron pot. Gimmel was there, and a man he called Anton, who bore little resemblance to his sister Motka, but there was no sign of the others. Feeney didn't look good: he'd been sobbing on and off for hours. From the towpath came the sound of mules braying, which usually meant that the barge would move again soon.

"Where are we going?" Norris said to Gimmel.

"Going?" Gimmel said. "You are in a hurry?" He stood at the foot of the companionway, looking up into pilothouse. The darkening sky that was visible above the stern was overcast, threatening more rain. There was something different about his voice; it was slow and resolved—he sounded like a man who had calculated the odds, didn't like the result, but decided to proceed anyway. He didn't bother to look at Norris or Feeney, as though they were immaterial, their fates already determined.

"What happens next?" Norris asked.

Gimmel didn't seem to hear. Anton, on the other hand, moved about the cabin, trying to keep busy. Clearly, he was nervous. Gimmel said, almost to himself, "They'll try Czolgosz—the papers say it will be quick, a few days at most—and then they'll execute him. Perhaps we should execute you as a response."

Norris put down his spoon and said, "That's one option."

"Yes," Gimmel said, turning to them. "One at a time."

Feeney's hands paused over the stew. "It's gonna be me." His voice was high, breaking. "I know it is."

Norris shook his head and lowered his eyes to the pot, meaning: *Eat, just eat.* Obediently, Feeney used both hands to spoon vegetables and gravy into his mouth.

There was a perpetual sameness to Gimmel's expression: part awe, part sardonic grin. "Most likely. It's a question of worth, and Norris is worth more than you."

"How?" Norris said to Gimmel. "How would this execution be carried out?"

"Interesting question." Gimmel rested his back against the companionway ladder, and as he placed his hands on his knees, a thick knot of rope—a monkey fist—was visible, protruding from his belt. "Let's consider how the state handles executions. Traditionally, in this country, hanging has been popular. You know back in '86 I was in Chicago during the Haymarket riot. The nice thing about hanging is it's such a public spectacle. There's a stage, just as in a theater, and the crowd is allowed to gather before the scaffolding as though they were going to witness some grand performance. The victim—*you* would call him the convicted—is marched up a set of stairs, and there's a moment where he faces the crowd."

"With or without a sack over his head," Norris offered.

"True," Gimmel said. "The sack, of course, might be construed to be an attempt to incorporate an element of decency in the proceedings, but in fact it only whets the crowd's appetite. They have come not to see justice done, but to see the face of the victim in that moment when he drops through the floor and his neck snaps. They want to know if it will be instantaneous—and therefore merciful—or if there will be a dance to death. In fact, I think the sack only sparks the imagination. I've seen enough hangings, Norris. They're usually swift and efficient, and there's little by way of entertainment—just a body dangling from a crooked head. But see, if you cover the head, it allows the audience to imagine the worst. And that's what you want from an execution, the opportunity for people—your citizens—to be able to imagine the worst form of suffering. That's what it's really all about—the imagination, not putting the poor bastard to death. You've already got him off the streets and you could simply throw him in a jail cell, to die of starvation, unseen. No, you've got to have your citizens *see* the sentence carried out. The worse, the better. It is, really, prescriptive."

"You're going to hang us?" Feeney said.

Gimmel looked at Feeney, disappointed. "But of course you know that in New York State they don't hang convicts any longer."

Feeney glanced over at Norris, who only nodded in an effort to show calm. "In New York," Norris said, "they use electrocution."

"Right," Gimmel said. "Very modern, efficient, and—"

"Expensive," Norris said.

"It requires Thomas Edison."

"So," Feeney said. "How? How you going do it?"

Gimmel studied Feeney with detachment now, but he didn't say anything, and Feeney began to rock from side to side in his seat—until Gimmel said to Anton, "Take him forward."

Feeney was still, his face childishly horrified. "You ain't gonna to tell me?"

Gimmel said to Anton, "Tie him up good, hands and feet."

Anton didn't move for a moment, and then he asked, "What about—"

Gimmel considered Norris and then said, "No, he stays here."

Feeney's head moved quickly now as he looked at Norris, at Gimmel, at Anton, who came to the table. At first, it seemed that Feeney would resist because there was something childlike and desperate in his face. His eyes sought something—anything—from them that might save him from this moment.

Anton took hold of his upper arm and said, "Come on." His voice was frightened, too, and even apologetic.

Feeney held still, looking as though he would fight any effort to make him stand up.

"You come," Anton said, pleading. "No much trouble, okay?"

"Feeney," Norris said, "don't."

But Feeney's face was turning red as he breathed in short desperate gasps, and he began to writhe as though some foreign, evil agent had taken possession of his body. He pulled away from Anton's grip and spittle streamed from his mouth. When Anton took hold of his arm with both hands, Feeney released a high, keening wail that didn't sound human. He kicked the table legs until the iron pot went over the edge, its contents spilling across the floor.

Anton stepped away from him, his boots and pants covered with gravy, but still Feeney twisted and kicked in his seat, and Gimmel came toward him now, yanking out the monkey fist from inside his belt. Norris stood up quickly and swung both arms together so that his bound fists struck Gimmel's face. Gim-

mel staggered backward, but then caught his balance. Blood ran
from his disfigured nose. He swung his arm low, and the monkey fist hit Norris's stomach hard. Norris doubled over, the wind
knocked out of him, and he fell to his hands and knees. For a
moment he was in such pain and so desperate to breathe that he
wasn't aware of anything else in the cabin. But then he raised his
head and watched Gimmel beat Feeney with the rope.

"You'll *kill* him," Anton said.

Feeney was on his knees, his face pulpy and bloodied, but
Gimmel didn't stop hitting him. Overhead, there were running
footsteps on the deck, and the large German, Bruener, scuttled
down the companionway, shouting for Gimmel to stop. Bruener
caught the arm holding the monkey fist, and then pulled Gimmel
away from Feeney.

Everyone was suddenly still, and the cabin was filled with the
sound of their gasping for breath. Finally, Gimmel shook himself
free of Bruener's arms. "All *right*," he said. He jammed the monkey fist back inside his belt and tugged at the bottom of his coat.
"All right, you get him up in the bow, or I'll kill him right here."

Anton and Bruener hoisted Feeney by his arms, and dragged
him through the door.

Gimmel dropped into the seat Feeney had occupied and
put his arms on his knees. He wiped his nose and mouth
with the back of his hand, and then sat back, exhausted. "That
man," he said, a little laugh gurgling in his throat, "has an inordinate fear of death." When he caught his breath, he said, "It's
curious. There's been no mention of either of you in the evening
papers."

Norris studied Gimmel, realizing what they had in common.
They were both capable of sudden violent outbursts, yet as soon
as they were finished it was as though nothing had happened.
Norris had discovered this about himself when he was young,
and he recognized that it was a valuable tool; often it made other
men circumspect. "Are you disappointed?" he asked.

"No, but perhaps you should be," Gimmel said.

"I suppose it could mean that two Pinkerton detectives really have no worth."

"True. Or they don't want to inflate your value—because you know what journalists would do with such a story."

"In that case I guess I should be flattered."

"Somebody's keeping this quiet. Who would that be, Norris? Would there be somebody who would know what you and Feeney are really worth?"

"You mean somebody to negotiate with?"

"Yes, perhaps."

"I see. That would be Captain Lloyd Savin. He organized Czolgosz's transfer."

"Do you think he'd negotiate?"

"Not if he were a Pinkerton. We don't negotiate with anarchists," Norris said. "But Savin's Buffalo police—so I can't say."

Anton and Bruener came back into the cabin, and Bruener said, "I told you we should throw these shit-ass Pinkertons in the lake."

"No," Gimmel said. "I think we'll contact this Captain Savin of the Buffalo police department. I would be interested to know what two Pinkerton agents are worth, if anything." Anton came over to Norris with the sack, but Gimmel held up his hand. "Norris, another outburst like Feeney's and you'll get more than a beating."

He nodded to Anton and the sack was yanked down over Norris's head.

⤜∽⤚

AFTER the public viewing, the president's coffin was returned to the Milburn house Sunday evening. The staff was served a light

supper in the dining room. Cortelyou discussed the final preparations for the train journey to Washington in the morning. It had
been an exhausting day and most everyone retired early; however, shortly after ten o'clock Dr. Rixey requested that a carriage
be brought around. He was taken back to city hall and admitted
to the prison directly across the street.

"You've another visitor, Leon," the guard said almost apologetically as he unlocked the cell door.

The prisoner lay on a cot suspended from the stone wall, his
hands folded behind his head. He didn't move as the door swung
open on a dry, creaking hinge. Rixey said, "Thank you, officer."
When the guard didn't move, the doctor added, "I'd like to be
alone with him."

The guard smiled, as though they shared a private joke.
"You want to go inside there? You're one of those, eh? No, I
don't mind." And looking in at Czolgosz, he asked, "You mind,
Leon?"

The prisoner still didn't answer, didn't move on the cot.

The guard walked to the table farther down the corridor,
where the other guard was sitting, reading a newspaper.

Rixey removed his hat. He was taller than the cell door and
he ducked as he stepped inside the cell, where he could straighten
up—his head came to within a couple of inches of the stone ceiling. He sat on the stool, the only piece of furniture in the cell,
which couldn't have been ten feet long. "I'm Dr. Presley Rixey,"
he said.

"I seen all the doctors I need to see." Czolgosz's voice was flat,
lifeless. "They already decided I was sane."

"That's not why I'm here."

Czolgosz lay still for a moment, and then suddenly he swung
his legs off the cot and sat up, leaning his back against the wall. "I
don't have to talk to you." He stared straight ahead at the opposite
wall.

"No, you don't."

Rixey let his right shoulder rest against the stone wall and he sat still, facing the end of the cell, where there was a bucket on the floor beneath a small window. There was the sound of rain outside. Rixey didn't move. He simply sat there, his forearms resting on his thighs, holding his hat in his left hand.

Minutes passed, and it brought about a curious silence from the two guards, who realized that there was something unusual going on inside the cell. At one point the guard who had unlocked the door whispered, "They just sitting there?"

"Shut up," the other said. He folded his paper and put it down on the table.

After that all four men were still, except for the occasional creak of a chair as one of the guards shifted his weight.

∽つC∼

Dr. Presley Rixey.

This doctor just sat on the stool and neither of them moved. It went on so long Czolgosz could tell it was making the two guards nervous. He thought he could wait the doctor out.

Dr. Presley Rixey.

Czolgosz had seen or heard that name, but he couldn't remember where.

After a while it was clear that Dr. Presley Rixey wasn't going to move from that stool, he wasn't going to give in. Czolgosz finally looked at him. He was a tall man with a full mustache, and his eyes were weary, yet clear and intelligent. It was nearly dark in the cell, and beads of water on his overcoat caught the light from the corridor. They made Czolgosz think of pearls.

∽つC∼

"I'VE never seen a pearl," Czolgosz said finally, "except in a photograph." He stared intently at Rixey's right shoulder. "They come from the sea."

"I believe they do."

Czolgosz's eyes turned doubtful. "That's what they say."

"I've seen it while on duty in the navy. We were in Valparaíso, our ship taking on supplies. There were these local boys, they dove off these rocks into the ocean. The water was so clear that you could see them swim to the bottom. They'd stay down for a long time, several minutes—I've never seen anybody stay under water that long—and they'd come up with this little sack in their fist. If they'd found a pearl, they'd hold the sack above their heads triumphantly and shout to the other boys on the rocks."

"It's just a grain of sand, right? In a shell, a clam shell."

"That's right. It all starts with a grain of sand."

Czolgosz thought about this a moment, and then nodded his head slowly. "I never seen one," he said. "Why are you here?" Before Rixey could answer, Czolgosz said, "All you doctors. You want to know why I did this thing, but you can't know. It's not something you can ever understand. You may have all kinds of education, but you can't know this. It's beyond you. I am a free man. Even though I sit in the cell, I am freer than you will ever be. And you will never understand it."

Rixey gazed down at his hat, which rested on one thigh. It seemed that to look directly at Czolgosz now would somehow push him back. "You're right," he said. "I don't understand. That's why I'm here." His fingers stroked the satin band in his hat.

"You never worked in no wire factory, did you?" Czolgosz said. "You never blew glass, you never felt the heat from those ovens. Hours, day after day. You never put in a day like that. All you can do is survive it, hope to get some rest, and go back again the next day, and the next. And when they don't need you, or when you're injured or sick, or when you raise any question about how little you're being paid, or how many hours you work, they let you go. They just let you go, Doctor. But not me, they never let me go because I was useful, I was a good worker and I could fix machines. Did you know that? I can fix just about any machine, always could. But there's no hope to it. I never been somewhere that a boy can dive under water and come up with a pearl in a shell." He thought a moment, staring straight ahead intently. Rixey had read about his eyes, his blue-eyed stare, but he'd never seen anything like the way they seemed illuminated from within by some pale, mystical light.

When Czolgosz spoke again, it startled the doctor. "And a man ought not walk around well fed and with soft, clean hands while there are people fixing machines for barely enough money to live on. Not even the president. Particularly the president. That's why I done this thing, and I don't give a damn if it don't make sense to you. It's the truth." He folded his arms as though he were chilled.

"Are you cold?" Rixey asked, but Czolgosz shook his head.

There was a blanket, neatly folded at the foot of the cot. Rixey was certain that Czolgosz was not a slovenly man, that he cleaned himself when given the chance. He had a sense of order and tidiness about him. He followed a regimen. He was, really, like many of the sailors Rixey had known in the navy, solitary men who lived according to clearly defined rules, men who performed their expected tasks. Men that Rixey had learned to trust to do their jobs efficiently, which was necessary aboard ship. But as an officer he had not been one of them. He wished it had been otherwise.

Rixey leaned forward on the stool and slowly got to his feet. Czolgosz became very still, as though he might leap. Rixey picked up the blanket, let it unfurl, and carefully draped it over the prisoner. "This rain—you'll catch a chill," he said, sitting on the stool again.

"Emma Goldman can explain it. She understands it. She knows what's in our hearts, and when she speaks it's as though she pulls it right out of us." He looked toward Rixey suddenly, and the doctor turned his head and stared back at him. "They're holding her in Chicago and it's wrong. She had nothing to do with this. I've said before: you can't find her guilty for having ideas. Can you?" Rixey didn't move. "You *can't*," Czolgosz said, louder. "If you believe *that*, you are no better than the rest of them."

He was so young. His face was still that of an adolescent. People would find him pretty, innocent-looking. They would never look at him and say, *Here is the face of an assassin, someone who changed the course of history. Here is someone so tortured, so angry, so full of conviction that he would shoot anyone, even the president of the United States.* It was confusing—appalling, really—the way this man looked. But the eyes, those bright, fathomless eyes, they were deep set, and the skin around them was dark. Clearly, he was under great strain.

"They tell me I will go to court tomorrow," he said.

"Yes," Rixey said. "While the president's body will be placed on a train bound for Washington, you will be arraigned and charged with his murder."

"I'm guilty—I do not dispute that, so there is no point to a trial." His hand drew the blanket tighter around his shoulders. "You will testify in court?"

"I have not been asked to, and frankly I'm glad of that. Other doctors will testify. I will accompany the president's body and look after his wife. That is my job." Czolgosz didn't seem to understand. "I am the McKinleys' physician," Rixey explained.

Something changed in the boy's eyes, a recollection, it seemed. "The bone felon," he said. "It was you that treated her for the bone felon. I read about it in the newspaper. Out west last spring, when they were traveling, she had this problem with her finger and you treated it. She almost died, and all of the president's plans were canceled."

"Yes," Rixey said. "That's right."

"I don't know what that is, a bone felon."

"A growth, an abnormal growth. It can become infected."

"Then they spent the summer at their house in Canton. She

recovered, and he was rescheduled to come here, and then I knew what I had to do." After a moment, he added, "You know I'm from Ohio, too?"

Something seemed to flood Rixey. A sorrow. An acceptance. This boy from Cleveland reading in the papers that the president would reschedule his trip to Buffalo, and his conclusion was to kill him. Rixey had been right—it was too dangerous for McKinley to attend the exposition. But Cortelyou was right, too: you can't keep the president from the people. That simply wasn't acceptable. McKinley understood that. Few people knew that about him. He understood their need to see him, to hear him. Furthermore, he needed to see them. "It was a terrible sacrifice," Rixey said.

Czolgosz didn't seem to understand. He looked curious.

"I was with him as he dressed the morning you shot him. The president was . . . He was in such a good frame of mind. I realize now why he seemed content, even jovial that morning: he would be meeting citizens, ordinary Americans. You have no idea how isolated a man like that is. He joked—I remember this now—he joked about having very little money in his pocket, not even two dollars, and he joked about the president being caught dead with so little money on him."

"I didn't rob him," Czolgosz said. "And to some people two dollars is everything."

"You're missing my point."

"You're missing mine. Those boys, diving for expensive pearls—were they paid well? I don't think so."

"I'm not talking about pearls," Rixey said. "There are things that you don't understand—you don't understand the sacrifice involved."

For a moment the young man's eyes were angry. "I have understood sacrifice for a long time. I done my duty."

"Is that what this was, duty?"

"Yes."

Rixey shook his head.

"*Yes.*"

"Another president has already been sworn in. You killed the man, a good man, a man I much revered, but there is still the president. You could not deny this country that. Its citizens, you see, they made him president. The presidency still exists—you could not take that away from us."

"And I would kill that one, too, if I had the chance."

"I believe you." Rixey was suddenly sweating, and his hard collar was uncomfortably tight. "Now I do believe you."

"And the next one after that."

Rixey moved his feet, intending to stand up.

"I know sacrifice," Czolgosz said. "I have known it for a long time. I seen it many years ago. When I was a boy my mother died giving birth to my sister. It was her eighth child. She died at forty, when I was ten years old. That was how I learned sacrifice."

Rixey got to his feet, the stool legs scraping the floor, and leaned over the cot. He slapped the boy's face. Then he straightened up, stunned by what he had done. The boy didn't move, wrapped in his blanket, nor did the guards in the corridor. There was only the sound of the rain outside the stone walls.

His left hand felt warm and stung slightly. He turned toward the open cell door, but paused and said, "Your mother, she is fortunate not to be alive now. She would be ashamed. You know that, don't you? You do know that?"

When he ducked his head and stepped out of the cell, the two guards got up from the table in a hurry. Rixey put on his hat and tugged it down on his head. "Now, show me the way out," he said.

~ つC ~

WITHIN the city of Buffalo there was an intricate web of water-ways—canals such as the Erie, the Main-Hamburg, and the Clark-Skinner—and off these ran branches, known as slips, such as the Commercial, the Prime, and the Ohio. During the day the *Glockenspiel* kept moving, and Bruener would tie her up after dark. During the night it rained on and off, and Hyde, Anton, and Josef took turns standing watch.

At dawn, Gimmel came up on deck. He nodded his head, indicating he wanted Hyde to join him in the stern. "All the newspapers—they're full of articles about McKinley, about Czolgosz, but there has been no mention of problems during Czolgosz's transfer."

"I know, not one word about the Pinkertons."

"It's as though it didn't happen," Gimmel said as they watched the first light coming up on the canal. "Tell me something, Hyde. Bruener says you were raised in an orphanage."

"St. John's Protectory."

"Terrible places, they are. I survived one myself in Illinois." Gimmel's eyes briefly drifted toward Hyde, and then he stared out at the river again. "But the experience prepares one for the realities of life. Family ties only complicate and confuse. You have no wife, no children?"

"No."

"Bruener says you are a good canawler."

"I have worked between Buffalo and Albany many years."

"Don't own your own barge."

"They're often handed down, father to son. It's one of the benefits of family."

"But you are unburdened. Can come and go as you please."

"You make it sound like I was a man of wealth and privilege."

"In some ways you are. You and I both, we possess a rare freedom, one not often afforded the working class." Gimmel took a step closer. "This is why I'm so disappointed. You said you knew Czolgosz. You failed me—you were supposed to help me get him." He watched the canal so long that Hyde thought that the conversation was over, that he had been dismissed. But then Gimmel said, "At a place like St. John's they must have instilled in you the concept of sin and redemption?"

"The nuns and priests did. That's why I ran away when I was twelve."

"You understand that you need to redeem yourself now?"

After a moment Hyde said, "What do you want me to do?"

"I want to send a message to someone in the police department," Gimmel whispered. "Norris says there's a Captain Savin. He was riding in the first carriage and had Czolgosz lying at his feet. And now he's kept the Pinkertons out of the newspapers. Clever fellow, this Savin. So this is what I want you to do: go talk to Savin. Tell him I want to exchange these two for Czolgosz."

"He won't do that," Hyde said.

"I know, but you tell him that first," Gimmel said. "Then you tell him that if he refuses these two Pinkertons will be end up dead, and this time I'll make sure the papers know about it, and that Savin had a chance to save them. Savin will realize he has to do something—he has no choice because this entire corrupt society is built upon the value of one life. A man doesn't do something to save that one life, he's considered a savage. But the truth is that we are all savages."

"He'll never give up Czolgosz," Hyde said.

"No, I know he won't."

"What do you really want for these two Pinkertons?"

"We're talking about two 'innocent' men, two defenders of the law. Savin's responsible for them. You tell him the price for these two Pinkertons is a thousand dollars."

"A thousand dollars?" Hyde said.

"Bring back his reply without having half the Buffalo police force follow you—can you do that?"

"Yes. Where?"

"Bruener says tonight we'll tie up just north of Black Rock Harbor. You'll probably need these just to get to see Savin." He handed two cards to Hyde. "These are their Pinkerton identification cards."

~シC~

IT was midmorning when Hyde arrived at city hall. Dozens of police guarded the front entrance of the building, admitting people, mostly newspaper reporters. Hyde stood in line in the rain and when the sergeant demanded his credentials he handed over the two Pinkerton identification cards.

"What's this?" the sergeant asked impatiently. He was Irish and his soft jowls reminded Hyde of the rolls of bread dough he'd seen the day before in the Trenton Avenue bakery.

"Show them to Captain Lloyd Savin. He'll want to see me. My name is Hyde."

The sergeant's blue eyes were skeptical, but then he went inside the entrance and showed the cards to another officer.

Behind Hyde two reporters had been complaining about editors and deadlines. Now, as they watched the policemen guarding the front doors, one of them said, "I tell you, this security's tighter for Czolgosz than it was for old man McKinley."

"Maybe we should get out our handkerchiefs, Lundt," the other reporter said. "Wrap them around our fists and see if that gets us inside out of this rain."

"Right," Lundt said. He had a flask, which he sipped from, and his whiskey breath cut through the raw air. "This is America and everyone's packing a gun now. You hear about Mr. Hearst? All of his editorials that have been critical of McKinley—they've come back to haunt him, particularly when he hinted that the situation was so dire that political assassination was warranted. Since the president has died, there's been a mob outside his office in New York, wanting at Hearst. The bastard's so afraid he keeps a pistol on his desk all the time." Lundt took another pull from his flask.

The Irish sergeant came back out to the steps. "Here, boyo," he said to Hyde. "Come with me."

Hyde glanced over his shoulder at the two reporters, their

faces stunned and resentful, and then he followed the policeman inside to the first-floor lobby. They climbed the marble staircase beneath an enormous portrait of McKinley, and on the second floor pushed through a crowd gathered outside the courtroom. The sergeant led Hyde around the balcony to the front of the building, and opened a door to a reception hall. "You wait in here," he said, and then he pulled the door shut.

Hyde had never been in such a large room. Chandeliers hung from a ceiling trimmed with gilt moldings. Tall windows were covered with red velvet drapes edged with gold fringe and tassels. He crossed the parquet floor, his footsteps echoing, and stood next to a grand piano. Out the window he could see the crowd waiting in the rain. Behind him, one of the doors opened. Captain Savin came in and walked toward the piano, seeming unimpressed by the size of the room. When he reached the piano, he leaned the Pinkerton identification cards against the music stand, and then he sat on the bench and tapped out the melody to "Mary Had a Little Lamb."

"My mother," he said. "She paid Mrs. Flannigan, who lived downstairs, to give me piano lessons, but I refused to go after a couple of months." He took his hand off the keys. "Tell me, which would you rather: to be able to afford a fine instrument like this, or to be able to play Chopin?"

"I'm not the least bit musical," Hyde said.

"Can't carry a tune myself. My father had a wonderful tenor, and my mother thought she could give me a little bit of culture. Poor woman, I became a cop anyway." He opened up his suit coat and took out a pack of Turkish Delights. "Tell me where they are, Hyde."

"They're being held by a group of anarchists."

"I gather that. Where?"

Hyde looked down into the street, where the line of reporters still waited to get into Leon Czolgosz's arraignment. But there were hundreds of other men milling about, and they looked as though they might storm the doors of city hall at any moment.

"It's Herman Gimmel, isn't it?" Savin said.

"Yes."

"We've sought him for years. What's he want?"

"To exchange Norris and Feeney for Czolgosz." Savin said nothing. "And he wants a thousand dollars."

Savin put the cigarette in his mouth, picked up Norris's identification card, and squinted at it through smoke. Once he deposited ash into the potted plant next to the piano. When he put the card back on the piano, he said, "And if I refuse, they die."

"And Gimmel will make sure those reporters down there in the street find out that you could have saved them."

"Everybody wants something." Savin got up from the piano bench and went to the window. "I want to be police chief one day. What do you want, Hyde?" After watching the crowd below for a moment, he said, "What do you want for Herman Gimmel?"

Hyde didn't answer.

"I was the one who set you up with Norris."

"It's not that easy, and you know it."

Savin nodded as though he were convinced that he should take a different approach. "You find it curious that an avowed anarchist demands ransom money? Do you see the contradiction there?"

"No. He'll buy dynamite with it."

"Of course. Norris says you're good, and I could see you were smart right off—for a canawler. At least you've managed to stay alive longer than that whore Clementine. But you know what your problem is, Hyde?"

"I have only one?"

"You have too many loyalties. I think deep down you're an idealist, which is always a mistake. But you're not a true anarchist—that's an important distinction."

Hyde gazed at the parquet floor.

"You're even loyal to that Russian whore."

Reluctantly, Hyde raised his eyes.

"Ah, *there* it is," Savin whispered. His smile was greedy, victorious. "This is not loyalty, but love?"

"We were talking about Herman Gimmel."

"We still are." For a moment Savin massaged his temples with his fingers. "We're hearing all sorts of rumors about anarchist plots. You know, this would be a lot easier if you'd just tell me where they are."

"It's not that easy."

"You're saying, 'I free them, what happens to me?'" Savin lowered his head and brushed cigarette ash off his lapels. "You want to know the truth? I can't stand Norris, and wouldn't mind if I never lay eyes on him again. Pinkertons kidnapped is one thing. But this isn't just any Pinkerton—it's Jake Norris, who's been sent out from Washington specifically because the president was coming to Buffalo. Men like Norris turn up dead, somebody's going to be held accountable. In this case, that's me." He gazed up at Hyde. "So what is it *you* want, Hyde?"

"That Russian is named Motka Ascher—"

"Yes, quite the beauty."

"I want to get her out of Big Maud's—bought, so Maud doesn't send someone after her. And then I'll take her out of Buffalo."

"You'll need money, of course." Savin raised a hand to smooth back his glossy hair. "All right. You take me to Gimmel, and I'll buy your Russian girl."

"No," Hyde said. "You'll buy her, and then I'll take you to Gimmel."

"I'll tell you something, Hyde. Norris wanted to tie her—you and her—to Czolgosz."

"She's got nothing to do with it."

"Nevertheless, it's something to keep in mind. It's still possible. All I have to do is suggest it to one reporter." The two men gazed at each other for a long moment. Finally, Savin turned away as he crushed his cigarette out in the potted fern, and for the first time looked around at the reception hall, scanning the ceiling and chandeliers, the large portraits hung on the walls. "All right,

Hyde. We'll meet at Big Maud's, tonight at eleven. We buy your pretty redhead, and then you take me to Gimmel." He ran his fingers across the piano keys, striking a few discordant notes. "I can understand a socialist, or even a communist. They believe in something, they believe in changing the way things are—they're even fool enough to think that can make things better. But anarchists, what do they believe in? Nothing."

"They believe in a world where everyone is free, where there are no policemen, and they're willing to kill anyone who opposes them."

"How do you explain it, Hyde?"

"I can't. I'm not an anarchist."

"No? Then what are you?" Savin didn't wait for an answer, but turned away dismissively and crossed the parquet floor.

∽ↄC∼

CZOLGOSZ barely slept Sunday night. He couldn't stop thinking about Dr. Rixey's slap—he couldn't understand why it bothered him so, but then he began to admit that he felt admiration for the doctor. When he came to that realization, he was relieved, and he finally managed to sink into the oblivion of sleep in the early-morning hours.

After breakfast Solomon and Geary took him to a room where an iron bathtub had been prepared. They left him alone to bathe, and then brought a clean shirt and collar.

"Thank you. I'm tired of wearing my own dirty shirt."

"We want you to look good for the courtroom," Geary said.

"Though not much'll happen today," Solomon added. "It's only an arraignment, and it won't be necessary to bring you in until near the end."

"Why should I be present at my own arraignment at all?"

It was as though Solomon didn't hear him. "You'll be charged with murder and a trial date will be set," he said. "Soon, I imagine. First-degree murder of the president of the United States."

Geary said, "You don't seem too concerned, Leon."

As he pulled on his coat, Czolgosz said, "Had this suit made in Chicago in July."

"I know," Solomon said. "At first the Chicago police said they wanted it sent out there for examination. They wanted anything that might help them link Emma Goldman to you, but seems they've dropped that. I mean, how could a suit link you to her?"

"I wore it when I met her in Chicago," Czolgosz said, "and I wore it when I shot the president. Does that make her an accomplice?"

"Penney has been trying to get her extradited to New York," Geary said. "But Chicago won't give her up. The judge there says there's no evidence of her involvement. Since when do you need hard evidence to arrest an anarchist? A Chicago judge should understand that."

"Politics," Solomon explained. "It's all politics. They'll let that woman walk."

"That's because she's as innocent as you are," Czolgosz said. They seemed angered by this, but then he realized that this morning they were a bit nervous. He felt the need to make it easier for them, and as he buttoned the striped gray jacket he added, "You realize this will be a famous suit? It'll be worth something after I'm dead. Maybe I'll give it to you as a going-away present."

They glanced at each other.

"You get the chair, Leon," Geary said, "they'll burn all your clothes."

"The chair?"

"The electric chair," Solomon said. "It's how we do it now in New York State. They'll take you to the prison over in Auburn."

"Where's that?"

"Oh, it's east of here," Solomon said. "Little town, not quite to Syracuse. If you wanted to get yourself hung you should have shot the president in some other state, someplace like Kansas."

Solomon took his handcuffs from his coat pocket. "Leon, you know the court has appointed you two lawyers. Why do you refuse to talk to them?"

"It ain't necessary," Czolgosz said. "None of this is necessary."

They left him in his cell for hours. He slept. He was brought lunch. He slept some more. Finally Solomon and Geary returned and he was handcuffed to both of them. This had become a familiar routine, where Geary usually led and Solomon followed when they passed through doors and down narrow stairs. Czolgosz walked with one shackled arm extended before him, the other behind.

"Like elephants in the circus," Geary said.

"This courtroom thing," Solomon asked. "You going to turn it into a circus?"

Czolgosz didn't answer, and they took him down to the basement to a damp tunnel. Their footsteps echoed off the stone walls.

Solomon said, "This runs three hundred feet under Delaware Avenue to city hall, so we can avoid that crowd. You ever hear of the Bridge of Sighs, Leon?"

"No."

"It's very famous," Solomon explained. "It's this old bridge that spans one of the canals in Venice. It connects the courtroom with the prison, where criminals were sent to serve life sentences or to be executed. We call this the Tunnel of Tears."

A group of men, including Chief Bull, were waiting at the

other end of the tunnel, and Czolgosz was surrounded as they climbed the stairs to the courtroom. There was a balcony above the stairs, and hanging between two marble columns was a large picture of the dead president. Czolgosz had seen that portrait many times; it was the one often used in newspapers. McKinley looked stern, dignified, but his eyes possessed a certain avuncular fondness.

Czolgosz hesitated on the stairs, causing the other men to stop. Thomas Penney seemed disturbed at first, but then when he saw Czolgosz staring up at the president's image, he said, "Take a good look. He's why we're all here."

They climbed the stairs and encountered a large crowd gathered on the second floor. When they saw Czolgosz, they hissed and booed and shouted, their voices reverberating off the marble walls. They surged toward him and were barely restrained by the dozens of uniformed policemen. There was much pushing and shoving as Geary and Solomon took him into the courtroom, which was not crowded—it was, oddly, quiet as a church. But those who were sitting there—nearly all men—shifted about for a better view of him. As he walked to a table before the judge's bench, he lowered his head and didn't look directly at anyone.

Solomon had difficulty with his set of handcuffs. The key would fit into the lock but he couldn't turn it. Minutes passed. Solomon kept trying and everyone else watched in silence. There was a palpable tension in the room, which tended to make Czolgosz calmer. When the lock finally opened, there was an audible sigh of relief, and Czolgosz sat between the two detectives. His lawyers, Robert Titus and Loran Lewis, two retired judges, positioned themselves at the far end of the table, as though they were embarrassed to sit near their client. When one of them finally looked toward him to say something, Czolgosz closed his eyes and turned his head away.

Men spoke but he didn't pay attention. He knew he was being

charged with the murder of the president, but he just sat still, staring at the floorboards by his feet. The whorls in the knots were quite intricate—if he looked at them long enough, they would seem to shift and move. After about ten minutes it was over and the detectives put the handcuffs on him again.

VI

MONDAY DR. RIXEY accompanied Mrs. McKinley on the train from Buffalo to Washington, D.C. The president's coffin rode in an observation car with glass walls that allowed people alongside the tracks to see it, draped with an American flag. Thousands lined the route, singing hymns, particularly "Nearer, My God, to Thee." The train slowed for each town as it traveled south through western New York, into Pennsylvania, down the Susquehanna River valley, to Harrisburg and Baltimore, until it arrived finally in the capital.

The rain never stopped. The skies were so leaden that it seemed as though it would rain forever. During the trip, the week's plans were presented to Mrs. McKinley by Cortelyou and several cabinet members, with Dr. Rixey in attendance. They explained that Monday night the casket would lie in state in the East Room of the Executive Mansion, protected by military guard. Tuesday there would be a procession down Pennsylvania Avenue to the Capitol, where there would be a public viewing of the deceased president in the rotunda. This, again, was of deepest concern to the first lady. Rixey gathered it was part jealousy, part the desire to protect her husband's remains from gawkers. Carefully, Cortelyou explained to her that, as in Buffalo, thousands of citizens would wait in line for hours so they could take a few moments to pay their respects. Tuesday evening the casket would be put aboard the train again for the slow journey west to Canton, Ohio. Final ceremonies would take place Thursday, September 19.

While all this was explained, Mrs. McKinley remained calm. She sat in her chair, her frail figure nearly lost in her black dress, her hands preoccupied with knitting yet another slipper. When the meeting was concluded, she said she wished to rest, and Cortelyou led the others out of the car, leaving Rixey and two nurses with the first lady.

"What about you, Presley?" she asked. "What happens to you after Thursday?"

"Mr. Roosevelt has requested that I stay on in my present position, but indicated that I should remain with you until you are properly settled in Ohio."

"How thoughtful," she said flatly. "I will not live in that little house on North Main the Major and I have in Canton. It was going to be our retirement home after his term of office ended, but I couldn't bear to be there without him. I'm going move into my family's house, where I grew up."

"I understand." Rixey pulled back a window curtain. They were passing through yet another small town and people were lined up alongside the track. Many held candles, shielding them from the rain with their hands.

One of the nurses, Mrs. Chase, gasped and he turned. The younger nurse, Miss Iggers, had opened a small trunk, which contained the clothes that the McKinleys had brought to Buffalo. On top were several of the president's neatly folded white shirts. Seeing them, Mrs. McKinley had dropped her knitting, and her face was twitching badly.

He went to her, took his handkerchief from his suit-coat pocket, and draped it over her contorted face. "Water," he said to Miss Iggers.

He sat in the straight-back chair next to Mrs. McKinley and waited; this had always been the president's role, concealing his wife's face until the fit passed. Rixey took hold of her hands, which lay shaking in her lap, and rubbed them gently. After a minute, he could feel her calming down. The nurse put a glass of water on the table next to the rocking chair.

"Get the oxygen ready, Mrs. Chase," he said, nodding toward the tank that stood on a dolly in the corner.

Mrs. McKinley's face was still now and he removed the handkerchief. Her eyes were closed and her mouth was set in a frown, which created deep wrinkles in her chin. She might have been asleep.

"Take some water, Ida," he said.

He held the glass up to her mouth but she didn't drink. Slowly she opened her eyes, and it took a moment for her to focus on him. Her left eyelid remained partially closed, and her breathing was shallow.

"You've never called me Ida before," she whispered.

"My apologies," he said.

She took the glass of water in both hands and drank. "No need," she said. "It was just the sight of his shirts," she said. "It's all we have really. Clothes. And that little house in Canton." Looking back at Rixey, she attempted to smile. "Can you imagine how many trunks the Roosevelts will need to move into the Executive Mansion?"

Rixey shook his head. He glanced up at Miss Iggers and saw that she was uncertain how to react to Mrs. McKinley's attempt at humor.

"And Teddy's horses." Mrs. McKinley laughed. "Do you suppose he'll bring them right into the house? Perhaps they could be exercised in the East Wing."

Mrs. Chase, a stout woman who stood by the oxygen tank, also seemed alarmed by this conversation. Rixey nodded and she wheeled the tank toward them.

"No," Mrs. McKinley said, her voice weak but stern. "Not yet." She took another sip of water, and then handed the glass to Rixey. "The doctors who performed the operation on the Major," she said. "I understand they are now the subject of much criticism. The press, other doctors—they're saying they didn't do all they could."

"There is much speculation," he said. "I guess there was bound to be." He put the glass on the table. "Some of them—Mann and Park and the others—are considering filing a lawsuit."

Her eyes were clear now. "I believe they did everything they could. It was very difficult for you, consulting with all of them. Sometimes I think doctors have bigger egos than politicians."

"Surgeons, perhaps," Rixey said.

"Do you know that years ago, when the Major was governor, our apartment was directly across the street from his office in Columbus, and every day precisely at three o'clock in the afternoon I would go to the front window and he would appear in his window and wave to me. Then he'd return to business." For a moment, her face seemed to collapse with remorse. "I was such a burden to him."

Rixey leaned toward her. "I've never seen a man so devoted to his wife."

She closed her eyes and nodded. Her breathing was still very shallow. Rixey stood up and nodded to Mrs. Chase, who rolled the oxygen tank closer to the first lady's chair.

A little after eleven that night Hyde followed Savin through Big Maud's front door. The madam shuttled across the vestibule, her palms pressed together in front of her powdered bosom, as though in thankful prayer. She embraced the captain, kissing him on both cheeks, a gesture that Savin seemed compelled to endure out of some sense of decorum.

"Darling," Maud said, taking his arm. "Come in, and let me

fix you a drink and introduce you to my wonderful girls—though perhaps I might be so fortunate as to . . . reminisce . . . with you awhile?"

"Maud"—Savin hesitated, politely—"we've come for Motka."

"Oh." Her surprise was as delicate as it was false. "You're not here for my little Russian redhead again?"

"No, she's leaving. For good."

For the first time Maud took note of Hyde's presence, and she was suddenly confused. "What is it? Moses Hyde here, he's in no trouble, is he?"

Savin smiled at her attempt to deflect. "No, Maud, it's about— do you suppose we could talk privately while we conduct this transaction?"

"Of course." Maud seemed distant and formal, now that a business deal was about to be negotiated. She walked Savin down the front hall, past the entry to the parlor, and through the door to her office.

Hyde took the stairs two at a time. When he reached the second floor, he heard opera coming from Bella Donna's room, and bedsprings were thwanging in time to the music. Then, slowly, he climbed to the third floor, and waited outside Motka's door, listening. There was a cacophony of music—ragtime piano and opera—echoing up the staircase, but he couldn't hear any sound from Motka's room. Finally he knocked. No response. He opened the door and found Motka lying on the bed, in the light from one candle on the nightstand. Her hair was piled loosely on her head and she only wore a velvet band that encircled her slender neck. She was holding still, her arms behind her head, one hip arched, as though modeling for a painter. Next to the bed a fat man was hunched over in the straight-back chair, facing her; he was fully clothed in a suit with a starched cravat, and he appeared to be merely staring at her. But there was movement, his fist bobbing up and down above his open trousers.

Seeing Hyde, Motka raised herself up on one elbow, alarmed.

The man glanced at Hyde—his ruddy face was desperate, and somehow familiar—and then he looked at Motka again, his hand moving with greater urgency, his breathing now turning to a wheeze.

Hyde realized he had seen the man's face in the newspapers. He was often included in photographs taken at balls and dinners, social occasions where women wore gowns and men wore boiled shirts over their bellies as though they were shields. "Get out, now," Hyde said.

"I *can't*." His hand moved faster and, looking again at Hyde, he said, "I don't touch her. I never touch her."

Suddenly he was thrown back in his chair as his legs went rigid, while Motka collapsed on the bed in exasperation. Hyde turned away in embarrassment and occupied himself by removing a paint chip from the doorjamb with his thumbnail.

The man in the chair shuddered and whimpered in disgust, and then he became silent and still. Hyde looked now, as the man was slumped over, exhausted. "See what you've made me do?" He removed a handkerchief from inside his coat and began daubing at his trousers.

"The police are downstairs," Hyde said.

"*What?*"

"Captain Savin—you know him?—he's in Big Maud's office at the moment—"

"Savin?" He shoved the handkerchief into his pocket.

"Better hurry."

He got to his feet, hoisting his pants about his girth, trying to fasten things as he veered across the room. Hyde stepped out of his way, and slammed the door behind him.

Motka sat up, pulling the sheet over her as she muttered angrily in Russian. He took the chair and set it aside, and then sat down on the bed, causing it to groan—a familiar sound—and quickly her slender arm came out from beneath the sheet and she slapped him on the left cheek. The force turned his head away.

After a moment, he looked back at her, and she slapped him again, harder.

This time he kept his head turned away. "Get dressed and pack everything."

"What can you be saying?"

"You're leaving here. For good."

She leaned toward him, took hold of his head, and kissed him hard on the mouth. "It is true?"

"You didn't used to do this, kissing," he said.

"You don't like me kissing?"

"I do. I like it better than slapping. If I leave Buffalo, will you go with me?"

"Go where?"

"Does it matter?"

"No. But *how*? Where would we go?"

"I don't know that yet," he said.

"North? They say Canada's winters are worse than here. But I like the winter. When I was a girl, the winters in Smolensk were beautiful, until spring when everything becomes the mud. But I cannot just *leave*. A girl named Sarah, she run away and Big Maud sent Mr. Varney to find her. He brought her back from Toledo—this is west, no?—and she had a broken arm, bruises, missing the teeth. Terrible pain. It take me and Bella Donna many days to make her better."

"Big Maud, she sell her girls?"

"Sometimes. But usually when they are no use no more. Drunk, or worse. Me, she would not let go. Unless for a lot of money. You could not get this much money, I'm afraid. She once sold a girl for two hundred and eighty dollars, plus a horse."

There was something tender and broken in her voice, and pulling her hair back off her face, he saw that she was crying. She pressed her face into his shoulder, and her tears were warm on his neck.

"I have the money," he said. "It's being arranged now."

She raised her head, her eyes luminous, reflecting candlelight. "Now? You have this kind of money?"

"I won't need horses."

Everything had fit into one small valise. He helped her with her coat, and then she leaned over the nightstand and blew out the candle. When Hyde opened the door, shifting light came up the stairway, and he realized that the music had stopped downstairs. Instead there was the swift padding of bare feet, as though children were sneaking out of bed, and the shadows that danced on the walls were from the other girls who had gathered down on the second floor. At the bottom of the stairs, they were met by expectant, joyful faces. Bella Donna, sobbing, took Motka in her arms and kissed her on both cheeks. *"Buona fortuna,"* she cried.

Motka moved toward the staircase, the girls touching her, whispering goodbye, and then she led Hyde down to the vestibule. Big Maud stood in the parlor entryway, her eyes averted. Motka paused in front of the madam, who appeared to be devastated by sudden bad news. In the parlor, everyone, men and women, looked on in silence. And then, without really looking at Motka, Maud said, "Well, you brought me a decent price." She turned away and drifted into the parlor, where she said, clapping her hands, "What's happened to our music?"

As Hyde followed Motka to the front door, the piano keys began to dance and voices swelled so that he felt they were being pushed out of the house. Motka hesitated on the stoop. She looked as though she'd forgotten something and began to turn around, but he took hold of her elbow and guided her down to the street. There was reluctance in her step. As they walked toward the waiting carriage, she tried to stop again but he held her arm tighter.

"I can't." She paused and pulled her arm free of his grip, and then looked over her shoulder. Some of the girls were peering

out from behind the parlor drapes, and on the second floor, Bella
Donna stood in her bedroom window, a handkerchief to her face.
"I cannot leave them."

"You don't have any choice," Savin said from the carriage.
"You belong to me now."

She looked at Hyde in the dim light cast from the windows
of Big Maud's. He realized he'd never seen her outside of the
house—she'd only once stepped out on the stoop, the night her
brother came out of the dark, fighting.

"We're going to find Anton," he said. "We have to. You have
to, Motka."

The light fell across her face, illuminating one eye, large,
frightened. "Anton?"

"He needs you now. We're going to go find him."

She took one look back at the house, then turned and walked
toward the waiting carriage. Hyde followed behind her. When she
reached the carriage step, Savin offered his hand, but she refused
it and climbed inside without assistance.

The streets of Buffalo were empty, fogbound. They were followed
by two other carriages, and once Motka glanced out the small
rear window and asked, "Who are they?"

"My men," Savin said.

"What for so many?"

"With anarchists, you never have enough."

"Anton is not the anarchist," she said.

Savin wouldn't look at her.

They didn't speak again until they reached the canal, north
of where it fed into Black Rock Harbor. Savin flicked his cigarette
out the window and said to Hyde, "Well?"

"Stop along here, and then we should walk down toward a
warehouse owned by the Shanley brothers."

"They're inside?"

"No. The barge will meet me there."

"The *Glockenspiel*," Savin said. "Bruener's boat."

"Yes."

"I had a notion. I've had my men looking for her, but no luck. She keeps moving. It's perfect. Hundreds of boats on the canal." He rapped his knuckles on the carriage ceiling and the horses began to slow. "You," he said to Motka. "I want you to stay here with one of my men."

"You are going to find Anton?" she asked.

"Yes. It will be all right," Savin said.

She looked at Hyde. "You will bring my brother back? Safe."

"For a prostitute, you have high expectations," Savin said.

Angry and frightened, she turned to Hyde, who said, "I'll find Anton. I promise."

The carriage came to a halt. Savin and Hyde climbed down, and there were eight uniformed policemen emerging from the other carriages, each armed with a pistol or a rifle. They gathered around Savin while he gave them instructions. Hyde looked down on the canal—it was quiet and still, and the fog made it difficult to see the buildings on the far side.

The policemen broke into two groups. Five of them walked past the Shanleys' warehouse and took a footbridge to the other side, disappearing into the fog. Savin led Hyde and the others along the front of the warehouse, indicating places—dark doorways— where each man should be posted. At the corner of the building they came to an alley, and Savin, Hyde, and one policeman waited in a shadow.

They stared out at the canal for more than half an hour. Savin didn't move, didn't even light a cigarette. Finally he said to the policeman, "Cullen, you walk that way a bit, and see if anything's coming down toward the harbor."

Cullen stepped out of the alley and walked north.

Savin took his pocket watch from his vest and opened it. "A little after one."

"They've been on time before," Hyde said.

"And how many of them are there?"

"Bruener, his son, and Gimmel. Anton. And Norris and the other Pinkerton."

Savin snapped the watch closed and tucked it back in his vest pocket. They stared out at the fog. After about ten minutes a dog came along, sniffing. When it saw them in the alley it turned around and ran off.

A few minutes later they heard footsteps and Cullen appeared out of the fog. "It's up there, sir." He was a large man with a handlebar mustache. "Several hundred yards, just after a bend where there's a slaughterhouse. Didn't see nobody, though, and the cabin's dark."

"All right." Savin stepped out in the alley and began walking north. Hyde and Cullen followed, and the footsteps of the other policemen could be heard across the water. They moved through the fog without speaking until they reached the bend in the canal, where Savin stopped. "Hate the smell of pigs," he said. Looking back toward the others, he said, "Quietly now," and then he led them past the sty, where pigs could be heard grunting and rooting around in the mud and rubbing themselves against slats in the fence.

When they came in sight of the *Glockenspiel,* they stopped, and Hyde said, "Strange, I don't see the mules. They should be ready to tow."

Savin said, "Where are Norris and Feeney?"

"Kept forward, up in the bow."

Savin watched the barge for a moment and then said, "You go ahead."

Hyde didn't move.

"You heard me," Savin said. "You go on aboard. See if you can get them to come up top—tell them something, something wrong with the hull."

Hyde glanced at Cullen but the policeman wouldn't return his stare.

"You have no choice," Savin said. "It's not a matter of trust. You have no choice—you promised the girl. Besides, I would like Gimmel alive." Hyde looked toward several policemen, who were lying on the ground, their rifles aimed at the barge. "We won't fire," Savin said, "unless they fire first."

Hyde started to walk toward the barge. There was no movement, no sound, no light on board. He could not see any of the policemen on the far side of the canal. He went down the plank to the deck and moved toward the pilothouse. Someone should have been on watch, but there was no one in sight. Below, the lanterns weren't lit in the cabin. It could be that Gimmel and Bruener knew he was bringing the police and were just waiting for him.

"Bruener," he said quietly. "Gimmel."

There was no sound from below.

Hyde moved to the top of the companionway, leaned over, and looked down into the dark cabin. Then he heard something from up near the bow. He went out on the deck and walked forward. And then he saw Anton, lying curled up on his side next to an open hatch. A marlin spike—a large wooden needle used to splice rope—was buried in the side of his skull, and the fingers of his right hand twitched as though trying to grasp something.

"Where are they, Anton?"

Anton coughed, and then he whispered something that Hyde couldn't understand.

"What? English. Speak English, Anton."

"Awe-burr."

Hyde could hear the sound of a carriage moving along the towpath. "Motka, she's here. Do you want to see her?"

Briefly one eyelid rolled up.

"What happened? Where did they go?"

Anton's eye closed and his hand stopped twitching as his body flattened out on the deck.

There was the sound of footsteps and Savin came to the top of the berm, accompanied by Cullen. Behind them, Hyde could see Motka as she was being restrained by two policemen. *"Anton,"* she cried, and then she spoke furiously in Russian to the men holding her.

Hyde went back up the plank, but Cullen stood in the way when he tried to approach Savin. "They killed him," Hyde said. "He was no anarchist, Savin." He tried to get around Cullen, but the policeman grabbed him by the shoulders and pushed him back.

"You lost them, Hyde," Savin said.

"I brought you down here."

Savin looked at his men who were holding Motka. "Take her back to the carriage."

She screamed as they dragged her back along the towpath.

Hyde moved toward Savin again, and when Cullen stood in his way Hyde shoved him. The sergeant drew his revolver and took aim at Hyde's chest.

"*Cullen,*" Savin said, and after a moment the policeman lowered his gun. "Have your men take care of that, Cullen." He looked down at the barge. "I still don't have my Pinkertons, do I, Hyde? I bought her, so I get to keep her." He walked along the towpath toward the waiting carriage.

∽⟩C⟨∼

THEY had been traveling for hours over country roads. Norris's back ached, but at least his hands were now bound in front of him and his head wasn't covered. It was night, raining, and they were sitting in the back of a milk wagon. All he could see was the dull glint of metal canisters, knocking against each other with dull bell tones. There was an awful smell: milk.

"We've been traveling all night," Feeney said. "We must be well out of Buffalo. That sound—the sound of milk sloshing in them canisters, it's gonna give me the squirty shits."

The wagon wheels banged over rough road, and the horses—

there were two sets of hooves—plodded on with determination. "I hate milk," Norris said.

He could barely see Bruener, slumped on a milk canister, his head lolling back against the wall as he snored. Gimmel was seated on a wood crate—the one that contained the sticks of dynamite—and his head was turned away as he stared out the one small window in the rear door of the wagon.

They were running. They were running because of Moses Hyde, and they realized they couldn't stay on the barge any longer. Despite rain drumming on the deck overhead, Norris had been able to hear Gimmel and Bruener arguing—mostly in German— in the cabin. Then someone came into the berth and removed the sack from Norris's head. He was staring up at Anton, who looked as though he wanted to divulge a secret, but he couldn't find the words, and it made him look nervous and remorseful. Then he began to cut the rope binding their hands. "We climb out one of the forward hatches," he whispered.

"What's happened back there?" Norris asked.

"Gimmel's very mad. Hyde was sent to police to make a deal for you and—"

"Hyde?"

"Yes."

"Good," Norris said.

"You know him?" Anton asked.

"I know Moses Hyde."

"He is not returned," Anton said. "Gimmel says he's been arrested or maybe paid off, and he will bring the police. So we must leave the canal now. So this is your best chance, while the rain is hard." Anton opened the door and led them into the hold. He opened one of the hatches and climbed up into the pouring rain. Norris and Feeney followed, and when they were all on the deck the boy Josef stepped out of the pilothouse, holding a pistol. Norris, Anton, and Feeney raised their hands.

Josef stamped his foot on the deck. Gimmel and Bruener came out of the pilothouse. Gimmel also had a pistol. He said something in German, and Bruener walked toward Anton, pulling something long and thin from his pocket—a marlin spike. Bruener raised his arm and brought it down swiftly, burying the marlin spike deep in the side of Anton's head, dropping him to the deck.

In the distance they could hear the sound of horses and a wagon coming along the towpath. Bruener tied Norris's and Feeney's hands again, and then they were taken off the barge. Anton still lay writhing on the deck in the pouring rain.

Now the milk wagon stopped and immediately there was the sound of horse piss striking packed dirt. Bruener opened the door and fresh, cool air filled the wagon. It was a moonless night, but Norris could see across a cornfield to a stand of woods.

"We'll wait here," Gimmel said.

They all got out and everyone pissed in the dark.

"You're running," Norris said.

Gimmel buttoned himself up. "I am always running."

"They are tracking down anarchists everywhere. They're throwing them in jail. In some places they're lynching them."

"For every one they kill, two will take his place." Gimmel took a flask from his coat pocket and tipped it up to his mouth. The smell of whiskey seemed to cauterize the sour smell of milk in Norris's nostrils. "You think I was sent here to perpetrate an isolated act?" Gimmel asked. "No, we must take full advantage of the situation Czolgosz has created. In the next week there will be bombs elsewhere—all over the country. It's our responsibility to provide the spark." He unlocked the crate that he'd been sitting on, opened the lid, and took out a stick of dynamite. "We'll let them know what we think of their notion of justice."

"Where?" Norris asked. "Out here? No, Gimmel, you've been chased out of Buffalo, where you might have blown something up, but now you're running. You've failed."

"Norris, your concept of failure and success—they are meaningless. What you don't have is the *attentat,* the deed—you lack conviction."

"I have plenty of conviction. People like you give it to me."

Gimmel put the stick of dynamite back in the crate and shut the lid. "No, you don't, really. Mine began years ago. When I was young I read Johann Most's pamphlets on revolutionary war science. It was a handbook on nitroglycerine, dynamite, gun cotton, fulminate of mercury. He called explosives the 'proletariat's artillery.' Dynamite is the great equalizer. But you know who really taught me how to make a bomb? Louis Lingg. His stature, it was incredible. People said they'd never seen such a strong, handsome man. The day of the Haymarket riot, Lingg and another carpenter named Seliger spent hours putting bombs together. I was still in my teens—and I helped. Lingg treated me like a younger brother—we all believed we were going to die soon, together. He spoke little English but he liked to call me 'Galoot.' When they were all put on trial, they tried to prove that it was Lingg who actually threw the bomb that killed all those policemen. But it wasn't Lingg. It was the Galoot. I threw that bomb. I threw that bomb, and my only regret is that I was not tried with Spies and Parsons and the others. The eloquence of those men—their speeches defended the workers' rights and the role of anarchism. Parsons's speech went on for two days! That fool judge allowed them to speak because he knew they were going to hang." He took a last pull on his flask, and then tucked it back inside his coat.

"But Lingg," Norris said. "He didn't hang."

"That's right," Gimmel said. "During the trial they found bombs in Lingg's cell, and they could never determine how they got there. The newspapers called him the 'anarchist tiger.' But just before they were all sentenced to death, Lingg was killed by an exploding cap that was hidden inside a cigar."

"I remember," Norris said. "He wasn't killed immediately."

"In Chicago people said it was the police, it was their form of revenge, and Lingg lay in a hospital, his face blown open, dying, unable to speak. But it was another anarchist, Dyer Lum. I helped him put the cap in the cigar, and then during a visit at the police station he managed to pass it to Lingg. And you know why?"

"It's what Lingg wanted," Norris said.

"He was too dignified to hang," Gimmel said as he took out the whiskey bottle again. "None of the four men they hung— Spies, Parsons, Engel, Fischer—not one of them died of a broken neck. They all strangled. It took more than seven minutes for all of them to die. For Lingg, hanging would have been a disgrace. And it's the same for Czolgosz. He deserves to die honorably, not in some electric chair." Gimmel tipped the bottle to his mouth.

"Martyred."

"Czolgosz knows his role. Anything to inspire others."

There was the sound of a horse approaching and they both looked toward the first light rising beyond the trees. A boy riding bareback was coming down the dirt road toward the milk wagon. He pulled up on the reins and said something in German to Bruener.

"So what are you going to do?" Norris asked.

"Keep going." Gimmel gestured toward the wagon. "Be patient. Wait."

~つC~

WHEN Solomon and Geary came for Czolgosz they didn't handcuff him. They climbed two flights of stairs to a room with only a wooden table and four chairs in the center. Solomon indicated that he should sit down, and then he went and stood next to Geary by the door.

"Another alienist?" Czolgosz asked.

Neither detective spoke at first; then Geary said, "No, better."

They waited without speaking for perhaps five minutes. There were tall windows behind Czolgosz and he turned in his chair to watch the rain, the way it ran down the long wavy panes of glass. Even the light of such a gray overcast day felt warm compared to the darkness of his cell.

When the door opened, Chief Bull and District Attorney Penney came in first; they were followed by Motka, the girl from Big Maud's, and another officer Czolgosz had seen before named Savin—he always seemed to be smoking a cigarette. Taking her gently by the upper arm, Savin guided Motka into the chair across the table from Czolgosz.

"I believe you two know each other?" he said, sitting at one end, while Penney sat at the other end. Chief Bull, as he usually did, remained standing; he went to the windows and stared out, his hands clasped behind his back.

"You recognize this man?" Penney said to Motka.

She stared at Czolgosz, frightened. Her hands were shaking. She was wearing a green dress beneath a long black wool coat with frayed cuffs. Her presence made both Geary and Solomon seem alert. Geary was particularly affected, and he stole fleeting glances, as though he feared being caught.

Czolgosz turned to Penney. "Even if she does, it doesn't mean anything. She works in a whorehouse. Many men know her."

"And we know you have accomplices," Penney said. He nodded toward the other man at the table. "Captain Savin here suspects that she assisted you."

"I told you—no accomplices," Czolgosz said. He turned toward the windows and said, "So you make one up." Chief Bull didn't answer and continued to stare out at the rain.

"But, Leon," Savin said. He was studying the long ash that had developed on his cigarette. "She has met with you, recently." Savin considered Motka a moment. "Tell me, what was the nature of these meetings?"

"Nature?" she asked. "I do not understand this very well."

Savin appeared satisfied as his finger tapped the cigarette, causing the ash drop to the hardwood floor. "You entertain men in a bordello." She only stared at him.

"That doesn't make her an accomplice," Czolgosz said.

"How many times?" Savin said. "How many times did he visit you?" She shook her head. "Did he use his name, Leon Czolgosz? Or perhaps Fred Nieman?" He took a drag on his cigarette. "And what did you do during these meetings, besides . . . entertain?"

"I saw her a few times," Czolgosz said.

"Saw her?" Savin said. "You first went there with a man named Moses Hyde."

Czolgosz looked at Motka, but she shook her head.

Savin continued. "But you went there on your own as well, according to Big Maud. Isn't that so?" He leaned toward her. "How exactly did you assist him? Perhaps you are in contact with other anarchists? I'm sure they frequent establishments such as Big Maud's. What services—other than the customary forms of entertainment—do you provide?" When he realized she didn't understand, or was pretending not to understand, he said impatiently, "What did you *do* when he visited you at Big Maud's?"

Motka glanced at Czolgosz as if to say that she could not hold out any longer, and then turning to Savin, she said, "Read."

"*Read?*" Savin said. "Read *what*?"

"English. He teaches me to read better English."

At the window, Chief Bull cleared his throat. "That's true." Everyone turned toward him, though he still continued to stare out at the rain. "It's consistent with what he told one of the alienists."

Seemingly disappointed, Savin dropped his cigarette butt on the floor and crushed it out with his shoe. There was only the sound of the rain against the windows. "I have learned something interesting, Leon," Savin said, finally, without looking up from the floor. "We found Motka's brother, Anton, on a barge in the canal—same barge as where a whore named Clementine was killed. You know what a marlin spike is, Leon?"

"A tool. For splicing rope."

"Exactly. Someone drove a marlin spike into Anton's skull."

Czolgosz watched Motka, who stared straight ahead, her mouth trembling now.

Savin got up, his chair legs scraping loudly on the floor. "He was an accomplice, too?"

"No," Czolgosz said. "I don't know the man."

"You do," Savin said. "You were assisted by both of them, and by Klaus Bruener, who owns the barge. And perhaps his son, Josef, too." Savin placed both hands on the table and leaned down toward Czolgosz. "And a man from Chicago. Herman Gimmel—a man we know has worked closely with Emma Goldman. They all helped you, didn't they, Leon?"

There was no point in answering and Czolgosz looked away.

Savin straightened up and said, "But something went wrong because her brother was killed."

The tears streamed from Motka's eyes. Savin walked toward the door, which Solomon opened for him. When the door was closed behind Savin, everyone in the room was silent, until Penney said, "So what do we do with her?"

"I understand Savin purchased her," Chief Bull said without looking away from the window. "It's really up to him. Take her back to her cell."

~✑~

THE president's funeral took place Thursday, in Canton. McKinley's hearse was followed by a parade that included eight thousand of Ohio's militia, along with members of the Masonic orders, Knights Templar, Odd Fellows, and the Grand Army of the Republic. President Roosevelt had declared that it would be a national day of mourning, and at the moment that the coffin was lowered into the ground in West Lawn Cemetery there was a five-minute period of silence throughout the country; telephone service was suspended and factories shut down their machinery as millions of Americans stood with bowed heads.

That night Mrs. McKinley took her dinner in her bedroom. The evening was cool but Dr. Rixey sat alone on the porch and smoked a cigar as the light faded in the western sky. He was distinctly aware of not being on the East Coast, where he had spent much of his life. The horizon in Ohio in some way reminded him of when he had been at sea, and how the sun would set on that hard blue edge of ocean.

A carriage pulled up in front of the house. As a man in a black wool overcoat got out and came up the front walk, Rixey went to the top of the steps. The man was slightly older, perhaps sixty, and his graying beard was trimmed into a pointed goatee. He removed his hat.

"Dr. Rixey, I'm Leonard Cousins, with the State Department. You may not recall, but we have met at several functions in Washington."

"Yes, of course," Rixey said. He didn't remember the man. "Are you here to see Mrs. McKinley? Because I'm afraid she has retired for the evening."

"No, Doctor, I came to discuss a matter with you, if you have the time?"

"Certainly." Rixey indicated that they could sit at the far end of the porch. It was nearly dark and lamps from the living-room windows cast soft oblongs of light across the floor. Rixey took a chair with his back to the house so he could see Cousins's face in the light. "Cigar, Mr. Cousins?"

"No, thank you, Doctor."

"If you'd like, I can have someone prepare you something to drink."

"No, really, I'm fine." Cousins leaned forward slightly. "Doctor, I've been sent out to Illinois, and on the way it was requested that I stop and see you."

"By whom?"

The question seemed to perturb Cousins. "Well, the

government—people in the State Department. They—we understand how difficult all this has been for you, and, well, we want you to know that your efforts are not unappreciated."

"Thank you, Mr. Cousins. You're very kind to deliver such a sentiment in person."

"The physicians who cared for the president will be compensated, of course," Cousins said. "There is a plan to submit to Congress a bill that would allow appropriate remuneration for their services."

"That is all well and good," Rixey said. "Many of the other doctors traveled great distances to be in Buffalo, and certainly they had to cancel other appointments and obligations. But there's no need for me to be a part of that—I already receive a sufficient stipend as personal physician to the McKinleys. So I really must insist—"

"If you don't mind my saying so, your duties recently went well beyond any normal—"

"Well I do insist. I was only doing my duty."

"Yes, we assumed that you would feel that way," Cousins said. He tugged on the point of his beard. "So, Doctor, we were wondering if—well, I don't quite know how to put this, really— but we were wondering if we might not provide you with a unique opportunity. As a means of showing our appreciation, that is."

"It's really not necessary, but thank you."

Rixey almost expected Cousins to get up and make his departure. Instead, he leaned forward until he was on the edge of his seat. He glanced toward the house, as though to make sure no one might be near the windows listening. "Doctor, I've never had to convey such a thing to anyone before, and it's rather delicate. I just hope that what I'm about to say is taken in the spirit that it's offered."

"Of course, Mr. Cousins."

"In the morning I'm continuing by train on to Chicago,

where I have some business to conduct, and then I will go down to Springfield, Illinois," Cousins said. His voice now dropped to a whisper and it was quite formal, as though he were making a statement for the record. "I'm going there because next week the coffin of President Lincoln is going to be moved to what we anticipate to be his final resting place." He paused as though to give Rixey the time to appreciate the significance of such an event. "At that time, the president's casket will be opened briefly and the remains viewed by a select few. We would like to offer you the opportunity to be a member of that party, if you wish."

Rixey took the cigar from his mouth and whispered, "My God."

Cousins sat back in his chair. "We thought the only appropriate way to make such an offer was by doing so in person."

"My God," Rixey said again. Then he crushed out his cigar in the ashtray on the table next to his chair. "I had no idea that this . . ."

Out in the street the carriage horse shook its head, causing its harness to jingle.

Rixey got to his feet, and Cousins did also. "I . . ." Rixey wasn't sure he could go on, but then he cleared his throat and said, "Mr. Cousins, I appreciate your stopping on your journey to speak with me personally, but I must decline."

Cousins now seemed annoyed, even insulted. "We merely thought it was the rarest of opportunities. They asked me to come here on my way to Chicago."

"Don't you understand? I just buried one president, a man I deeply, deeply revered. To go off to look upon the face of—it's unconscionable."

"Well, then, I'll be on my way. I'll tell them that you were otherwise engaged—"

"Mr. Cousins, you can tell them it's unconscionable."

Cousins gazed at him a moment, then put on his hat, and with a nod of the head he walked down the porch to the stairs.

Rixey went to the railing and watched the man climb into his carriage, which then moved down the street, the horse's hooves clopping loudly in the evening air. Suddenly it overcame him—as though the events of the past few weeks had finally reached him all at once. Leaning over, he placed both hands on the railing and sobbed uncontrollably, but as quietly as possible so as not to disturb anyone in the house.

~ɔϲ~

HYDE spent a couple of days on the canal, asking if anyone had seen Klaus Bruener or his son, Josef. Most canawlers had heard about the police raid on the *Glockenspiel* and the man found killed with a marlin spike. But fear brings reticence. Nobody had much to say because they'd all heard what happened to that fake limey huckster. Quimby had been found hanging from a warehouse rafter, a one-way train ticket to Denver in his pocket, and the head of seagull stuffed in his mouth.

~ɔϲ~

BY the angle of the sun, Norris figured that the milk wagon was headed east. On the third night when they stopped he heard the sound of chickens, a dog barking. Gimmel opened the wagon door and Norris could see across a barnyard to a clapboard farmhouse. A woman stood on the porch, with her teenage daughter and two small children, as a man in denim overalls and a straw hat walked toward the wagon. Gimmel and Bruener climbed out. They spoke with the man, while the chickens pecked at the dirt around them.

When Bruener came back to the wagon, he said to the milk-man, "Okay, Tuck, put it in the barn."

Norris was taken out and tied to a post in a horse stall. Feeney was placed in the next stall. One of the children, a boy with a blond cowlick, climbed up on the gate and looked down at Norris.

"Mister, why're your hands tied up?"

"Why do you think?"

"You're a criminal, wanted by the law."

"I am the law," Norris said.

The boy was unprepared for this, but then he announced, "My pa says the law is for rich men like J. P. Morgan and they all should be skinned alive for what they done to this country. He said you work for Teddy Roosevelt."

"That's true. He's my cousin." The boy was awestruck. "And that fellow there in the next stall? He's Teddy's nephew."

The boy jumped off the gate and ran out of the barn. Within minutes Norris fell asleep to the sound of mourning doves cooing in the rafters.

It was dark when he was untied from the post and brought out of the stall. There was a plank laid across two barrels and they sat on hay bales while the woman and her daughter served them a chicken dinner with yams and peas. The women couldn't have been much more than thirty but she'd already lost most of her teeth. The girl had long blond hair that hadn't yet gone stringy, and Josef kept stealing glances at her while she moved about the men.

Gimmel hardly ate and he kept a whiskey bottle in front of him, which he shared with Bruener and Tuck.

"How'd you come to being a Pinkerton?" Tuck had a handlebar mustache that he kept teasing out with his fingers, which were greasy from the chicken.

"My parents died when our house in Wisconsin burned

down," Norris said, "and I was sent out to live with an aunt and uncle who had a farm in Lone Tree, south of Iowa City. One day my uncle Lute comes back from a business trip to Omaha and says his train was robbed. He'd lost a lot of money and the family nearly lost the farm that year. I was about fifteen but I was already bigger'n you. I asked Lute who robbed the train, and he sort of laughs, and says, 'Train robbers,' like I'm some idiot. 'They wear masks, you know, bandannas so you can't see their faces, and they carry guns.' Then I heard about these men called the Pinkertons in Chicago. There had been so many train robberies that the railroad hired these Pinkertons to ride on some trains—guns, horses, and all—and if robbers stopped the train, well, didn't *they* get a surprise? So when I was eighteen I took a train to Chicago, found the office of these Pinkertons, and I talked them into letting me ride on those trains out west. I was a big strong farm boy and I was good with a gun."

Tuck twisted the end of his mustache. "You've killed train robbers?"

"Killed me a bunch of people. But I started out with two train robbers. Shot both right smack in the center of the forehead. One kind of looked like he just went to sleep, and the other got this look of surprise in his eyes. Sort of like 'I ain't thought this whole enterprise through and *now* look at me!'"

All the other men laughed, except Gimmel.

⁓

SEVERAL times Czolgosz was brought to meet with his lawyers, Lewis and Titus, in Chief Bull's office. Other than the fact that one's beard was white and the other's black, Czolgosz found them indistinguishable and he ignored their attempts to speak with him. It was clear that neither man wanted to take the case.

Saturday afternoon a man arrived and looked through the cell-door window. "Leon, my name is Dr. Carlos MacDonald." The man's face was broad, his blue eyes friendly and sincere. His white beard was flawlessly trimmed. "I am a professor of mental diseases and medical jurisprudence at Bellevue Hospital Medical College in New York City."

"You're an alienist." Czolgosz was sitting on his cot. "I've seen plenty of them."

One of the guards opened the cell door. MacDonald stepped inside and sat on the stool, his knees almost touching the cot. The alienist was wearing cologne.

This doctor's eyes suggested that he was capable of understanding things that the others didn't want to hear about. "If we're going to talk," Czolgosz said, "I want to talk to you alone."

MacDonald appeared gratified. "I think that would be fine, Leon." He said to the guards, "We would like to be alone." He waited until they moved down the corridor and sat at a table where they ate their meals. Then he turned back to Czolgosz and said, "That's better."

"You came all the way from New York City?"

"Yes."

"Why?"

"Because I'm interested in your case," MacDonald said. "For some time I have been interested in the legal definition of insanity and how it influences cases such as yours. I've been involved with other assassins, Leon. Are you familiar with the name Guiteau?"

"I know he killed President Garfield."

"Yes, twenty years ago. Guiteau was a lawyer of sorts, and he defended himself, with the help of his brother-in-law. In court the case got bogged down in absurd questions of protocol. The question of Guiteau's sanity was raised."

"I don't have a brother-in-law to represent me."

MacDonald smiled. "You have a sense of humor."

"Does that mean I'm sane?"

"It might—I need to know more about you." MacDonald placed his hands on his knees. "I'm told that you have a good appetite, though lately you've hardly eaten. You're Catholic, but you've given up the faith. You like a cigar—"

"Will you give me a cigar?"

"I can't—I don't have any with me," MacDonald said. "I understand that you smoke them daily, and that you drink, but only in moderation." He paused and stared at Czolgosz. He would not look away—so many people did when they stared into Czolgosz's eyes. Once someone told him that his eyes made them uncomfortable because they were too honest. But this alienist looked right back at him. He said, "Do you have intercourse with women?"

"Does that matter in a murder trial?"

"Everything matters, to me," MacDonald said.

"I have had intercourse with women, yes."

"Is there any one woman that you feel particularly attracted to?"

"What do you mean, sexually?"

"Are you in love with any woman?"

"In love?"

"There have been newspaper stories about a woman who jilted you."

"Absolutely not true."

"Some reporters say you married a woman in West Virginia."

"Never even been there. Newspapermen make these things up. You know that."

"Do you realize that you're a hero to some people—miners, farmers, factory workers, folks like that?"

"They are workers. They understand what I did."

"I believe that's so," the doctor said. "Do you masturbate or participate in any other unnatural practices?"

Czolgosz thought about this for a moment. "If a man does something, how can it be 'unnatural'?"

"I suppose you could look at it that way. You can read and write, quite well, I understand, in English and in Polish."

"True," Czolgosz said. "That must mean I'm sane."

MacDonald stroked his beard a moment. "To be sane, in my opinion, Leon, is more than knowing right from wrong—and this is where I differ with many of my colleagues. I believe that a sane person also has the ability to *choose* the right and *avoid* the wrong. Do you see the distinction?"

"Sure."

"Why did you shoot the president?"

"Is it necessary for you to ask that question?"

MacDonald lowered his hand and rested it on his knee. His fingers were thick and he had very long, well-manicured nails. "I'd like to hear your reason."

"I thought it would be clear to someone like you."

"Perhaps I'm wrong," MacDonald said. "I'd rather hear it straight from you."

Czolgosz leaned forward on the cot and spoke very quietly. "McKinley was always talking about prosperity when there was no prosperity for the poor man." He cleared his throat. "I am not afraid to die. We all have to die sometime."

"Did you act alone?"

"Yes." Czolgosz rested his back against the wall again.

"This is what I find interesting," MacDonald said. "Your refusal to acknowledge your co-conspirators, other anarchists."

"There aren't any co-conspirators. There are plenty of anarchists."

"I think you might be delusional—but it is a political delusion. Because if you are insane, then all anarchists are insane, and I don't believe that. This is what makes you so interesting. You're perfectly rational. People like you will be a great threat in the future."

"You are right to be concerned about the future," Czolgosz said. "You make the future that you get."

For the first time MacDonald seemed baffled, and perhaps even slightly angry.

"I still don't understand why you asked whether I've had intercourse with women."

"It's worth knowing." MacDonald seemed to have come to a decision and he looked grim, determined. "Monday you go on trial—the authorities want to move very quickly. If you are convicted of first-degree murder, do you know what will happen to you?"

"I'll get the chair. I'd rather hang. I don't have a choice?"

"No."

"John Wilkes Booth. They hung him."

"That was almost forty years ago. A dozen years ago New York State began to use the chair, when they electrocuted William Kemmler."

"You know that for a fact?"

"I was there."

"Really? What did he do?"

"Killed the woman he lived with."

"Do you suppose he had intercourse with her?"

"Seems she was a terrible nag. He used an ax."

"Are you saying she deserved it?"

"I'm saying the man broke the law. Leon, I didn't really come to talk about this—electrocution. We can talk about something else."

"No. I find it interesting."

"All right. They have improved the procedure since Kemmler."

"How do you mean?"

"They should only have to do it once now—throw the switch."

"How many times did they throw it for Kemmler?"

"Twice," MacDonald said. "The facilities were very crude, very insufficient then. The equipment—there were no useful gauges, no ammeter or voltmeter."

"They strapped him in a chair."

"Yes, a special chair, and he was very obliging, making sure as much of his body was in contact with the chair as possible. Then they ran fifteen hundred volts of alternating current through him for ten seconds. And then—"

"What did he look like?"

"Well, his body went into spasm. Rigid spasm." MacDonald tugged at an earlobe for a moment as he stared down at the floor. "He developed bruises on his face, and the skin on his fingers split open and bled. There were blisters. But his heart was still beating, so they threw the switch again." He raised his head and there was a kindness in his eyes. "My colleague, Dr. Spitzka, was horrified. He argued that the state should use the guillotine for such situations, but I disagreed. There were certain defects of a minor character that needed to be eliminated. Significant improvements have been made."

"Improvements? Meaning the switch will only have to be thrown once."

"That's right, Leon. More voltage for a longer duration."

"You'll be there?"

"Would that be all right with you?" MacDonald asked.

"Yes. I'd like that."

"All right then."

They didn't speak for a while, and Czolgosz thought that the session was over, but then MacDonald looked troubled as he scratched the back of his head. "Who have you had sex with last, if you don't mind my asking?"

"No, I don't mind."

"Was it recent?"

"Fairly. It was here, in Buffalo. It was with a prostitute who called herself Motka." Czolgosz hesitated—somehow that wasn't enough. "I was going—you see, I was going to help her to learn how to read English."

MacDonald appeared not to comprehend what he was saying. "You were teaching her to read?" Czolgosz nodded, and

MacDonald seemed to collect himself; he placed his hands on his knees, leaned forward, and got up off the stool. "It's interesting that you can perform such a compassionate act, and then shoot the president."

"I know," Czolgosz said. "It's insane, really."

~ɔꞔ~

"YOU know what they're going to do?" Feeney whispered.

Norris could see through a gap in the boards into the next stall. Feeney was lying on his side on a bed of straw. He was facing the stall gate and his bound hands were tied to the post.

"We're waiting—waiting for something, but I don't know what."

Feeney tried to look over his shoulder toward Norris, but he could only manage to stare straight up. Straw clung to his clothes, his hair. "That crate he sits on, all that dynamite, he's going to set it off."

"They left the barge because it was no longer safe," Norris said. "Where are we?"

"Well east of Buffalo. I figure we could be on any farm between Rochester and Syracuse. I don't understand why we don't keep moving."

"Me neither."

"Gimmel must be planning to blow something up."

"But what's out here, cows and crops?"

"It's gonna happened soon." Feeney's voice was adamant and tight with fear. "I can feel it. And we're going up with it."

In the evening the wife and daughter brought a pot of soup and bread out to the barn. Norris and Feeney were untied and allowed to sit at the makeshift table to eat, and then they were put back in their stalls but not immediately tied to a post. A bucket had been placed in each stall, and while Feeney used his, he whispered, "I got me something, something sharp. A piece of a file they use on hooves."

"Wait till they start drinking."

After dark Gimmel, Bruener, and Tuck, as always, got into the whiskey. The light from their lantern cast long shadows up into the rafters. They spoke mostly in German, getting louder as the evening wore on. Horses stirred in their stalls. Norris could hear Feeney slowly sawing away at the rope that bound his wrists. Then there came another sound, somewhere from behind the barn. At first Norris thought it was an animal rubbing itself against a post, but then he heard a suppressed sigh.

Feeney paused in his sawing and whispered, "What's that?"

"It's that girl and Josef," Norris said. She was about seventeen, a few years younger that Josef. "You could see her making eyes at him while she ladled out the soup. Get it while she's still got all her teeth."

At the front of the barn Tuck began playing a mouth harp, and Bruener slapped his thighs in time. Feeney started working again.

"How you doing?"

"Nearly there."

Straw crackled beneath Feeney as he sawed the rope, and then he suddenly stopped. He crawled over to the wall that separated their stalls and he slid the file through a gap in the boards.

Norris's hands were bound tight to the gatepost. "I can't reach it."

He could see through the gap in the wall as Feeney got to his knees and lifted the latch. Slowly he opened the gate just wide enough for him to slip out on his hands and knees. He crawled to the outside of Norris's gate. "I could cut it from this side." He looked toward the front of the barn, and then began sawing at the rope that bound Norris to the gatepost. The lantern at the front of the barn cast flickering shadows, and intermittently Norris could see the rusty file and Feeney's hands, which were covered in blood. From behind the barn Josef and the girl were both gasping as though they were running. They grunted and whimpered, louder and faster. The animals in nearby stalls were becoming agitated, their hooves knocking on the hard dirt floor. A mule brayed. The girl cried out as though in agonizing pain. Bruener, dancing a jig, sang in German—something about a fräulein. Feeney kept working at the rope, until it suddenly broke away from the gatepost. Norris quickly freed his wrists, which were raw with rope burns.

He opened the gate and crawled out of the stall, following Feeney toward the back of the barn. When they reached the open door they lay still on the ground, looking out on a cow pasture under a starry sky. The air was cool and rich with the smell of manure. Josef and the girl were quiet now. As Norris's eyes adjusted to the dark, he saw them leaning up against the side of a shed. The girl's skirts were raised, revealing a long pale leg that entwined Josef's haunch. She turned her head toward the barn, and then she screamed.

Norris and Feeney got to their feet. Turning to their right, away from the shed, they began to run, but then stopped when they saw what had startled the girl: Gimmel stood at the corner of the barn, holding a pistol at his side. He took aim, and Norris and Feeney stopped and raised their hands. There were running footsteps in the barn, and Bruener and Tuck came outside, the lantern swinging. Cows in the pasture were frightened and they lumbered away into the safety of the dark.

Norris looked at Gimmel. "You were watching them," he said, curious. "Just like when he was in the shed by the canal with Clementine."

Bruener went up to Feeney and took hold of one of his bloody hands, forcing him to drop the rusty file. Bruener pulled a knife from the sheath on his belt and quickly drew the blade across Feeney's throat. Feeney gasped as he fell to his knees. For a long moment he seemed to be confused as blood flowed down his throat and soaked the front of his shirt. A burbling sound issued from his mouth, his nose, and then he fell forward in the dirt.

Bruener went over to Norris, raising his knife, but Gimmel said, "No."

So Bruener wiped the bloody blade on the thigh of his pants and slid it back in its sheath as he walked over to the shed, where Josef now stood next to the girl. Bruener slapped the boy's face hard, and then shoved him toward the barn. The girl fainted, her back sliding down the shed wall until she was squatting on the ground, her skirt hiked up over her white shins, her bony knees.

~⌒~

MONDAY morning Czolgosz was handcuffed to Geary and Solomon as they took him through the Tunnel of Tears to city hall. On the second floor they were confronted by an angry crowd— larger than the day of his arraignment. The police had formed a cordon and Czolgosz was hustled into the courtroom and then the doors were slammed shut. Inside, several hundred people shifted about for a better view of him as he was brought to one of two long tables in front of the judge's bench. His handcuffs were removed, this time without difficulty, and he sat between Solomon and Geary. His lawyers, Titus and Lewis, were seated at the far end of the table; neither looked in his direction. District Attorney Penney and several other men were gathered at the other table—some of them were the alienists who had examined Czolgosz, but he only remembered the name of one, Dr. MacDonald. To one side of the judge's bench, there was a group of about fifty men seated in rows that allowed them a clear view of the proceedings. Most of them were scribbling in notebooks, which created a scratching sound that reminded Czolgosz of mice trapped in a wall.

When Judge Truman White entered the room from a door behind the bench, everyone stood up. After the judge took his seat, they all sat down, and he said, "Mr. District Attorney, have you any business for the court?"

Penney stood up and said, "I desire to arraign the prisoner Leon F. Czolgosz, Your Honor. Mr. Czolgosz, you have been indicted on the charge of murder in the first degree, committed on the sixth day of September of this year, in that you unlawfully killed one William McKinley, contrary to law. How do you plead?"

Judge White looked at Czolgosz for the first time. He appeared curious, and Czolgosz suddenly felt the urge to speak to him. He leaned forward slightly, but his attorney Lewis got to his feet and said, "If the court please, we desire—"

The judge said, "I think the prisoner was about to speak. Czolgosz, did you understand what the district attorney said to you?"

"I didn't hear it," Czolgosz said.

Penney seemed agitated. He said loudly, "You are indicted and charged with having committed the *crime* of murder in the first *degree*. It is al*leged* that you on the sixth day of September of this year unlawfully *shot* and *killed* William McKinley, contrary to *law*. How do you *plead*?"

Czolgosz said, "Guilty."

Angry voices echoed through the courtroom and Judge White pounded his gavel until there was order again. Then he said, "That plea cannot be accepted in this court. The clerk will enter a plea of 'not guilty' and we will proceed with the trial."

Czolgosz leaned back in his chair.

They proceeded to select a jury. The first man questioned was a sixty-year-old plumber. There were also farmers, a man who sold butter and eggs, a blacksmith. All of them were asked questions about their opinion of the case, about their employment and family life, about their views of insanity, and about capital punishment. Some people were accepted by both sets of attorneys, while others were not, and the process of selection was tedious, yet conducted with efficiency.

Czolgosz paid little attention. He stared at the floor. He watched the newspaper reporters as they diligently took notes. He studied the judge's hands. They were pale, the fingers thin. There were no nicks, cuts, bruises, or calluses. They were the hands of an old man who did no manual labor. When the judge realized that Czolgosz was staring at his hands, he pulled them inside the loose sleeves of his robe.

Czolgosz had admitted his guilt. There was no reason for all these people to be in this courtroom. They were accomplishing nothing. Yet the lawyers droned on, and he was reminded of sermons given by priests during mass. As a boy he would drift off as soon as the priest stepped up to the pulpit. In those days he had pleasant reveries involving hunting and fishing, but now he couldn't conjure such images, so he merely stared at the floor and concentrated on the sound of the rain against the windows.

Occasionally he heard people behind him whispering, and he realized that they were surprised by how tranquil he was— and when they said this, there was disappointment in their voices. They wanted a madman, a raging lunatic, disrupting the proceedings and spewing anarchist slogans. But he wasn't like that at all, and this had a sobering effect on the audience in the courtroom. One voice—a woman's—whispered, "He's so quiet and detached, and his face is so youthful. Perhaps they have the wrong man?"

After lunch recess the jury selection was concluded and the prosecution began its case. A series of witnesses established the facts of the shooting. A large sketch and several photographs of the floor plan of the Temple of Music were used to establish the location of the crime. Most of the time Czolgosz stared at the floor until a Dr. Mann was called to testify. The doctor was small, tidy, and arrogant. His responses were abrupt, as though the questions put to him were an impertinence he shouldn't have to suffer. There was a great deal of discussion about gangrene, which he claimed was caused by germs and pancreatic fluid. At one point, the doctor said, "The president probably was not in very good physical condition. He was somewhat weakened by hard work, want of exercise, and conditions of that kind."

He and District Attorney Penney discussed whether the bullet had actually struck the pancreas. Mann didn't think it had, but serious damage had been caused by concussion to the organ as the bullet passed through the stomach. During this point in the testimony, Czolgosz realized he was sweating and he wiped his face with a handkerchief. He did this quickly, not wanting to give the impression that he was disturbed by the graphic details of the president's wounds. And then he realized that since being arrested he had not once really thought about the actual shooting; it was as though it had been erased from his mind—he knew he did it, he knew why he was being held, but the event itself seemed to have disappeared from his memory. But now he saw it all again, particularly the first shot, the hole in the president's starched white shirtfront. That bullet, Czolgosz realized now, was not the one that had done any damage; it was the second bullet—striking the president lower in his enormous stomach—that killed him. Czolgosz felt like he had somehow drifted out of his own body, if only momentarily, and he could see himself standing before William McKinley, his arm extended and the .32-caliber Iver Johnson wrapped in a handkerchief. It was not a big pistol—it fit easily into his hand—and he wondered if such a small weapon was sufficient to kill such a large man. Too, he saw the president's eyes: during that brief moment between the first and second shot, McKinley's eyes became startled and alert. He didn't seem to be in pain so much as surprised. And again, Czolgosz knew—he was absolutely certain now—that there was a moment when something in the president's expression was sincere, even grateful.

Penney and this Dr. Mann talked about the second bullet at great length, and never once could the doctor state the obvious: it had killed the president. Czolgosz wanted to stand up then. He wanted to get to his feet and shout at them, tell them all how absurd this was—he had shot the president, the second bullet entered his stomach, and a week later the man died. What more did these people want?

~ↄᴄ~

HYDE sat at the table in the Three Brothers Café where he had first met Norris. As he read about the first day of the trial, he held the newspaper so that he could occasionally glance out the window at the man leaning against the lamppost in front of the apothecary. Hyde had first noticed him outside a saloon on the canal the day before; he wore the clothes of a canawler but he'd never spent a day walking behind a mule team. It was the way he watched everything, as though he'd never seen it before; it was the patches on his coat, which were too recently stitched; most of all, it was his hands, pale and soft. Now he watched the morning commerce on Market Street and never once appeared to look directly at the café.

Hyde finished his coffee, folded up his newspaper, and tucked it under his arm. He went outside and crossed the street, waiting for a wagon laden with barrels to pass. When the man saw that Hyde was headed straight for him, he took his weight off the lamppost and began to walk away.

"I know you've been following me," Hyde said. "Savin sent you, right?"

The man kept walking. He was younger than Hyde, in his early twenties, and his neck was marred with acne.

"You listen to me," Hyde said, taking hold of his forearm. The man turned and looked at him, indignant. "You've got to go to Savin and tell him I think I know where Gimmel has taken the Pinkertons." The man looked about, pretending to be confused. "We don't have *time* for this," Hyde said, pulling him closer. "You been tailing me for at least a day, but now you have to get word to Savin. They'll never let me through the police surrounding headquarters—you know that."

The man yanked his arm free and brushed his sleeve as though it had been soiled.

"Look, it's here in the newspaper," Hyde said, shoving his folded copy of the *Courier* in the man's hands. "You tell Savin the last thing Anton said before he died was 'Auburn.' " He tapped the front page of the paper with his finger. "I thought he was say-ing something in Russian, but it's right there, in that piece about the Czolgosz trial."

Reluctantly, the man looked down at the paper. "What is?"

"Auburn," Hyde said. "It says that the Czolgosz trial will be swift—it might even be over today—and that he will be taken to the prison in Auburn because that's where they have one of these electric chairs. Do you understand? It's pointless for you to follow me. You need to let Savin know that Gimmel's taken them to Auburn."

"Herman Gimmel?"

"That's better—you've heard of him," Hyde said. "You know, you're not bad. I bet you been following me for days. What's your name?"

The man now looked uncertain. His mouth was small and tight, and there was something off-kilter about his jaw. "Thorpe. Jeb Thorpe."

"Well, Jeb Thorpe, I don't know what rank you are in the police but if you want a promotion you need to tell Savin I'm going to Auburn, and he needs to get there as quickly as possible."

Thorpe's posture stiffened and his eyes looked doubtful.

"All right, follow me, if you want. Come with me to Auburn, but first call Savin and tell him where we're going."

"Call him?" Thorpe said.

"Yes, let's do that," Hyde said. "Do you realize I've never used a telephone—never. You make the call and let me talk to him."

Thorpe looked down at the newspaper in his hand again. "Why would they take the Pinkertons to Auburn?"

"They have explosives."

Thorpe's jaw went slack. "I'll bet they have a telephone over at that apothecary."

They went inside the apothecary, which had a creaking hardwood floor and rows of shelves stocked with medical supplies. Hyde waited in an aisle full of elixirs as Thorpe went up to the counter at the back of the store. A stout man in a white smock looked skeptical as Thorpe produced his wallet with his badge. They spoke for a moment, and then went to the end of the counter, where there was a telephone box on the wall. Thorpe took the receiver off the hook, turned the crank on the side of the box, and spoke into the black cone that was attached to the box. Hyde worked his way down the aisle, watching Thorpe. Your voice goes into the box, then along a thin wire that's suspended from poles above the streets, until it reaches another telephone, perhaps miles away. Yet Thorpe was speaking softly. After a minute, he turned and nodded to Hyde, offering the receiver. "I've got Savin on the line," he said.

Hyde went over and took the receiver; it was heavier than he expected. He leaned toward the telephone, until his mouth nearly touched the cone, and said, "*Savin, you there?*" The man in the smock looked at Thorpe, alarmed.

"No need to shout, Hyde," Savin said. His voice seemed to be squeezed out of the receiver. "I can hear you fine."

"Well, I can hear you, too."

"That's better. So you've met Thorpe and now you want to tell me something?"

"Auburn, Gimmel's taken them to Auburn. That's what Motka's brother was trying to tell me before he died. Czolgosz will be taken there, and that's where your Pinkertons will be. Gimmel's got a lot of dynamite."

"I see."

"I'm going there."

"Yes, all right," Savin said. "Tell Thorpe I want him back here at headquarters."

Hyde cleared his throat. "What about Motka?"

"What about her?"

"Is she all right?"

"She comfortable enough."

"What do you mean 'enough'?"

Savin didn't answer immediately and for a moment Hyde wondered if they'd been cut off. But then Savin said, "I mean she's in a cell by herself and she's being properly fed. She's not getting fucked all day long."

"When will you let her go?"

"That's a good question, Hyde. Keep in mind that I bought her. I own her. Right now you get to the train station. I'll meet you there."

"You don't own her, Savin."

"I paid for her. I got her out of Big Maud's." There was a pause until Savin said impatiently, "Hyde."

"What?"

"You can ring off now."

Hyde turned to Thorpe, who took the receiver away from his ear and hung it on the hook. "Alexander Graham Bell," Thorpe said, and then he grinned.

~つC~

THE second day of the trial the defense cross-examined Dr. Matthew Mann, and then several security guards were questioned about the shooting. Again, Czolgosz paid little attention, until one man named Gallaher was asked to produce the handkerchief that had concealed the weapon. The bullet holes and burn marks were clearly evident in the fabric, and the large audience stirred uncomfortably, as though the piece of cloth were itself a dangerous weapon.

Later another guard demonstrated the Iver Johnson revolver that had been used to shoot the president. Penney had a tendency to repeat the same question, as though the witness were holding back some important detail. There were no important details, and no one ever asked how it was possible that a man with a revolver in his hand and held against his chest in full view, merely wrapped in a handkerchief, could file past dozens of security personnel, approach the president of the United States, and fire two shots at close range.

Something else was missing from their stories, and Czolgosz didn't know what it was, until one of the guards was asked about a man named Parker. He was the Negro who had been standing directly behind Czolgosz in the reception line, and the guard admitted that Parker was the first one to knock the gunman to the floor and keep him from taking more than two shots at the president. But the other witnesses would not even acknowledge that a Negro had been in that line—it seemed they had all agreed in advance to erase Parker from the events in the Temple of Music. The men responsible for the president's security, though they had failed miserably, had apparently agreed to alter their stories to make it appear that they, and they alone, had restrained the assassin. They were all testifying under oath, and they couldn't even be honest about this detail.

A man named James Quackenbush was called to the witness stand, and it was established that he had been present when Czolgosz confessed only hours after the shooting. Czolgosz vaguely remembered the man; he was not a member of the police force, apparently, but had something to do with organizing the Pan-American Exposition. Czolgosz thought it curious that Quackenbush, rather than a member of the Buffalo police, was the one who testified about the confession.

When Penney asked Quackenbush, "Can you recall anything

he said on the subject of why he killed the president?" Czolgosz turned his head toward the witness stand.

"He said he did not believe in government," Quackenbush said, "that he thought the president was a tyrant and should be removed. He said that the day before the shooting when he saw the president in the grounds that he thought that no one man should receive such services and all the others regard it as a privilege to stand by and render services. That is the substance, I think, not the words, although he used the word 'services.' He said he had for several years been studying the doctrines of anarchy, that he believed in no government, no marriage relation, and that he attended church for some time but they talked nonsense and he discontinued that."

"He said that, did he—that he did not believe in church or state?" Penney asked.

"Yes," Quackenbush said, "and that he did not believe in the marriage relation, that he believed in free love. He gave the names of several papers which he had read—Polish names which I cannot recall, four of them—and he mentioned one known as *Free Society*."

Penney asked, "He mentioned some places that he had been where he had heard these subjects discussed, didn't he?"

"Yes, places in Cleveland, Ohio," Quackenbush said. "He stated before he came to Buffalo he had been in Chicago. He said he had been influenced by the teaching of Emma Goldman."

Her name caused a murmur to erupt in the courtroom. The judge pounded his gavel, demanding quiet. Czolgosz looked at the floor. He understood then: this trial wasn't really about him; it was about Emma Goldman. They simply didn't believe that he could conceive of what he did on his own. He had told them that her ideas had influenced him, but that wasn't good enough. They needed to prove that Goldman had conspired with him to shoot the president—that it was her idea. All of her speeches, all of her

articles, all of the riots that her public appearances had caused—
they needed to believe that Emma Goldman was the root of the
problem, and that if they could get rid of her the entire anarchist
movement would be eradicated.

Czolgosz closed his eyes. He was suddenly light-headed, and
he felt himself sway in his chair.

What they would never know, what they would never understand, was that shooting the president had really been an act of
love.

At noon Judge White declared a recess until two o'clock.
Czolgosz, Geary, and Solomon returned to the prison across the
street, where they sat at the table down the corridor from the cell
and ate cold roast beef, potatoes, and carrots.

"Won't be long now," Geary said as he cut up the meat on
Czolgosz's plate. "Another hour or so."

"You ever seen a murder trial this quick?" Czolgosz asked.

Solomon shook his head. "Never."

"It's too long," Czolgosz said.

"You in some kind of hurry, Leon?" Solomon asked.

"They could take a year and they'd never understand it."

"That so?" Solomon said. "Well, this afternoon I'm sure
they'll get Chief Bull on the stand because he's been responsible
for holding you." He looked at Geary. "The old Bull's got to get his
time on the stand because you can see Savin is angling for a piece
of the limelight."

"He's after his job, he is," Geary said.

Solomon forked some potatoes into his mouth, and said to
Czolgosz, "Then maybe they'll put some of those alienists up
there to talk about whether or not you're sane."

"Why don't they put you on the stand?" Czolgosz asked. "Both
of you know how sane I am. And if you can, I'd like you to convince them to let me have a fork to eat with. I hate eating with a

spoon." He smiled, but the two detectives glanced warily at each other, and then resumed eating. "What?" he said.

"Leon?" Geary seemed embarrassed and he didn't look up from his plate. "I got to ask you. Quackenbush said you don't believe in marriage. You really believe in this free love business?"

"If somebody puts his hand on a Bible and says so, I guess it's got to be true."

"You practice it?" Solomon asked.

When he finished chewing a piece of roast beef, Czolgosz said, "The idea that it's 'free,' I suppose, isn't accurate. But that's what they call it."

"What do you mean?" Geary asked.

"I've never had a woman, you know, *free.*"

"You pay for it," Solomon said. "You go to a whorehouse and pay for it?"

Geary added, "Like with that little redhead they brung in yesterday?"

"You never been to a whorehouse?" Czolgosz asked.

Geary laid his fork down and held up both palms. "Whoa, there."

"Maybe you're married?" Czolgosz said. "I don't know, you've never mentioned a wife. If you got one, then you don't need to go whoring."

"Right," Solomon said. "We can get it anytime we want. But is there any law that says a married man can't enter a registered house of assignation?" Geary looked toward his partner uncertainly. "I been to brothels," Solomon said. "There's nothing free about it. But a few times it sure was worth it."

"Where *you* been?" Geary asked.

"You know there's dozens of places just off Market Street. I used to work that beat."

"They do it for *free*?" Geary asked.

"No, I always insisted on paying," Solomon said. "Don't want them to be able to take advantage, right? But being police, they would give me special treatment, if you know what I mean."

"You *dog*," Geary said.

Solomon nodded toward his partner. "You see, Geary's not only married, he goes to church every damn Sunday."

Ignoring Solomon, Geary said, "Leon, you never married then, never considered it?"

"No."

"Well," Solomon said, "a good whore can help you there."

"Maybe," Czolgosz said. He finished the last of his roast beef. When he raised his head, they were still both staring intently at him.

Solomon leaned forward and whispered, "Leon, you ever do it with Red Emma?"

He didn't answer.

Geary leaned forward, too. "She any *good*?"

He just stared back at them.

"I'll bet she'll take your peter in her mouth," Geary said. "All them radical women, they'll suck on it, right?"

Czolgosz put down his spoon.

Disappointed, Geary said, "He ain't gonna tell us nothing."

"Look at him," Solomon said. "You can see the killer in him now. He'd like as kill both of us if he had the means to do it. Why, if he had a fork he'd go right for your neck. It's that Red Emma, that's what it is. She turned this boy's head around."

"I'll go back to my cell now and rest a bit before the afternoon session." Czolgosz got up and walked down the corridor.

"They arrested her in Chicago," Geary said. "Penney tried his damnedest to get her extradited to New York, but they wouldn't budge, and now she's off scot-free."

"Too bad," Solomon said. "If they got her here, they could've tried the two of them together. Like the eight anarchists that were tried for the Haymarket bombing. You know I heard that when the death penalty was handed down one of the defendants was standing by a window, and he tied a little noose in the cord hanging from the shade, and that's how the crowd outside the courthouse learned the verdict."

"Leon," Geary said. "Come on back here. We're just having a little fun. Leon?"

Czolgosz stepped inside his cell and pulled the heavy door closed.

There was a delay at the start of the afternoon session while the lawyers gathered in the front of the room. Czolgosz couldn't hear what they were saying; several times one of them turned toward Dr. MacDonald and the other alienists, who were seated in the first rows behind the prosecution's table. Finally, the lawyers took their seats and Chief Bull was the first to take the stand. His testimony merely repeated what had been stated by previous witnesses. At one point the crowded courtroom became particularly quiet when Penney asked if the defendant believed in marriage.

Chief Bull said, "He did not believe in marriage. He was a free lover, and the Free Love Society—as I understand it—this was a Free Love Society."

After Bull's testimony, the prosecution rested its case. Czolgosz understood now what the conference at the beginning of the session had been about: the lawyers had decided not to call the alienists to the witness stand.

Lewis looked at Czolgosz and said, "Do you wish to take the stand and testify?"

Czolgosz shook his head.

Slowly, Lewis stood up. "If Your Honor please," he said, "the defense has no witnesses to call, so that the testimony is closed at the close of the testimony of the People. We are somewhat embarrassed, disappointed, in the People's testimony closing at this point. My associate and myself have not had very much consultation as to the course to be pursued, but from the slight conversation that we have had we are inclined to ask Your Honor to permit each of us, both of us, to make some remarks to the jury in summing up this case. They will be on my part very brief, and I presume so on the part of my associate."

Judge White nodded his consent. As Lewis began to speak Czolgosz looked at the clock on the wall. Lewis spoke for nearly half an hour, until his voice broke with emotion, and he said, "Now, gentlemen, I have said about all I care to say about this case. The president of the United States was a man for whom I had the very profoundest respect. I have watched his career from the time he entered Congress—it must be twenty or more years ago—until his last breath here in the city of Buffalo, and every act of the man, so far as I could judge, had been the act of one of the noblest men that God ever made. His policy—we care nothing about that so far as we may differ as to his policy, but his policy has always met with my profoundest admiration in every respect. I have known him not only as a statesman, but I have known him, through the public press and otherwise, as a citizen, a man of irreproachable character, a loving husband, a grand man in every aspect that you could conceive of, and his death has been the saddest blow to me that has occurred in many years." Lewis sat down, put his handkerchief to his face, and wept.

The other defense attorney, Titus, stood up and said, "If the court please, the remarks of my distinguished associate have so fully and completely covered the ground and so largely anticipated what I intended to present to the jury myself, that it seems entirely unnecessary for me to reiterate what has already been said upon this subject, and we, therefore, rest with the remarks made by Judge Lewis." Titus sat down but did not have the need of a handkerchief.

Then it was Penney's turn, and it was clear from the start that he would not be brief. Penney talked a great deal about Czolgosz's sanity, and at one point asked, "What evidence is there in this case that the man is not sane?" When he concluded, Czolgosz noted that seventeen minutes had passed.

Then Judge White stood up, and told the jury to do the same. Czolgosz hoped that the fact that the old judge was standing meant his comments would be brief. But he spoke for twenty-one minutes. As with the other speeches, there was praise for President McKinley, and considerable discussion of the relationship between sanity and guilt, and with justice as opposed to what he called "lynch law." When the judge finished, his voice was quivering, and he sat down with tears in his eyes.

Czolgosz thought that that was the end of it, but there was still some discussion between the lawyers and the judge concerning the fine points of the law regarding sanity until, finally, Judge White said to the jury, "You gentlemen may now retire with the officers."

The jury and the judge left the courtroom at 3:50. At first Czolgosz thought that he would be taken back to his cell, but Solomon and Geary made no move to leave. Everyone else remained in their seats. There was a commotion in the back of the courtroom and Czolgosz looked around: though every seat was taken, more people were filing through the doors and standing along the walls.

At 4:17 the tipstaff thumped the floor twice, Judge White returned to the bench, and then the jury filed back to their seats. The judge told Czolgosz to stand up, and he got to his feet. His lawyers remained seated.

The clerk called the names of each juror, and then asked, "Gentlemen of the jury, have you reached a verdict?"

The jury foreman stood up and said, "We have."

"How do you find?" the clerk asked.

A fly landed on Czolgosz's right cheek, which he brushed off with his hand.

The foreman unfolded a slip of paper and read, "Guilty of murder in the first degree as charged in the indictment."

The clerk asked, "So say you all?"

The twelve jurors said together, "We do."

There was silence for a moment, and then a din of voices burst out in the courtroom despite the rapping of the judge's gavel.

Czolgosz sat down. The trial had taken a little more than eight hours, and the jury had taken less than a half hour to reach its verdict.

~ↃC~

NORRIS couldn't tell how much time had passed. He was in a stall again, curled up on the hard cold ground, tied to the gatepost. His head throbbed and dried blood encrusted his mouth. He was certain his nose was broken. He could barely see out of his left eye. After Feeney's throat had been cut, they made Norris dig a hole out in the pasture and bury the body. This took a long time and Norris nearly collapsed from the work. It was first light when he was through, and then Gimmel beat him with the monkey fist.

~ↃC~

CZOLGOSZ was brought back into the courtroom at two o'clock on Thursday, and again the room was packed. Only Titus sat at the defense table with Czolgosz, Geary, and Solomon. Once court was in session, District Attorney Penney told Czolgosz to stand up. He hesitated, and then got to his feet. The clerk came over to him with the Bible, but he didn't put his hand on it. The clerk looked at Judge White, who nodded impatiently, and Czolgosz was sworn in without his hand being on the Bible.

Penney came out from behind the prosecution's table. He asked Czolgosz a series of questions—his age, where he was born, his last place of residence, his marital status. Czolgosz answered quietly, so much so that he was asked repeatedly to speak up. He would not. When they asked if he had a trade or was a laborer, he said he was a laborer. He grew weary of questions they already knew the answers to, and he had only one thing to say.

Penney asked, "Have you been convicted of any crime before this?"

"No, sir," Czolgosz said.

There was a pause, and for a moment it seemed no one knew what to do next, until the clerk said, "Have you any legal cause to show why sentence of the court should not now be pronounced against you?"

The courtroom resounded with murmurs, and Czolgosz said, "Can't hear that."

Judge White said loudly, "People in the room should remain absolutely quiet and those who are unwilling to do that until the proceeding here is terminated should retire from the room at this time."

The crowd fell silent, and the clerk said, "Have you any legal cause to show why sentence of the court should not now be pronounced against you?"

Czolgosz looked at District Attorney Penney and said, "I would rather have this gentleman speak, over here."

For a moment Penney seemed to appreciate the request, and then he said gently, "The clerk asks you if you have any legal cause to show why sentence should not now be pronounced against you. Do you understand?"

"No, sir."

"He wants to know if you have any reason to tell the court why you should not now be sentenced—say anything to the judge. Have you anything to say to the judge before sentence? Say yes or no, if you have."

"Yes," Czolgosz whispered.

"Make your statement, then."

Judge White leaned forward and asked, "Does he answer?"

Penney said, "He says, yes, he has something to say."

The judge said, "In that behalf, Czolgosz, what you have a right to say—"

Czolgosz said, "I want to say this much—"

"Wait a moment," the judge said.

Penney leaned toward Czolgosz and said, "Listen to the judge."

Judge White said, "The legal causes which the law provides that you may claim in exempting you from having judgment pronounced against you at this time are defined by statute. The first is that you may claim that you were insane. The next is that you have good cause to offer either in arrest of the judgment about to be pronounced against you or for a new trial. Those are the grounds specified by statute upon which you have the right to speak at this time, and you are at perfect liberty to do so freely."

Czolgosz whispered, "I have nothing to say about that."

Penney turned to the judge and said, "He says, 'I have nothing to say about that.'"

Judge White said to the district attorney, "Are you ready?"

"I am through, sir," Penney said.

The judge looked at Czolgosz. "Nothing to say?"

"I want to say something about my family."

Titus looked at the judge. "I think he ought to be permitted to make a statement in exculpation of his family, if the court will permit it."

"Yes," the judge said. "Proceed, Czolgosz."

"I would like to say this much," Czolgosz said, raising his head slightly, "that the crime was committed by no one else but me. No one told me to do it and I never told anybody to do it."

Titus said, "Your father and mother had nothing to do with it?"

"No, sir," Czolgosz said very quietly. These people didn't even know that his mother had died years ago. "Not only my father and mother, but there hasn't been anybody else had nothing to do with this."

Judge White looked at Titus. "What does he say?"

"He says no one had anything to do with the commission of this crime but himself, that his father or mother or no one else had anything to do with it." Titus turned to Czolgosz. "Did they know anything about it?"

"No, sir, they didn't know about it." Czolgosz spoke so quietly that Titus, who was standing next to him, had to lean closer to hear. "I never told anything of that kind—I never thought of that until a couple of days before I committed the crime."

Titus turned to the judge and said, "He never told anybody that he intended to commit the crime, nor did not intend to until a couple of days before its commission."

"Anything further, Czolgosz?" the judge asked.

"No, sir."

There was a burst of noise in the courtroom. The judge scanned the crowd and pounded his gavel until there was absolute silence again. Then he faced the defense table. "Czolgosz, in taking the life of our beloved president you committed a crime which shocked and outraged the moral sense of the civilized world. You have confessed your guilt, and, after learning all that can at this time be learned of the facts and circumstances of the case, twelve good men have pronounced your confession and have found you guilty of murder in the first degree. You declare, according to the testimony of credible witnesses, that no other person aided or abetted you in the commission of this terrible act. God grant it may be so. The penalty for the crime of which you stand convicted is fixed by statute, and it now becomes my duty to pronounce its judgment against you. The sentence of the court is that in the week beginning October 28, 1901, at the place, in the manner, and by the means prescribed by law, you suffer the punishment of death." Judge White leaned back in his chair. "Remove the prisoner."

Czolgosz's legs felt weak, and both Geary and Solomon took his arms and eased him down into his chair. He was looking at the floor, but realized after a moment that Titus had taken his right hand in his and was shaking it. "Goodbye," the old man said.

Then the two detectives handcuffed him and lifted him by his arms out of his chair.

BOOK III

I DONE MY DUTY

Anarchists were in favor of violence or bomb throwing. She [Emma Goldman] declared that nothing was further from the principles they support. She went on, however, into a detailed explanation of the different crimes committed by Anarchists lately, declaring that the motive was good in each case, and that these acts were merely a matter of temperament.

Some men were so constituted, she said, that they were unable to stand idly by and see the wrong that was being endured by their fellow-mortals. She herself did not believe in these methods but she did not think they should be condemned in view of the high and noble motives which prompted their perpetration. She continued: "Some believe we should first obtain by force and let the intelligence and education come afterward."

Chicago Tribune
Sunday, September 8, 1901

VII

HYDE SAW THEM for just a moment: two horses, the bay ridden by a girl, the sorrel by a boy. The horses were sauntering down the main street in Auburn, and Hyde caught a glimpse of them as they turned a corner two blocks to the east and disappeared behind Zemmin's Feed Grain Store. It was evening, last light of day, and warm for so late in September. Hyde had been resting in his room on the second floor of the boardinghouse operated by Mrs. Czyznski. When he saw the horses from the window, he left his room and rushed down the hall toward the back of the house.

He and Savin had arrived by train the previous afternoon. They had talked with the local police. They had gone to every boardinghouse and hotel in the town. No one had seen anyone who resembled Herman Gimmel. In the afternoon they ate dinner in the Osborne House, the largest hotel in town. Savin was upset that they had made the trip all the way out to Auburn. He was convinced that Gimmel's gang was still in Buffalo, and after finishing his steak he went into the hotel lobby and placed a telephone call to Chief Bull. Hyde sat on a leather couch and watched Savin as he talked a long time on the telephone. When he finally hung up he crossed the lobby and entered the bar. Hyde joined him and they both had a whiskey. Savin was so angry he could hardly speak, but he did mention that the police were following some new leads in Buffalo. When he finished his drink he said, "And I'm stuck out here with you," and then he left the bar and walked back to Mrs. Czyznski's house. It was only a few blocks, and Hyde followed at a safe distance.

Now he knocked on Savin's door and listened to bedsprings and footsteps; when Savin opened the door he was in his union suit. "What?"

"They're here," Hyde said. "I just saw Bruener's boy on horseback, with a girl."

"You sure?"

"I'm pretty sure. He's a tall thin kid."

"I imagine there are a few of those in Auburn."

"They had sacks on their horses—they must have come into town for supplies."

"You never mentioned anything about a girl."

"There is no girl," Hyde said. "She must be from around here. We could ask in the stores along the street."

Savin seemed greatly disappointed, as though such a routine exercise in police work were beneath him, but as he started to close the door he said, "Meet me downstairs in five minutes."

The second store they went to was a grocer's a block from the boardinghouse. An elderly woman sat on a stool by the cash register, while a man who appeared to be her son was cutting meat on a butcher block. "I was upstairs." The woman's gnarly hands fondled the head of her cane. Turning to her son, she asked, "George, that the Rumson girl come by here earlier?"

George, must have been in his late thirties and he simply looked at both men as he put down his cleaver and wiped his bloody hands on his apron. Savin took out his wallet, flipped it open, and displayed his badge. "It was the Rumson girl, all right," George said.

"Blond girl," Hyde said. "With a boy—you know him?"

"A boy?" George said. "Her cousin?"

"You know him?" Savin asked.

George shook his head. "No, she just said he was visiting. He didn't say a word the whole spell they were in here."

"He can't," Hyde said. "He's a mute."

George gazed down at the meat on the block a moment. "That's why she kept using her hands and spoke to him loud like. I thought he mighta been, you know, simple."

"What's she done?" George's mother asked.

"Nothing," Savin said. "We just want to ask some questions."

The old woman didn't seem satisfied.

"It's about a horse," Hyde said. "Somebody reported a stolen horse."

Savin turned to him, barely concealing his surprise.

The old woman laughed. "Them Rumsons may be a lot of things but they ain't horse thieves, though I reckon they're poor enough." She shrugged as she looked at George.

He seemed to make a decision, one he knew would displease his mother, and he said, "Their farm's maybe three miles south of town. Place is on the right side of the road. Small house, big barn, and a silo with a faded *R* painted on it. Can't miss it."

Savin led Hyde to the door, but they stopped when the woman asked, "There be any reward for this information?"

"Absolutely," Savin said. "It was a good horse."

When they were outside, Savin paused on the sidewalk to light a cigarette. "You know, Hyde, Norris was right about you. You ever be interested in police work?"

"I'm a canawler."

"No future in it. That canal won't last long."

"Why?"

"It's 1901, that's why." Savin took out his wallet and gave a five-dollar bill to Hyde as he nodded toward the western end of the block. "We're going to need horses to get out to that farm. You go over to that livery stable and rent us two, and meet me back at Mrs. Czyznski's."

"You going to tell the local police?"

"I'd rather not. They'd just get in the way." Hyde stared at him as he took a deep drag on his cigarette. "But we'd be outnumbered— there's Gimmel, Bruener, and his son, and I suppose you have to figure the farmer into this, too." He dropped his cigarette and crushed it with his shoe. "I might give them a call." He started across the street and walked toward their boardinghouse.

Half an hour later Hyde was sitting on a roan mare in front of Mrs. Czyznski's house, holding the reins of Savin's bay. The horses kept their heads close together as though they were conspiring.

Savin came out the front door of the house and paused on the porch when he saw Hyde's reaction. "What?"

He was wearing a khaki riding jacket with epaulets, jodh- purs, tall riding boots, and a bush hat with one side of the brim snapped up against the crown. A holster was strapped to his hip, and a leather satchel slung over his shoulder.

"You look like one of Teddy's Rough Riders," Hyde said.

"I was." Savin came down the steps, his boot heels knock- ing loudly. "You don't think I'm going to sit a horse in my good suit?"

Hyde gave him the reins to the bay. "Thought never crossed my mind."

Savin mounted his horse with ease and led Hyde down the main street; at the corner they stopped in front of a small brick building with AUBURN POLICE written in arcing gilt letters across the window. An older man in need of a shave pushed open the door and stepped outside; his uniform tunic was unbuttoned to accommodate a substantial belly.

"Afternoon, Sergeant," Savin said.

The sergeant spit a black wad out into the street. "Captain, you going out after anarchists, here?"

"You said on the telephone you could spare me a man."

The sergeant appeared both amused and disgusted. "I got a train coming here in the early-morning hours, delivering this assassin fella to the prison, and I'm hearing talk about a lynch mob. I can't really spare you even one man while you go riding off into the countryside like the damned cavalry." He spit again, and this time a strand of black juice clung to his grizzled chin.

From around the corner of the building came a horse, ridden by a uniformed policeman. He looked to be still in his teens.

"So consider it a professional courtesy," the sergeant said, as he turned to go back inside the station. "Just don't get him shot or nothing 'cause he's the son of my wife's cousin and I'd catch hell for it." He slammed the door behind him.

Savin looked the policeman over and asked, "And what's your name?"

"Mance Rutherford, sir."

"Well, Mr. Rutherford," Savin said, "at least you come armed." He dropped the leather satchel down off his shoulder, opened it, and removed a holster and revolver, which he gave to Hyde. "Strap this on, canawler." After Hyde buckled the holster about his waist, Savin rummaged around in the satchel once more and took out a box of shells. "How you fixed for ammunition, Mr. Rutherford?"

"Fine, sir."

"Ever shoot at a man?"

"No, sir," Rutherford said.

"Ever shoot anything?" Savin asked.

"Rabbits, sir."

"I see." Savin tossed the box of shells to Hyde, and then hung the satchel over his pommel. "The thing to do, Mr. Rutherford, is to think of anarchists as rabbits."

They walked their horses back to the main street, went east a block, and then turned on the road where Hyde had seen Josef and the girl. South of town they broke into a trot, on a dirt road that wound through rolling pastures. An enormous full moon was rising above the distant hills. There was the smell of manure in the air, spiced by the sweetness of rotting apples.

"What makes you say the canal won't last long?" Hyde asked.

"River commerce, canals—even your horse," Savin said. "All will become things of the past. I read about it in a newspaper article. You've seen these automobiles in the streets of Buffalo? A hundred years from now that's what we'll be riding."

It seemed, to Hyde, so incredible that he almost pulled up on his reins. "All of us?" The horse sensed his indecision and snorted so that he could feel her ribs contract between his legs.

"And roads," Savin said with confidence. "They'll have to be paved, and there'll have to be a lot more of them."

Mance Rutherford glanced at Savin warily but didn't say a word. He only now seemed to appreciate what he'd gotten himself into, and his eyes were clouded with confusion and not a little fear.

Finally, Savin said, "Mr. Rutherford."

"Yes, sir?"

"You ever been to Buffalo?"

"No, sir."

"Somehow I suspected as much. How about Rochester?"

"No, sir. I've been to Utica."

"Utica," Savin said with interest. "You have a question about our mission, about your role in all this?" When the boy hesitated, Savin said, "Just do as you're told, son. Understand?"

"Yes, sir."

They passed several farms and after a couple of miles could see the barn and a silo above a copse at the edge of a field. Savin drew up his horse and waited for the others to do the same. From his breast pocket he produced a small pair of binoculars, which he used to survey the terrain. "It's best that we not be seen or heard approaching the farmhouse," he said, putting the binoculars away. He pointed toward the barn and silo, the woods in the foreground. "So we'll ride across this pasture and enter those trees. Then we'll see how close we can get on foot."

They turned their horses off the road, easing down into a narrow culvert, and once they climbed out Savin give a kick and led as they rode hard across the pasture. Cows ambled out of the way and birds, hidden in the grass, lifted up into the night sky. When they reached the trees they dismounted and walked on into the copse. Finally they stopped and tied their horses to a stand of birch, and then continued on, until they reached the far edge of the woods. They could see the farm a hundred yards across a pasture, bathed in moonlight. There was the sound of trickling water, and to their left a creek emerged from the woods, ran along the edge of the field, and passed to the west of the farm. Savin drew his gun, waited till the others did, too, and then led them down into the creek. The water was low and they walked through mud and sand, crouched down beneath the lip of the bank. Some of the nearby cattle paused in their grazing. The barn doors were open and weak lantern light cast moving shadows across the chickens in the yard. Savin raised his hand and they all stopped.

"I'm guessing that's them moving about in the barn." Savin looked over his shoulder at Rutherford. "You stay here. Anyone comes out of that house armed, you take them down. Can you do that?"

"Yes, sir."

"What if they're not armed?" Hyde said.

Savin seemed disappointed by such impertinence, and he kept his eyes on Rutherford. "You draw a bead on them. If they see us, or if they are headed into the barn, you fire a warning shot. If they are armed, we shoot."

"Yes, sir." Rutherford cleared his throat. "You wouldn't want me to go back to town for more men?"

"I was under the distinct impression that your sergeant wasn't

.willing to grant me any." Savin's grin was quick, vicious. "I am fortunate he let me have you." The grin disappeared, and he said, "Your sergeant is so worried about getting Czolgosz off the train? We came in at that station—it's right across the street from the prison. It's not even fifty yards." He looked at Hyde for support. "Auburn look like a town capable of mustering a lynch mob?"

"He murdered the president," Hyde said. "You saw the crowds in Buffalo."

Rebuffed, Savin gazed toward the farm. "Never mind. You come with me, Hyde."

They crept along the creek bed, moving to their right. Every time Hyde glanced over the top of the bank he could see that they were getting closer to the barn. Suddenly there was a sound from the house—a door opening on a squeaky hinge—and they stopped. They looked through pasture grass, saw a smudge of white moving toward them, and they dropped down behind the bank.

"It's the girl," Hyde whispered. "The one that came into town with Josef."

"Damn."

They held perfectly still, listening to her approaching footsteps in the grass. Then she stopped and there was silence, followed by the sound of water. Looking over the edge of the bank, Hyde could see her squatting in the grass, her long skirt gathered in one hand. She was blond, slender, and in the moonlight her pretty face seemed complicated by uncertainty. When she was finished, she stood and continued walking, though not directly toward them, but off to their right, and then she disappeared as she climbed down the bank to the creek bed. She wasn't ten yards away, just around a bend in the creek.

And then there were more footsteps, these running through the grass, and Hyde saw Josef sprinting toward the edge of the pasture. He climbed down the bank where the girl was, and there was absolute silence.

Hyde and Savin stood motionless, their guns pointed at the sky. Minutes passed and nothing seemed to happen. Hyde waited for Savin to give him some signal, but his face was within inches of the muddy bank, and he continued to look at the snare of roots that were in the soil. Then, from around the bend in the creek, came the faintest sound—a soft, feminine sigh—followed by a moan and a gasp, and then there was breathing, rapid, rhythmic, in time with the hard slap of flesh.

Savin raised his free hand, made a fist, and pumped it twice.

The sounds of their coupling tended toward a greater concentration, until there was a brief explosion of noise, the girl yelping, and Josef gasping in utter desperation. It was the only time Hyde had ever heard the boy make any kind of verbal sound, and toward the end it almost seemed as though he were trying to speak some foreign language. Hyde wondered at the fact that their orgasm sounded so close to anguish.

And then it was over, and they were quiet. It was like they weren't there, around the bend, until suddenly the girl pleaded, urgently, in a half whisper, "*Please*, Josef, we have to leave, we have to tonight—right now. If you stay here, you know you'll die. You know what they're going to do. You won't live through it, I know you won't. Let's just go. Take me away from here—anywhere, I don't care. Somewhere they'll never find us."

She stopped at the sound of the door to the house closing, followed by a set of footsteps, first coming across the barnyard, scattering chickens, and then sweeping through the grass. Hyde ventured a look, and though it was very dark—the moon had passed behind clouds—he could see a man walking toward the creek. He stopped ten yards away and said, "You come up out of there, hear me?" His arms hung loose at his side and he wore a rumpled straw hat.

Finally there was the sound of feet scrambling for purchase in the muddy bank as the girl and Josef climbed up out of the creek and stood at the edge of the pasture. The girl's blond hair was in disarray and her blouse was untucked from her skirt. Her pale feet were covered with mud.

"Daddy, *please*," she said.

"Step aside, Lydia."

"You have to understand." She took a step forward.

The man raised his right arm—he gripped a pistol in his hand. The man said nothing. Josef stood still. And then there was a shot, which snapped the man's head to the side, sending his straw hat flying as his body fell to the ground.

The girl screamed as she went to her father. Josef turned and stared toward the woods, and then he began running for the barn. Three men appeared in the open door, backlit by lamplight. One of them, Bruener, shouted something in German to Josef.

Savin stood up, took aim, his free hand bracing his elbow, and fired. The girl, kneeling over her father, shrieked. Gimmel and Bruener disappeared into the barn. Savin fired again. Josef stumbled, but then managed to hobble into the barn and out of sight.

~ꝰ⌒~

NORRIS was awakened by the first gunshot. Animals in the barn took fright, their feet prancing nervously on packed earth. Bruener shouted in German.

A second and then third shot sounded closer.

Norris shifted, pressing his forehead against the stall fence, and through a gap in the boards he could see Bruener standing inside the large, open front door of the barn. Then Josef staggered into the barn and sprawled on the ground, clutching his left thigh. Gimmel led Tuck to the rear of the milk wagon. As he collected firearms—a rifle and several pistols—Gimmel said, "Hitch up the team."

Gimmel returned to the front door, where Bruener was kneeling over his son. They argued in German, but finally Bruener and Josef took guns and positioned themselves on both sides of the open entrance to the barn. Bruener fired two rounds with the rifle. Gimmel picked up the lantern and returned to the milk wagon, where he climbed in the back and pulled the doors shut. The barn went dark, and outside it was quiet except somewhere the girl was sobbing as the moon passed from behind a cloud.

~つC~

GEARY and Solomon weren't eating, but they sat in the room with Czolgosz while he ate a ham dinner with potatoes and lima beans.

"See? His appetite's good," Geary said. "He had just that little moment there in the courtroom, but he's fine now."

"A special train will take you to the prison in Auburn," Solomon said.

Czolgosz ate some potatoes and beans, and then put down his spoon. "Tonight?"

"Ten o'clock," Solomon said. "Once they get security set up, you'll be taken out to the train. It's not a hundred yards from city hall."

"You won't be going with me?"

"No," Solomon said. "You'll be in the custody of the sheriff of Erie County."

"We've made sure that they have cigars for you on the train," Geary offered.

Solomon got out of his chair and he opened the door before looking back at Czolgosz. "It was good thing, you speaking for your family there in the courtroom," he said, and then he went out into the hall.

Geary stared at his folded hands on the table. "For the rest of my life, Leon . . ." He seemed chagrined at his choice of words.

"I told you, I was the one that caught the president after he was shot and eased him back into a chair. I wanted this assignment. I wanted to hate you. I will never understand why you did this thing. You seem like a good sort to me. I mean, if we had met somewhere, had a drink or a meal, I think we would have—"

"You probably wouldn't even speak to me," Czolgosz said.

"You don't know that," Geary said, but then his face became angry, and he was clearly embarrassed by this. "We don't know— we'll *never* know." He was having some difficulty breathing and his voice was higher than usual. "But you made a decision and now there's no getting around it: you're going to get on the train to Auburn. I don't know that many men would be as calm as you through all this. Something in that I admire—I know I shouldn't say it." He got to his feet and extended his right hand. "Goodbye, Leon."

Czolgosz didn't stand up, but he shook Geary's hand—there was a moment when Geary didn't seem able to let go, but then he did and he went out through the door quickly. Czolgosz listened to his footsteps, along with Solomon's, disappear down the hall.

Czolgosz stared at his dinner; there was more ham but he pushed the plate toward the middle of the table. He heard movement outside the door and, raising his head, watched a man step inside the room—and another man, older, in his late fifties, stop out in the hall. "My name's Sheriff Caldwell, and this is Detective Mitchell, and we're going to escort you on the train." Both men wore bowlers and raincoats over their suits. Caldwell was tall and quite stooped in the shoulders; Mitchell was built like a prizefighter and he seemed quite pleased with himself. Czolgosz was reminded again that this duty was something of a privilege. All these policemen would be distinguished from others because they had been assigned to guard the man who had assassinated President McKinley.

"I'd rather have Solomon and Geary take me," he said.

"I'm afraid that's not up to you," Caldwell said.

They went to his cell, where there was a pan of warm water, a shaving kit, and towels. While he washed and shaved, Caldwell and Mitchell watched as though they had never seen a man shave before. At one point he paused and said, "I ain't going to slit my throat, you know."

When it was time to go, he was handcuffed to Mitchell and taken outside. Dozens of policemen lined their route. Czolgosz boarded the Pullman car and sat next to Mitchell. Caldwell joined a group of detectives at the front of the car. There were at least thirty men on board, and Czolgosz recognized some of them but didn't know their names.

Once the train got under way the men began to relax; there were sandwiches, pickles, a wheel of cheese, and they sat in small groups eating and talking. Czolgosz was allowed a cigar and he stared out the window as the train crept through the neighborhoods of Buffalo. Though it was dark outside, he could see that there was no crowd, no mob.

"All this security for nothing," he said.

"That's why we're moving you at night," Mitchell said. "But word is out that you're being taken to Auburn. It's impossible to keep something like this quiet."

"Once the verdict and sentence are pronounced, it doesn't matter to anyone."

"I hope you're right. We have a ways to go. Should arrive in Auburn at three a.m."

Czolgosz looked out the window again. "I've always loved trains."

A man who had been speaking to Caldwell came up the aisle and sat down in the seat facing Czolgosz. He crossed his long legs, being careful of his tweed suit. "Leon, my name's Louis Seibold. I'm a correspondent for the *New York World*. Mind if I ask you a few questions?"

Czolgosz stared at him through cigar smoke. "It cost you to get on this train?"

Seibold glanced at Mitchell and said, "Dearly." He took a small notebook and pen from inside his coat. "The police have been picking up anarchists all over the country." He spoke quickly, as though he were afraid of running out of time. "This will be the end of anarchism."

"Or the beginning of the workers' revolt."

"Well, I suppose you have to believe that," Seibold said. "Did you hear about the man they nabbed in St. Louis who claims he tied the handkerchief around the gun for you?"

"I haven't heard anything about a man in St. Louis." Czolgosz drew on his cigar. "I know what you want me to say. The handkerchief wasn't tied. I wrapped the gun in the bandage myself, and then I got in line to meet the president." As the reporter wrote in his notebook, Czolgosz realized that the scratching sound of a fountain pen had always bothered him. "My father—I am sorry I left such a bad name for him."

Seibold looked up from the notebook. "So you're sorry for the crime?"

Czolgosz hesitated. Something had changed since he had been sentenced; it was over now except for the execution, and he wasn't ready yet to think on that. He couldn't say what was different, but he knew it was there. Gazing out the window, he said, "I am sorry I did it." He watched the smoke drift off the tip of his cigar, and then added, "One thing more I want to tell. I would give my life, if it were mine to give, if I could help Mrs. McKinley. That is the saddest part of it. But what is the use talking about that now? The law is right, it is just. It was just to me and I have no complaint, only regret."

Seibold didn't write anything now, as though he understood that it might jeopardize the conversation. "If you had to do it over again, would you do it?"

"No, I would not," Czolgosz said. "It was a mistake."

"Was your mind influenced by the reading of anarchist newspapers or books?"

"I don't know."

"Do you know anybody in Paterson, New Jersey, any anarchists?"

"No, I don't know anybody there."

"Was your trial fair?"

Czolgosz stared at the reporter. "Yes, it was fairer than I thought I would get. The judge could not help doing what he did. The jury could not—the law made them do it. I don't want to say now it was wrong. It was fair to me and it was right." He looked back at his reflection in the window. "I have nothing to say about it."

Seibold began writing again, swiftly, and when he was finished Mitchell nodded his head. Seibold stood up, tucking his notebook and pen inside the outside pocket of his suit coat, and stepped into the aisle. Czolgosz watched the reporter's reflection in the glass: he paused, putting one hand on the back of the seat to help keep his balance. Turning back to Czolgosz, he said, "I understand you're Catholic but don't go to mass anymore. Will you see a priest . . . before?"

Without looking away from the window, Czolgosz said, "I don't want to be ashamed. Maybe I will see a priest." He needed to stop talking now. He needed to hold on until it passed. "It is worse than I thought it would be." He looked up at Seibold.

The reporter averted his eyes; he didn't seem to comprehend what he'd heard, and it made him frightened, anxious to get away. As the train rocked from side to side, he walked unsteadily up the aisle toward the front of the car, grabbing the backs of seats and pulling himself along, as though he were climbing some great height.

Czolgosz gazed out the window again and smoked his cigar. The train passed slowly through neighborhoods with clapboard tenements, warehouses, open fields. Occasionally there were small groups of people standing alongside the track. Their somber faces were illuminated by the light cast from the coach, and sometimes he heard shouts, their voices murderously shrill above the clatter of the wheels. When the train ran beneath an embankment, there were people standing on top of a brick wall, holding lanterns. Their mouths were open, and he realized they were singing.

"How'd they know I'm on this train?" Czolgosz asked.

"Don't know," Mitchell said. "Word gets around, no matter what we do. It's people want to see you dead and gone." Mitchell fingered the hard brim of his bowler. "It's Americans."

"I'm an American," Czolgosz said.

Mitchell only stared at him.

~✺~

THE girl cried for so long that Savin finally turned to Hyde and whispered, "Jesus, if she doesn't shut up *I'm* going to shoot her."

From the house, a woman called out, "Lydia, you come up here this minute."

"They shot him," the girl said. "He's dead, Momma."

"Come up to the house now." Something in the woman's voice suggested that she had expected this all along.

"And they shot Josef, too." The girl got to her feet and began walking toward the barn. Her gait was coltish and graceful, and her skirt swung easily about her ankles. "Josef?" she yelled. "You hurt, too?"

"He's all right," Bruener shouted. "Just do like your momma says."

But the girl continued toward the barn, until her mother came out into the yard, took her daughter by the shoulders, and guided her into the house.

There was a sound to Hyde's left, and he looked down the

creek to see Rutherford approaching, crouched down below the bank. When he reached them, Savin seemed both disappointed and amused.

"Well, Mr. Rutherford," Savin said. "That was quite a shot. Looks like you put it right in his ear canal. You learn to shoot like that hunting rabbits?"

"Yes, sir. My father told me to aim for the head so as not to spoil the meat."

"I see," Savin said. "It's a good thing, obeying your daddy. But did anyone tell you to leave your position?"

"No, sir."

"Well, that is what you did, Mr. Rutherford. I don't cotton to insubordination, but I'll let it go this once." Savin took a moment to survey the farm. "There's at least four of them. The thing is not to let them know there's only three of us. We need to spread out, give them the impression there's more of us." He looked at Rutherford. "Now I want you to go back to where you came from in the woods—but not the exact same place, so they'll think there might be at least two of you out there. Get yourself a good view of the front of the barn." Turning to Hyde, he said, "You stay here while I go down the creek that way"—with his pistol, he waved in the other direction—"and see if I can get around behind the barn. I'll try to flush them out into the yard so you can get a clear shot."

"What about the Pinkertons?" Hyde asked.

"What about them, Hyde?" Savin said.

"You told me Norris was important."

"He is." Savin seemed embarrassed that the subject had even been raised. "But what's more important at this point is that dynamite."

"Dynamite, sir?" Rutherford said.

"Right," Savin said. "According to Hyde, they've got dynamite, which they intend to use to kill Leon Czolgosz when his train arrives in Auburn later tonight. Their idea is to make a martyr of him. It's a hell of a notion—this is the kind of people we're dealing with here. I want to get the Pinkertons out alive, but the dynamite is now our priority, understand?" He stared at Rutherford and Hyde, waiting for a response, and when there was none, he said, "Now, let's move."

⁓ↄC⁓

TUCK opened the back doors of the milk wagon. Gimmel had put the lantern out, and Norris could barely see him climb out and open a stall where one of the horses was kept. As he bridled the horse, he gave orders in German. He spoke rapidly and no one questioned him. There seemed a resignation in their silence.

Tuck came over to Norris's stall and knelt on one knee; with a knife he cut the rope that held Norris to the gatepost. Norris got to his feet with some difficulty, as his hands were still bound in front of him. Tuck opened the gate and then motioned with the knife. Norris stepped outside the stall and walked to the back of the wagon, where he turned and sat on the floor, and then leaned back so he could swing his legs inside. He watched Gimmel throw a saddle up on the horse's back.

"What are you doing, Gimmel?" he asked.

"You're going for a little ride, Pinkerton."

"Where?"

Gimmel didn't answer as he concentrated on tightening cinches, but when he was finished he said, "I suppose you believe in some form of eternity."

"Don't really give it much thought," Norris said. "I find the here and now occupies all of my time."

"Perhaps we have that in common." Gimmel climbed up into the saddle and walked the horse a few steps toward the milk wagon. "Whatever's at the end of here and now, Norris, that's about where you're headed." He nodded, as a gesture of farewell, it seemed, and then Tuck closed the wagon doors.

Again, Norris found himself sitting in the dark breathing that sickening smell of milk.

~ひC~

THERE was noise in the barn suddenly—pounding hooves, wheels, yelling—and then a wagon came through the open doors, scattering chickens in the yard. The moonlight was bright enough that Hyde could see three men sitting on the driver's bench, Bruener on the left, Josef on the right—both firing pistols in the direction of the creek, while the man between them slapped the reins on the horse's haunches. Hyde stretched out his arm and began shooting. The wagon bucked over the rutted path that ran alongside the pasture, making it difficult to draw a bead. Mewling cows trotted in a panic across Hyde's line of fire. He could hear Rutherford's shots, muffled by the woods, and a burst of gunfire came from the far side of the barn. The smell of gunpowder filled the night air.

As the wagon neared the house, someone stepped out on the porch—it wasn't the girl, but the older woman, her mother. She carried a rifle on her hip, which she fired twice, taking down the horse. The wagon ran up on the animal's hindquarters and for a moment it was poised at an angle on two wheels before it fell over on its left side. All three men were thrown to the ground, where they lay hurt, and a fourth tumbled out of the back of the wagon.

The woman sat down on the porch step and began to cry. The girl and two small children came out and hovered around her. Hyde climbed up over the bank of the creek and ran across the pasture. He could tell that the man thrown from the back of the wagon was Norris; his hands were tied in front of him but he managed to get to his feet. He limped badly as he went to the nearest man—Klaus Bruener—picked up a gun that lay on the ground, aimed, and fired. Bruener cried out and began crawling back toward the barn. Norris fired twice more and Bruener stopped moving. Norris hobbled over to the man who had been driving the wagon and shot him once in the head.

"*Norris*," Hyde shouted when he reached the barnyard.

Norris was working his way toward the boy, Josef, who was writhing on the ground, holding his leg. "I'm going to finish them, Hyde." He seemed oddly gleeful. But then he knelt down and sat back in the dirt, clutching his injured foot. "Goddamn, I think I must have busted my ankle." Looking around, he said, "I don't see Gimmel. You already shoot that bastard?"

From the open barn door Savin said, "He rode off." He walked out into the yard, holding his left arm tight to his body as though in fear that he might somehow drop it. His forearm was slick with blood which glistened in the moonlight. "I believe I have lost a good portion of my elbow."

"Gimmel shoot you?" Norris asked.

"He rode a horse out the back of the barn," Savin said.

Norris nodded toward a crate that lay on its side near the back of the wagon. "He took some of the dynamite."

They were silent for a moment, and the only sound in the yard was of Josef grinding his heel in the dirt. The girl had gone to him, but she didn't seem to know what to do.

"Where is that boy with our horses?" Savin asked.

As if in response they heard the sound of hooves; turning, they watched Rutherford lead their horses out of the woods and across the creek at a point where its banks were low, and then they trotted up the pasture. They came into the yard and stopped, breathing heavily and snorting.

"You're losing a lot of blood," Hyde said.

"Gimmel's on his way to Auburn," Savin said.

"You need to have that looked after," Hyde said.

"There's an old doctor," the girl said. "Lives two farms to the south."

"Rutherford," Hyde said, "you fetch that doctor." He went over and climbed up on his horse.

"What do you think you're doing, Hyde?" Savin asked.

"Somebody's got to go to Auburn."

~⌒ᗝᑕ⌒~

THE train made a brief stop in Rochester, where a conductor and a porter boarded the Pullman car. They told Sheriff Caldwell that they'd received a wire saying that a large crowd was gathering in Auburn. After that the policemen seemed more somber; they talked quietly and the car was filled with cigar smoke. At the station in Victor a series of bloodred lanterns had been hung above the platform, and in Canandaigua another group of people stood alongside the tracks.

Sheriff Caldwell came down the aisle and again sat across from Czolgosz. "If there's a mob in Auburn," Mitchell said, "they might tear him apart." He spoke as though Czolgosz weren't sitting next to him.

The sheriff nodded. "Maybe so."

"We could go on through," Mitchell offered, "not stop at Auburn. Wait it out till the mob breaks up and sneak him into the prison."

Sheriff Caldwell considered this for a long moment, and then he leaned toward Czolgosz. "You want another cigar?" he asked. "You might not get any more once the train arrives."

For some reason Czolgosz couldn't decide whether he wanted a cigar or not, and he just stared back at Caldwell. Finally the sheriff prepared the cigar, clipping the tip with his pocketknife and then lighting it for him. "You know, Leon," he said, drawing hard, causing the match flame to be sucked into the rolled end of the cigar. "I do think you look the least bit nervous. I understand you've been real calm about everything in Buffalo." He handed the lit cigar over.

Czolgosz took a puff; it was a mild cigar, not too harsh. "These are good," he said. "The president, he liked Garcias. These are good but they're no Garcias."

"Your guards gave them to me back in Buffalo." Caldwell got to his feet. He began to turn up the aisle, but looked back at Czolgosz. "This train stops at Auburn. We'll get you in prison—I don't care how big a mob there is. We're not traveling five hours from Buffalo just to skip out on delivering our man." Without waiting for a response, he began to make his way toward the front of the car.

"I was raised on a pig farm outside of Elmira." Mitchell closed his eyes as he slid down and made himself more comfortable, his feet propped on the opposite bench. "I had a cousin Jody that fell off the fence and knocked hisself out. Them hogs tore'm apart. We heard him screaming something awful, but by the time my pa got there it was too late. They was dragging him around the pen by his intestines. Never seen nothing like it."

Czolgosz leaned toward the window again, until his forehead touched the glass. His chest was tight and he found that he had to breathe carefully. The last time he felt this way he had been at Big Maud's—the night before he shot the president. Moses Hyde had come upstairs to Motka's room, drunk. Czolgosz was half asleep when his Iver Johnson revolver fell on the floor. Brand-new, loaded, but never been fired. Hyde picked up the gun and aimed it at Czolgosz. There was a moment as he sat up in bed, staring at the end of the barrel, when Czolgosz's chest seized up so tight he couldn't get any air down into his lungs. But then Motka crowned Hyde with the chamber pot, and Czolgosz was able to take a deep breath. A Russian immigrant girl trapped in the attic of a whorehouse, with a chamber pot—it was a moment that changed everything, it changed history. But now, as he stared out at a moonlit cornfield, Czolgosz wished Hyde had pulled the trigger. Only Hyde had known what he was capable of, what was in his heart. He could have ended it all there.

~✺~

ORDINARILY the streets of Auburn would have been empty after two a.m., but tonight men were everywhere, walking in groups, talking among themselves. Lamps burned in windows; women and children stood on front porches and in doorways, watching. On the main street, Hyde dismounted and tied his horse to a post. He fell in stride with the others, who seemed drawn as if by a siren's call. They were walking toward the prison, which loomed high above a stone wall. A mob—perhaps a thousand people or more—was gathering in the street between the front gate of the prison and the train station. Some men held torches and there was a collective murmur that seemed both angry and joyous. Occasional shouts and bits of song rose up from small groups. The night had turned cool and there was the smell of whiskey in the air. Hyde was reminded of the crowds that gathered around the baseball field in Buffalo, there as much for the chance of a good brawl as for watching the game.

He tried to study each face but it was hopeless. Even with his grossly disfigured features, Gimmel could easily get lost in such a mob. Still, Hyde pushed his way through, toward the station platform. Most likely Gimmel would strike quickly, soon after the train arrived. Hyde finally reached the platform, where the crowd was more agitated and boisterous, as though they were on the brink of some great ritualistic ceremony. The uniformed policemen who tried to keep order were merely shoved and jostled about by the swarming mass.

There was a large wooden box next to one of the lampposts;

SAND was painted on the side. Two boys stood on the closed lid, watching the crowd, and there was just room for one more— Hyde hoisted himself up and stood behind them. They were per- haps twelve years old, both wearing knickers and wool caps, and they regarded him as an intruder.

"Listen," he said, taking some coins from his pocket, "I need to find a man here and I'll give you a dime to help me out." He placed a coin in each of their hands, and they exchanged startled glances. "My friend has scars on his face, terrible scars, and if I don't get him home quickly his wife will—well, she'll give him a good thrashing, understand? So let's see if we can spot him, all right?"

The boys nodded, and then they began to scan the crowd. Minutes passed. The crowd grew larger, more densely packed on the platform, which flanked both sides of the tracks. A man stepped outside of the station and shouted, *"Ten minutes!"* which brought cheers.

The taller of the two boys tugged on Hyde's coat sleeve. "There?"

A man with a deep scar down his cheek stood at the edge of the platform.

"No," Hyde said. "Keep looking."

"How 'bout that one, mister?" the other boy said. He pointed across the tracks, and Hyde saw Gimmel standing near the edge of the platform on the far side.

Hyde put several more coins in the boys' hands and leaped down from the box. He shouldered his way to the front of the platform. As he crossed the tracks Gimmel saw him, and dis- appeared into the crowd. Hyde followed, though he was unable to see Gimmel. There were fewer men on this side of the tracks, and soon Hyde reached a wooden fence; he caught a glimpse of Gimmel climbing over the fence and plunging into some tall bushes. Hyde placed his hands on the top rail of the fence, vaulted over, and then crashed through the bushes, branches whipping and scraping his face. He emerged into a street and heard footsteps to his left. Gimmel looked over his shoulder as he turned a street corner. Hyde pulled his revolver from his belt and ran after him.

He went down a narrow street lined with small houses. Ahead, Gimmel's coat bulged, and he ran as though he were weighed down—Hyde was sure he had dynamite strapped about his torso. People watched from their porches and front yards. At the end of two blocks there was an open field and Hyde stopped next to the trunk of a tree and listened—he heard nothing but the distant sound of the crowd back at the station. As he stepped away from the tree, there was a gunshot from the other side of the field and chips of bark sprayed his face. He stepped back behind the trunk, and rubbed his stinging right eye. Then, looking across the field, he saw Gimmel for a moment as he lumbered toward a row of weeping willows. Hyde crossed the field, which was covered with corn slash, and when he reached the willows the land dropped off to a stream. To his right he could hear Gimmel's feet push through water. Hyde went down into the stream, the water cold, the bottom silt and littered with fallen branches. After about fifty yards, he rounded a bend in the stream and could no longer hear Gimmel ahead of him.

He climbed up out of the stream and dropped to one knee on the muddy bank. He could see that the stream went over a low falls and fed into a pool. Next to the falls was a building with a partially collapsed roof and the remnants of a wheel hanging above the cascading water. Gimmel fired again, the flash of his muzzle coming from between the paddles in the wheel, and then he went behind the building.

Hyde got to his feet and worked his way slowly down alongside the stream. He could only hear the relentless hiss of the water pouring over the falls. The windows had been removed from the building, leaving tall oblong openings, and Hyde watched the second story. The footing became difficult as he moved over slick rocks. Just as he neared the falls, he saw movement in the opening at the left corner of the building. Gimmel called out, but Hyde couldn't understand a word over the sound of the waterfall. Gimmel shouted louder, his voice both desperate and angry. Hyde thought he heard the word "strife." Or perhaps it had been "life." Then Gimmel fired twice.

Hyde lost his footing, and as he fell backward his gun went off just as his head struck rock. The pain brought white streaks to his vision, and he lay on his back, dazed. Above him, Gimmel seemed oddly poised and then he took a step forward. Hyde realized he had dropped his gun—he rolled onto his side and ran his hands over the rocks, but couldn't find it. Raising his head, he saw Gimmel fall from the window and plunge into the pool, sending up a wall of whitewater. There was no sound, no sight of him.

Hyde got to his feet and walked to the edge of the pool.

Gimmel broke the surface, flailing his arms, and he had difficulty keeping his head above water. He sounded like he was choking as he pawed at the water frantically—but the weight of the dynamite was too great, and he suddenly disappeared. Hyde waited, but Gimmel didn't come up again. The surface of the pool calmed and Hyde could see a wavering reflection of the moon. In the distance there was the sound of a train whistle.

~⊃C~

AS the train passed slowly through the outskirts of Auburn, Czolgosz felt as though he were stationary while houses and buildings were moving past his window, an optical illusion that caused a hollow sensation in the pit of his stomach. He was still handcuffed to Mitchell, who was dozing. Sitting across from him, Sheriff Caldwell periodically took a nip of whiskey from a flask he kept inside his overcoat.

Mitchell opened his eyes. "What time is it?"

"Just about three o'clock," Caldwell said.

The train slowed to a crawl, allowing four guards to board the

Pullman car, and as soon as they came inside one of them said loudly, "They're waiting for him, boys."

Sheriff Caldwell got to his feet. "How many?"

"Oh, God. Easily over a thousand." The man, like most of the detectives, was broad in the shoulders and he wore an overcoat and a good suit. He was trying not to show fear, but it was in his eyes. "Prison's just across the street from the station, but we got to get him through them." His voice cracked a bit. "It ain't far to the front gate, but there's a lot of them and they're hungry."

"I'm telling you, we could still pass on through," Mitchell said. "Stop at the next town and bring him back once the crowd gives up."

Czolgosz looked at the sheriff, who ignored him—sitting with his hand cupping his chin, his forefinger pressed against his lips. "No," Caldwell said, "we'll proceed as planned."

An involuntary trembling developed in Czolgosz's arms and legs, and as the train pulled into the station he could see hundreds of men gathered alongside the tracks, shouting and screaming. Some carried torches, which illuminated their angry faces.

Sheriff Caldwell got to his feet and hollered, "Listen now, boys. We'll go out the back door here. Surround the prisoner and don't stop—keep moving toward the prison gate." He looked up and down the car, studying each man. "And whatever you do, no guns."

The train came to a halt, clouds of steam drifting past the windows. The detectives filed down the aisle and out the door. Mitchell got up and led Czolgosz—his legs rubbery and awkward—toward the back of the car, their right arms linked by the handcuffs. They stepped out onto the rear platform of the car and there was a roar from the crowd. Mitchell pulled Czolgosz down the steps and they entered the center of a phalanx of detectives and uniformed policemen gathered on the platform. There was a great deal of pushing and shoving, but the detectives moved forward slowly, jostling the crowd, which only seemed to become louder, more agitated. As they reached the street Czolgosz thought that the detectives would not be able to hold. Men broke through and hit him with their fists. They spit on him, and clutched at his clothes and hair. At one point he was being yanked away from Mitchell and he thought his arm would come out of its socket. But some policemen wielded nightsticks. They continued slowly across the street, stepping over men who lay in the street, their heads bloodied. Czolgosz was carried along as several detectives held him by his arms, often lifting his feet off the ground. There was much yelling, and Czolgosz could feel their hatred, their desire to kill him with their bare hands. He tried to protect his head with his free forearm, but fists kept pummeling him, fingers gouged him. His face ached and his mouth and nose were filled with blood.

As the phalanx neared the tall wrought-iron gate in front of the prison, the mob became frantic. At one point Czolgosz fell to his knees, where he was kicked repeatedly in the sides and back. But he was hauled up onto his feet by Mitchell, while another man took hold of his free arm. Turning, he looked into a familiar face—Moses Hyde. His cheek and forehead were badly scratched, and he had blood running from one nostril. With all his strength Hyde lifted Czolgosz and helped Mitchell carry him toward the gate.

The gate opened just enough to allow them inside the prison grounds. The crowd reached through the bars and spat on Czolgosz. Glass bottles were thrown over the fence, breaking on the pavement. Czolgosz could no longer walk and several men now carried him through the front door of the prison. His handcuffs were unlocked and he sprawled on the hardwood floor. Many of the guards were injured and everyone was shouting. He went into a fit of crying and screaming. Several guards held his arms and legs, but he couldn't stop kicking and writhing. Finally they peeled off his torn coat and rolled up his shirtsleeve. One man knelt over him, hypodermic needle in hand. Hyde stepped back and Czolgosz could only keep screaming, the sound pouring up out of him as though he had been holding it in for years. The hypodermic needle was stabbed into his upper arm, and the injection brought a swift flooding sensation; the trembling ceased, his limbs became leaden, and he felt as though he were falling away from the bloody faces that stared down at him. He strained to see Hyde, now standing behind a group of detectives. Unlike the others, his eyes were not angry. There was something else, something Czolgosz couldn't fathom—it wasn't a look of satisfaction so much as of relief, and there was something horrifying in Hyde's stare.

VIII

DR. RIXEY REMAINED in Canton to care for Mrs. McKinley until mid-October. The night he had been packing for the trip back to Washington, D.C., he was summoned by a young policeman, who drove him in a carriage out to the cemetery. It was after eight o'clock but there were a number of lanterns glowing on the knoll where the president had been buried. Two policemen came down to the carriage to greet him.

The taller of them was a plainclothesman, who said, "Dr. Rixey, I'm Captain Biddle, and this is Private Deprend. Apparently, someone made an attack on President McKinley's tomb." In the lamplight Biddle's face had deeply lined cheeks.

"What kind of attack?" Rixey asked.

Biddle said to the younger policeman, "Tell him, Deprend."

"Yes, sir," Deprend said. He was young and nervous, and he spoke very fast. "It was about seven thirty, Doctor, and I was on guard right beside the vault. I saw this figure—I believe it was a man—he was standing behind a tree. He didn't do anything for about twenty minutes. I let him be—lots of people have been coming around to just look at the president's tomb—but when he moved to another tree about ten yards closer I told him to come out in the open and identify himself. He made no reply, but he stepped out from behind the tree and came closer. I called to him a second time, but still he didn't respond. Then he was close enough for me to see that he was carrying a box—it was dark, but it was a white box, I'm certain of it. I raised my gun and took aim, and again demanded that the man stop and identify himself." The young policeman glanced at Biddle, and then continued. "Suddenly I was attacked from the side by another man—he reached for my gun and it discharged once. We struggled on the ground but I could not see his face because he was wearing a mask. And he tried to stab me with a knife." The policeman turned and showed the doctor the side of his overcoat; there was a long slash that had gone through the coat and his shirt underneath.

"Are you wounded?" Rixey asked. "I can't see any blood."

"No, I wasn't cut, sir. But I have bruises because when he knocked me down I rolled all the way to the bottom of the hill there."

"And the two men?"

"Gone," Captain Biddle said.

Rixey stared at the captain, who turned to Deprend. "That will be all, Private."

The young man looked grateful. "Yes, sir." He climbed back up the knoll to the vault.

"Captain," Rixey said, "is he reliable?"

"He's been on the force about four months. I have no reason to doubt him."

"Did anyone else see either of these men?"

"No, sir. Some of my other men reached the vault within seconds and we searched the grounds, but it was dark and we found no trace of them."

Rixey gazed up toward the vault a moment. "Have any reporters been here?"

"Not yet," Biddle said. "But I expect word will get out."

"I appreciate it that you sent for me, Captain." Rixey began to turn away, but then stopped and faced Biddle again. "What do you think of the white box?"

"I think it was explosives."

"I see. Someone wanted to blow up the president's vault."

"I would say so, sir."

Rixey started up the knoll.

"Doctor, would you like a lantern?" the captain asked.

"No, thank you."

Rixey climbed up to the vault and walked around it once. Then he stopped and placed his hand on the marble. Nothing, he realized, would be the same from now on. The country had changed in the short time since McKinley's death. There was something frantic, even rabid, in the way people had responded to the assassination. It was in the faces he had seen when McKinley's body was returned to Canton. It was in the newspapers, where the stories seemed almost exuberant in their ability to shock. There was a great cacophony of voices, strident, sorrowful, wanting, and angry, which had only been waiting for this one event to set them free. The marble was cool beneath his hand, and somehow he found it soothing, even reassuring.

～ჂⅭ～

ON Auburn's death row the cell walls were lined with metal plates. Czolgosz often laid his hands against the steel, marveling at its cold impenetrability. His nose and cheeks were bandaged so that his vision was limited. He had bruises on his torso, arms, and legs. There was constant pain deep in his muscles, burning aches in his joints; his left shoulder felt as though it had been dislocated. Security was tighter than in Buffalo. There were always two guards seated just outside his cell door. And he knew there were four other men in cells down the hall; they talked to one another but rarely to him, and he understood that they resented the fact that he received special attention. He spent most of the time lying or sitting on the cot, covered with blankets because the cell was cool. His appetite was still good and he looked forward to each meal, after which he would sleep soundly for hours. He welcomed the oblivion of sleep. Only a faint residue of his dreams remained after he awoke. There were moments when his solitude seemed perfect. His mind could stop and, lying still, this was what he hoped death would be like. In these moments he looked forward to death.

Early one morning Moses Hyde sat next to him on the cot.

You don't seem to mind the size of the cell.

No, Hyde said.

We have that in common.

When you sleep on a barge, you are usually in a tight berth, not much more space than a coffin. Sometimes you sleep in a hammock, so that you are curled up like a pea in a pod.

This must be why I always preferred trains.

They both laughed, and then they were silent for a while.

I should have shot you when I had the chance.

That's the difference between you and me, Hyde. You hesitated. There was a moment when I couldn't breathe, and I waited for the pain of the bullet, but then Motka hit you with the chamber pot. You couldn't bring yourself to do it. That helped me because the next day as I waited in line to be greeted by the president, I knew I could not hesitate.

It is difficult to deliberately shoot someone, particularly a man who is unarmed, who is no threat to you. That is why I hesitated—that and the drink. If I had not hesitated, the president would be alive.

Perhaps, but if I had not shot him, then someone else would have. Eventually. We are at war and there is always someone prepared to do what is necessary.

I don't believe that.

I know you don't.

What is even harder for me to understand is that you have no remorse.

Not now. I did have a moment. It was on the train to Auburn. I was frightened. I had been sentenced to death that afternoon and I told a reporter that I regretted what I had done. I said I felt sympathy for Mrs. McKinley. Somehow I thought saying such things might end my fear. But it didn't.

You still have it, fear?

No.

What did end it?

Pain. I was nearly killed by that mob when I arrived here and for days afterward the pain was terrible. I'm better now, but I still hurt. It's because of such pain that I have no fear of death. It will be the end of my pain.

Hyde thought about this for a long while. You frighten me, the way you think.

I do it to free you.

Then you have failed.

You are not free?

Not in the way you imagine. No one is free in the way you imagine. You want everyone to be without obligation, responsibility, guilt, regret. You might as well tell people to go back to the Garden of Eden. You don't understand that each of us needs his burden. Labor. Love. Devotion to another. These are all hard to bear, but without them we would not be alive. We would have no reason to live.

I cannot listen to this any longer. I will not believe that. I done my duty. That's what I shouted right after shooting the president, and I still believe it. I done my duty.

Hyde got up off the cot, but paused at the door. And I have done mine.

The afternoon before Czolgosz was to be executed his brother Waldeck was brought to the cell. They greeted each other in

Polish, but the guard said that they had to speak English or Waldeck would not be allowed to stay. Waldeck was very nervous and somber. He said the entire family was being hounded by reporters and the police. They were trying to prove that Waldeck had assisted in the assassination. The family was treated differently by neighbors, and they had to shop in stores where they were not known. And yet they all had agreed to wear pins with Leon's picture on them, to demonstrate that they were not embarrassed. At one point Waldeck broke down and cried. He said that he had brought some papers for Warden Mead to sign— there was a small life insurance policy that their father had on Leon, and they needed the money. And the warden had told Waldeck that he would not be allowed to take his brother's body back to Cleveland for burial. Czolgosz assured him that everything was all right. The guards only allowed them to talk for a short while, perhaps ten minutes. He was glad to be alone after Waldeck left. He wanted only to be alone. He wanted to be alone and he wanted to eat. The hard thing was waiting for dinner to be brought to his cell. He was always hungry.

He was sound asleep when he suddenly realized that the cell door had opened. Several men stared in at him. He recognized some of them—Dr. MacDonald, Warden Mead, and Superintendent Collins—but the others he'd never seen before.

"It's time, Leon," Mead said.

He got up off the cot as Collins unfolded a piece of paper. His fingers were old and his nails well manicured. He put on a pair of spectacles, cleared his throat, and began reading: it was the death warrant, which sounded like the legal nonsense they had read often at the trial. When he was finished, he looked up and nodded his head.

Czolgosz stepped out of the cell. One of the guards took him by the left arm—it was almost a friendly grasp. A small man in a brown suit knelt down and with a pair of scissors cut his pants legs from the cuffs to the knees. Czolgosz felt the slightest chill rise from the concrete floor and spread up his shins.

"Can I see my brother again?" he asked the warden.

"No," Mead said.

"I want to make a statement."

Superintendent Collins cleared his throat. "What do you want to say, Czolgosz?"

"I want to make a statement with a lot of people around."

Mead looked at Collins, who shook his head.

"Well, then, I won't talk at all," Czolgosz said.

When the man had finished cutting the pants legs, he stood up and said, "Lean forward and lower your head, please."

Czolgosz did so and felt the man begin to cut away the hair on the crown of his skull. No one spoke and there was only the sound of the scissors. He watched curly tufts of hair drift to the floor.

When the small man was finished, he stepped back. Czolgosz straightened up and watched another guard come forward and take his right arm. They walked three abreast down the hall toward a brick archway. There was small threshold beneath the archway and Czolgosz caught his foot on it; he would have stumbled but the guards held him up. He paused a moment, and then walked on without difficulty.

The room was about twenty-five feet long and almost as wide. There were two windows; as in his cell, they faced the front gate and were covered with bars and surrounded by ivy. In the center of the room a group of men sat on wooden chairs in a semicircle facing the electric chair, which stood on a low platform in front of the far wall. There were more leather straps than he had expected. The platform, he realized, was covered with rubber. They reached the end of the room and the guards released his arms. He immediately turned and sat down. The men sitting in the semicircle stared back at him, their eyes curious, somber. A few lowered their heads and avoided looking at him. It seemed odd that someone would agree to attend an execution and then refuse to watch.

The guards began to fasten the straps about his chest, arms, and legs. One guard's hands were shaking and he had difficulty with the chest buckle. Finally he got it done, and he seemed greatly relieved. When all the straps were fit snugly about him, the guards stepped back and another man in a suit proceeded to wet Czolgosz's scalp with a sponge. The cold water ran through the hair on the back of his head and down his neck, sending goose bumps down his back. The man then picked up a metal cap with wires, fit it on Czolgosz's head, and secured it with a strap under his chin. It was heavy and uncomfortable. The metal was cool on the place where his scalp had been shaved and wetted.

"I am not sorry," Czolgosz said. He spoke calmly but loudly so that everyone could hear him. "I did this for the working people." For a moment some of the men facing him appeared confused, while others seemed disturbed that he had spoken at all. "My only regret," he said, "is that I haven't been able to see my father."

Out of the corner of his eye, Czolgosz saw movement as Warden Mead raised his arm, held it there, and then let it drop.

~つC~

IN November, while on a hunting trip in the Appalachians, the president took two deer. It snowed the day they broke Camp Roosevelt and traveled twenty miles of mountain trail on horseback to the nearest train depot. By evening the president's entourage of more than forty men—mostly government officials, foreign envoys, and journalists—had taken over the Larchmont Hotel in Charleston, West Virginia, as though they were holding a forward position in battle.

Despite Dr. Rixey's reservations, the president insisted that they all take a walk through town after dinner. Roosevelt had, to say the least, a prodigious appetite, and vigorous and lengthy constitutionals were part of his daily regimen. He led the party through the streets, despite thunder, lightning, and cold rain; half an hour into their trek they were briefly pelted with hail. At the head of the column, the president's frequent laughter was eerily high and gleeful. By the time they returned to the hotel, everyone was drenched and exhausted. After they changed into dry clothes they convened in the lobby, which soon filled with the smell of port and cigars.

Rixey noticed that when George Cortelyou finally reentered the lobby he was followed by two porters who proceeded to set up a motion-picture projector and a screen. Chairs and sofas were arranged before the screen and the men settled down. A couple of times Rixey caught Cortelyou's eye, but his expression seemed to say, *Don't ask.*

Rixey was one of the last to sit, near the back, and when he looked to his right the man who nodded to him was Detective Norris, whom he recalled meeting briefly in the Milburn house in Buffalo.

The lights were turned off in the lobby and as the projector whirred to life, Roosevelt stood up and said, "Gentlemen, this short film is compliments of Mr. Thomas Edison. This is a simulation, I'm told, produced by his company."

As the president sat down, images flickered on the screen: a train sliding by a high wall, and some buildings in the distance. The clarity of the film was poor and the images blended into one another, but this seemed to lend a surprising artistry to the production. The film cut to a group of men standing in front of a wall. The men appeared deeply somber and their movements were stiff. There was no sound to the film. The rhythmic clattering of the projector reminded Rixey of a train. Occasionally the images jumped forward, as though a small piece of time had been cut out of sequence. The prisoner, wearing a dark jacket, was led to an oversized wooden chair with armrests, which was entangled in a series of straps and wires. Voluntarily he sat in the chair and the guards proceeded to fasten the straps about his torso, legs, and arms. When a metal bowl-shaped contraption sprouting wires was fit on the prisoner's head, one of the journalists sitting toward the back of the lobby whispered, "It's a coronation." There was a moment of subdued laughter, but as there was no response from the front row, where the president sat, there quickly followed a tense silence.

When the guards stepped back from the prisoner in the chair, Rixey leaned forward until he could see Roosevelt. The president's head was tilted slightly so that he appeared to be watching the screen with his right eye. Rixey knew that he was having increasing difficulty with his left eye; he had informed the president that he feared he might lose sight in that eye, particularly if he continued to spar in boxing rings. The president accepted this prognosis with unusual reticence, but then he told Rixey that under no circumstances was there to be any mention of his eye to anyone. The doctor had complied, and to his knowledge the only other person to be aware of the president's condition was his wife, Edith.

Rixey sat back and looked at the screen again. For a long moment, nothing seemed to happen. The prisoner sat in his chair, facing the camera. Lines and dots then flashed through the film, giving the air around the condemned man what appeared to be an electrically charged atmosphere, as his body went into several brief spasms, and then he slumped down in the chair, dead.

The film ended and there was absolute silence in the lobby. Clearly, the men were uncertain whether or not they should applaud. They just sat there and no one seemed to think of turning on the lights.

Finally, the president got to his feet. He stood and his burly physique was silhouetted upon the blank white screen. Every other man in the lobby remained absolutely still, staring at Roosevelt. Rixey had noticed this on numerous occasions, how this man by his mere presence could somehow transfix everyone around him. His effect upon them was peculiar—there was fear, to be sure, and yet they were also helplessly drawn to him. Since he had moved into the White House—no longer to be called the Executive Mansion—everything had changed, everything was new, and despite the constant whispered reservations and doubts, it was clear that all those who worked around Roosevelt could not deny that he had already projected a resolute and unbridled energy that would affect the entire country. After a moment, the president squared his shoulders and walked across the room, and every head turned to watch him go. A waiter opened the door for him, and he disappeared.

"Simulation," Norris said in disgust. "In the film, he didn't even look like Czolgosz."

Norris got to his feet with effort, and using a cane he favored his left leg—clearly, there was restricted articulation of the ankle—as he walked toward the lobby doors. Rixey got out of his chair as well and accompanied him to the sidewalk. They stood beneath the awning over the hotel entrance and smoked cigars in the cool, damp air.

"Ever see a moving picture before?" Rixey said.

"Once."

"Really? What was the subject?"

"A man and woman copulating," Norris said. "Every position imaginable."

There was a silence that Rixey found awkward, and finally he managed to say, "Next thing you know, men will be flying."

"If they want to make use of motion pictures, they should have set the camera up in right in front of Czolgosz and filmed the whole thing as it happened. Let every American see it, let them see how justice is done."

Rixey stared down at Norris a moment. He didn't seem quite as beefy and imposing as he had in Buffalo; however, there was something even more arrogant and pugnacious about him, as though he'd been dealt an indelible slight for which he could find no proper redress. It was beginning to rain, and Rixey was inclined to bid the man good night and return to the lobby, but then he said, "I heard that you had some real trouble with anarchists out there."

"We got them, Doctor," Norris said tightly. "We got them in the end."

"Yes, well, you Pinkertons have that reputation."

"I'm no longer with them." Norris's voice was now both proud and resentful. "My leg, you know. And they didn't like the fact that I shot them. Point-blank, unarmed. They said they could have been brought to justice. I said they received what they deserved, shot while crawling away on their bellies." He put his cigar in his mouth and clamped his teeth down on the soggy end. "Even the Pinkertons are going soft."

"I see," Rixey said. "What are you doing now?"

"Can't really say." Norris looked as though he wanted to smile but couldn't quite bring himself to it, so he merely worked his cigar over to the other side of his mouth. "I'm employed by the government now."

"Spies, that sort of thing?"

"Security," Norris said, disappointed.

Rixey realized that he really was no longer the brutal, ruthless man he had appeared to be in Buffalo. "Tell me, that spy I met in Buffalo, that young fellow with the bruised head, what happened to him?"

Something in Norris's shoulders froze and he refused to look away from the rain, which was coming down harder, drumming on the awning overhead. Norris clearly didn't want to address the question, and seemed insulted that it had been raised at all.

"Hyde, wasn't that his name?" Rixey said. "Yes, I believe it was—Moses Hyde."

"You have a good memory, Doctor." Norris looked directly at him, and then took another puff on his cigar before tossing it out into the street. "You know who Herman Gimmel is?"

"Of course. They've been hunting him for years and it finally appears that the man drowned—strange, there wasn't much about it in the papers."

"Hyde stopped Gimmel." This seemed difficult for Norris to say. "Killed him."

"Killed him?"

"In Auburn."

"Sounds to me . . ." But then Rixey went on, feeling that it had to be said. "Moses Hyde must have done something rather heroic."

Ever so slightly, Norris rocked back on his heels, using his cane to maintain his balance. He lowered his head and murmured, "Perhaps." Turning slowly, he went back toward the hotel doors and for the brief moment that the doorman swung open the brass door there was a burst of warmth and light and the smell of port. Norris paused and glanced over his shoulder, his eyes deep pools of resentment, and then the door was closed behind him.

Out on the sidewalk there was only the rain, now pouring in a steady sheet off the edge of the awning and splashing on the curbstone—Rixey loved the sound of it. The water created an absolute wall, solid yet moving, and he could feel its cool mist on his face.

~⊃C~

AT first light they completed the final preparations for the passage to Albany. After a long winter in Buffalo, the first days of April were unusually warm, and Hyde had heard reports that the canal was free of ice as far east as Syracuse. As he came out of the pilothouse, he saw Lloyd Savin crossing the footbridge slowly, his left arm hanging useless at his side. Savin came down to the towpath and walked alongside the barge, nodding to Motka, who was working the dock lines in the bow. When he reached the stern deck, he said to Hyde, "Permission to come aboard."

"Granted."

"Should I call you captain?"

"It's not necessary, Captain Savin."

"Well, it seems only appropriate, now that it is your boat." Savin came down the plank and stepped aboard. He took the cigarette from his mouth and with a flick of the middle finger sent it spinning into the canal. As always, he was wearing a good suit. "I wanted to see you off. Maiden voyage and all that."

"You're just in time, then," Hyde said. "We'll be away soon."

"Your hold full?"

"Building supplies mostly. Shingles, nails, lumber. In Rome we're taking on a piano to be delivered to a doctor in Albany."

Savin looked the barge over, bow to stern. "A fresh coat of paint and she looks like a new boat."

"Bruener built it himself, and she's one solid barge."

Savin glanced up at the name painted above the pilothouse door and said, "You've renamed her *Clementine*."

"It was her idea." Hyde nodded toward the bow, where Motka was securing a hatch. Towlines ran a hundred feet up to a harnessed team of horses on the towpath. A young boy in knickers held their reins.

"Who's the hoggee?" Savin asked.

"Anton's boy. His wife and new baby have gone to live with relatives in Rochester, but Pavel's twelve and he wants to try work on the canal." Hyde looked at Savin. "What about Bruener's boy, Josef?"

"The court may try to keep a boy his age out of prison," Savin said. "There's talk about sending him west on an orphan train. He's a strong kid, and I suspect that some farming family out on the plains might take him in."

"I ran away from St. John's Protectory because I didn't want to end up on an orphan train," Hyde said. "Farmwork never appealed to me."

"You're a canawler." Savin studied Hyde a moment. "You know when we saw Clementine's body, right here on the deck, Norris told me he would need someone to replace her. He insisted on a canawler. When I picked you, I figured you for dead, too."

"Maybe I'll outlive the canal," Hyde said. "I hear it doesn't have much of a future."

Savin smiled. "Which is another reason why you should

consider joining the police. I've told you I can help get you in. You have a knack for detective work."

"You've helped enough, arranging it so I could buy this boat." Looking forward, he said loudly, "All right, it's time we were away."

Savin started up the plank to the towpath, but paused and looked forward. For a moment he watched as Motka walked the length of the deck, releasing dock lines. "She seems different now," he said, "not so delicate and pale—but still beautiful."

Since she and Hyde had moved aboard the barge, Motka had put on weight and her face was certainly fuller, the skin a soft russet color from so much outside work. Though the quarters were tight, she'd converted the cabin into a clean, efficient home, with porthole curtains and a tablecloth at suppertime. And rules: dirty boots were left topside and Mondays clean laundry dried on a line above the deck. Often the smells of baking bread, onions, or fried fish emitted from the galley. After she'd locked down the last hatch, she paused to look at the sun rising on the canal, a hand rubbing her lower back. Her hair, swept across one shoulder by the breeze, was aflame in the morning light.

"She's due in September," Hyde said.

"That explains it." Savin continued up the plank but paused to look the barge over once more. "Not bad, Hyde, for an orphan. You've got your boat, and you've got the makings of a family. They say the child of an orphan will always have a home."

"You read that somewhere."

"I did," Savin said. "Newspaper, I think." As he climbed to the towpath he glanced down at Motka, touching his hat brim, and there was something in his gesture that suggested that he might be envious of their journey.

Hyde released the stern line, coiling the rope neatly on the deck. He took hold of the tiller, and then raised his free hand. Pavel slapped his reins and the horses started along the path, their heads bobbing with each step. When the slack on the tow-lines was taken up the slightest jolt ran back through the hull, and the barge began to move. Below, there was a good deal of creaking and groaning as crates shifted and settled in the hold. Hyde pushed the tiller to starboard and the bow swung away from the embankment. Motka came astern and leaned against the rail next to him. She pointed toward the embankment, which was covered with patches of snow that were broken by clusters of green stems with yellow buds, and asked, "What is the English?"

"Crocuses," Hyde said.

"Yes," she said. "We have this word in Russian, too. Interesting, one language for flowers. Always is so beautiful, crocuses coming up through the snow."

Hyde said, "Low bridge. There will be many on this trip."

As the barge passed slowly beneath the footbridge, he and Motka leaned forward so that the wood beams just cleared their heads. In the shade the air was cold and there was a distinct echo to the sound of water running alongside the hull. When the barge emerged into the sunlight, they straightened up, their faces warmed by the reflection off the canal.

Author's Note

Historical records regarding Leon Czolgosz are scant, murky, and contradictory. What is clear is that he viewed himself as a martyr to the anarchist cause, with no illusions about escaping his fate; thus he was, perhaps, the perfect assassin.

His plan was as bold as it was simple. Considering the security measures employed during the president's visit to Buffalo, Czolgosz should never have been able to get within arm's length of William McKinley with gun in hand. But he did, primarily because he was so quiet, so secretive, so youthful and innocent in appearance, and, apparently, because he acted alone (whether he was in league with co-conspirators has been a matter of intense debate during the last century). What may be most intriguing about Czolgosz, and what contributed to his success, is that he did not seem to fit notions of a "ruthless killer." During his incarceration the authorities were baffled by his mild nature and poise. He was bright and respectful (usually), and he exhibited little concern for his own well-being, despite the fact that he was beaten while in jail. Perhaps most disconcerting was his honesty; he offered no alibis, made no attempt to exonerate himself or seek mercy for his actions, and freely expressed his commitment to anarchism.

At the beginning of the twentieth century the popularity of the anarchists' extreme views is an indication of how deep the division was between social classes. There are similarities between anarchism and today's terrorism; however, it would be a mistake to say they are identical. Anarchists weren't motivated by any deep religious or nationalistic impulse; they saw the working class as being greatly oppressed (as they were), and they determined that the only solution was to destroy the political and economic system that caused such blatant inequities. In their view, public officials, corporate officers, and civic leaders naturally represented—and benefited from—that oppression, so it was merely logical to eliminate them. Members of the working class, which had become an economic engine designed to increase the wealth of the few, were dying every day in the streets and factories of industrialized societies. Thus, political assassination was justifiable, and attempts were made on numerous influential figures (royalty, government leaders, industrialists, for example) in the United States and throughout Europe.

True anarchists did not offer any viable solutions to existing social problems; they didn't want to replace the current economic and political system with something that they thought would be better. Philosophically they believed that any system, be it religious, cultural, legal, or otherwise, restricted the freedom of the individual. Czolgosz's assassination of William McKinley had great historical ramifications, perhaps none more significant than Theodore Roosevelt's elevation to the presidency. Ironically, during Roosevelt's administration, laws were passed that helped precipitate the end of the anarchist movement in America, at least in its ability to unite and motivate the working class.

Yet more than a century later, the anarchists' impulse still may resonate with those who dream of a world unfettered by laws, governments, and institutions that spawn inequity and hypocrisy. It is an idealized version of anarchism, certainly, one that doesn't necessitate violence but is no more realistic than visions of a world without war and strife—which leads to a sad conundrum: Why do such lofty aspirations of freedom so often lead to bloodshed?

Acknowledgments

Historians understand that the pursuit of total accuracy, though a worthy and even valiant enterprise, is ultimately futile. Likewise, the fiction writer who mines the past for a story may attempt to be faithful to historical record, but to believe that one can actually succeed is the greatest fiction of all. Historical novels are, by nature, a unique amalgam of fact and fiction, conjecture and illusion, and *The Anarchist* is no exception.

My deepest gratitude goes to many people who have been extraordinarily supportive and helpful along the way. Some I don't even know by name, such as particular librarians at the Harold Washington Library Center in Chicago and at the Buffalo and Erie County Public Library. I also wish to thank Northern Michigan University for the faculty research grant that provided the funds for me to travel to Chicago and Buffalo.

I am also truly grateful to the following:

For his thoughtful insights regarding Polish culture and language, Marek Haltof. For sending to me all kinds of Xeroxed material found in the public library in Auburn, New York, Tom Hodgson. For their tolerance of my sorry attempts at writing and speaking Italian, *la bella lingua,* Livio and Sara Stabile. For their help in finding rare books, as well as their dedication to the everlasting printed word, Ray Nurmi, Diane Patrick, and Dana Schulz at Snowbound Books in Marquette, Michigan.

I wish to thank Shaye Areheart for her absolute devotion to publishing books that are beautiful to behold, inside and out; thanks also to her dedicated staff for their care and professionalism, with especial appreciation to Kate Kennedy, the pride of Bowdoin, Maine.

Once again, I am truly grateful to my literary agent, Noah Lukeman, for his fortitude and generous insights.

Regarding what the Irish writer William Trevor refers to as "nature's strict economy," my love to the families of friends who died while this book was being written: Harold "Bud" Hines, who was more than a great hockey coach; and to Marion Mustard, who was more than an inspiration to everyone who had the good fortune to know her.

And in remembrance of one good dog named (among other things) Dammie, and one bad cat from Canada named Bob.

My love to my brothers Peter and Michael, and my sister Elizabeth, and their families and loved ones.

Always and forever, with love to my wife, Reesha, *La Guida*.

About the Author

John Smolens has published five novels and a collection of short stories. In 2006 he was the recipient of a Distinguished Faculty Award from Northern Michigan University, where he is a professor of English. He and his wife, Reesha, live in Marquette, Michigan.

ALSO BY JOHN SMOLENS

Cold *takes us deep into an intricate, fascinating tale, where love, greed, and the promise of a last chance compel six people toward a chilling and inevitable reckoning.*

$12.00 paper (Canada: $18.00)
ISBN 978-1-4000-5087-1

Written in spare, graceful prose, Fire Point *is a thrilling and suspenseful story of love, vengeance, and renewal, set against the pristine beauty of one of America's great inland seas.*

$12.00 paper (Canada: $17.00)
ISBN 978-1-4000-8323-7

Available from Three Rivers Press wherever books are sold